Praise for Sharon Lathan's Darcy Saga:

"Ms. Lathan's writing is lyrical and perfect for this genre… Jane Austen would be proud."

—*The Good, The Bad and The Unread*

"Engaging, fast paced, and searingly romantic."

—*Austenprose*

"If you love *Pride and Prejudice* sequels, then this series should be on the top of your list!"

—*Royal Reviews*

"Exquisitely told… I was swept up by the romance."

—*Rundpinne*

"A heartfelt, enjoyable story filled with passion and warmth. Beautifully written."

—*Anna's Book Blog*

"Sharon Lathan really knows how to make Regency come alive."

—*Love Romance Passion*

"The passion between Elizabeth and Darcy has kept me captivated over five books, and I can't imagine ever tiring of it."

—*Queen of Happy Endings*

"I highly recommend it to Austen fans, Regency romance connoisseurs, and all readers who believe in the happily ever after of well-written escapist literature."

—*Suite 101 Romance Fiction*

"A look inside the hot, steamy love affair between two very passionate people."

—*A Bibliophile's Bookshelf*

"It's a book that I found almost impossible to put down until I finished it and then immediately read it again. And when I closed the covers after the first reading—I felt satisfied that things were now as they should be."

—*A Curious Statistical Anomaly*

"Lathan's genius is to spin the everyday occurrences of married life into a page-turner. In a world full of strife, this book full of happiness is a treat for all."

—*Linda Banche Romance Author*

"The way Ms. Lathan allows the relationship between Darcy and Elizabeth to evolve is wonderful and will surely induce a contented sigh from all romantics."

—*Once Upon a Romance*

"Jane Austen fan or not—you're going to love this author's interpretation of life after the wedding… Very highly recommended reading."

—*CK2's Kwips and Kritiques*

"It's easy to see why Lathan's Darcy Saga is so successful. Just as romantic and engaging as ever, this is one sequel you won't want to miss."

—*Austenprose*

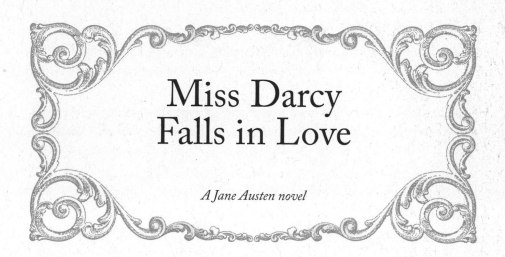

Miss Darcy
Falls in Love

A Jane Austen novel

Sharon Lathan

sourcebooks
landmark

Published by Sourcebooks Landmark, an imprint of Sourcebooks, Inc.
P.O. Box 4410, Naperville, Illinois 60567-4410
(630) 961-3900
FAX: (630) 961-2168
www.sourcebooks.com

Library of Congress Cataloging-in-Publication Data

Lathan, Sharon.
  Miss Darcy falls in love / by Sharon Lathan.
      p. cm.
  1. Darcy, Fitzwilliam (Fictitious character)—Fiction. 2. Bennet, Elizabeth (Fictitious
character)—Fiction. 3. England—Social life and customs—19th century—Fiction. 4.
Domestic fiction. I. Title.
  PS3612.A869M57 2011
  813'.6—dc23
                                    2011036459

Printed and bound in the United States of America
         VP 10 9 8 7 6 5 4 3 2 1

The Darcy Saga

BY SHARON LATHAN

This novel is dedicated to my most faithful fans,
those ladies who have been with me since
the beginning of my online posting days.
Dubbed the TSBO Devotees—short for
"Two Shall Become One" as my saga was originally titled—
their encouragement and inspiration has never wavered.
Simone, who steered me toward Sourcebooks and
has become my dearest long-distance pal.
Vee, who coined the TSBO phrase and
is saving a spot for me on a beach in OZ.
May and Kathy SF, who forever sing the praises
of Matthew Macfadyen on Topix.
Elly, Julie C, Susanne, Jen W, Esther Ann, Seli, and Jeane A,
all of whom never let a week pass by
without saying hello and lifting me up.
I love you!

Table of Contents

FIRST MOVEMENT

Introduction

CHAPTER ONE

Overture in Lyon

*M*ISS *GEORGIANA DARCY* WAS written on the outside flap of the folded parchment envelope in fine calligraphy. The addressee fingered the dried ink before turning the envelope and noting the wax seal. A bold *M* circled by what appeared to be holly.

Interesting, Georgiana thought.

Not too long ago, the concept of receiving what was undoubtedly an invitation addressed directly to her by people unknown would have flabbergasted her. Half a year of traveling through Europe had altered her expectations and such invitations were so common an occurrence that she barely noted the absurdity of it. Furthermore, she was actually rather surprised that this was the first as yet conveyed since she had arrived in Lyon three days ago.

Her smile deepened, a low chuckle escaping as she shook her head. *How Fitzwilliam would laugh at me*, she mused, the thought rising unbidden and causing a sharp pang that pierced her heart. The smile faded, but she rapidly smothered her homesickness, walking to the wide, cushioned seat recessed into the window alcove where the stunning view would lift her spirits. She sat, taking a moment to gaze over the perfectly symmetrical rows of grapevines that stretched in an unbroken sweep to the distant river. All were barren of growth and she fleetingly wished it were spring or summer rather than deep winter, but then she squelched that ridiculous notion, thankful that her excursion abroad would encompass all four seasons ere her return to England in April.

Yes, I am a little homesick. Her smile returned as her attention was given to the missive held in her hand.

> *The Marquis and Douairière-Marquise de Marcov request the presence of Miss Georgiana Darcy for* dîner de gala *at the Château la Rochebelin on 21 January of 1820 at hour seven.*

As she suspected, the de Marcovs were unknown to her. She shrugged, certain that her aunt and uncle would be familiar with the family. She was under their jurisdiction for this leg of the journey and trusted them explicitly. Thus far, there had been no cause for doubt or dismay, every partaken entertainment delightful. She rested her head against the cold wall, her thick plaited coil of golden hair acting as a cushion. Her reflection shimmered on the polished surface of the glass, her densely lashed large eyes so vividly blue that they mocked the dull sky of winter. Not the tiniest wrinkle of unhappiness marred the smooth perfection of her high forehead, honeyed brows arching delicately over round eyes that surveyed the landscape stretching before her. The chilled air infused rosiness in her cheeks, the only hint of color on her creamy skin, and she drew the wrap closer about her arms.

The Château Plessis-Rhône, home of the Vicomte de Valday, sat on a gentle rise surrounded by fertile fields. Even in the winter the countryside was verdant with enormous evergreen trees and bushes randomly distributed amongst the dormant vines, leafless trees, and dulled lawns. The waters of the Saône glittered turquoise in the muted daylight of what was a typically sullen day, the residuals of misty fog lingering in places. The intermittent rain from the day before continued to threaten, lurking darkly in the patchy clouds that obscured the sun. Georgiana much preferred the warmth and brightness of a summer day, but the play of grays and shadows amid the nimbostratus clouds mixing with the colors on the ground was beautiful in its own way.

Sunshine or gloom, the joy of being stationary and surrounded by stout walls was priceless.

Georgiana had discovered during the Channel crossing from England the previous spring that sea voyages did not disturb her as they did her unfortunate brother. Therefore, as difficult as it was to say *arrivederci* to Italy, she had relished the complication-free voyage across the Mediterranean. Unfortunately, the inclement weather that had not plagued them during the voyage had beset them once on terra firma. Crossing the Alps of Switzerland last June was as easy as a country stroll compared to the rigors of the overland journey from Genoa to Lyon. Incessant rains and wind-blown debris required frequent halts and accommodations in less than luxurious coaching inns. The cold was unrelenting, their sturdy carriage and piles of blankets and furs seemingly worthless against the chill. The bedraggled travelers arrived at the massive estate owned by the de Valdays, never before experiencing such joy to see a house!

Simply being warm and clean had lifted Georgiana's sagging spirits immeasurably. Now if she could only ease the ache in her heart.

Georgiana sighed, gazing at the cloud formations suspiciously. A sudden flurry of activity to the right captured her attention and brought a laugh to her lips. A dozen birds had burst forth from a copse of low bushes with dead leaves flying crazily, the agitating predator unseen but the squawks indicative of some sort of fright. It was a simple thing, of course, and nothing she may not have witnessed at Pemberley, but the landscape was so unique and served to remind her of how fortunate she was—and how amazing the journey was, in spite of the pangs of homesickness and grief.

A clamor in French from the hallway broke her reverie, seconds later the door bursting open and three figures tumbling into the parlor.

"Dearest Georgiana, finally! Hiding away already, are you? Frédéric insisted that we hunt you down and rescue from your solitary daydreams!"

The speaker was a young woman of nineteen. She was short, barely reaching Georgiana's shoulders, with a voluptuous figure finely accentuated by an exquisitely tailored gown of purple velvet. Her lavender-tinted eyes blazed vibrantly amid a round face. Mischief and impertinence were etched upon her entire countenance from the tiny tapping foot to the mass of tightly coiled ebony curls audaciously escaping jeweled pins. She was in all ways a vision of supreme, sensual loveliness that could wrest the breath away from everyone who beheld her, male or female. Her name was Zoë, and her lush beauty was so ineffable that it was impossible to imagine that another could match it.

Yet the woman standing near her was indeed a match.

Her twin, Yvette, was nearly a duplicate. It was only the small mole located just to the right of her upper lip that easily revealed her unique identity. The combined essence of these two extraordinary creatures was a captivating assault upon one's senses. The blessing from the Maker in allowing the creation of two entrancing offspring would presumably then exhaust any hope of further divine favor upon their parents, but this was not the case.

Frédéric, nearly eighteen, was as stunning and forceful a presence as his elder sisters. With his curls styled foppishly about his face, his enormous deep-blue eyes, and his plump mouth, he had a slight feminine air to his look that was aided by his shorter stature and stout fleshiness. But this was only at first glance. As soon as he moved or spoke a word, the effeminate vision was swept away by a personality, voice, and bearing that exuded confident masculinity. The three de Valdays were bewitching and somewhat exhausting, but Georgiana adored them already.

Frédéric bowed gallantly, spearing Georgiana with an unconsciously sensuous gaze. "Rescuing damsels is a gentleman's sworn duty, is it not, beautiful lady? Especially she who is fated to be one's love for all eternity?"

Georgiana laughed, shaking her head as he kissed her hand.

"Foolish child!" Yvette declared, shoving her brother aside. "How many women have you declared undying, passionate love to this week?" Frédéric merely shrugged, his grin brilliant and unrepentant. Yvette sniffed, turning to Georgiana and opening her mouth to speak, but Zoë beat her to it.

"I see you have your own invitation to the de Marcov's gala. *Magnifique!*" She fluttered the parchment paper addressed to her in the air while performing a sequence of graceful pirouettes about the room, gleefully singing, "Dancing, dancing, dancing! Until dawn! With endless parades of handsome men!"

"Shall you save one dance for me, sweet sister?"

"I said 'handsome men,' dear brother, not 'homely child.'" She continued to dance about the room, Frédéric laughing and fluidly twirling toward her, engaging in an elegant *pas de deux*.

Yvette sat onto the window seat beside Georgiana. She held her invitation in her hand, face alit with the same sparkling joy as her sister's. "Is it not marvelous? You shall meet dozens upon dozens of men, the finest noble *gentilshommes* of the Rhône-Alpes. Perhaps you shall fall madly in love and never wish to return home!"

"That is doubtful, my dear Yvette."

"I shall not give up hope, my friend! Why return to dreary England?"

Georgiana laughed. "You have never been there, and should be hesitant to call any other place dreary considering the weather here."

Yvette shrugged and then suddenly gasped, eyes wide as she grasped Georgiana's hand. "They say the grand ball is in honor of Lord de Marcov's betrothed, an Englishwoman! Perhaps you know her!"

"Highly unlikely. Dreary England is a vast continent. Do you know all in France?"

Yvette laughed gaily, deep dimples flashing, rising to commence her own sweeping ballet across the room. "Not as yet, but someday I shall. Famous I will be! An actress or prima ballerina or wife to the greatest duke in the Empire!"

"Come, Georgiana! Practice the dance with us!" Zoë dragged her from the window seat, Georgiana blushing and shaking her head, but swiftly getting caught up in the frivolity of the moment. One could never maintain a dour attitude for long when surrounded by the de Valday siblings.

"I deduce the invitations have been delivered."

The gay voice, accented English in a melodious tone, interrupted Georgiana's silliness. Her cheeks flushed in embarrassment but the three de Valdays continued to twirl.

"Yes, mother dearest! Dancing and flirting and dancing!"

"Will there be handsome Englishmen, Mama? Men with exotic accents and clear blue eyes like Georgiana?"

"Not every man in England has blue eyes," Georgiana explained with a laugh, but the girls ignored her.

"With luck the mysterious Englishwoman will have a dozen sisters for Frédéric to flirt and fall in love with."

Frédéric grinned at Yvette, but declared emphatically, "My heart has been lost to the glorious Miss Darcy and I shall never gaze upon another!"

The Vicomtesse de Valday waved her hand airily, winking at Lady Matlock as the two of them entered the room and crossed to the sofa. "Of course, Frédéric," his mother said with exaggerated conviction, sitting onto the cushion before answering her daughters. "I do not know if there shall be dozens of English men or women for you three to charm. Nevertheless, I am sure there shall be dozens and dozens of eligible French dance partners, since the de Marcovs never celebrate by halves."

"Pish!" Yvette pouted, lower lip protruding becomingly. "We have charmed all the available men in Lyon. None are remotely interesting, are they, Zoë?" Her twin nodded, curls bobbing and pout as adorable. "We *must* travel to Paris or Vienna or London for fresh conquests."

Zoë fell in a graceful heap at her mother's feet. "Oh yes, Mama. Lyon is so dreadfully dull! Surely you saw hundreds of gorgeous Englishmen when you lived in England?"

"Perhaps," Lady de Valday responded with a secretive smile, "but if you remember, silly girl, I met your father while dwelling in England, at Lady Matlock's home, in fact, so other handsome men vanished from my memories."

"Oh yes!" Yvette joined her sister in a pool of skirts at their mother's feet. "Tell us the story of how you and Papa met and fell so desperately in love!"

"Oh so romantic!" Zoë added with a dramatic clutch to her heart and a feigned swoon.

The vicomtesse laughed and shook her head. "You have heard the tale a million times and yet still add your own flourishes to a mundane meeting. Silly girls!"

The chorus of *please*s rose to the gilded ceiling, but it was Georgiana's softly spoken reminder that she had not heard the story that prompted the two older women to jointly recount how they first met.

"It was in the years prior to the Revolution," Lady de Valday began, her voice serious and sad. "My father was a loyal royalist and refused to leave as the Terror grew. It would prove to be an unwise choice, as there was no halting the blood thirst of the masses and his efforts to spread rationality only earned him an appointment with the guillotine."

She paused, wiping a tear from her eye before able to put aside the endless grief. "He was not, however, completely foolish or trusting. He secured our wealth, secreting the bulk of our family heirlooms, and then he sent us away to England. My mother cried and refused to leave him, but he insisted. It saved us all."

Her voice broke, the memories still raw. Lady Matlock squeezed her friend's hand and took up the tale. "I was a young wife then, living at Rivallain with my husband, and we opened our home to French refugees. Inès and her family came to us, her mother and mine related distantly. They dwelt with us for nearly four years, and Inès and I grew close."

She smiled affectionately at Lady de Valday, who smiled back as long ago memories washed over them. "It was a wonderful experience," Lady Matlock resumed, gazing at her friend. "I perfected my French, learned many new musical techniques and compositions as well as artistic talents, since Inès is brilliantly accomplished. We became dearest friends."

"What Madeline does not say is that she is an incredible painter who could never teach me to hold a brush the correct way, let alone actually create an image of worth, and that she soundly beat me at every sport we engaged in! Her archery skills are incomparable."

"I shall concede the truth of that, although we were equal equestrians and a generous portion of our days were spent exploring on horseback. But of course the most memorable time was when Césaire, your father, came with his family."

Inès blushed, much like an adolescent with her first crush, and took up the narrative. "He was so handsome. He still is, of course, but then? *Ah, magnifique!* His grandfather knew the previous Lord Matlock; I cannot quite recollect how the connection originated, but it did not matter. My heart was instantly captivated."

"And Papa? Was he as captivated?" Yvette asked breathlessly, as if she had never heard the story.

"Alas, no. He was intrigued, but far too capricious to willingly settle based on a summer acquaintance."

"But you were persistent, *oui*, Mama?"

"A huntress determined to capture the man of your dreams! Your will firmly set to acquire what your heart needed to survive!"

Lady de Valday laughed at her girls' exclamations, shaking her head as she replied, "To a point, I suppose. We females can be quite tenacious. But in truth, it was our parents who finagled matters. Unbeknownst to us, they agreed the match was to be. All your father and I knew was that once the war ended, with Napoleon restoring a semblance of order so we could return to France, our families were suddenly the best of friends!"

"It took nearly a year, Inès's letters to me filled with her romantic machinations."

"Poor Papa never had a chance," Frédéric declared. "How could he resist your charms, Mama?"

"How could he indeed!" Yvette agreed. "He merely needed time, as all men are pathetically obtuse in matters of *amour*."

Frédéric huffed derisively, Zoë speaking before he could counter that assertion. "It is a wonderful story. So full of love and longing, romance and drama." She sighed. "And because of your friendship with Madame Countess de Matlock, forged via the fires of war and heartbreak, we now have our own refugee to harbor…"

"I am not a ref—" Georgiana began, Yvette's breathless *oui* interrupting her protest.

"*Oui!* Thus it is our sworn duty to entertain our lost friend, and, as fate is destined to be repeated, lead her to finding her true love!"

"Oh, how delicious a tale it will be," Zoë squealed, her curls bouncing with her emphatic nodding. "Mademoiselle Darcy's heart succumbs to deep, passionate love while dancing in Lyon, or"—she suddenly gasped—"better yet, Paris!"

"Please!" Georgiana laughed. "I assure you my heart is perfectly safe and not intending to succumb to anyone, in Lyon or Paris."

Frédéric groaned, pantomiming a dagger to the heart, his death taking a dreadfully long time as he staggered about the room. Georgiana merely shook her head at the dramatic display.

"Surely you do not mean you will not dance or *flirt*?" Yvette asked, her eyes wide with astonishment at such a bizarre concept.

"I will dance, yes, but I do not flirt."

Yvette remained incredulous, but Zoë waved her hand dismissively. "Every girl flirts. It is natural. As is falling in love, especially in Paris where love is tangible in the very air you breathe."

"Well, I did not fall in love while in Paris last summer, nor have I become even remotely smitten while in Austria or Italy, so I fear I shall disappoint, my dear Zoë."

Zoë shrugged, clearly not convinced. In fact, she wore a rather devious expression that caused Georgiana no small amount of alarm!

Yvette recovered from her amazement, springing up from her knees. "I certainly shall flirt. Flirt and dance, dance, dance! We shall teach you how it is done, sweet Georgiana." She grabbed her "dead" brother, where he laid draped over a chair, and the heartbroken lover was instantly resurrected and began gaily waltzing with his sister.

Georgiana was yanked from her chair by Zoë, the latter apparently deciding that the woefully ignorant Georgiana needed lessons in coquettish behavior begun immediately. Within minutes, all three de Valdays encircled their protégé, the eyelash fluttering, simpering smiles, and seductive gazes only causing Georgiana to laugh.

Lady Matlock and Lady de Valday shared a glance, the unspoken communication inherent in most long-term relationships easily comprehended. With nods of silent agreement, it was decided not to share what they knew of Lord de Marcov's fiancée, his "English Rose" as he called the lovely Lady Vivienne.

Indeed, it would be much more fun to have the connections discovered at the ball.

The Château la Rochebelin, ancestral home of the de Marcovs, was simply stunning. Georgiana could think of no other word to describe it. Lit with hundreds of lamps dotting the drive, fence posts, tree branches, windows, terrace railings, pinnacles, and a dozen other surfaces, the mansion was a dazzling spectacle. A surpassing example of Renaissance architecture with Gothic influences, the massive building of nearly three hundred rooms was the largest in the county. The host of carriages and bejeweled guests lining the wide drive and spacious walkways were dwarfed by the *magnificance* of the surrounding structure.

Yet, as eye-catching as the château was, Georgiana was captured by the legion of glitteringly attired people who became visible as they exited their carriages and milled about the lawns and terraces.

Attending balls was no longer the frightening experience it once was. The two years since her debut in London had provided numerous occasions for the inherently shy young woman to learn ways to overcome her nervousness. It would never be as easy for her to mingle and vamp as it was for some, such as the three de Valday youths, but it was not the tortuous circumstance for her it was for her brother. In fact, as she alit from the carriage, heard the strains of music wafting amongst the chatter of conversation, and was buffeted by the energy created from so much gaiety, her enthusiasm fizzed.

Zoë and Yvette each grasped an arm, Frédéric imperiously leading the way with a grand flourish. Together the threesome escorted Georgiana into the vaulted foyer as if she was the Empress herself. Lord and Lady Matlock, accompanied by the Vicomte and Vicomtesse de Valday, fell into step in their wake while sharing amused smiles.

"Let the children play with their new toy," Inès murmured to Madeline, all of the adults laughing at the jest.

The guests mingled about, gradually advancing through the press of bodies to where the evening's hosts were greeting them, in the reception area in the grand salon. The formal receiving line was long, protocol calling for fastidious arranging of the honored guests in order of rank and association with the *noblesse d'épée* de Marcov family. Thus, the marquis and marquise stood at the head of the long line, their eldest son and his betrothed beside, with her parents, Lord and Lady Essenton, flanking. The lesser-ranked relatives trailed behind, the precision formation losing order as people conversed.

Zoë, Yvette, and Frédéric kept Georgiana entertained and distracted during the long wait with witty banter, gossip, and innumerable introductions. They apparently knew everyone, Georgiana never bored as they inched closer to their hosts.

A nudge and whisper from her Aunt Madeline brought Georgiana's attention to the next person in line, the young woman pivoting about and finding herself a mere foot from a tall, handsome young man with blonde curls.

"Oh, Mr. Butler!" She stepped back a pace, smoothly recovering with a graceful curtsy. "What an amazing surprise. How fare you, sir, and what brings you to Lyon?"

Mr. Sebastian Butler smiled, thick tawny brows rising in amusement, but bowing elegantly before answering with a question. "Do you frequent balls often, Miss Darcy, without knowing who your hosts are?"

Georgiana flushed, momentarily nonplussed as she searched his gray-colored eyes for mockery. But all she saw there was harmless teasing. She laughed. "You have justly perceived my faults, Mr. Butler. I am convicted. I confess I am caught up in the frivolity of the occasion and unpardonably ignorant of the particulars. All I know is a marriage approaches." Her blush deepened, but Mr. Butler chuckled, his merry countenance easing her embarrassment.

"No conviction is laid at your feet, Miss Darcy. I would much prefer to be freely attending to the joys of the festivities, but, alas, family duty beckons. And to answer your first query, I fare very well. I trust the same is true for you?"

"Indeed, yes. Very much so."

"As to the particulars, it is my sister who is affianced to Lord de Marcov. Since I am largely to blame for his fate, having introduced the two while de

Marcov and I roomed together at Oxford, I have been conscripted to be the best man. That explains my partial hosting obligations, position in the receiving line, and presence in obscure Lyon. What of you, Miss Darcy? I had heard that the Darcys were touring the Continent, but I assuredly did not expect to encounter you here."

Georgiana tilted her head, unable to resist a return tease. "Am I to understand, sir, that as host you are unfamiliar with your invited guests?"

He threw back his head and laughed. "Tried and convicted, Miss Darcy! Well played. My only defense is that I am of minor importance. My sister, the future Lady de Marcov, is the true star. She prefers to have her pesky older brother remember his place, which is behind the piano preparing the wedding music."

"That is a vitally important duty. Her trust must be immense." She smiled. "Then you are still pursuing your music?"

"Most aggressively, yes. However, I do find time for the occasional occupation upon the ballroom floor. May I have the honor of a dance, Miss Darcy, if your card is not yet filled by dashing Frenchmen?"

"I have a slot or two, Mr. Butler."

"The first waltz, if it pleases you?"

She nodded, her mind suddenly blank as she scrambled to think of something else to say while his intriguing eyes boldly scanned her face.

"You must introduce us to your friend!" It was Zoë and Yvette, speaking in tandem, eyes brazenly assessing every attribute of the striking Englishman being monopolized by their friend. Frédéric was humorously watching Georgiana, his roguish smirk and quirked brow indicting her unabashed flirting. Georgiana flushed belatedly, the realization that she had indeed been flirting shamelessly, however unconsciously, bringing her diffidence to the fore.

Georgiana welcomed the interruption, slipping into French and performing the introductions dutifully as her face cooled and nervous flutters eased. "Monsieur Butler, allow me to introduce my friends, Mademoiselle Zoë and Mademoiselle Yvette de Valday, and Monsieur Frédéric de Valday. This is Monsieur Butler, a kinsman of mine."

"Ooh! A kinsman, you say? How utterly intriguing and coincidental!" Yvette held her hand out, bobbing a curtsy and flashing an alluring smile.

Georgiana rolled her eyes, but Mr. Butler bowed, kissing the gloved fingers with due pomp and a serious, "*Enchantè*, mademoiselle."

Zoë's hand was quick to follow, her gaze blatantly seductive. "Please tell us, monsieur, how you and the lovely Mademoiselle Darcy are related?"

Mr. Butler's smile burst forth, his mischievous gaze touching Georgiana. "My grandmother, the Marchioness of Warrow"—he indicated an elderly but lushly beautiful woman further down the line—"is the youngest sister of Mademoiselle Darcy's grandfather, the late Mr. James Darcy. Alas, despite the familial connection, our paths never crossed until two summers ago in London at a ball to honor Mademoiselle Darcy's debut."

"And since then we seem to be treading close upon each other's steps." Georgiana laughed at his puzzled expression. "My family passed last May at the Swiss estate of my Aunt Mary, the Baroness of Oeggl, while apparently you and Lady Warrow dwelt at their manor in Vienna."

"Indeed we did. And, yes, we heard of your visit to the château when they returned to Vienna in the autumn. I would very much like to hear of your Alps crossing, Miss Darcy. I have not been brave enough, nor had the time, to attempt such a feat. I am highly impressed at your fortitude."

Georgiana blushed at his warm, respectful inspection, and tried to ignore the teasing expressions worn by the de Valdays. It was not that hard, actually, Georgiana discovering her attention was quite captured by Mr. Butler.

Sebastian Butler stood well over six feet, his body lean and masculine. His stylishly trimmed, thick, golden-blond hair was naturally erratic with soft curls. His handsome face was narrow, the jawline firm with a faintly pointed chin, almond-shaped eyes of slate gray, and a thin nose set above a full mouth; all was perfectly balanced within a complexion fair from too many hours inside though with ruddy cheeks from abrupt exposure to the sun. Later the twins would point out the flecks of blue in his eyes, the small scar on his left earlobe, the slightly crooked smile, and so on, but then, they enumerated such miscellany about most of the men at the assembly! It would be several weeks before Georgiana added their discovered minutia to her own list of incidentals.

Another gentle nudge from her aunt brought her back to reality. The gap in the reception line ahead of them was wide; Georgiana again flushed as she dropped a brief curtsy and herded the fawning twins away from the amused Englishman. There were a couple of backward glances, Mr. Butler meeting her smile each time, but very soon his form was lost in the surging crowd.

Dance partners were in abundance, for both sexes, so it did not take long for Georgiana to secure gentlemen for every dance in the first sets. When the waltz was called, she glanced about with some trepidation, having not laid eyes on Mr. Butler since the receiving line. But then he was beside her, his pale gray eyes sparkling with mirth as he offered his arm.

They took their places on the polished wooden floor, his touch light as they assumed a proper waltz form. His smile was friendly, putting her at ease.

"I recall seeing you dance the waltz with Colonel Fitzwilliam at the Darcys' ball two years ago."

"Therefore you feel secure that I shall not step on your feet?" He chuckled, nodding. Georgiana continued, "My brother taught me, but I fear he will only now waltz with his wife. I must rely upon the charity of others now that my lifelong dance instructor has moved on."

"I am certain none see it as charity, Miss Darcy." The music began, Mr. Butler leading into a flawless turn. He waited until the initial steps flowed into a smooth promenade before speaking. "How long have you been touring Europe, Miss Darcy?"

"Since March last. Mr. and Mrs. Darcy, and my uncle, Dr. Darcy, traveled with us for nearly three months before returning home. We were quite the entourage!"

"I can imagine. But it is most delightful to travel with friends and family, is it not?"

"Very true."

"Why did the Darcys and Dr. Darcy return home? Did they not wish to see Italy? Surely Mr. Darcy did not fear the rigorous crossing?"

"No," Georgiana replied as she laughed at his tease, "although my uncle would have flatly refused to ascend into snowcapped trails if Fitzwilliam had suggested it, I assure you. No, they needed to return home prior to the birth of my second nephew."

"I see. Then congratulations are in order, Miss Darcy. I was unaware of the addition to your family, but then, news of such common nature rarely makes it this far to the east."

"Thank you, Mr. Butler. It is a joy, naturally, but I fear oddly nebulous to me, since I have not seen him as yet."

He heard the sadness in her voice, and his tone was comforting as he said, "When shall you return home?"

"April, tentatively. We are meeting my cousin, Colonel Fitzwilliam, and his wife in Paris next month. After that we will make our final plans, and I confess to being torn between anxiousness to be home and the delights Paris has to offer."

"At least you shall be again surrounded by loved ones. It eases the heart, I have found. Until arriving in Lyon for my sister's wedding, I too have been away from my parents and sisters. At times homesickness has assaulted me."

She nodded, holding his gaze as they performed the steps automatically. "Are you very close to your sisters?"

"Immensely. I am the eldest with five sisters after me. I know it is rather unattractive, but I do admit to relishing the devotion! They universally adore me as their personal knight in shining armor and I miss the idolization. My ego has taken a hit."

"Humility is good for us all, Mr. Butler," she piously intoned, her eyes twinkling. "But I do know what you mean. My brother has been my rock through all of my life and I am extremely close to Mrs. Darcy and my nephew Alexander. It is painful to be so far removed."

"It is only for a short time, Miss Darcy, even if it seems never ending. Forgive me for spouting off as if a wise older brother, but time away from those we depend upon is usually best for building character and independence. I have discovered this to be true."

"Yes, indeed, you are correct. You have traveled only with your grand-mother, then?"

"From time to time various friends from university have joined me, but I have primarily been accompanied by my grandmother, Lady Warrow. Of course, she appears to be on intimate terms with half of Europe, so I have yet to experience overwhelming loneliness."

Georgiana chuckled. "I can imagine that is so. I had never met my famous relative until two years ago, at the ball you spoke of, but the tales are numerous."

"She was likely wisely barred from corrupting Pemberley Estate." His voice was light, clearly conveying the deep affection he held for his eccentric grandmother.

"Not at all," she denied with mock scolding. "My uncle has regaled us with stories of visits during his youth, when his father, Lady Warrow's brother, was yet alive. Unfortunately distances grow greater as time passes."

"And the Warrow estates are in Somerset. Makes for difficulty in frequent traveling. I am told that my grandmother's third husband was averse to travel and refused to board a ship. Clearly my grandmother is making up for lost time. Upon occasion she exhausts me with her stamina." He smiled fondly. "Then, she pretends to be weary, a claim I know to be untrue, and sends me off on a solitary quest for a spell."

"Is this for your benefit or hers?"

He laughed lightly and executed another beautifully led reverse turn with a fleckerl at the end. Georgiana followed flawlessly, rotating with a swirl of her skirts, catching his waiting arms, and resuming the traditional steps with fluid ease. Mr. Butler grinned, teeth flashing, and inclined his head in approval.

"The truth is," he resumed their prior discussion, "the point of my trip to Europe has been primarily educational. I confess to shamelessly exploiting my grandmother's connections in order to study music. She insisted, of course, much to my father's dismay, but one does not easily argue with Lady Warrow. I owe her more than I can possibly ever repay." He finished with a gentle tone, moving Georgiana with his clear devotion.

"So this was not the typical Grand Tour?"

Again he laughed, his resonant tones reminding her so much of Fitzwilliam. "Indeed not. I am sure the majority of gentlemen of our class would see me as a tremendous disappointment. Essentially, I am a sedentary individual with minimal wanderlust to cool, and I did not travel to Italy. I would love to, mind you, as I adore art, and opera has such strong roots there. But the call to study with master composers and pianists was far preferable to wasting time in extensive travel."

Georgiana's eyes lit up, her breath catching. "The masters? Such as who?"

Mr. Butler noted her intense expression with some surprise, opening his mouth to speak, but the music halted with the final twirl completed. With some reluctance, he let her go, bowing deeply before stepping back a pace. To his further astonishment she bobbed an abstracted curtsy, unconsciously bridging the narrow gap between their bodies.

"Where did you study? With whom? Was it marvelous?" Her eager face was lifted to his, gloved hands clenched by her breast as if in supplication.

He smiled, offering his arm. "Are you thirsty, Miss Darcy? Perhaps a drink and some air while I regale you with stories of Hummel and Moscheles?"

She gasped. "Did you meet… Beethoven?"

"Most impressive, Miss Darcy. Few outside of Germany know these men, let alone that they are friends with Beethoven."

"Were you serious? About Hummel and Moscheles that is?"

"Indeed, I was serious. However, I must be honest and confess that I was attempting humor and did not anticipate your interest. I rather expected a blank stare and beg your forgiveness for assuming your ignorance. Most young ladies gaze at me as if I have suddenly sprouted an additional head when I veer into 'music-speak' as my sisters call it."

She took the offered glass of punch absently. "No, I am truly intrigued. I have played the pianoforte all my life and adore learning of new compositions, especially those of unique quality. Plus, I find that knowing the background and influence of a composer, what he has endured, or whom he has involved himself with lend an understanding to the piece that aids in performing it. Do you agree?"

"Sometimes, yes. Certainly an artist grows by association and concourse with other artists. I think the truly gifted are blessed with their own intrinsic character, their voice, if you will. Study, experiences, and relationships can inspire and affect, but one must not lose their sense of self, what makes them unique."

"I recall vividly the compositions you played at my brother's house in London two years ago, Mr. Butler. Very romantic and cantabile but also strong and audacious. Your work moved me. Has your style been affected by your studies and time abroad?"

"To a degree, I imagine. I like to try my hand at new techniques." He shrugged, grinning roguishly. "Playing or composing, I am never bored."

"When I play I try to imagine what the composer was feeling, what he is attempting to convey in the music. This may be difficult in your case, if you scurry all over the place."

He chuckled. "Have no fear, madam. Music is birthed by the composer, true. And the orchestra will follow the notes and instructions with each conductor placing his mark upon the arrangement. Every listener will interpret and emote singularly. You must allow your personal sentiments to be fed by your life, Miss Darcy. Your playing will thrive exponentially if you seek inward rather than concentrate without."

"Thank you for the advice, Mr. Butler, but perhaps that is partially the problem. I am twenty and barely stepping beyond the borders of Pemberley. I have no life experiences to draw from."

"Yet." He raised his glass in a salute.

"Yet." She clicked his glass and took a sip of her punch. "In the meanwhile, as I scour the Continent for escapades to broaden myself, will you satisfy my curiosity as promised?"

"Gossip, Miss Darcy? Shall I tell you that Meyerbeer snores louder than any man I have ever encountered and that Giuliani smokes the most disgusting Cuban cigars?"

"Not unless it contributes to their musical thesis." She smiled, playfully wagging her finger his direction. "Careful, Mr. Butler. Such comments will brand you discriminatory toward the opposite sex. I wish to hear of intellectual theories, your keen observances, the gleaned wisdom of the masters, all of it! The gossip can be covered afterwards," she finished dryly.

"Again, I accept your conviction of the flaws to my character." He bowed humbly, face seriously set although the sparkle in his eyes and bubbling amusement in his voice negated the effort. "You frighten me, madam."

"Me?"

"Indeed. By now you should be running away screaming, or at least searching your numbed mind for a plausible excuse to get as far away as possible. Most people do when I dig too deeply into my craft. There are few of us in this vast world who comprehend the mechanics behind the joy of music." His tone conveyed amusement but also respect and fascination.

"Sorry to disappoint, sir."

"I am not disappointed. In fact, this is rather thrilling and to my great advantage." At her puzzled expression he inclined his head toward two girls who were approaching the isolated corner they had gravitated to. "Wait and bear with me." He winked at Georgiana and then smoothed his features as he turned to the girls.

"Brother, you promised me a dance!" the youngest proclaimed without preamble, bouncing on her toes.

"Indeed, I did and have not forgotten. But remember your manners, Adele. Allow me to introduce Miss Georgiana Darcy, a relation of ours. Miss Darcy, two of my sisters, Lady Adele and Lady Reine Butler."

They curtsied, Adele sprightly and Reine dignified.

It was Reine who spoke, her voice controlled and subdued, "We met in the receiving line, brother. Miss Darcy, we are the annoying younger sisters. Give him time and he shall tell you so himself." She glanced to a solemnly nodding Sebastian, the merest hint of a twitch to her lips. "We felt it our duty as kinsman to rescue you from the fate worse than death—that is being tortured mercilessly with talk of notes and scores. The poor boy has no life beyond a pianoforte."

"No life at all," Adele agreed, dimples flashing. "He is, however, an excellent dancer. Do you not agree, Miss Darcy?"

"Most excellent."

"No need to flatter, Adele. A promise is a promise, although why I should have to suffer having my feet mangled when it was my persuasion that convinced father to let you stay for the dancing is beyond my comprehension."

She tossed her head, curls bobbing adorably, laughing and reaching to kiss her brother on the cheek. "He is the best brother in the world! And not completely dull, Miss Darcy, truly."

"Actually, we were having a fascinating discussion about Moscheles and musical philosophy when you arrived. We are kindred spirits with a shared passion for music it appears."

Both girls stared at her uncomprehendingly.

"As typical, you woefully misjudge your brother," he said with a long-suffering sigh. "Some women do believe me charming and interesting."

"Well, one anyway," Reine offered with a smirk. "In that case, since Sebastian has miraculously unearthed a like soul, you must join us for tea tomorrow, Miss Darcy. We can entertain with tales of our dear brother while you two entertain with song."

"Oh yes! You must!" Adele declared with a clap.

Georgiana glanced from one smiling face to the other. "If you are sure it is not an imposition?"

"Not at all!" Sebastian assured. "Besides, I have yet to cover any gossip or musical philosophy." He grinned a crooked grin, bowing with a flourish before whisking Adele off to the dance floor, leaving a laughing duo in their wake.

Chapter Two

Harmonics of Compromise

THE BUTLER OF THE Château la Rochebelin was still brushing the raindrops off Mr. Butler's overcoat and Sebastian wiping the water off his boots when Lord Adrien de Marcov's voice boomed from the upper landing of the curved staircase.

"There you are, Butler!" The tall Frenchman bounded down the stairs, taking two at a time, greeting his friend in the middle of the vaulted foyer. "You clearly need a drink," he indicated the water dripping off Butler's limp curls onto his drooping cravat. "What possessed you to leave the house in this weather, and on horseback no less?"

"I had an engagement I could not break. I was playing with Miss Darcy."

The marquis lifted a brow. "Oh *really*," he smirked, drawing out the vowels.

"Poor choice of phrase"—Sebastian cringed—"but you can remove that libidinous grin from your face as you knew what I meant."

"Butler, I am a week from marrying a woman I love passionately. She may be focused on the wedding day, but I am focused on the wedding night. Libidinous grins are an unconscious, uncontrollable gesture, all things considered."

"Please do not remind me." Sebastian stepped past his friend, walking toward the parlor with de Marcov trailing.

"Of course, after the wedding night I am confident the new Lady de Marcov will also be wearing a satisfied smile."

"Must you?"

De Marcov spread his hands, the innocent expression unconvincing. "Merely wanting to reassure you that your dear sister will not be discontented in any way as my wife. What kind of a husband would I be if my bride was not properly ravished?"

"Thankfully, I shall not be around to witness any indications of my sister having been 'properly ravished.'" He poured a glass of cognac and drank it in one swallow, ignoring de Marcov's laughter. "Is torturing me why you were hunting me down?"

"Not entirely, although you must admit you walked right into it this time. Playing with Miss Darcy indeed! How could I resist?" He refreshed Sebastian's drink and then poured his own glass of cognac. Sebastian shook his head and laughed as they sat onto chairs across from each other.

The two men had met at Oxford five years prior and formed an instant friendship. Sebastian had met few men in his life as witty and entertaining as Adrien de Marcov. Within a month they switched dormitory rooms, bunking together and proceeding to have a marvelous cohabitation while completing their educations. In a host of ways they were very different, yet their bond was as tight as brothers born from the same mother. The teasing was ingrained, but the reality was that nothing delighted Sebastian more than the fact that, thanks to the transforming, deep love between Adrien and Vivienne, two of his favorite people in the entire world were happy and soon to be bonded. And de Marcov would then truly be his brother.

"Very well. I will concede that I opened myself up for a fair dose of mockery. I should have said, 'I was at the Château Plessis-Rhône calling upon Miss Darcy who then impressed me with her pianoforte playing.'"

"*Oui*, I may have had difficulty twisting that about to benefit my need to needle you," de Marcov said as he nodded, posing as a man deep in thought. "Of course, I might then point out that this is the third day in a row you have called upon Miss Darcy. Alone. Dare I jump to an intriguing conclusion, Mr. Butler?"

Sebastian grunted. "I have spent far more time than that in the company of your sister, Lord de Marcov."

"Gabriella is fifteen, so I am not worried. Yet. You do, however, have a tendency to monopolize women. Why is that, do you think?"

"*You* asking *me* about monopolizing women? Now that is rich!" Lord de Marcov laughed aloud and made no attempt to deny the charge. Sebastian continued with a soft smile, "I imagine growing up with five sisters has some bearing on my gravitating toward the company of women. However, in the case of Miss Darcy, it largely is due to our mutual appreciation for music. She is quite talented and hungry to learn." He paused, staring into the amber liquid for several seconds before resuming in a subdued tone. "It may be wholly selfish but after months, hell, years, of single-minded study to advance my knowledge and expertise, it is refreshing and… rewarding to teach another. Especially someone as eager as Miss Darcy."

The marquis nodded, all traces of teasing erased from his face. "Indeed, I can sympathize. You wear your typical airy grin and gay attitude, but I know you well, my brother. I am acutely aware how disturbing the atmosphere is under the present circumstances."

Sebastian's mouth twisted. "That is an understatement. Perhaps avoiding unpleasantness is a portion of the impetus for deserting the house. With Miss Darcy I have no fear of harsh criticism and verbalized disappointment."

"Enjoying being worshipped, are you?"

"Spare me some latitude, as being worshipped by a woman who is not my sister is a new phenomenon for me. I know you are familiar with being equated with a deity but not I."

Now it was de Marcov's turn to wince at Sebastian's taunting. "Shall we keep that information amongst ourselves, please? My betrothed may not appreciate every detail of my past indiscretions." His friend's grin was devious, Lord de Marcov's eyes narrowing but voice remaining humorous. "I sense blackmail looming." Sebastian merely continued to grin, de Marcov chuckling and shaking his head as he continued. "Delighted to know I amuse you. Threats notwithstanding, I am forever your friend and brother, and as such, I know the particulars of your heart and situation. Thus I am not so sure whether you will be pleased or additionally harried by the main reason I was hunting for you all morning. But here it is."

He pulled a sealed envelope from his inner jacket pocket, handing it to Sebastian. "It arrived three hours ago by express courier. I do not know the contents for certain, but have no doubt the positive response nevertheless. Whether you share the news with Lord Essenton is your decision."

Sebastian's hands were visibly trembling, his eyes locked onto the sender's address for several seconds before turning it over to break the seal. He read the enclosed letter slowly, his face impassive for a long while. Lord de Marcov was about to rip the sheet out of his hands impatiently when Sebastian finally broke into a brilliant smile and looked up.

"I have been accepted."

"I had no doubts," de Marcov responded blandly, but his smile was nearly as broad.

"For the fall session. Do you know what this means? How… happy… honored… how… I do not have the words," he ended simply.

"You have met Herr Beethoven numerous times, taken lessons even, studied with Franz Schubert, and worked with the Gesellschaft der Musikfreunde, yet *this* overwhelms you?"

"I was overwhelmed by those as well." He shook his head dazedly. "My good fortune continually staggers me. I keep anticipating the streak to break, yet it only soars higher. A whole year, perhaps more, at the Conservatoire de Musique in Paris is the pinnacle of my dreams, Adrien. Imagine what I shall learn. The talent I will be surrounded by and playing with and learning from."

"They are the fortunate ones, as far as I am concerned."

"Your devotion touches my heart, but you know that is not the truth."

"I beg to differ! You are incredibly talented and will be an asset."

Sebastian again shook his head, this time in amusement. "Be that as it may, I will persist in lauding my luck and striving to prove my worthiness. I have a great deal to prove, first, as an Englishman admitted into a primarily French school and, second, to my father."

"How do you imagine he will respond to this development?"

"With his typical scathing remarks at how I belong in England at Whistlenell Hall and not wasting my time on pointless dalliances with ridiculous music. Sometimes I think he would prefer I was philandering with women of ill repute or gambling away my fortune, as if those are legitimate activities for a man my age." He shrugged and chuckled, eyes bright as he looked at his friend.

"Well," de Marcov countered, stretching his legs, "I cannot argue with *that* philosophy! I have been encouraging you to do more of that for ages, but you have no respect for your elders' advice."

"You are one year my senior, so you do not count."

"Perhaps chronologically, but in the joys of living, and women, I trump you by decades. So, are you going to share the fabulous news?"

"I may avoid my father from time to time to preserve my sanity and the peace, but I have never cowardly retreated. He knew I applied at the Conservatoire, so it will not be a shock. Even if I had been rejected, as I am sure he was supplementing the saints above to arrange, I would not have returned to England yet. Italy beckons me still, and I would have chosen traveling there as an alternative. No, I will tell him, unless you would rather I delay until after the wedding? I do not wish to distress Vivienne."

"She supports your study, as does Lady Warrow. Better get it over with while you have all of us here to vocalize our joy and drown Lord Essenton's anger. In fact, it sounds like the opportunity is upon you."

They both paused, looking toward the open parlor doors where voices drifted closer. Seconds later they stood, crossing to greet Lord and Lady Essenton, Lady Warrow, Lord de Marcov's widowed mother, and Vivienne Butler. The latter skipped gracefully over the threshold, her feet seeming to float inches above the floor as she headed directly toward her fiancé. Lord de Marcov instantly grasped her hands, bringing both to his lips for a lingering kiss before tucking Vivienne close to his side, their dotty expressions and smiles identical.

"Nauseating," Sebastian muttered with a dramatic roll of his eyes, earning a playful kick to his shin from Vivienne. He sidestepped the accompanying punch to his arm, reaching to assist his grandmother into her chair.

"Thank you, my dear boy. What a perfect gentleman you are." She lifted her cheek for the soft kiss she knew he would bestow, clasping his hand for an affectionate squeeze that crunched the parchment he unconsciously held. "What is this? Oh! From the Conservatoire!" Her gaze flashed from the sender's address to his face, hopeful joy infusing her ageless eyes as she waited for his affirmative news.

"What is this? You mean the Conservatoire in Paris?" Lord Essenton flared.

A slight tightening at the corner of Lady Warrow's eyes was the only indication of her annoyance at herself for blurting without thinking, but Sebastian understood and winked before turning to respond to his father. Lady Warrow was his greatest advocate and frequently engaged her son in verbal lashings in defense of her grandson's chosen course in life. Nevertheless, she knew

Sebastian capable of dealing with his father's stubbornness and that he preferred to confront these discussions independently.

"The letter came today, sir." He handed the parchment to Lord Essenton, who snatched it out of his fingers and commenced reading with a frown while Sebastian silently waited. Extolling the honor in his acceptance or expressing his happiness was pointless, as he knew from experience.

"So you are obstinately determined to shirk your responsibilities for another year of studying music?" Lord Essenton sneered the last word as if uttering a vile curse, his spine stiff where he stood next to his wife's chair.

"My wishes have not changed, no. This is a duty I must follow, Father."

"Duty? How is this nonsense a duty? What possible benefit will it give you, other than to brag of your achievements and entertain guests at Whistlenell?"

"Essenton, please refrain…"

Lord Essenton's curt hand gesture silenced his wife, Lady Essenton flinching involuntarily and bowing her head.

Sebastian ignored his mother's humiliation with effort, the commonness of the action not making it easier to disregard. Instead, he kept his voice level, his stare bold upon his father's face, and his expression calm if firm, as he answered, "The benefit, sir, is in exploring an art necessary to my soul. Ceasing my pursuits would be as accomplishable as ceasing breathing. I apologize for failing in my attempts to convey this necessity adequately."

"Do not patronize me, boy," Lord Essenton growled. "I have listened to your preaching on this need of yours for years. I have tolerated your pounding on the pianoforte all hours of the night and day, paid for your lessons, silently heeded endless conversations between you and your mother on the subject, and agreed to this course while at Oxford and abroad, always with the promise that your future at Whistlenell Hall was most important. Yet here you are extending your absence from home for another year. When will it end?"

Sebastian fought the urge to smile at his father's words, every one of which had not only been spoken a thousand times in the past, but were also grossly inaccurate, as never had Lord Essenton tolerated, been silent, or agreed to his son's plans. Yet his humor did not displace the rising vexation.

"I intend for it never to end, my lord, at least not in the way you wish. Music will forever be a large aspect of my life. I will not allow my talent to be crushed."

His eyes flickered to his mother, Lord Essenton noting the miniscule movement and flushing angrily.

"Is that what you think? That I desire to crush you? Is this why you despise me so, Sebastian, and refuse to assume your place at my side or assume the title offered to you?"

The room was silent as the grave except for the nearly audible tension crackling in the air around Lord Essenton and Sebastian. Neither man looked away to the parlor's occupants, although Sebastian knew how each was responding to the familiar discourse. Lady Warrow would be fuming and biting her tongue. Lady Essenton would be quietly dabbing at teary eyes. Vivienne would be clutching Lord de Marcov's arm with a mixture of frustrated irritation and sadness while Adrien would be bristling as strongly as Lady Warrow. The dowager Marquise de Marcov would be frowning in confusion. They need not worry, however. The contentions were old ones, Sebastian nearly impervious to the guilt and irritation engendered. Additionally, he was well aware of how best to deal with his father.

He softened his voice, answering with the perfect blend of contrition and determination. "Father, of course I do not believe you wish to crush my creativity. I know you have my best interests at heart and I could never despise you. Please believe my asserted promise to return home in due course, but this is something I must do, now while I have the freedom from estate responsibilities and only myself to care for."

"Freedom and independence are important to you, I see," Lord Essenton offered after a pause, his mien suddenly altered from anger to something resembling curiosity or perhaps dawning admiration. "Self-reliance is a respectable trait, Sebastian. I can appreciate this, even if I do not agree with how you are expressing it. I will never understand your drive to learn a craft wholly useless to an earl, but I see that attempts to divert merely strength your resolve and force you further along this path."

Sebastian shifted his feet, the beginning tendrils of uneasiness and suspicion tingling up his spine. Lord Essenton continued, actually smiling slightly, "Accepting my assistance, monetarily or otherwise, clearly violates your ethics. Why this is the case remains a mystery, since you have no issue with accepting your grandmother's—"

"Just a minute, Albert," Lady Warrow interrupted with heat. "You know very well that Sebastian pays his portion and is invaluable as my companion. Nay, he is necessary for me to travel abroad as I want to, and this journey was initially my idea. He takes nothing from me."

"I enjoy grandmother's company and confess that her familiarity with the Continent is valuable, but my personal wealth is sufficient to fund my travels, Father."

Lord Essenton nodded. "Indeed, I cannot deny either truth. Nevertheless, the influence of the Marchioness of Warrow surely helps in your... pursuits."

"Grandmother's acquaintance with numerous persons of importance is certainly a benefit," Sebastian agreed, his mind scrambling to decipher how the expected argument had taken this rational turn. And why.

"Introducing Sebastian to friends is one thing," Lady Warrow disagreed, her gaze suspiciously upon her son, "but it is Sebastian's talent that enables him to pursue his education. I have nothing to do with that."

Lord Essenton raised his brows, looking at his mother in perplexity. "Are you honestly telling us that he is not introduced as the grandson of the Marchioness of Warrow? Do people believe him to be a servant or, heaven forbid, something more disreputable?"

Lady Essenton's gasp of shock was audible and Vivienne shouted, "Father!"

Sebastian clenched his fists, horrified amazement rendering him mute, but Lady Warrow rose slowly to her feet. She barely reached her son's breastbone, but her diminutive stature was negated by her stiff spine and regal bearing as she glared icily upwards, radiating a calm fury formidable to behold.

"Albert," she said, nothing particularly ominous in her tone or the word itself, yet they all flinched, even the addressee, although the reaction was controlled and he held her murderous gaze boldly. "You will beg my pardon for such an insinuation this very instant. Remember, I warn you, that as a marchioness *suo jure* I outrank you, *and* I am your mother. Tread carefully, Lord Essenton."

He inclined his head. "I beg your pardon, Marchioness. I meant no disrespect, Mother, but spoke only from honest confusion."

"Do not think to placate me so easily, Albert, or to fool me with your feigned contrition and confusion. You know perfectly well that I would never harm our family name in such a way. All know whom Mr. Sebastian Butler is when he serves as my escort. Introductions are specific, I assure you."

"This is comforting," the earl said as he nodded, turning his eyes toward a still fuming Sebastian, "yet I am truly baffled as to why it is acceptable to align yourself with the famed Marchioness of Warrow yet not your father, the Earl of Essenton."

"Are we back to that old discussion?" Sebastian asked with a harsh laugh. "Is that where this conversation has been leading? To you harping on me for choosing not to accept my courtesy title?"

"I have never comprehended your reluctance, Son, and I confess it continues to pain me that you deny your heritage and birthright."

"I deny nothing, Father. How can you not understand? Or at least accept that I wish to be taken seriously on my own merits and not because I am the Viscount Nell?"

"I fail to see how wearing your title proudly is different than standing in the shadow of the Marchioness of Warrow. In the end it is your 'talent' that advances you, as indicated by your recent accomplishment." He lifted the letter of acceptance from the Conservatoire still clutched in his hand. "Have you not adequately proven yourself?"

Sebastian did not respond, Lord Essenton finally smiling and handing the parchment to him. "I suggest we attempt a compromise to end these futile hostilities."

"What sort of compromise?"

"I will no longer express my derision for this course, will even congratulate you and boast of your endeavors. All I ask is your renewed promise to complete your education as swiftly as possible without any distractions delaying your progress. You said one year was the typical enrollment at the Conservatoire?"

"One is minimal, three years at most."

"Very good, then! Three years I shall extend with not a hint of disagreement."

"If?"

"If you assume your title while here, as an acknowledgment of who you are and assurance to me that you do recognize what is most important. Then return home to learn from me and assume your place, marry immediately, and safely secure an heir." His voice fell, the tone tender and sincere. "You must try to understand how vital this is, Sebastian."

They stared at each other in lengthening silence, for the first time in ages both of them quashing their prejudices and ingrained enmity to examine the topic scrupulously.

Sebastian spoke first. "Very well, sir. I agree. With my own caveat. I will marry, but on my own terms and of my own choosing. And it will not be Lady Cassandra! On that point I will never compromise."

Lord Essenton smiled as he extended his hand. "We can decide on the appropriate lady of nobility at a later date, although Lady Cassandra's charms may alter your opinion in due time."

Sebastian shuddered even as he shook his father's hand. "She has no charms, Father, which is why you are so certain she will remain unattached until I return. Unless you count her dowry as a charm, as I suspect you do, but clearly that is insufficient for me or any other man in England."

"She is waiting for you specifically, Sebastian. But," he spoke louder to forestall Sebastian's rebuttal, "we do not need to talk about it now. For the present, we can turn our hearts to another marriage. Vivienne, I hear the dresses arrived today?"

And he walked to his daughter, peace and gaiety gradually seeped in and displaced the tension. Sebastian shook off his warring emotions slowly. His heart wanted to believe his father sincere and finally willing to relinquish his animosity. But somehow he knew it would not be that simple.

❧

The perfunctory knock and rushed entrance of Lord Essenton before a verbal invitation was given did not surprise Lady Essenton. Under the circumstances, she had expected him to visit that evening. She knew her arrogant husband would go to his grave without ever admitting it, but he inevitably sought her when he was irritated or distraught. One might suppose that fact gave her comfort. Knowing that he probably did not share his innermost thoughts with his two mistresses—the two she was aware of that is—or his favorite girls at the London brothel he frequented should have been some solace. Unfortunately, this was not the case.

She stifled a sigh and stood from the chair she sat curled in, dropping a proper curtsy as he approached. "My lord husband, I am honored to welcome you into my bedchamber. Would you like anything besides your brandy?"

She indicated the glass of amber liquid he held in his hand, but he shook his head. "Nothing now. I want to discuss Sebastian with you." He dropped into the chair she had recently vacated, on purpose she knew, and swept a hand to the other identical chair across from the ottoman. "Sit, woman," he commanded, following it with a large swallow of brandy.

Lady Essenton complied, sitting docilely on the edge. "Conversation is always agreeable, my lord. I am at your service in whatever capacity you desire."

He grunted. "I will wait to see how the conversation proceeds before discussing any desires. God, why do you wear such hideous nightgowns? No wonder I feel no yearning to visit your bedchamber unless I have no alternative."

She did not flinch, although his words hurt, and instead remained calm and silent. Lord Essenton was silent as well, his eyes steady upon her gown-covered bosom despite his spoken indifference. Sewn from soft linen dyed pale rose with lace edgings and gathers designed to exhibit her assets, she knew his words were false. She had worn the gown in hopes he would visit, but with or without a pretty gown, Lord Essenton knew her body quite well.

Once upon a time he had been a frequent visitor to her bedchamber, but years eroded her youthful beauty and birthing six children left marks and extra flesh that he found repellent. Competing with the numerous younger women available at the snap of a fingertip to a man of Lord Essenton's wealth was nearly impossible. Lady Essenton held limited power over her husband, but she was aware of his attraction to her miraculously firm and bounteous breasts. He was probably attracted to any woman with large breasts, she amended, but when one was desperately in love with a man who did not return that love, one latched on to any advantage.

It had been over a month since their last conjugal assignation, that one induced by too much liquor and her proximity, which happened to be convenient for his needs. Lady Essenton held no delusions as to her importance in his life, or any hope for a better future. No, she could only accept and be a wife when and how he chose. She knew he was only here now to gripe and scheme about Sebastian and, once done with that, might very well leave and satisfy his lust elsewhere. As often as not, that was the scenario. With luck and a bit of womanly wiles, perhaps the night would evolve as she wished.

"So," he finally blurted, pulling his eyes away from her chest and taking another gulp of brandy, "how can we make sure our errant son returns home and marries Lady Cassandra?"

"Sebastian has a strong will, much as his father does. We must tread carefully."

"I must tread carefully, you mean. You are thrilled to see him wasting away his life with this nonsense and would just as soon forget Lady Cassandra."

"You are mistaken, my lord. I am pleased that Sebastian is happy, but I do want him to marry and return home soon."

"Just not now or with Lady Cassandra. I know you dislike her as intensely as he does."

"I am indifferent to Lady Cassandra, my lord. I merely believe another lady will prove more favorable to our son."

"You have prospects, I suppose? And quit 'my lording' me. I have a name you are allowed to use, Maria."

"As you wish, Albert." She rose, retrieving the bottle of brandy she kept at hand for him, and bent low as she refilled his glass, the gown gaping and affording him a nice view. "I know of a dozen young ladies of virtue, eminence, and substantial dowries."

"Write them down for me and I will consider the alternatives. However, Lady Cassandra is my choice and is, in all ways, perfect as the wife of an earl. An obedient son, and wife, would not argue with me over it."

He scowled fiercely, Lady Essenton resuming her poised, and hopefully seductive, perch on the chair. She did not point out, this time, that his "perfect" choice was unattractive, fat, and dull as a post.

"Sebastian has reservations regarding Lady Cassandra based on valid concerns. However, I cautiously suggest that his vehement denial might be lessened if you did not harass him."

Lord Essenton frowned in confusion. He was not a stupid man, but subtle scheming was not his forte. "But how can he not see the logic in marrying her? It frustrates me to no end! She is sole heir to a lucrative estate that will fall to her husband—an estate, as he knows, that lies adjacent to ours. The financial benefits are substantial and it will increase our family's landholdings significantly. Additionally, she wants to marry him! That fact continues to placate Lord Webbing, but even his forbearance will cease if Sebastian does not accept our arrangement soon. I am running out of excuses."

"As pointed out, you have adequately informed our son of these facts. Sebastian does not need to be lectured again. He needs space and freedom. If he is not browbeaten and instantly placed on the defensive, then perhaps he will come to the same conclusion." *When hell freezes over*, she thought. "Gentle persuasion may serve better, and I shall apply myself to the endeavor, but I still suggest you consider alternatives."

"I suppose you think you can persuade him better than I?" When she did not answer his mocking question, he grunted, waving his hand condescendingly. "Do what you think you can do. Just make sure he is betrothed before too much longer or I will sign the papers myself and drag him to the church."

She nodded and steered the conversation away from talk of bargaining a wife for their son as one bargained for a prized stallion. "I was surprised at your compromise. I hope that you are sincere and finally accepting of music as a necessity to our son."

"The 'compromise' was to shut him up. Oh bloody hell, Maria! I am sick to death of fighting with him! I swear he purposely goes the opposite direction from what I ask of him. If I thought it would do any good, I would pay the authorities at the Conservatoire to revoke his acceptance."

"He would only pursue another course, probably heading to Italy."

"Precisely." Lord Essenton sighed, unguarded for a moment and showing a man confused and frustrated. He stared into the brandy, gentle hand motions causing it to swirl. "I hate music. Hate it with a passion. Why I ever allowed you to bully me into teaching the children is beyond me."

"Ladies must be able to play. It is a requirement of our class along with other artistic capabilities. Our daughters would not be as valued if not fully accomplished. Artistic talents and refinement are vital for a good marriage. We have seen this already with Clarisse's marriage to the Duke of Tichbourne and Guinevere's betrothal to Lord Rycroft."

"Yes, I have heard all the arguments and went along with it even at the risk of one of them being like my sister," he spat, draining the glass and hastily reaching for the decanter. "And after being careful to hire instructors aged or hideous to look at, and limiting their exposure to any one art, who is it that ends up betraying me and running off as she did? My only son!"

"He has not betrayed you, Albert. And he is not running off with his instructor as your sister did."

"He might as well have, living amongst poor musicians in shabby tenements and frequenting unsavory music halls and pubs. It is disgusting and shames the family just as her behavior did."

Lady Essenton could not stop her laughter, even when her husband glared at her with the tips of his ears turning red. "Oh, Essenton! You do have an overactive imagination! Sebastian is studying with the finest, most respected artists of our generation. Why the Conservatoire is a highly prestigious institution with impeccable standards."

"Yet what benefit is it to him?" he shouted, launching from the chair. "In the end he will have nothing to do with it except play in base locales just to feed this 'need' of his."

"How many times have we sat in the best parlors and salons of London or Paris and been entertained by pianists or flutists? All of them have been men of renown and elegance, some with titles and family connections of the highest caliber."

"Minor titles and none of our class or with our responsibilities."

"You are shortsighted, my husband."

"And you are a foolish woman, blinded by your maternal pride," he snarled. "You forget the other danger of his philandering. What if he sires a horde of bastards before a legitimate heir?"

He is not like you was what Lady Essenton wanted to say, but she kept quiet, not that he gave her a chance to reply.

"Or worse yet, what if some fortune hunter entangles him in a web and he marries without my permission? What if he falls in love," he said with a sneer, "with a woman utterly unacceptable, like Miss Darcy?"

"What is wrong with Miss Darcy?"

"Are you a simpleton? She has no title and her dowry is paltry compared to Lady Cassandra. She is completely unsuitable and the sooner she leaves Lyon the better."

"Well, I think she is a delightful young lady, from what I have seen."

"Good thing these decisions are not up to you, then. Sebastian *will* marry a lady of breeding and nobility, not the daughter of a minor landowner. I will not allow it."

Lady Essenton clamped her lips tight. It was useless to argue the matter. His mind was set. However, she also knew her son to be very like the man who sired him, at least in the area of his intractability and determination. Sadly, this probably meant there were battles ahead, regardless of the "compromise" forged that afternoon.

"One problem at a time," he said in a quieter tone, his eyes again focused on his wife's chest. "I have his promise to concentrate on his studies, as ludicrous as they are, and since he takes them so seriously, I doubt he will stray far. I will work to secure a proper betrothal as soon as possible so a marriage can take place immediately upon his return. Hell, if I work it right, and convincingly play the contrite father who wants the heritage secure, which is true, I may get him married sooner. A short trip home to stand before the altar and consummate the marriage can be done in a few weeks. Maybe he will even leave her pregnant and then he can cavort all he wants."

"Your plan may have greater success if you give up on Lady Cassandra. I rather doubt that will happen."

"I have not given up, although I am beginning to agree with that," he said after some hesitation. "I guess it was worth my time coming to you after all. Do your part in persuading Sebastian. Use that mothering bond you two have to convince him. Now, since that is settled…"

He grabbed her wrist, jerking her up from the chair and twisting the arm behind her back while pulling her against his chest. He bent for a harsh kiss, Lady Essenton melting into his body.

"Get this ghastly thing off," he rasped, taking hold of the bodice's edge, ripping the gown down the middle, and tossing it aside. "Much better," he said, scanning her body with purest lust in his eyes. "Still heavier than I like, but you do have fine breasts, Maria. Now get in bed and show me you can still satisfy your husband."

SECOND MOVEMENT

Exposition

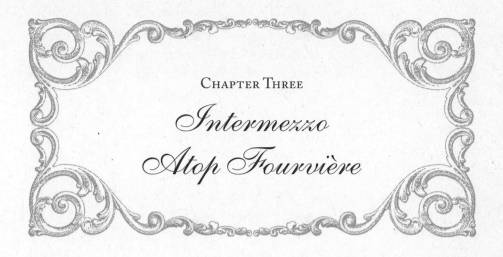

CHAPTER THREE

*Intermezzo
Atop Fourvière*

THE RAINS CEASED THAT night, the next day dawning with clear skies and a strong sun that commenced drying the soggy dirt. The ground was far from completely dry and the warmth transferred through the January air was minimal, but it was enough to satisfy the young people inhabiting the Châteaus la Rochebelin and Plessis-Rhône. Days of forced inactivity behind solid walls and roofs were making everyone edgy with the need for fresh air and exercise.

The only exceptions to the extreme irritability from gloomy weather were Miss Darcy and Mr. Butler.

Each day Sebastian braved the wind and rain, traveling the short distance to Plessis-Rhône for several hours of pleasant company. The de Valday siblings joined in for roughly thirty minutes of conversation and snacks, but that was the maximum amount of time that ever elapsed before the topic of music or composing was broached. At that point, the discourse went rapidly downhill as far as they were concerned. When Georgiana and Sebastian drifted to the pianoforte—an inevitability that averaged two minutes and twenty-three seconds after the talk turned to music, according to Frédéric who amusedly counted—that was their signal to exit the parlor, an exodus they doubted either of the musicians noted.

They were correct in that assessment, a fact Mrs. Annesley could have told them if they had asked her. Georgiana's companion acted as chaperone, sitting in a far corner with a sewing project in her hands, softly smiling and enjoying the youthful banter. She was delighted to observe her charge and the gentleman sharing their mutual fervency for music. It was rare to see the shy Miss Darcy relax so thoroughly and rarer still for her to openly perform and express her opinions. But there was something about Mr. Butler's demeanor that instantly eased her in a manner never witnessed by Mrs. Annesley. The developing friendship was clearly beneficial and lovely to behold as they exchanged knowledge and played musical pieces.

Nevertheless, as completely absorbed as they were in the joys of music—to the point of losing track of time until reminded that hours had passed and it was now lunchtime or beyond—Georgiana and Sebastian welcomed the break in the weather that allowed for an excursion outside.

A horse ride was decided upon with baskets of food and thick blankets carried along for what was planned as a full day. Lord de Marcov recommended heading west to Fourvière, an idea greeted with enthusiasm by the French residents and curiosity by the English.

"Fourvière is an ancient hill," Lord de Marcov began, his horse leading the way with the others clomping near enough to hear his informative speech. "You can see it rising before us"—his hand swept the western horizon as they left the city behind, the tree covered slopes looming ahead—"over four hundred feet above the Saône. The summit is where our history as a city begins; it was founded when the Romans settled here, as a strategic position between the sea and mountains with the two navigable rivers aiding the transit of goods and armies. They named it Lugdunum, the capital of Gaul."

Their horses wove between the thick trees and brush, following the well-trod and snaking trails that gradually ascended the hill. Aside from hooves striking stones and the human voices, the only other sounds were natural ones of leaves rustling, wildlife twittering, and rivulets splashing.

Lord de Marcov continued, "It remained a thriving city extending to Croix-Rousse Hill until the Empire's fall, after which came centuries of upheaval, until the eleventh century when the church revived our prestige by declaring Lyon, as it was by then called in the Latin tongue, as the seat for the Primate of Gaul. We have moved forward since, but none forget that our origins lie on Fourvière Hill."

"Tell them of the ruins, my lord," Yvette encouraged.

"Ah, the ruins, *oui*, mademoiselle, are intriguing. Stone walls and structures dot the plateau, piercing through the soil and grasses in bizarre patterns that invite archeologists from time to time. Excavations frequently occur with coins, jewelry, shards of pottery, and the like unearthed. Remnants of what is believed to be aqueducts have been partially revealed, but the complete history remains buried."

"Perhaps a day will dawn when the hidden treasures are finally uncovered."

"*Oui*, I pray you are correct, Miss Darcy, although I doubt it shall be in my lifetime. However, if we gaze downward we may espy an artifact upon the ground. It happens often."

"Well, I intend to race across the fields with the wind whipping against my face," Frédéric asserted. "Moldy coins hold no interest to me. Will you race me, my dearest Georgiana?"

"Can your ego survive a defeat, Monsieur de Valday? I warn you I am a skilled rider."

"Ha!" He tossed his head at Georgiana's tease. "I fear nothing!"

Sebastian laughed. "Do not be too confident, my friend. The Darcy reputation for horsemanship is renowned in England. I find myself trembling at the concept of daring a Darcy."

"A mere female?" Frédéric asked with overdrawn incredulity, following the gesture with a wink for Georgiana who was blushing at Mr. Butler's praise.

Vivienne harrumphed, but Sebastian answered. "I believe you need three more sisters to erase any idea of females being 'mere' in any way. I have never known my sisters to fail in a quest."

"Precisely right," Vivienne said, nodding.

"Even if they must succeed by cleverly finagling a male's assistance, *oui*, heart of my heart?" Lord de Marcov grinned at his betrothed.

Vivienne smiled, her eyes crafty and tone smug as she replied, "Skills of coercion are to be valued, my love."

The marquis laughed along with the others, a verbal comparison of special skills following as he led the way along the summit's ridge. Finally, they exited the wood onto a flat expanse of grasses and weeds. The valley and rivers spread out far below, the rooftops of Lyon stretching for miles in a dizzying display. Not far from the rim sat a ring of stones, many quite large and jutting through the earth. Most were flat, smooth, and cushioned with moss, but some had broken or decayed, leaving behind jagged edges. They dismounted beside a cluster of level rocks, unloading the baskets and covering the damp rocks with the blankets.

Spirits were gay, as evidenced by the degree of laughter and joking. They strolled around the area and nibbled a few cold treats, but in no time at all they were again astride their mounts for the earlier challenged race.

The de Valdays proved to be poor riders in general, or perhaps were simply lazier, and fell behind quickly. Mademoiselle Gabriella de Marcov also halted, though it was doubtful that a lack of horsemanship was the reason, since she was an accomplished rider; it was more likely being due to her obvious infatuation with Frédéric de Valday! Lady Adele and Lady Reine Butler halted when the others did, preferring the company of adolescents.

Vivienne and Adrien rode neck-and-neck with Sebastian and Georgiana, their horses stretched in a row as they flashed over the uneven ground, leaping over or veering around obstacles. Sebastian shouted in triumph when he and Georgiana pulled into the lead, but the sense of victory was short lived when a quick backward glance revealed the lovers purposefully shifting course toward the thick trees to the west.

He laughed, shaking his head and turning to Georgiana. "We have been deserted," he yelled against the rushing wind.

"Then it is between you and I," she yelled back, following with a sharp command to her mount. The mare responded with a burst of speed, Georgiana flattening her body onto the back as the animal pulled ahead with ease. Racing with Sebastian in her wake, horse and rider kept to a straight path heading directly toward a stone wall nearly four feet high.

Sebastian gasped, panic rising as he watched her smoothly jump the barrier, her horse landing beyond the wall without the slightest hitch in stride and continuing the race toward the distant tree line. His horse followed her jump, as Sebastian's fear was replaced with delight and esteem, and a broad grin lit his face when he joined her in the cool shadows of the trees.

He reined in, bowing deeply from his seat in the sweating animal's saddle before meeting her glittering eyes. She was breathing heavily and several strands of golden hair had escaped her brimmed hat to fall loose over her glistening neck and flushed cheeks. Her face was suffused with exhilaration, and in that moment, she was the most beautiful woman he had ever beheld. For a time he could not speak, staring fixedly at her countenance and breathing heavily along with her, although whether from the race or his reaction to her he could not say.

Finally he wheezed, "My assessment was correct. Darcys are formidable riders. My respect is immense, Miss Darcy."

"Thank you, kind sir. However, if ever you encounter my brother, please resist relating your respect, as he would surely have a seizure to learn of my recklessness."

"I promise to keep your secret of daredevil exploits, but one must presume this is not your first bout of reckless riding?"

She laughed and shook her head. "I have, from time to time, managed to evade the escorts William insists on. And then, of course, he is not with me now and I am fortunate that my aunt and uncle are not as protective. This too is a well kept secret or even the Earl of Matlock would be in serious trouble."

"I have no wish to be in trouble with Mr. Darcy, so you may trust my silence on the topic. I am not, however, above a little blackmail, so be warned."

She laughed again, steering her horse to a rock so she could dismount. Sebastian leapt to the ground and hastened to her side just as she slid off the saddle. His gloved hands grasped one elbow and leather-clad palm, pressing her body into the horse's side and for a short time in his embrace. For too long after her feet were firmly planted on the ground the pose held. Sebastian finally collected himself, released her, and stepped away. The tingling sensation elicited by the contact radiated through his arm and into his whole body, the scent of roses and perspiration invading his nostrils for a combination that worsened his disorientation.

Georgiana's head was bowed, not allowing Sebastian to gauge her reaction. Then she murmured *thank you* and turned away to pick a path through the brush. He gaped at her back for another second or two before returning to his wandering horse. He needed the moments to collect his composure, whispering and brushing a hand over the strong neck of his mount until his hands quit shaking. Then for good measure, he busied himself at the saddlebag, eventually withdrawing two carefully wrapped cheese stuffed meat rolls and walking to where she stood near the plateau's edge.

Wordlessly, he handed one to Georgiana, careful to avoid touching her fingers, and in silence they strolled over the grass, welcoming the weak warmth offered by the sun as they ate their snack.

"I have waited for a solitary moment to share this with you, Miss Darcy," he broke into the quiet, drawing a folded envelope from his inner jacket pocket and handing it to her. "It was delivered yesterday while I was visiting with you. Lord de Marcov awaited my return impatiently and I have impatiently waited for the opportunity to inform you of my news."

Georgiana skimmed the calligraphy, her eyes widening and delight evident as she exclaimed, "Oh my! The Conservatoire! How utterly phenomenal, Mr. Butler! However have you contained your happiness all this time?"

"With difficulty, I assure you."

"Englishmen are so rarely admitted, so I am to understand."

"That is true. I am still in a state of wonderment at my fortune."

"Fortunate indeed, but I believe your skill plays a larger part in this accomplishment."

"You are very kind, and nearly as devoted as de Marcov, who insists the Conservatoire is benefitting the greater. Nonsense, of course. I am humbled by the admission and intend to prove my worth at every turn." He sighed, gazing at the letter now in his hands with an expression of awe and sincerity. "Studying at the Conservatoire has been a dream and ultimate goal for as long as I can remember," he finished softly.

"Then I am doubly thrilled for you. Your family must be bursting with pride."

He hesitated a fraction of a second before agreeing that they were indeed quite proud, his eyes instinctively darting downward and hand tugging on his cravat in a nervous gesture typical whenever he fibbed. Georgiana said nothing, but he saw the creases that flashed across her brow and he smiled gaily to ease any distress. He resumed their stroll, stooping to pick a broken twig off the ground and twisting the flexible wood with his fingers as he spoke. "My mother, grandmother, and sisters are most supportive and delighted for me. My father is a different matter, I fear. I hinted of his attitude at the de Marcov's gala if you recall." She nodded. "I wish I could say he appreciated my endeavors but, alas, that would be an untruth."

"Does he oppose your choices?"

He shrugged. "To a degree, yes. I am man enough to stay my course, and at times I think that annoys him while simultaneously making him proud. He admires strength and fortitude even while annoyed that it is coming from me in this matter. He simply wishes I displayed those traits in areas he prefers and remained at home."

Again he smiled, his voice light, but she sensed the pain underneath and wished she knew what to say. Sebastian seemed to read her thoughts. "Do not concern yourself, Miss Darcy. I should not have burdened you with my affairs. My father is a good man and our love will survive these disagreements. They are not the first and likely will not be the last! Yet you can see why my drive to pursue my studies now—before duty pulls me in another direction—and to prove myself capable is critical."

"Forgive my boldness, Mr. Butler, but I find I am curious as to what you do plan to do with this education? Not to align myself with Lord Essenton's discouragement, since it pains me greatly to imagine your talent wasted and never shared with those who appreciate fine music, however, I can, to a degree, comprehend his reasoning."

Sebastian did not answer immediately. He stepped onto a fallen log, tossing the shreds of bark from the twig he had been stripping into the bushes that covered the descending slope of Fourvière, and stared solemnly at the distant horizon. Georgiana began to fear she had angered him and was preparing to apologize when he spoke.

"I ask those questions of myself frequently, Miss Darcy. I regret my father's attitude, wish he were more understanding and supportive, and even feel angry upon occasion. Yet, logically, I know he has a point. What can I do with this… gift? Will I ever be able to use it other than to entertain my family and our guests?"

The question hung on the air, Sebastian finally tossing the mutilated twig over the edge and turning to look at Georgiana, his gray eyes hard as slate and his voice firm. "I may not know my entire future, Miss Darcy, but I do know that someday I will be Lord Essenton, with an estate I love as my responsibility. I will have a wife and children. I will serve in the House of Lords. And I *will* play and compose music. I *cannot* separate and deny portions of who I am and all that is central to my happiness," he finished with a shake of his head.

They stared at each other for a long stretch. Sebastian's countenance was as serious as she had ever seen. Gone was the amused twinkle that perpetually lit his gray eyes and the characteristic lilt to his full lips. Suddenly he appeared years older than three and twenty, intense and sure. It was as if he strained to communicate nonverbally to her, sensing that she would understand his heart. And the oddity was that she did, at least to an extent. As a woman with a set future before her, indulging in pointless whimsies, no matter how passionately felt, was easily tempered.

Or were they?

For years her dreams had been invaded with desires for more. Denial became second nature, knowing that for her, those dreams could never be realized. Mr. Butler, however, was a man, thus having no reason to reject his passions or accept inevitabilities.

She nodded, holding his gaze. "I do understand, Mr. Butler. Perfectly. I applaud your persistence. Perhaps it is my naïveté and optimism, but I think your father will eventually understand and be as proud of you as the others in your family."

"Perhaps," he agreed. "Someday." Then he smiled, the jovial Mr. Butler she was beginning to know well snapping back into place. "Now, we should return to the others before they send out the hounds."

"Or eat all the food."

Their ride back across the hill's crest was slower. They laughed and conversed, the subjects general and light, while inspecting the scenery and enjoying the fresh, crisp air. As expected, the others were already gathered about the stone ring and spread blankets, the food baskets open.

"About time," Lord de Marcov greeted them. "A moment later and all the food would have been gone."

"Not quite," Yvette soothed, patting the covered basket situated between her and Zoë. "We made sure *l'enfant* ate not all of it."

"I may starve as a sacrifice, my heart, but for you I would perish with joy," Frédéric countered, his hand spread over his heart as a pledge.

Mademoiselle Gabriella de Marcov frowned at Frédéric's fervent declaration, the former sitting on the same blanket Frédéric lay upon. The latter stretched in comfortable repose, smiling upward at Georgiana and seemingly ignoring the younger girl, but none were fooled by his nonchalance. Frédéric de Valday was a masculine magnet and was well aware of his appeal. And he loved it.

"I, for one, appreciate your sacrifice, Monsieur de Valday." Sebastian helped himself to a heaping plate of cold food, serving Georgiana before settling beside Gabriella with due pomp, the fifteen-year-old blushing prettily at the attention.

"Butler, my sister reminded me of the small museum of musical instruments at the Catholic Church in Issoire. I have not been there in years, but Gabriella visited several months ago and said it has grown and been renovated with some remarkable pieces to view. I am sure I would be bored to tears, but imagine you and Mademoiselle Darcy would feel otherwise."

"If Mademoiselle de Marcov recommends it, then I trust her opinion. Miss Darcy?"

"It sounds very interesting."

"Tomorrow, then? If you are not too busy preparing for your departure to Paris?"

"Indeed, I was going to ask a similar question of you, sir. I believe you have a wedding to prepare for?"

Vivienne waved her hand. "Please, take him away! Too many men underfoot are annoying. Adrien should go with you to keep me from strangling him!"

"Exactly why I am going hunting tomorrow, dearest. Butler was invited, but heaven forbid he damage a digit or strain a wrist."

"Absolutely! Can you imagine the trouble I would be in if I could not play the wedding music? My sister would disown me and we would never have the opportunity to hunt together ever again. Better I practice the pieces and do nothing more strenuous than stroll through a dusty museum with Miss Darcy."

CHAPTER FOUR

Composing a Friendship

LONG FINGERS MOVED EFFORTLESSLY over the keys, the melody pouring from the piano harmonious and emotive. Georgiana stood to the side of the fine instrument, palms flat upon the gleaming wood to feel the vibration, eyes closed, and body swaying slightly as the music flowed through her. Sebastian Butler watched her with a pleased smile as he played.

Composing and playing music was a compulsion for him, an obsession, if you will, that had been a driving force for as far back as his memories existed. Lady Essenton was musically inclined, quite skilled in fact, although unable to utilize her talent other than teaching her children. She had created an environment consisting of songs and instruments, demanding that all of her six children learn the basics. Lord Essenton agreed that the girls needed to play and sing, considering the accomplishment a worthy one for entertaining family and guests, but he discouraged his son from learning what he deemed a female pursuit.

However, it was Sebastian who had shown a true gift, and by the time he was ten, his skill had far surpassed anyone else in the household. There were few instruments he could not play. Strings, drums, woodwinds, pipes—he was curious about everything, picking up any instrument he found and learning how to play whether by instruction or instinct. The pianoforte and piano were his chosen preferences, but he could manage nearly any instrument.

Rare was the piece of music he was unable to master within days. His voice, a fluid baritone with an octave from high bass notes to low tenor, was an inborn gift that only improved with training. His compositions, while perhaps not brilliant or revolutionary, were beautiful and varied in style. For all of this, he owed the greatest debt to his mother, and now his grandmother as well. They had presented a united force against his father, who thought Sebastian's musical studies a waste of time. They insisted he fulfill his dreams now, while the duty of estate management was not a burden he needed to bear. The current tenuous peace with his father had been harshly bought.

Over time, he had discovered that as tremendous as his joy was in learning about and creating music, a higher pleasure was felt in observing the response of others as he performed. Being able to share the transcendent bliss he experienced via music was indescribable. Clearly Miss Darcy was enjoying the composition. He snuck a peak at Mrs. Annesley, Miss Darcy's companion and chaperone, and his surge of contentment redoubled, as she was sitting in the far corner, embroidery forgotten in her lap and eyes glazed as she enjoyed the music.

He lifted his voice, adding French lyrics of love and eternity. Georgiana opened her eyes, smiling happily as he completed the ballad. She clapped her hands, Sebastian bowing his head with a grin.

"Do you think she will be pleased?"

"Oh, how could she not? It was beautiful. Lady Vivienne will be overjoyed and weeping hysterically!"

"That, I am afraid, is not a conclusive sign of praise, as my sentimental sister cries at the drop of a hat," he said with a laugh. "She shall be a dewy mess all through the ceremony is my guess. Luckily, de Marcov is aware of her propensity for tears and loves her anyway, poor sod."

"Well, I am certain a portion shall be due to your song, Mr. Butler. Tomorrow will be a day of remembrance on numerous levels."

"I do wonder about this part," he said, playing a set of chords. "It feels, not quite perfect. Like it needs a… dissonance." Georgiana said the last word simultaneously, Sebastian meeting her eyes with an exuberant grin. "You hear it as well!"

"Yes. Something to add an emphasis as to what is coming, to draw attention. But not too harsh, Mr. Butler."

"Indeed, no. And only for maybe two or three chords. How about this?" He played the section again, altering the notes ever so slightly, the subtle instability of the new arrangement underscored by the lifting tone and blending smoothly with the composition, while evoking a visceral charge in the listener. It was incredible and transformed the entire piece.

"Bravo!" Georgiana clapped. "Stupendous. Your sister will indeed be a puddle of tears! May I, please?"

"Of course!" He rose from the bench, waving his hand in front of the piano. "You know the piece as well as I, and it helps to hear it from another's fingertips." She assumed his place on the bench, fingers brushing over the keys as he leaned over her right shoulder to arrange the sheets of music properly. "There. Start from the top and play it through to the end, if you do not mind, Miss Darcy."

She nodded her head. "My pleasure," she murmured, fingers testing the initial notes as she concentrated on the papers before her.

Sebastian smiled, glancing downward as he straightened. Completely unconsciously, he had positioned himself so that he was afforded a direct view of her generous bosom, the soft swell and dark line of her cleavage readily visible. The sweet aroma of her flowery perfume rose from her ivory skin. A jolt surged through his body. Desire assaulted every muscle like a tidal wave that rushed and surged chaotically, settling in his gut and groin with a painful crash.

He stifled a gasp, stepped hastily backward several paces, and willed his racing heart to slow. His reaction was so utterly unexpected that his befuddled mind froze. Numbed yet excruciatingly aroused, he could only breathe deeply and wait for the tremors to pass.

She is beautiful, he reasoned, a fact he had recognized two years ago, at her debut ball in London at Darcy House. Sebastian Butler was assuredly a man who appreciated and desired those of the opposite sex, but for so long his focus has been on study. Matters of serious courtship were never considered, and sexuality was largely suppressed except for a handful of brief dalliances. His genial fraternization with persons of both genders was natural and rarely led to thoughts of sex. Never had he experienced a powerful reaction to a woman, as he had now twice with Miss Darcy, and it was disturbing.

He closed his eyes, allowing the waves of music and her sweet soprano to wash the troubles away, swiftly deciding that it was nothing more than a purely physical response heightened by his long abstinence.

Georgiana finished the cantata, turning to Mr. Butler for his opinion.

He had regained his equilibrium, the flush of arousal passed, and he bowed appreciatively. "Beautiful! You should play it rather than I."

She stood, shaking her head and laughing. "I shall be in Paris while you are dazzling the wedding guests, Mr. Butler. Perhaps someday you can amuse me with the tale of how weepy the assembly was."

"I shall see you in Paris, will I not, Miss Darcy?" He ignored the faint tightness of dismay that banded about his chest and kept his friendly smile intact. "I promised to take you to the Conservatoire, remember?"

"Indeed, you did, but I would not hold you to such a promise, sir, if your schedule does not permit excessive free time for recreation. Your studies are far more important than entertaining me."

"My studies will not commence in earnestness until autumn. Entertaining you is a prospect I hold in high regard, I promise. It will be my pleasure."

"Thank you. I do appreciate the offer and confess I would be saddened to miss a private tour of the Conservatoire. Nevertheless, it is undoubtedly fortunate I will be departing before long, since I fear my curiosity to hear of your every adventure is inexhaustible. If given free rein, I would monopolize your every waking minute with questions!"

"And I would not complain," he assured, resuming his seat at the pianoforte and pretending to study the keys while tapping an improvised tune. "Are you anxious to return to England? Are you weary of traveling?"

"Not the traveling exactly," she answered after a pause to consider. "I have thoroughly enjoyed seeing places I've previously only read about and meeting people from such diverse cultures. However, I have realized that I prefer familiarity surrounding me."

"You miss your home."

"I do. Pemberley and, to a lesser degree, Darcy House have been the only dwelling places I have ever known. Our hosts have been hospitable and our lodgings comfortable, for the most part. Yet there is a sense of security and belonging that I have not felt since leaving our shores. I suppose that sounds odd."

"No. I understand your meaning. I have felt the same unease upon occasion, and I experience my moments of pining for home. However, I started young with boarding school and then Oxford, always with the plan to travel abroad set within my mind and preparing my heart."

"Or perhaps you do possess a portion of wanderlust despite your denial."

"Indeed! Perhaps you are correct, but I shall avoid confronting the truth, in case I decide it is an attribute I possess and I am then struck with an uncontrollable urge to sail to the Orient!"

"Ah, but this might be an excellent urge. You could learn from the Kunqu and Sichuan opera masters, incorporate German and French influences, thus creating a masterpiece unparalleled."

"And unwatchable, I am sure." He shook his head, laughing and gazing at her with respect. "Chinese opera. Who would have thought? Is there anything you do not know, Miss Darcy?"

"Very little," she declared, hiding her smile, "and what I do not yet know I shall extract from your brain. I did warn you, Mr. Butler."

"Yes, you did. Extract as you wish and then use that knowledge to compose your own Chinese-German opera. I am beginning to believe you may be wrong in which of us should move about the world."

He wagged his finger at her, Georgiana batting it playfully away and shaking her head. "I confess that I imagine watching a Chinese opera would be a spectacular experience, but the lengthy journey there is utterly unappealing. The green fields of Derbyshire are calling to me. I shall leave the traveling to those better suited for the lifestyle—after I monopolize their precious time, that is."

He opened his mouth to assert that he considered spending time with her as precious, but the parlor door opened, revealing a footman.

"Sir, the carriage is prepared and awaiting your pleasure."

The foul weather of the week before had left behind air that was crisp and replete with the fresh aromas of damp soil and washed foliage. It remained cold, but the sky was an endless blue, free of any clouds to obscure the sun's warming rays, making the short ride a very pleasant one. The whitewashed, brick church was larger than either had expected based on de Marcov's description. It was undoubtedly very old, the paint chipped in numerous places and gaps present in the mortar, but the garden was well tended and the pathways clear. Located on the northern edge of the small village of Issoire, on the outskirts of Lyon, it was surrounded by homes and businesses. The dirt and cobbled streets were far from busy, but enough people roamed about to indicate a thriving community.

The *musée de la musique* was housed in a long, two-story building that had once been a convent, but new quarters for the resident nuns had been built some fifty years ago. The vacated rooms began as storage, the priests and nuns finally realizing that the accumulation of old instruments, sheet music, and other relics could be arranged into a semblance of order. The modest museum that began as a simple way to increase the church's revenue, rapidly evolved into a full-scale museum, as local residents, many who were exceedingly wealthy, donated to the collection.

Georgiana and Mr. Butler were immediately impressed. "It will never compete with the Louvre, but it is nice," Mr. Butler noted with wry humor and a grin.

They wandered together, Mrs. Annesley allowing them the space to talk without fear of eavesdropping, although neither paid the companion much mind, their attention drawn to the displays and the conversation evoked.

"Can you play the harpsichord, Miss Darcy?" he asked, as they stood before a seventeenth-century Blanchet.

"Yes. We have one at Pemberley. My mother was quite adept, so I am told. I only vaguely remember her playing it. More of a sense, actually, most likely fabricated in my mind due to stories I have heard."

"Perhaps, although I believe music is a strong stimulus to memory. Meaning that, if your mother did play the harpsichord frequently when you were young, your memory is sparked when you hear the unique tones produced by the instrument."

"Yes, I can see the logic in that. Same with smells. I have always envisioned her when I smell roses, yet I was not told until years later that rose water was her favored perfume."

"Is that why you favor the fragrance of roses?"

She blushed, surprised that he had noticed, and nodded.

"I am sorry you lost your mother so young," he said softly, his gaze tender. "I cannot imagine. Do you have vivid memories of her?"

Georgiana shook her head. "Nothing vivid, sadly. Or at least I am unsure if what I recall are true remembrances or images conjured. There are several portraits within the house." She paused, smiling fondly. "My father was deeply devoted to my mother and desired capturing her image as frequently as possible. Thus, my brother and I now have a wealth of reminders throughout the manor. I was only four when she died, but William was older and has forever sought to keep her alive for me. He recounts hundreds of stories, enumerating the tiniest details, conveying feelings as well as facts, all so clearly that sometimes it seems impossible that they are his memories and not mine."

She looked up into Sebastian's pale eyes that watched her with sympathy. "I am fortunate, from a certain perspective, that I was blessed with many more years with my father."

"Was he a kind man? A devoted parent?"

She nodded her head emphatically. "Oh yes indeed, he was, but also extremely sad. He never recovered from mother's death. William has told me of how altered he was after. I have no memory of him from before. To me, he was always affectionate, ready with a laugh and a tight embrace. Yet, I knew of his pain. He would tell me of mother, speaking of her as if she was still alive, which I suppose she was to him, in his heart. His voice would be sad, yet oddly joyful. He told me once that she gave him purpose and happiness, and that the best gifts of his life came from her. When I asked him what those gifts were, he said it was Fitzwilliam and me." She smiled brightly, eyes moist. "Is that not beautiful?"

"Indeed, it is. And very true, I daresay."

"I miss him, but content myself in knowing that he is with mother, the woman he loved so completely. He must be overjoyed and at peace, and they are no longer alone. Do you believe in such an afterlife, Mr. Butler?"

"I do. I am sure you are correct in your assumption, Miss Darcy. And I am thankful that God blessed you with a brother who is so devoted. Nevertheless, I am saddened at your losses at so young an age." He smiled ruefully. "My father can annoy me no end, but I do revere and love him. I cannot fathom the day he will pass away, and not only because I will then be Lord Essenton and forced to relinquish my wayward existence."

She chuckled, appreciating his lightening of the sad subject, and decided it was time to change the topic. "Oh, look. Hymnals. My, some of these are quite old."

"I love hymns. They seem more… spiritual than sacred music alone." He shrugged. "I suppose that makes no sense."

"On the contrary. It makes perfect sense. The focus of a hymn is on praise and worship of God. The words are felt deep in your soul."

"Have you heard many of the hymns of Charles Wesley?"

"Indeed, I have! They are among my favorites. Our rector at Pemberley Chapel met both the Wesley brothers and studied with them for a time. Theologically, I believe he greatly agreed with Mr. John Wesley, but in the end could not bear to break with the Church, but our services draw upon many tenets of the Methodist Movement." She glanced over to see how Mr. Butler was accepting that borderline heresy, but he was staring at her with deep interest and no obvious censure. "My brother is better educated than I, but we Darcys have a strong faith."

"Yes. My grandmother speaks reverently of her family's devotion to religion, even if she has not precisely followed a strict moral code." Again, the strong affection was evident in his voice, even when teasing about Lady Warrow's eccentricities. "You may be interested, Miss Darcy, in some of the psalms I have placed to music."

"Indeed, I am."

He shook his head at her awed enthusiasm. "It is a hobby, one might say. Amid more serious compositions and study, I have been methodically compiling short hymns from the scriptures. I have often wondered how the creations of David may have sounded as originally placed to music." He laughed. "Presumptuous, I know. And of course they did not have pianos two millennia ago, so very different than my humble offerings to be sure."

"All instruments are pleasing to God, Mr. Butler. And I would love to hear your hymns."

"Once we are settled in Paris, I will dig them out for you to peruse. I would be greatly honored, and benefited, if you sang a few of them for me. Some are written for a soprano and your voice is beautiful."

She flushed, nodding once before turning to the object beside the harpsichord. "A Silbermann pianoforte. Oh, this is a beautiful specimen, if a bit battered. We have a Silbermann at Pemberley, although it is a far later model than this one."

"These markings here date it at 1737. They've improved the design considerably since then. Do you prefer the pianoforte to the piano?"

She pursed her lips, thinking carefully as she ran her hand over the smooth wood. "They are different. I like the softness, the tonal quality, and the sustain of a pianoforte. For my seventeenth birthday, my brother gifted me with a Stein from Vienna. Four years prior he had purchased a Broadwood piano with six octaves! Oh, it is a wonder and I adore it. It was a horrible extravagance to buy a second instrument of such magnitude so soon after the other, but he knew how I appreciated the varied registers of the pianoforte. He spoils me horribly."

"He loves you immensely," he corrected. "Have you read that Broadwood has invented a seven-octave piano?"

Her brows rose. "Truly? That must be amazing. You should write for such an instrument."

He laughed. "Eventually, perhaps. I do plan to tour the Érard establishment while in Paris. He is on the innovative edge of piano development." He glanced around, noting Mrs. Annesley unobtrusively standing at a far window, and leaned toward Georgiana, whispering conspiratorially, "I have penned a six-octave fugue, but do not think it very good, so do not tell anyone." He winked.

She leaned closer, whispering back, "I wrote a six-octave sonata and think it quite good."

His eyes opened wide, his mouth dropped open, and his hand instinctively moved to lightly grasp her forearm as his voice rose in surprise. "You wrote a sonata? How could you not tell me this? I am so proud of you! All this time talking about music, with me droning on egotistically about my achievements, and here you are a composer!"

"It is nothing compared to your accomplishments, Mr. Butler, truly. But"—she looked at him through her downcast eyes, her cheeks scarlet—"if it is not too much trouble… that is, if you have the time, later… maybe I could play my melodies for you? For your critique?"

He lifted her chin gently, his voice low and smile genuine. "We are friends, are we not, Miss Darcy? I would be privileged to hear your creations, and knowing your skill, I doubt if my critique is necessary."

They stared into each other's eyes with their faces less than a foot apart. He held her chin, fighting the urge to stroke his thumb over the warm softness of her flesh or, better yet, the inviting moistness of her lips. The lips that parted slightly, affording a glimpse of her teeth and the tongue behind, Sebastian vividly imagining how incredible it would feel to press his lips against hers, insert his tongue between, and touch…

With a shake he removed his fingers from her chin, clearing his throat gruffly as he straightened. "Well, I see that we have much to cover once settled in Paris: the Conservatoire, all this music to listen to, the Louvre, Érard's, hymnals, my sister's weeping. You shall grow quite ill of me, madam."

"Unlikely, sir. Besides, I shall be leaving Paris by mid-April at the latest." She was surprised to hear a normal voice escaping her dried throat, the words distinct even though she did not consciously form them. How could she when the only thought inhabiting her brain was to wonder how it would feel to kiss Mr. Butler? She was scandalized by the impression, her heart pounding at the shock of such a notion. She slid her arm away from under his hand and pressed her palms flat onto the surface of the harpsichord, willing them not to tremble or betray her thoughts by caressing the skin where his bare hand had lain. Somehow she had to ignore the desire that burned over her flesh that begged to be touched.

"Oh? Your plans have become set?"

"A letter arrived today from my friend Miss Bennet. She is Mrs. Darcy's sister and has recently become engaged. The wedding is scheduled for late April, and I must be there. So you see, I shall not long be around to distract your studies for the hassle of fulfilling promises, made in the heat of the moment, that you are too much of a gentleman to break. Honestly, Mr. Butler, please do not allow me to invade your purpose. You owe me nothing."

"I enjoy our time together, Miss Darcy. It is in no way an imposition and none of the invitations I extended were hastily rendered. I quite know my own mind. And besides, my serious studies do not begin until the fall, when my enrollment at the Conservatoire begins. Until then, I am free to be spontaneous."

Smiling gaily, he waved his arms in the air, using the gesture to shake off the lingering stupor and smother the strange stab of breathless sadness that entered his heart at the thought of her leaving.

They continued to wander about the rooms, conversation light and pleasant as they enjoyed their companionship and mutual interest. Their balance was restored amid talk of music, but it was not only Mrs. Annesley who was aware of the constant separation of several feet and the careful avoidance of touching each other.

CHAPTER FIVE

Consonance of Purpose

IT WAS LATE AFTERNOON when they returned to Château la Rochebelin, Georgiana intending to depart to the de Valday château after biding a proper adieu and expressing her appreciation to Mr. Butler, but they were interrupted by his sister while yet standing in the foyer.

"Oh, there you are Sebastian! Finally," she exclaimed from the stairs, descending in a breathless rush. Her face was glowing, the permanent smile that seemed to be etched into her lovely face these days broader than usual. "Miss Darcy," she greeted with a perfunctory bob in Georgiana's direction, continuing on without pausing, "my sisters' dresses have arrived and Adrien is thoroughly indifferent to the fact! He persists in vexing me with his pathetic jests and pretended ignorance."

"I doubt if his ignorance is pretended, dear sister," Sebastian interrupted with a chuckle.

Vivienne waved her hand irritably, her face falling into an adorable pout, her eyes wide with astonishment. "How can he not recognize the supreme importance of gowns to a wedding ceremony? You must come and talk reason to him!" she pleaded, grasping his hand. "You comprehend these things and can communicate the significance!"

Sebastian rolled his eyes, glancing sidelong at a smiling Georgiana. "I have yet to decide if having five sisters is a blessing or a curse. Years of polite praise for their attire have somehow translated to an awareness of feminine sensibilities and superior fashion sense. God help me."

Vivienne tugged on his hand while reaching to clasp Georgiana's as well. "Come! You too, Miss Darcy. We females shall provide a united front against the stupid males devoid of basic common sense."

"I beg your pardon!"

But Mr. Butler was ignored as they were dragged to the parlor. A number of people sat and stood about the large chamber, but Georgiana was instantly overwhelmed by the profusion of ruffles and lace draped over two long sofas. She honestly could not count how many gowns there were. The piles were so voluminous that one would initially think there must have been a couple of dozen, but even a cursory observation of the prancing young woman modeling one of them gave pause to that idea. The dresses for the Butler sisters were a masterpiece of satin and velvet, melding an older style with the newer French passion for crinoline skirts, wider hemlines, and excessive adornments. The yards of fabrics and trimmings necessary to fashion such gowns was mind-boggling, and Georgiana could not help but wonder what the bride's gown looked like!

"Am I not fabulous, Sebastian?"

"Yes indeed, Adele. You are for certain the loveliest creature I have ever seen." Sebastian bowed grandly to his youngest sister, who beamed with satisfaction. "I fear you shall outshine the bride."

Vivienne snorted her disdain at that notion. Lord de Marcov laughed gaily, drawing his fiancée close to his side and patting her hand placatingly. "Adele, my sweet," he said, "you are a vision, but none on earth could compare with my precious Vivienne, owner of my heart." He brought Vivienne's fingers to his lips for a tender kiss, his bride-to-be smiling but quick with a retort.

"Flattery shall save you from severe punishment, Adrien, but total salvation will only be granted if you fawn gushingly over the dresses. I do not wish to marry an utter simpleton. Sebastian is here to assist you in comprehending your lunacy and error."

"Is he now?" Lord de Marcov looked to Sebastian with a raised brow, his grin broad. "Please, enlighten me, Butler. I have mentioned appreciating the frilly bits along the hem and the puffy sleeves, but apparently that is insufficient. Should a gentleman know the proper name of each button, cloth, and lacy

ribbon as well? Rather effeminate, is it not?" he finished with a mildly sugges-
tive smirk toward Sebastian, who only laughed.

"Poor soul," Sebastian said with mock pity. "You miss the point entirely, de
Marcov. Trust the man who has five sisters and a mother"—he bowed toward
Lady Essenton—"as possessing superior intelligence over the unfortunate man
with one sister. Your life shall be a happier one if you learn enough to feign
avid interest over womanly essentials. The proper amount of animation will
earn undying devotion and respect, you reaping the reward of unwavering favor
and coddling. It is a game and an art form that I have obviously perfected ably,
since my sister enlisted my help to penetrate your density."

"You boor!" Vivienne launched a small sofa pillow at her brother's head,
Sebastian catching it deftly. Laughter rang out, voices rising in amused conversation. Sebastian turned to Georgiana and winked, she hiding her mirth behind
her hand.

"How did you find the museum, Miss Darcy?"

"It was surprisingly comprehensive for so small an establishment. Thank
you for recommending it, Lord de Marcov. Mr. Butler and I greatly enjoyed
the diversion."

"I do pray you managed to acquire some sort of education while there, as
that is presumably the purpose to you tarrying on the Continent." It was Lord
Essenton, his voice mild as he addressed his son, but with an edge noted by all.

"Indeed, sir, it is my overall purpose, and my time at the museum was"—he
glanced to Georgiana with a soft smile—"enlightening."

Lord Essenton frowned. "Just do not lose sight of why you are here. You
have the year ahead of you to learn all you can and get this musical nonsense
out of your system before returning to England and your duties. Remember
our agreement."

Lady Warrow spoke up from her regal perch on an elaborately carved
Queen Anne chair. "Sebastian will stand by his word, Essenton, have no fear."
She smiled at her grandson, ignoring Lord Essenton's annoyance. "Study as
you wish, dear boy, but do not forget to play as well! Life should be enjoyed to
the fullest. Too much seriousness makes for horridly dull people." She gazed
pointedly at her son, standing erect and irked nearby.

"Thank you, Grandmother. Never fear, my intentions are intact, but this
time is for Vivienne. And a holiday is always good for fresh inspiration, I

daresay." His tone was gay, eyes sparkling as he attempted to lighten the mood inserted by his father, but Lord Essenton was not finished.

"I am to understand you are departing for Paris soon, Miss Darcy?"

"You are correct, my lord. We depart tomorrow and plan to stay in Paris until early April at the latest, then returning home."

He nodded, smiling pleasantly. "Well, it has been a delight encountering you here in Lyon. Please extend our best wishes for a safe journey home to Lord and Lady Matlock."

"I shall do that for you, Father, as I will be seeing Miss Darcy and the earl and countess while in Paris."

"Indeed. Well, that is excellent news." His voice was dry, belying the words. "Again, I do hope you will not forget to prepare for your stay at the Conservatoire and your current planned occupations."

"I shall not, but occasional diversions are abundantly welcomed." He smiled at Georgiana, who blushed, both of them missing the tight scowl that flashed across Lord Essenton's features before disappearing behind a serene façade.

The loud knock at the door revealed the twins and their brother. They filed in before permission was fully granted, not that Georgiana was surprised, since the ritual was a nightly one. Zoë carried a tray, balancing a silver teapot with steam rising from the spout, a tiny bowl of sugar, a small pitcher of cream, and four china cups. Yvette bore an identical tray laden with an assortment of pastries.

"Petits fours filled with caramel crème, baklava, and pumpkin custard tarts! Fresh today," Yvette sang, making yummy sounds as she set the tray onto the waiting table.

"And I have Beaumarchais to entertain!" Frédéric declared, waving the leather-bound book high in the air. "You fair maidens may repose as I dramatically play all the parts! Applause and accolades highly anticipated, just so you know."

Laughter, silliness, and gossip would rule for the next several hours. Georgiana had swiftly grown to anticipate these hours spent in foolishness and youthful companionship. The activity was nearly unknown to her, as her only sibling, although dearly adored, was far older. The only time in her twenty years she had experienced what it was like to have this brand of kinship was with Mary and Kitty Bennet. Then, as now, she treasured the frivolity and amity. However, that night was bittersweet because it was their last, since Georgiana and the Matlocks would be departing for Paris the following day.

"It is just not fair! How can our parents be so cruel as to bring you into our lives, sweet Georgiana, only to be wrested away in so short a time! It is unconscionable!"

"You *must* stay in France! How can we live without you?" Zoë interjected, every bit as dramatic as her sister.

"I am sure you will manage to survive quite well," Georgiana answered with a laugh and playful shove.

"Will you not miss us horribly?" Yvette asked with a sob.

"Most horribly, I assure you."

"If only you could have fallen madly in love. Then you would be forced to stay, as your heart would be ripped asunder otherwise!" Yvette declared with a passionate clutch to her left chest, sighing hugely and falling backward onto the pillows that were stacked before the fire.

Zoë snorted. "We tried, dear sister, introduced her to hundreds of gorgeous Frenchmen, even *l'enfant*"—she gestured to a smugly smiling Frédéric who was momentarily strangely quiet—"but she only had eyes for her divinely perfect Englishman."

"I did not! And he is not mine."

"Well, I cannot blame her," Yvette admitted dreamily, ignoring Georgiana's protest. "He is yummy enough to eat."

"Yvette!" Georgiana was dumbfounded, her face scarlet.

Zoë leered, voice falling into a seductive purr. "Eat, kiss, touch, squeeze. Hmmm. Just think of all the wonders to be enjoyed with such a man." She was gazing at the red, astonished face of her new friend with a teasing glint in her eyes. "Just imagine how stupendous he must be naked."

Georgiana was aghast, and not only because of Zoë's indecent words, but also because of the sudden vision of Mr. Butler unclothed that assaulted her mind and made her heart race painfully. Abruptly, the memory of his touch seared her mind, sensations confusing her while warmth spread across her skin and flutters invaded her belly. Her breath caught, but at which indelicacy she was not sure, and words utterly escaped her.

Frédéric and Yvette burst into gales of laughter. Zoë joined in, closing the space to envelop Georgiana in a snug embrace. "Oh! You should see your face! Sweet, innocent Georgiana!" The ribald hilarity continued unabated for some time, all three de Valdays spouting further sexual comments and witty double entendres between their breathless laughter. Georgiana could not decide whether to laugh or weep, the conjured images flashing through her mind both disturbing and pleasant.

"Do you love your Englishman, my friend?" Yvette abruptly asked in a serious tone.

"No! No. That is, he is a friend and no more."

Zoë harrumphed, reaching for a pumpkin tart. "Who needs to be friends with a man? Men are for love and protection, that is all."

"Is this so, oh wise one of the world?" Frédéric chuckled. "Is that why the Almighty created us males?"

"You, little boy, are the exception," Yvette assured him, planting a noisy kiss on his rosy cheek.

"*Merci.* Now, who wants to hear a secret?"

The twins gasped, eyes instantly sparkling, and they grabbed on to their brother's hands.

"Do tell!"

"Speak, you scoundrel! Keeping secrets all this time!"

He reveled in the moment, drawing it out as the twins begged and tickled. Georgiana's discomfiture eased in the merriment, her heart again brimming with the happiness found in these playful interludes. She knew the de Valdays meant no harm, their bawdy earthiness merely a harmless characteristic that hid a technical innocence the same as hers.

"I overheard mother and father—"

"Eavesdropping again?"

"Do you want to hear my news or not?" Zoë shrugged as if unconcerned, but Frédéric knew better, as did they all, so resumed with a grin. "They were speaking to the esteemed Lord and Lady Matlock. Father and mother offered our townhouse in Île Saint-Louis for them to stay rather than the hotel, and"—he paused dramatically, making sure all eyes were fixed upon him—"we shall be joining them later this month!"

The twins released identical squeals of glee. Yvette rose to commence dancing about the room, singing a song extolling the beauties of Paris, while Zoë gathered Georgiana into another tight embrace.

"*Magnifique!* We shall have more weeks to play! Dancing, parties, opera! And more time for us to observe you and your English *amour* fall passionately in love, and to teach you of the ways to woo and please your new lover!"

Georgiana opened her mouth to protest, but it was pointless, as Zoë had bounced up to join her sister and brother in wild capering about the room.

⁓

At the de Marcov château, Sebastian Butler and Adrien de Marcov sat alone in far more sedate companionship in the elegant drawing room, sipping wine, but having a surprisingly similar conversation.

"Was it difficult to bid adieu to Mademoiselle Darcy today?"

Sebastian glanced up in surprise, brows lifting. "No. Why should it be? We shall see each other in Paris."

"She is an absolutely lovely woman," de Marcov stated, watching his friend closely. "If I were not so besotted with my own sweet English Rose, I might consider making a play for her myself."

"Those days are long over, my friend. If, that is, you wish to keep your manliness intact, as my 'sweet' sister would likely castrate you for even entertaining such a notion."

De Marcov winced but then brightened. "By the end of this week, I assure you that castration will absolutely not be an option she would consider."

"Please, remember this is my baby sister we are speaking of. I think I shall persist in believing in her virtue with any eventual conceiving occurring immaculately."

"Very well, I shall control my instinctively roving eye. But I am not dead to female allurements, nor ever will be, so must again inquire how you can be so unmoved by the beauty and personality of Mademoiselle Darcy. I worry for you."

"Your concern warms my heart," Sebastian responded with overblown gratitude, "but you know I cannot allow myself to become romantically entangled at this time. I have an agenda, a plan for the present that does not include romance."

"You and your obsessive need to organize and choreograph every moment of your life." De Marcov shuddered. "How that clinical attitude lends itself to the creative artist is beyond my comprehension."

"This discussion again?" Sebastian asked humorously. "Are you still annoyed that my marks in mathematics and the sciences were as good as in the arts, while you barely survived from year to year without disgracing your parents?"

"My parents understood the importance of studies outside of traditional education. So, are you assiduously forcing yourself to not fall in love with the charming Mademoiselle Darcy?"

"That is not what I meant and you know it. She is my friend. We both appreciate the distinction and are content in the path our relationship has taken. Feelings cannot be fabricated if they do not exist."

The marquis stared at Sebastian, who placidly sipped his wine, not speaking for a full minute. Then he said, "That makes no sense whatsoever. And I think you are lying. It is unnatural to behold such beauty and not be moved by it."

"So says the man who seduced nearly every woman he ever met."

"Until my heart was enraptured by one Vivienne Butler. I owe you my present happiness and merely wish to assist you in matters of *amour*, especially since you are hopelessly inept." He grinned, Sebastian shaking his head as he laughed.

The differences in their characters when it came to sexuality were a long-standing joke between them. Lord de Marcov was the quintessential Frenchman with all the clichés. His list of lovers, all of who willingly went to his bed and left satiated, could fill an entire book. Sebastian was not a virgin, but his list would barely constitute a paragraph, a very short paragraph, in the Frenchman's book! Lord de Marcov's philandering had changed with the eventual commitment and binding love to Vivienne, but it had taken Sebastian some time to fully embrace the idea of his sister wedding someone so cavalier about sex, as much as he liked him. But he had been witness to the astounding, profound alteration in de Marcov's character after he met Vivienne. He could vouch for de Marcov's abstaining as he completed the final year at Oxford, was privy to the pining for her while they were apart, and knew the depths of the new marquis's despair when their marriage was postponed due to his father's unexpected death. The full extent of the love he felt was clear, the gushy Frenchman quite verbal on the topic.

In fact, he was quite verbal on most topics, Sebastian educated on bedroom matters well beyond his personal experience!

"You have taught me quite enough, thank you very much. I am sure when the time comes I shall be adequately prepared." Sebastian spoke dryly.

"But not as yet? And not with Mademoiselle Darcy? You are going to persist in this affirmation?"

"It is the truth, no matter how differently your current romantic soul may wish it to be otherwise. You, my brother, have love deeply etched into your brain these days."

"I think, lately, I have pure lust etched into my brain, if you must know the truth." He shook his head, gazing at Sebastian's grimace humorously. "Man was not meant to go so long without female companionship, Butler, especially when daily in the company of the exquisite example who owns one's heart. It has been far too long, and if this next week does not hurry past, I truly believe I shall explode. You should have burst into flames ages ago!"

"Very funny."

"Well then, I shall believe you if you say the two of you are just friends, although I cannot comprehend such an arrangement and judge it wholly unnatural…"

"You would," Sebastian interrupted.

"…nevertheless, I will be the first to say 'I told you so' when you finally admit you are in love with her."

Sebastian opened his mouth to protest, but Lord de Marcov smoothly changed the subject.

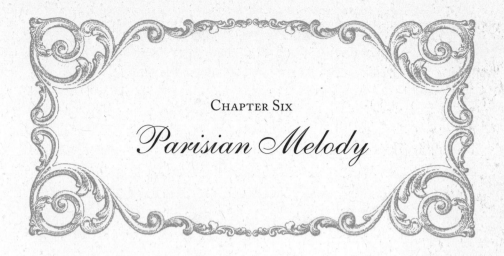

Chapter Six

Parisian Melody

THE BEAUTIFUL PARIS TOWNHOUSE of the de Valday family was located on the Quai d'Orléans of Île Saint-Louis. The numerous gilded balconies afforded stunning views of the slow-moving waters of the Seine and the stone arches of the Pont de la Tournelle that spanned the river, giving access to the island residential district. Georgiana and the Matlocks had arrived over a week before, discovering the luxurious city manor—belonging to the de Valday family for over one hundred years—prepared for their stay, with the staff welcoming and professional. Many of the Parisian nobility had chosen to relocate to newer districts in the western part of the vast city, deserting their fine mansions to financiers, magistrates, artisans, and others of the bourgeoisie. The isle was a tranquil nook amid the very heart of the boisterous city, the eclectic collection of residents adding to the novelty.

Georgiana's cousin and legal co-guardian, the retired Colonel Richard Fitzwilliam, had been residing in town since December with his wife, Lady Simone Fitzwilliam, and her youngest children from a previous marriage, Harry and Hugh Pomeroy. They had chosen to stay at one of the many sumptuous *hôtels* Paris was famous for, the distance a short buggy ride away. Georgiana had greeted her family with tremendous enthusiasm, not only because she had missed them terribly, especially her dear friend Richard, but also to ply them endlessly for details of her newest nephew, Michael Darcy.

The greatest misery for Georgiana during her long separation from her brother and sister-in-law, Elizabeth, was the knowledge that she would miss the birth and early months of their second child. After the announcement of his birth arrived unexpectedly in late September, letters from home became infrequent and uncommonly brief. Georgiana worried that something was amiss, strengthening the misty tendril of homesickness already wrapping around her heart. The colonel assured her that Michael's fragile health from his earlier-than-expected birth was resolved by the time of his christening. Between him and Simone, she was regaled with stories of the youngest, tempestuous Darcy, as well as the rapidly growing Alexander, now over two years of age, and her sadness was alleviated.

Georgiana was able to relax and relish the serene, diverse scenery of Île Saint-Louis. She walked along the narrow streets with Mrs. Annesley or Lady Matlock as weather allowed and engaged in a number of excursions beyond the tiny island, for sightseeing rambles or social events.

Some portion of the day was inevitably spent in quiet solitude, such as that day, since the Matlocks had departed for an appointment with friends, leaving their niece to her own devices. She chose to brave the bracing air, cooled further by the waters of the Seine, and sit on a cushioned settee on the terrace outside the salon. She was ostensibly reading, but found her attention frequently distracted by the various vessels passing along the river. Additionally, although she tried to ignore it, her thoughts drifted to Mr. Butler. She was not sure when he would arrive in Paris but knew that his sister's wedding had taken place four days prior, so assumed it may be at any moment. The number of times his image or voice intruded upon her as she went about her normal activities was too numerous to count. She recognized that she missed his company and anticipated his return, but stubbornly attributed it to the nature of a fledgling friendship. The fact that she rarely thought about Kitty Bennet or the de Valday twins or even her brother and sister with such intensity was a detail that had not occurred to her. Or at least she refused to acknowledge it.

She sighed, laying the book aside and giving up on the occupation. Instead, she gazed at the water in a half doze until the chill forced a retreat to the warmth of the salon. Yet rather than the hearth, she sat at the fine pianoforte to seek solace in music. Her delicate fingertips moved over the ivory keys, skillfully generating flawless, beautiful tones that rose into the air. She closed her eyes, reveling in the peace and happiness she inevitably attained while playing.

Instantly, the world faded away, her awareness of noises disappeared and concerns dwindled. Her heart lifted with the notes and her body warmed. It was a joyous place for the young woman who so adored music of all varieties, especially when playing favorite melodies. The rush of emotion was powerful. There were few times when she experienced greater surges of pleasure. She knew this and embraced the sensations as they flowed through her, not expecting that anything could ever supplant the jubilation.

"You play that song far better than I do," a voice interrupted, Georgiana's eyes flying open as an intense pulse of delight jolted through her body. She smiled brilliantly, a remaining shred of self-possession keeping her on the bench even as her heart soared and begged her body to leap upward.

"That is a blatant falsehood purely designed to flatter, but I shall accept the compliment, pointing out that my ego is now inflated frightfully. I pray you can bear the consequences."

"I am extremely tolerant. Nearly saint-like." He grinned, halting at the end of the bench and bowing low. "Miss Darcy, I trust I am finding you well?"

"Indeed, Mr. Butler, I am quite well." She offered her hand, which he took and brushed lightly with his lips. "You are the same?"

"Excellent, if a bit weary. It has been a busy week, and I am greatly anticipating a month or so of supreme laziness." He turned serious, his wide smile fading slightly. "Miss Darcy, I do apologize for appearing so suddenly without properly informing you of my presence in Paris. I pray you can forgive my unseemly haste, but"—he shrugged—"I have no actual excuse other than that I wished to see you. I was planning to merely leave a note, see I even have it here"—he fluttered a folded piece of paper extracted from his jacket pocket—"but when I heard you playing my composition I shamelessly bullied the butler into allowing me entry." He gestured toward the lurking and deeply frowning man standing in the doorway.

Georgiana assured the servant that it was fine to admit her guest. He bowed curtly, pointedly leaving the door open wide before he departed.

"Do you think he is skulking behind the wall just to be sure?" Sebastian whispered, eyes twinkling.

"Oh, I am sure of it."

"Well, I am relieved to know your safety is not an issue. Truly, I do not wish to intrude if you prefer your solitude."

"Not at all! I was actually rather bored and unable to concentrate on my book. Music soothes me. But conversation is preferred, and I know you have much to tell me." She rose. "Let me call for tea. Please, be seated Mr. Butler, and begin mentally preparing your update."

He laughed. "As you wish, madam."

The following hour was spent in humorous conversation. Sebastian recounted his sister's nuptials in incredible detail, even properly describing the wedding gown, so that it was easy for Georgiana to envision it. As he had anticipated, Vivienne did cry throughout the entire ceremony, especially when he sang the song written for her and his dear friend.

"Adrien had tears in his eyes as well," he said smugly, "but he refused to acknowledge the fact when I confronted him later. Now the newlyweds are on their way to Rome, drinking champagne, dancing, staring adoringly into each other's eyes for hours on end, and doing all the other things that those passionately in love do."

"Yes, I know the pose quite well," Georgiana murmured as she bent to pour more tea into their cups.

Sebastian's brows rose, the odd twist that invaded his heart shoved down as he asked teasingly, "Really? Who is the fortunate fellow?"

Georgiana laughed, waving her free hand in the air. "Oh, not me! Not as yet. I am speaking of my brother, Mr. Darcy, and his wife. And, I should add, my cousin Colonel Fitzwilliam and Lady Simone. One likes to think that they will never succumb to such ridiculous displays, but after witnessing love firsthand, especially from people one never thought would be so sentimental, and seeing the happiness ensuing"—she shrugged—"well, it does not seem so comical after all."

"I agree. And since a large amount of music and poetry is inspired by love, I suppose we artists should be thankful for the all-consuming emotion."

"Thank you," she said as she ducked her head modestly, cheeks rosy, "for including me in your reference to artists. I am not sure I deserve the designation."

"Oh, but you do, Miss Darcy. Your talent is remarkable. In fact, I think you should consider studying at the Conservatoire. Women do enroll, you know."

Georgiana truly looked stricken, even if her eyes did sparkle at the idea.

"Oh no, Mr. Butler! That is very kind of you to say, but I could never be away from my family for so long, and I am sure Mr. Darcy would not allow it!"

He smiled to ease her distress. "It was just a thought, of course, but you must never ignore your gift or allow anyone to tell you that music is inconsequential. That is a lesson I learned."

"Has it been difficult, Mr. Butler, dealing with your father's displeasure?"

He sighed, shrugging away his bitterness as he sat back into the sofa and stretched his long legs out. Neither gave any consideration to the relaxed, mildly improper posture they were engaged in, too comfortable with each other and caught up in conversation to notice. He gazed at the ceiling, hands clasped over his head, his voice introspective when he spoke.

"The worse part is that I cannot convince him that my love and devotion to music does not mean that I do not adore our estate, Whistlenell Park, and revere the title that I shall someday wear. He persists in seeing it as an all or nothing proposition. In his view, my passion for the arts therefore excludes the ability to have a passion for anything else, including my home. He fears that I shall run off to live in some artist's commune, embarking on a decadent lifestyle with prostitutes and degenerates, immersing myself in composing and playing until I am driven mad." He laughed, glancing at Georgiana. "He has a fanciful imagination, my father."

"Indeed, he must, as even I would assert the unlikelihood of you doing any of those things."

"You know me better than you may suppose, Miss Darcy. For some reason, I find my mouth babbling on when we are in conversation. I pray you do not mind overly?"

"Have I protested thus far, sir? Indeed, I am just as wordy, to my surprise. And you have already promised to keep my revelations to yourself, remember? I shall die of embarrassment otherwise."

"I definitely would not wish for that!" He chuckled, growing serious as he continued, "The truth is, Miss Darcy, as I have told you before, I know my musical gift is not a brilliant one." He waved a hand to halt her instant negation. "Do not say it! Believe me, I have long since accepted the reality. That is not to say I debase myself entirely, as I know I am talented far above most. See"—he winked—"I am still arrogant and egotistical! There are few Mozarts or Bachs or Beethovens, but many others have minimal success and are content to entertain or contribute humbly. I see no reason why I cannot enhance and explore what talent God has given me while also embracing my role as Lord Essenton, when that time comes. Especially since that, as my grandmother is quick to point out to my father, will likely not be for years."

"You are his only son, Mr. Butler. Despite your conviction that he shall live a long life, it is not always a certainty. He probably is not consciously dwelling on his mortality, but the truth is that we never know when God will call us home. I imagine he worries that you will be unprepared."

"Indeed, I know you are correct. I have thought of all this, Miss Darcy. I am not an unfeeling son."

"I know you are not! I apologize if I spoke imprudently."

He smiled at her obvious distress, his voice warm and soothing. "I spoke imprudently, Miss Darcy. Please forgive me. I know you meant no disrespect or were making allegations. In fact, what you say is utterly accurate!" He laughed. "I am a man, many of my friends are men, and thus I am well aware of how insensate the male species typically is, especially when surrounded by females who delight in pointing it out. I am referring to my sisters," he clarified to allay her instant self-recrimination. "Along with fabulous feminine fashion sense, I am also blessed with a heightened awareness of my own brainlessness in emotional matters, thanks to the hourly reminder, nearly from the moment Vivienne was able to speak."

Georgiana could not resist laughing. The mental image of a toddling Lady de Marcov badgering a child Mr. Butler was highly amusing!

"I am afraid our time together is too short for me to relate all the mistakes I have made that my dear sisters have kindly taken upon themselves to correct me on. But back to the original topic, I am abundantly prepared to assume the Earl of Essenton mantle, Miss Darcy. My father first began sitting me on a stool situated by his side as he conducted estate business with our steward when I was seven. Every day without fail, whenever I was home, I spent an afternoon in management instruction. Until I was fifteen, I was not allowed to speak, could not ask a single question, or offer an opinion. I vividly recall the day when he first turned to me after discussing a matter of crop rotation with Mr. Kline, inquiring what I thought." He smiled, eyes on the ceiling and faraway. "I knew it was a test, that if I said the wrong thing, or hesitated for a fraction of a second, another year would go by before he asked me again."

"What did you do?" Georgiana was raptly listening, mesmerized by the tale and the play of pleased emotions that ran over his handsome face.

"I told him. I stood up from my stool, held his hard gaze, and specifically delineated how they should fallow the hundred acres to the north, plant wheat on the Richmond's tenancy, and so on." He looked at her, pride glowing. "I passed the test. For the next two years, until I went to Oxford, and then whenever I was home, I worked with him as much as possible."

He paused, expression serious as he continued to gaze at her. When he spoke, it was with a powerful and steady timbre rarely heard. "Music is one of my passions, a great one to be sure, but no more than my love for our ancestral home. I *will* be an excellent Master of Whistlenell Park and Lord Essenton when the time comes, Miss Darcy. My father has no reason to fear that I will not make him, and all my ancestors, proud."

"So… you resent that he does not trust you? That after all you have shown him, after all the passion of your convictions, he doubts you?"

Sebastian sighed, nodding and finally looking away. "Yes, I suppose that is the crux of it. That, I confess, is where my bitterness lies. But I have accepted that I cannot convince him at this time, or probably ever. I could not choose to relinquish my dream of studying music and pursuing where that path leads me in favor of pleasing my father. That choice would surely lead to my misery. Thus I pray daily to the Almighty that time shall be in my favor, and I will be able to prove my trustworthiness and capability *after* fulfilling my personal satisfaction. I hope that does not make me sound horribly selfish?"

She shook her head slowly. "No. No, not at all. It is wise to know who we are and follow the path of fulfillment. One cannot please everyone anyway and will not be able to please anyone if unhappy." She thought of her brother, marrying Elizabeth who was considered unworthy by so many yet brought him immeasurable joy.

"Thank you. You are quite sensible, Miss Darcy, and for some reason your approval and understanding is important to me." He stared into her eyes, another interlude of silent communication passing between them. Sebastian flushed at his private confession, looking away as he continued, "For now, my father is staying quiet. I suppose the wedding and our compromise are mollifying him."

"Which compromise?"

"That I will assume my title as Viscount Nell while here and return home after a year or two at the Conservatoire to marry and take my place on the estate."

"He is anxious for you to marry then. Does he have a lady in mind?"

Sebastian nodded, still staring into space and not catching the odd flatness to the question. "Yes. I have resisted, but if he had his way we would already be wed. It is strange, really, since he did not marry my mother until well into his third decade. Rumor has it he enthusiastically enjoyed his bachelor years and was not concerned with thoughts of matrimony and an heir, even after becoming Lord Essenton. For another five years he continued his wild ways, yet he all but forced me to be shackled ere I finished Oxford!"

"Well, perhaps he saw the error of his choices and simply desires you not make those mistakes and find happiness as he did."

Sebastian barked a harsh laugh and returned his gaze to Georgiana. "How lovely it would be if that were the truth of it, Miss Darcy. My father and I probably have only one trait in common and that is not to rush into marriage, although our reasons for delay are different."

"What of your compromise?"

"A compromise is not a promise. There is always room to wiggle around. Lord Nell I shall be, and in a few years I will return home, and then I can deal with the properly aristocratic, titled lady he selects for me! Now"—he sat up abruptly, slapping his palms against his thighs—"we are becoming entirely too serious and stuffy. Would you care to accompany me in a walk to the church of Saint-Louis-en-l'Île? I hear it is quite remarkable but have never taken the time to view it."

"Well, then I shall have the upper hand in this adventure at least, as I have toured through the grounds and structure three times since arriving!"

He bowed with a flourish. "Excellent! I shall place myself into your capable hands, Miss Darcy."

They strolled casually along the Rue Saint-Louis-en-l'Île toward the classic seventeenth-century church dedicated to King Louis IX, mingling with the varied pedestrians attending to their pursuits. They chatted amiably, Georgiana pointing to the occasional architectural facet or historical intrigue. Sebastian was amused at her role as cicerone, knowing from their talks that she was no more fascinated by history and architecture than he was.

He paused at one point, indicating a blandly carved archway of boring brown stone over a servant's entrance to one townhouse, asking in a serious tone, "Now tell me, Miss Darcy, in your professional expertise, would this be a Baroque-style portal, or is it more Gothic?"

"Tease! Be thankful you are with me and not my brother. He would ponder your query, launching into a twenty-minute dissertation on the various differences between the two, and would then inform you that this is a perfect example of uniformed simplicity as well as probably giving the history of stonecutting and where this particular rock hailed from."

He laughed loudly, easily envisioning the prim Mr. Darcy doing just that. "Very well then. I applaud your restraint and will be forever appreciative that I am with this particular Darcy, for many superior reasons." He said the last with a respectful incline of his head, eyes glittering. Georgiana blushed, shaking her head as she gently propelled him forward.

The Jesuit church, built in the 1620s and much damaged during the Revolution, was greatly restored to its former glory. The collection of stained-glass windows alone would make the building worth visiting, but the round clock of iron that hung suspended from the steepled belfry and the golden-domed transept were additional spectacles.

"I may not share my brother's passion for architectural aesthetics, nor can I name more than a handful of famed designers," Georgiana whispered as they passed through the vestibule, "but we both love the peace that pervades such places. Do you, Mr. Butler?"

He nodded. "I do. Although I must say I have not spent too much time searching out unique places of worship as I traveled. Unless, of course, there was a famed pipe organ or glass harmonica to hear." He paused, gazing serenely at the statues, his voice low and reflective when he resumed. "There is a church in a modest village near Brussels. It is small, fairly nondescript compared to many, but the acoustics are amazing. The organ is rather large for a small place, an eccentric gift by a wealthy local patron some hundred years ago. It is an Arp Schnitger, if you can believe it. They actually allowed me to play it." He smiled, his face glowing with the memory. "It was incredible. I would love to share such an experience with you, Miss Darcy." He stopped abruptly, eyes darting to hers before averting his gaze in embarrassment for being so presumptuous. "That is to say," he stammered, "few I know would appreciate the tones and melody as you would."

He flashed a smile, walking a pace away to collect himself. For those brief seconds, his mind had readily conjured the image of the two of them side-by-side with their hands moving synchronously over the keys he so vividly remembered, as exquisite music created in unison rose to the heavens. The loss of such an enchanting vision, however unreal and impossible, was poignant and he needed to inhale vigorously to ease the tightening in his chest.

They wandered in silence, exiting the side door to the garden area beyond. A number of other visitors strolled about the grounds, Georgiana and Sebastian unconsciously veering toward a large elm by a small pond where a rope swing sat vacant. Sebastian gestured to the wooden platform, smiling contentedly as Georgiana sat down. Gradually conversation resumed as he pushed her gently, the afternoon shadows lengthening into dusk before they returned to the de Valday townhouse.

Lord and Lady Matlock greeted Mr. Butler with pleasure, quickly extending an invitation to dine with them that evening, but he begged their understanding in declining. "My grandmother is expecting me to dine with her tonight. She needs at least one night settling into town before all know she has arrived. By tomorrow her engagement calendar will be full and she shall no longer require my constant attention, unless it is to be as escort." He laughed. "She did enlist me to invite all of you to dine with us on a day of your choosing. Was quite imperious about it, in fact, and I would be forever in your debt, my lady, if you and Lord Matlock and Miss Darcy agreed to the offer. Colonel Fitzwilliam and Lady Simone are invited as well, of course. It would be an honor and a delight, as well as saving me from a tongue lashing for failing in my assigned task."

Lady Matlock laughed in understanding, promising to visit Lady Warrow on the morrow. "Georgiana, Lady Simone, and I will call upon her if she is agreeable, and we can plot our socialization schedules."

"Excellent! I shall tell her to expect you in the afternoon." He managed to avoid glancing at Georgiana too often during the conversation, not wanting to betray his happiness in seeing her again so soon, and in the promise that their paths would cross frequently in common pursuits. "Lord Matlock, if it meets with your approval, Miss Darcy has agreed to honor me two days hence in touring the Louvre. I have a friend who works in the antiquities wing, as well as knowing the musical sections adequately myself. Miss Darcy seemed to believe Wednesday did not interfere with any laid plans and my friend is working that day so could sneak us in to the restricted sections. Of course, I would be thrilled to act as guide if you and Lady Matlock wished to join us?"

Lord Matlock glanced to Georgiana. She stood placidly, her hands clasped and still, and her face composed. A faint rosiness highlighted her cheeks, and her eyes twinkled between her demurely downcast lashes, but otherwise she gave no clue to her inner thoughts. At these moments, he was struck by the similarities to her brother, despite the differences in their physical features.

"If she agrees, I have no issue with the appointment. I am not that fond of museums myself, although I appreciate the offer, Mr. Butler, and I know Lady Matlock has a prior engagement." He avoided looking at his wife, afraid that her face would betray surprise at the deception, since he well knew she had no plans for Wednesday. Yet apparently, they were aligned in their deviousness.

"I would have imagined the Conservatoire top on your list of places to visit, Georgiana," Lady Matlock ventured, "although I am sure the Louvre's offerings are interesting."

"I did not wish to be presumptuous or possessive, and was unsure if you had gone already," Mr. Butler began.

"I am most anxious to visit the Conservatoire, Mr. Butler, and confess I was awaiting your expertise and familiarity with the facility."

Georgiana's hasty interruption and entreating expression broadened his smile. "Name the day and it shall be done."

"Next week, if that is not too soon?"

"Shall we plan for Monday next?"

"Monday will be perfect."

He laughed at her giddy enthusiasm, inclining his head. "Monday it is then, with my pleasure."

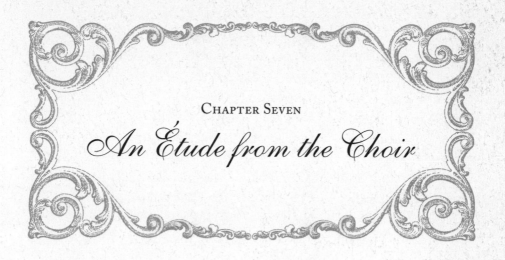

CHAPTER SEVEN

An Étude from the Choir

LATER THAT NIGHT, LADY Matlock entered the bedchamber assigned to her husband. Lord Matlock reclined upon stacked pillows, an open book on his lap, but he laid it aside and smiled as his wife approached. She slipped under the thick comforter, clasping his warm hand and bestowing a tender kiss onto his cheek.

He reached up and brushed a stray lock of her blonde hair away from her face, holding her eyes. "Paris, the city of love, yes, my dear?"

She released a sensual chuckle, kissing the fingertips that rested on her lips. "It appears that any city in France brings romance to the fore."

"Despite my happiness in this actuality from a personal standpoint, I suspect you are referring to our niece?"

"Partially." She leaned in for a long kiss, her husband humming his appreciation. "I am curious to hear your thoughts on the subject, especially after your misinformation this afternoon. Are you, Lord Matlock, playing matchmaker?"

"Only giving them the space to allow the natural course of things. You wish for my thoughts on whether Georgiana is falling in love with Mr. Butler and vice versa? Or my thoughts on the match in a general sense?"

"Both."

He sighed, stretching and leaning further into the pillows. "He is the heir to the Essenton earldom, reportedly worth as much or more than my own estate. The line is an excellent one, with the Duke of Dorset as second cousin. Lord Essenton is well respected in the House of Lords." He shrugged, looking at his wife. "You know as well as I, my dear, that there could be no impediments. Fitzwilliam could not wish for better."

"Fitzwilliam is not my concern."

"Ah. You refer to Lord Essenton's assertion that his heir is to marry Lady Cassandra? As far as I can tell, there is not a formal arrangement between the two."

"I know. But he is quite vocal on the choice, even while planting seeds amongst every family of nobility with an eligible daughter. None doubt his insistence that his son marry a lady of high rank, a requirement amenable to dozens I could name off the top of my head. Why, the name of Mr. Sebastian Butler, Viscount Nell, is whispered loudly around the ladies of my circle! I do not believe the earl would be agreeable to an untitled woman, no matter how large her dowry."

"Georgiana will be a fine wife, possesses a substantial dowry, and is a befitting Lady Essenton. If they mutually wished to be wed, I cannot imagine Lord Essenton denying them."

Lady Matlock nodded but did not feel the same conviction as her husband. In truth, Lord Matlock was not so sure either, his knowledge of Lord Essenton's avowals greater than his wife's.

"As for their romance," he went on, answering her other request for his opinion, "I fear I am no good at reading such emotions. You are the expert there. But they do clearly enjoy each other's company and have an incredible amount in common."

"I have watched Georgiana mature over these past years, especially during these months abroad. In all ways she is a young lady of exemplary character and beauty. Yet, it has been her blossoming as a musician that has astounded me, Malcolm. I truly never foresaw the talent she possesses, nor would have predicted her boldly proclaiming it."

"Indeed, I agree. And her confidence has grown exponentially just in this short time with Mr. Butler."

"His gift is formidable, to be sure. I know Georgiana thinks very highly of him, and his encouragement has so inspired her. She expresses great thankfulness and delight in their friendship."

Lord Matlock was studying his wife closely. "You fear she may misconstrue thankfulness for affection?"

Lady Matlock pursed her lips, eyes unfocused as she mused on the question. Finally, she shook her head. "No, I do not believe so. Quite the opposite is what I fear."

"What do you mean?"

"From what she has told me, and the interactions I have witnessed with a woman's perspective, I am convinced there is a mutual attraction. But they are both so determined to learn from each other, support the other's artistry, be friends who share a mutual passion, that I do not think they are allowing themselves to feel anything deeper."

"Perhaps there is nothing deeper, Madeline. Remember Mr. Giltenhelm?"

She laughed, squeezing his hand where it rested upon her knee. "Not still jealous, are you, husband?"

He grunted. "I was not jealous then, so shall not be so now. However, I did not appreciate the woman I hoped to marry maintaining a friendship with a man, even if he was nothing but a childhood playmate as close as a brother. The point is everyone thought he was perfect for you, that your long-standing relationship must be one of love. But you both knew otherwise. It took me many years to understand that you could be friends with a man, and I still regret that it was his death that led to full realization."

She patted his hand, smiling her forgiveness. "Far in the past. But I see your point. We must watch them closely. I hate to see her hurt if either of their feelings turns to love unreciprocated. However, it may never evolve into more."

"Now that we have hashed out another relationship crisis amongst our children, let us turn to our own relationship, shall we? Kiss me, my lady."

"As you wish and command, my lord."

The retired Colonel Richard Fitzwilliam was not at all surprised when his wife entered his bedchamber that night. Unlike his parents, who held to the tradition of separate sleeping quarters, Lady Simone welcomed her husband into her bed as a permanent fixture. The only nights they did not sleep together were when she was required to comfort one of her children or care for her stepson, the current Lord Fotherby.

Concern for the latter was the reason she was not already entangled amid rumpled sheets next to his bared body. A letter arriving that day from the eighteen-year-old Marquess of Fotherby, who remained safely ensconced at his estate in High Wycombe, Buckinghamshire, with a house full of servants, three friends from boarding school, and two physicians needed to be read to Harry and Hugh Pomeroy. Her nine- and six-year-old sons worried over the half brother they loved, and reassuring them that he was well took priority.

Richard understood this. Nevertheless, he was impatient for her return. Partly that was out of a desire to pull her onto the smooth sheets of their bed and engage in activity sure to thoroughly rumple them, but primarily it was to read the missive himself! His fondness for young Oliver was genuine and he too would be relieved to read of his well-being. Therefore, he jumped up when the door opened, greeting his wife with a kiss while exchanging a brandy glass for the folded parchment.

"Thank you, dear," she said, taking a sip of the warmed liquid.

Richard merely nodded, his eyes scanning the bold cursive dried onto the paper even as he encircled her slim waist and steered her toward the plumped pillows on the bed.

"This is very good news," he murmured. "He says he has not suffered any serious bouts since our departure, has been out riding twice, and attended Lord Farnsworth's ball. He does not say if he danced…"

"Knowing Oliver I rather doubt it," Simone interjected with a chuckle.

"Yes, true." Richard flipped to the next page. "The tonic Dr. Darcy prescribed appears to be working. Even Dr. Lowes has seen no need to bleed him, and that is a minor miracle that speaks for itself. Ah! He beat Trencher at darts! Well done, Oliver, well done."

"After all the practice he has gotten with you, he should be able to beat Aniston as well."

"I am sure in time he will."

Richard continued to read even as they settled onto the wide bed. Simone leaned against his side, daintily drinking the brandy while rereading Oliver's letter along with her husband.

"How interesting," Richard said after minutes of silent reading. "He writes that Trencher's family visited for a fortnight, pointedly mentioning Lady Janelle a good half dozen times. I wonder if he is infatuated with her?"

"Not that he has ever revealed to me."

"Well, he does a fair amount of appreciative gazing at the ladies, even if he is too shy to ask one to dance. Perhaps Lady Janelle will be the one to spur him into action," he suggested with a naughty chuckle.

"I am not sure he is capable of being spurred into action, as you delicately put it."

Richard lowered the letter onto his lap and turned toward his wife. A pall of sadness overshadowed her face, not diminishing her beauty but wrenching her husband's heart. He kissed her forehead, stroking over her cheek and replying with conviction, "You worry unnecessarily. Yes, he is shy and immature for his age due to his illness, this is true, but in the year I have known him, he has grown taller and wider in the chest. His voice is deeper. And he is much stronger, as evidenced by his successes on horseback and in shooting. Gradually he is becoming a man with a man's interests."

"Lord Fotherby was not so convinced," she countered, referring to her deceased first husband by his title, as she always did in conversation. "His revelations of Oliver's mother and her difficulties in… the marriage bed, in conceiving and carrying her pregnancies led him to believe their only child may not be able to… react as a man should."

Richard laughed at her hesitant, oblique way of summing up the sexual act, Simone blushing and hiding her face in his shoulder. They had been married for over a year, neither virgins when they wed and robust in the intimate realms of their life, yet she remained demure with a tendency to blush. He thought it charming and humorous.

"Let me see how far the rosiness has spread this time, Mrs. Fitzwilliam." He peeled the nightgown off her shoulder, exposing her breasts and lightly trailing his fingertips across them, Simone squirming and goose bumps rising. "Not as yet, ah! Wait! Yes, there it is, that beautiful flush touching your skin."

He bent to bestow several kisses to her pink bosoms, mumbling words of praise against the fullness before lifting to meet her adoring eyes.

"Erase your worries of Oliver. When we return I will have a man-to-man chat with him, although I am sure your fears are groundless."

Her eyes widened in surprise. "You would ask him bluntly if he… well, if he can…"

"Yes, I will ask him bluntly. I am a soldier, or was, so gritty conversations about manly pursuits do not disturb my sensibilities. Men are not as gentlemanly as they like to pretend, my lady, but I promise to be circumspect if you wish."

"Thank you. He may not be as willingly forthcoming as you suspect."

Richard grinned, shaking his head. "If you say so, Simone, but I think you would be surprised. And speaking of blunt conversations," he rushed on before she could disagree about Oliver, "did you or my mother have any luck with Georgiana?"

She shook her head. "Nothing of any certainty, no. She is fond of Mr. Butler, there can be no doubt of that, and she does tend to gush, but primarily in regards to his musical knowledge and expertise. I sense something more but cannot be sure."

"You did not simply ask her, 'Are you in love with Mr. Butler?' That would have been the easiest way."

"Richard," she chided, playfully swatting his arm, "that would have been a useless tactic."

He shrugged. "Maybe. She may not have answered directly or truthfully, but you would have discerned the answer in her eyes. Do women not have an intuitive sense about these matters? A clairvoyance betwixt the sexes we imperceptive men do not possess?"

"Where in the world did that fanciful idea spring from?" She shook her head and chuckled at his dramatic delivery—he was clutching his chest, his voice lifting into a dreamy intonation. "How ridiculous! Besides, you forget that my time with Miss Darcy has been short. She has barely arrived in Paris after months away, and we had scant time to become deeply acquainted in the month surrounding our wedding. Additionally, Mr. Butler only arrived today! It requires a span of greater length and intensity for the clairvoyant bond to be established."

"Ha!" He fell against the pillows in laughter. "I knew it!" He kissed her dimpling cheek.

"Really, Richard, if your mother is not sure of her sentiments, how am I to know? You are undoubtedly the best one to read her face in response to Mr. Butler. You can be the judge, since you know her best."

"When it comes to reading Georgie's emotions of love, I am clearly not the one to judge."

"Richard…"

"After all," he continued, his eyes averted, "I leapt to the conclusion that I felt passion for Georgiana when really I needed and wanted her to drown my grief over losing you, while improperly interpreting your emotions toward me. If I had not failed, many things would have been different." He returned his gaze to her face, squeezing the warm hands that were tightly clasped within his. "Now I see clearly. I see the fullness of your desire and heart. I see it in your eyes, my love, every time you look at me."

"How romantic," she said with a teasing lilt but also with an undertone of seriousness. "But as I have told you many, many times, my dearest, you are far too severe. Deep in your soul you knew I loved you and would never willingly leave. You also knew that what you and Georgiana felt for each other was not a strong passion. You did interpret correctly and that is why you did not force matters with Georgiana and why you came back to London."

"And why we are together now."

"Yes."

They stared at each other for a long while, their hearts bare with love that pulsed in a synchronized beat. Finally Richard smiled, dropping his eyes to her exposed chest and licking his lips.

"So, I guess what you are telling me is that the burden of discovery has been abdicated to me?"

"Oh, do not sound so put upon! You know your mother will not relent in her delving, and I am to understand Lord Matlock has developed a taste and talent for deception as well." Richard's brow lifted in question, Simone laughingly telling him of that encounter. "Yet in the end we may all be in error."

"Meaning?"

"Meaning they may be nothing more than friends who play the pianoforte together and talk of notes and scales. They hardly know each other!"

"Mother seems convinced there is something more."

"Perhaps, perhaps not. Maybe we will discern something when we actually meet the gentleman at dinner tomorrow night. I say save your speculations until after, proceeding with circumspection. And for heaven's sake, do not frighten the poor young man with any of your 'gritty conversations'!"

"No talk of 'manly pursuits' either? May I talk of manly pursuits now? Or preferably *not* talk about them and act upon them instead?"

Lady Simone's response—an affirmative one—was not verbalized either, action the preferable option for both of them.

～❦～

The young woman who was the center of this speculation sat on the padded bench of her vanity table in the bedchamber selected for her, at the far end of the hall, down from the larger quarters designed for married couples. The room was small, but warm and cozy and well-appointed. Georgiana was content with the arrangements, not that she was in a current state of mind to be discontented about anything.

She did not realize that she was humming under her breath, the tune suspiciously similar to the one she had been playing that afternoon when Mr. Butler arrived. She was aware that she was smiling, since she was staring at her reflection in the mirror, but that she attributed to the friendly chat she was engaged in with her companion, Mrs. Annesley.

The older woman was listening more than contributing to the conversation, a pleased smile upon her face as well. She pulled the stiff bristled brush through her charge's thick, waist-length hair, mentally counting each stroke while she harkened to the softly spoken words.

"I wish you had not left, Amanda, so you could have heard the Psalms of King David that Mr. Butler set to music and was so kind as to play for me. Lord and Lady Matlock returned to the chateau, our impromptu concert necessarily ending at that time, but he has accepted my invitation to tea on the morrow so you will hear the psalms for yourself."

"I shall delight in them, I am sure."

"I thought his interpretation was brilliant, but of course he would not accept such high praise." She shook her head, pausing to pour a palm full of Warren and Rosser's Milk of Roses from the glass bottle sitting on the linen-draped vanity tabletop, humming in the interim. She began smoothing the oil over her arms, returning to the topic after a slight laugh.

"He is so humble. This is an excellent trait, of course, but rather maddening at the same time. I am sure he will realize his potential once at the Conservatoire."

"You are pleased he is here." It was not a question, Mrs. Annesley continuing to brush while surreptitiously watching Georgiana's reaction.

Georgiana blushed. Quickly reaching to rub the soothing oil over her cheeks to hide the rosiness, she replied calmly, "Of course, it is nice to see a familiar face. His company is pleasing to be sure, but I also weary of constantly being forced to establish new associations and remember more names. I think my poor head shall burst with all the lords and ladies and convoluted French names! It is comforting to socialize with someone I have already gone through the preliminaries with, as it will comfort me when the de Valdays arrive."

"Although they do not possess your passion for music. It is lovely to see you sharing your interest in this way, Miss Georgiana."

"Is it not a wonder? So rarely does one find a kindred spirit and Mr. Butler is so knowledgeable! I could dig into his brain for ages and never uncover all he knows, I am sure of it."

"Did Mr. Butler restate his intention to escort you to the Conservatoire?"

"Oh yes! Monday next, and on Wednesday we are touring the Louvre. I hope you are prepared for the adventures?"

"I am sure it will be educational, if not embraced with the full glory of delight as it will be by you, my dear."

Georgiana laughed at Mrs. Annesley's mocking expression reflected in the mirror. "I may yet transform you into a woman who loves art and poetry, Amanda. I refuse to give up!"

"And I refuse to give up in enticing you to read one of my romantic novels. I am reading Mrs. Radcliffe's *The Romance of the Forest* now, if you wish me to read aloud?"

"Thank you for the kind offer, but I shall stay with Mr. Charles Burney's *History of Music* for the present."

"Is that the book Mr. Butler brought you?" She sniffed when Georgiana nodded. "Pity. I was hoping for something scandalous or titillating like Polidori's *The Vampyre*."

"Mrs. Annesley! Can you imagine how inappropriate that would be?"

"Then why are you laughing and your eyes shining, my dear? There, your hair has been brushed the obligatory one hundred strokes so it will shine as brilliantly as the sun, rendering you as breathlessly beautiful as an angel for Mr. Butler to feast his eyes upon while playing his psalms of heavenly glory!"

"Goodness, the ridiculous things you say! I should burn your fanciful novels ere all hope is lost."

"But you will not because you delight in my teasing. Now, off to bed with you! I will tidy up here, and probably still be at work when you fall asleep after one page of your dreary book."

Georgiana stood, leaning to kiss her friend and companion on the cheek before doing as ordered. Propped comfortably on several pillows, she began to read the volume given to her that afternoon by Mr. Butler, the gentleman stating simply that, "I finally found where I had tucked it in my trunk and knew you would like this Burney after quoting liberally from *The Present State of Music.*" In seconds she was engrossed, the smile intact and the humming recommenced.

Amanda Annesley silently moved about the room, picking up the few items dropped onto the floor or left out of place. It was an easy chore since Georgiana Darcy was extraordinarily neat. In reality, she tarried and fabricated tasks in order to observe the young lady circumspectly while mulling over the recent developments.

Five years ago, she had been hired to serve as a companion to Miss Darcy. Newly widowed and with limited resources, it was a sensible charge to accept. During her interview with the somewhat frightening and severe Mr. Darcy, all she had been told was that his sister had suffered a recent trauma and deception by someone close to her. His ominous speech and simmering anger gave her pause, but when she met Miss Darcy all she saw was a painfully timid girl of fifteen who, to her way of thinking, needed a motherly, or at least sisterly, touch.

It did not happen overnight to be sure. In time, however, Georgiana did warm to Mrs. Annesley, the warmth gradually leading to friendship. The presence of Mrs. Darcy in the family and the close relationship that evolved between the two initiated a true transformation. Other friendships with young ladies of her age and station, such as Mary and Kitty Bennet, Bertha Vernor, and Vera Stolesk aided her blossoming.

The story of Mr. Wickham and the near elopement was offered in stages, and by the time Mrs. Annesley heard the entire tale, it no longer held any significance. The reticent, awkward girl encountered when she accepted the post had grown into a graceful, clever, charming young woman with numerous acquaintances. She danced at balls and conversed with relative ease. She excelled at card games and engaged in intellectual discourse.

Yet traces of shyness and reserve lingered, especially with crowds or unfamiliar people. With gentlemen, her conversations were fleeting and superficial, engaged in on a dance floor or group setting, and never flirtatious or gregarious. The number of intimate friends was few and they were all female except for her cousin Richard.

And the latter thought caused Mrs. Annesley to pause in folding the shawl in her hands to gaze at her young friend. Georgiana continued to read, the smile fixed and musical humming ongoing. There was something indefinably altered in her countenance these past weeks, a glow of happiness and maturity not seen before.

Are you in love?

Mrs. Annesley wanted to ask the question. She had asked it of Miss Darcy once before. Then, it was in regards to Colonel Fitzwilliam, although she had already known the answer. Asking the question was for Georgiana's benefit, the bluntness necessary to force her to face the truth. The answer, of course, was *yes*, she loved him as her dearest friend, and *no*, not as a passionate lover. Facing the truth eased the pain of loss when he returned to Lady Simone. It was impossible to mourn the demise of a connection that had not truly existed. The relevant relationship of deep familial friendship remained intact.

Asking the question in regards to Mr. Butler at this juncture would be pointless. Mrs. Annesley knew her young lady well enough to recognize that Georgiana would be unable to answer with clarity. Georgiana did not know her heart, Mrs. Annesley perceived, but whether that was due to stubborn denial or because the sentiments were in their infancy she could not divine.

Despite Miss Darcy's maturity, she was yet an innocent. Her young lady was utterly unaware of Mr. Butler's flare of desire at the piano. *How long can her innocence last? Surely someone will pierce her heart and awaken the woman inside. Will it be Mr. Butler? And what are his feelings for Miss Darcy? Merely an intense friendship and nothing more?*

"Amanda? Is something amiss?"

Mrs. Annesley smiled, covering the jolt out of her contemplative reverie by applying another fold to the shawl. "Nothing, dear. Woolgathering. Do not stay up too late reading. It would not do to fall asleep mid psalm, now would it?"

THIRD MOVEMENT

Development

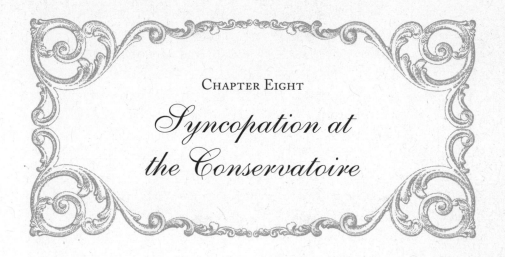

CHAPTER EIGHT

Syncopation at the Conservatoire

THE WEEKS PASSED IN a flurry of activity. The relaxed serenity of Georgiana's initial days in Paris ended. Every day and each evening there was a planned event of some type.

The *maisons* outside the limits of Paris proper, the numerous opulent *hôtels* catering to the wealthy traveler, and the abundant townhouses of the upper classes were overflowing with visitors from Europe. It was 1820, the Prince Regent was newly crowned as King George IV, and the return of semi-stability after decades of revolution and Napoleonic control—aided by the restoration of the Bourbon Dynasty with Louis XVIII on the throne—allowed for a resurgence in tourism. Political upheaval and debate continued to rage, King Louis not universally loved and adored, but the aristocracy and social elite generally ignored such intrigues for the draw of entertainments.

Droves of Englishmen, too long deprived of the glories of Paris and desiring to escape the colder climes of England, flocked to the more temperate zones of France in February. There was a celebratory atmosphere in this country in the midst of regeneration. Nothing, not weather or season or social class, inhibited the fun. Days were spent touring the gardens of the Tuileries and Luxembourg palaces, riding along the Avenue des Champs-Élysées or viewing the divers museum expositions. Nights were passed at the Opéra-Comique, Académie Royale de Musique, a fashionable ball, or salon.

Paris was a city that never seemed to sleep. Someone, somewhere, was hosting a gala or dinner party or exhibit or festivity, and the odds were high that the Marchioness of Warrow knew about it. And was invited. The Earl and Countess of Matlock, although not as notorious and familiar to the whole of Paris society, were certainly honored temporary residents whose presence was desired. Mr. Butler and Miss Darcy, esteemed in their own right as English dignitaries, nonetheless benefited from the acclaim of their elders.

Georgiana, accustomed to the cyclical social seasons of London, was somewhat taken aback to discover the Paris of winter nearly as bustling as in the previous summer when she had been visiting with William, Lizzy, and George Darcy. Now she was surrounded by Lord and Lady Matlock, the newlywed Fitzwilliams, and a host of new acquaintances. By late February, the de Valday siblings would join the shifting crowds of younger folk who inhabited the ballrooms, galleries, and gardens of Paris with their chaperones conspicuously present. New introductions were made on a daily basis, in large numbers, and previous friendships from the ton of London were renewed. At no time was there a lack of companionship and lively entertainment.

Yet, as in Lyon, Georgiana unconsciously gravitated toward Mr. Sebastian Butler and vice versa. The two rarely passed a day or evening, and never both, without seeing each other. They discovered their commonalities included more than just music. Dancing, plays, art exhibits, and horseback rides were among their other shared passions, partaken of in varying degrees, either with their new acquaintances accompanying or alone with Mrs. Annesley acting as chaperone.

Inevitably they managed to secure quiet periods in the music room, poring over sheets of scale-lined parchment either stamped with notes that they learned to play or blank until their quills etched created melodies. They neither planned the phenomenon nor spoke of it specifically, but collaboration had become the highlight of their lives.

"This scale here," Georgiana said, her fingers spread elegantly and the descant played as she watched his face.

He nodded, scribbling the notes hastily. "Yes, yes. That is good, very good. Perhaps then a… here, let me try."

He sat onto the bench, Georgiana scooting over to make room. Unerringly his hands repeated her previous chords, his longer and broader fingers every bit as delicate. The tones emitted were beautiful, lilting, and emotive, his ideas blending with her inspirations flawlessly. He closed his eyes, allowing the music to flow through him, adding fresh inspirations in the same cadence for several measures until suddenly, accidentally, slipping with a jarring dissonance.

They both winced and shuddered.

"That was truly awful," Georgiana declared with a grimace.

Sebastian chuckled. "Indeed. I would have to agree."

"And you were doing so well. What a pity. Look, goose pimples." She held up her smooth arm with a grin for his inspection.

He grunted, faking a severe frown. "Teasing, unforgiving woman! Give me another chance."

"Please do. And try to do better this time so the chills will disappear from my spine."

He nudged her with his shoulder, Georgiana giggling and nudging him back. Their eyes met briefly before he again attacked the keys, replaying from the beginning. He subtly altered the pitch and modulation, expertly capturing the andante tempo and soft terraced dynamics of the cowritten piece, the melody gentle and light.

She placed her hands upon the keys, matching his dolce playing for a while, and then adding a lyric refrain, a glissando, several staccato notes, and other improvised embellishments in harmony with his notes but in an accelerating beat.

He laughed, his own fingers following her pattern at the same increasing speed, melding perfectly. They shared a smiling look, hands continuing to move as their eyes held the other, until in synchrony they ended with a vibrant culmination.

"Ha! You turned our divertimento into a capriccio!"

She shrugged, laughter bubbling in her voice when she spoke. "It seemed fitting after your disaster."

"Miss Darcy saves the composition. Very well then, prove your superiority over the bungling man by writing down your brilliance, I dare you."

"Challenge accepted!" She rose amid the laughter, commencing furious writing as he grinningly replayed the finale.

"There," Georgiana proclaimed proudly, lifting the paper and blowing to dry the ink. "All done!"

"Let me see." He rose, standing beside her at the piano's edge, fingertip gliding over the surface as he read the freshly inscribed score. His lips silently mouthed the notes and head nodded slightly with the tune playing in his mind.

Georgiana watched his face, captivated by the intent expression and animated gestures playing over his handsome features as he read the music. For not the first time, she became aware of a fluttering in her heart, a quickening of her breathing, and mild flush to her cheeks as she stared at his profile and felt his arm brushing against hers. Innocent she may be, but she was not a fool. That she was becoming increasingly attracted to him in a way never experienced with another was no longer a question.

It was Sebastian who invaded her slumber and brought joy to her day. Urgency to see him was her waking thought, even while a blush spread over her cheeks as the nature of her dreams was recalled. Each night she fell asleep with a smile, as memories of their hours together replayed through her mind, even as a frown creased her brow by the dilemma of her sentiments.

She felt hypnotized by his presence in a way she knew was inappropriate under their unique circumstances. He was her friend, someone she admired and respected. Her affection for him was real and growing, but so was her awareness of his purpose. The last thing he wanted, or needed, was a romantic entanglement. She knew he did not see her as anything but a friend and fellow artist, and she would never allow her fancies to interfere with his goals.

Her heart constricted. The ache of longing weakened her knees and was visible upon her face. If he had chosen that second to turn her way, all would have been revealed, and she knew it.

She swallowed, smothered the silly impulses, and harshly shoved the feelings aside. With practiced Darcy steel, she smoothed her features and started to turn her eyes away from the rapt contemplation of his face.

But he chose that moment to lift his eyes and meet her stare. For a long second that stretched for illusory hours, their gazes locked.

Understanding and acceptance hovered at the edges. Emotions flared and danced in their eyes. Currents sizzled and sparked within the minuscule space that separated their bodies. The yearning to touch, to cross the invisible barrier, to speak the words tickling the tips of their tongues pounded through their bodies with gale force. Yet for some reason, the onslaught paralyzed them, and they stayed, neither moving nor speaking.

Georgiana broke the spell first, determinedly dragging her dazed blue eyes away from his face with a monumental effort. "Did you discover any errors?" Her voice was calm and her hand surprisingly steady when she picked up the sheet of music, stepping away several paces to pretend studied attentiveness to the pages.

"Yes. That is, no. No errors. It is excellent, as I expected."

His voice was husky, gray eyes following her movements. *What is happening to me?* Again the intense sensations of friendship, attraction, and sexual arousal chaotically crashed together and blotted out his reason. *Am I falling in love with her?* He cringed at the thought, not so much because he was adverse to the idea, but because he knew she did not feel the same. It was evident in how she moved away, in how serene her demeanor, in how blank her beautiful blue eyes. *If she felt the same, would I not detect a hint of desire or shaken composure?* Yet she was forever restrained, warm, and playfully teasing him, not unlike one of his sisters.

He cleared his throat, standing straighter as he mentally shook off the troubling thoughts and they reverted to their typical bantering. "We should play this for Professor Florange at the Conservatoire today. He would be greatly impressed."

"Flatterer! It is not nearly that good."

"It is brilliant, Miss Darcy. You truly must learn to trust me in this and trust in your talent. You are very gifted."

"Thank you, Mr. Butler. I appreciate the compliment, but it was a collaboration, so any brilliance in the piece is equally yours to boast of."

"Indeed, you are correct, madam! This means that as equal owner of the masterpiece, I can show it to Professor Florange!" He snatched the pages from her grasp, dancing away from her lunging hands nimbly with a mischievous laugh. "Now we shall have the unbiased opinion we are craving—"

"*You* are craving, not I!"

"As you wish. But I tell you, you are special, and you should know it."

"Mr. Butler, please. You must not say such things. And I do not desire scrutiny beyond yours."

"Why ever not?"

She shook her head, successfully grabbing the pages out of his hand. "I simply do not. Let us leave it at that, shall we?" He did not reply, staring at her with his brows twisted by a question as she tucked the sheets into his case. "Promise me you will desist in such talk, please?"

She lifted her gaze to his, holding steady until he finally nodded. "Very well, I promise."

❧

The broad corridors, immense musical chambers, and chair-lined classrooms of the Conservatoire National Supérieur de Musique in Paris were crowded with teachers and students of both sexes. Founded in 1795 by the National Convention, that temporary legislative government that ruled during the Revolution years, this free school of higher musical education was one of the most prestigious conservatoires in Europe. Tuition may be paid by the state, but admission was based on musical skill and the passing of rigorous exams. In this, Mr. Sebastian Butler had encountered no difficulties.

He had opted to enroll for the fall session, desiring some months of free study and enlightenment as he toured about Europe before settling into a regular schedule of classes.

"I am keeping my options loose," he explained to Georgiana as they drove along Rue Bergère toward the gigantic brick building housing the Conservatoire. "I would like to complete the full three-year term, but that may be impossible since my father is reluctantly allowing two years. It is not necessary to study longer, as I do not intend to pursue a living in music. I will never join the Opéra-Comique or Opéra de Paris. Have no desire to do so, as you know." He smiled at Georgiana from across the gently rocking carriage. "The truth, Miss Darcy, is that I am becoming a bit homesick. Do not divulge this to my father! You too, Mrs. Annesley, are sworn to secrecy."

Georgiana's companion smiled. "Your secret will go to my grave, sir."

"Much appreciated. The green fields of Staffordshire are calling to me. There are unique fragrances that only exist there, flora and fauna I adore, and landscapes etched upon my heart. Also, it is difficult to be away from my sisters, but for now I am content with this course and shall not battle Lord Essenton over the matter unless time reveals I must."

"Do you fear studying at the Conservatoire may appear tame after you pass the summer in Vienna?"

"The conservatory of Vienna is new and not well-established. I recently read that Antonio Salieri is the director, and it will be an honor to meet him. But Paris is where true learning is an art. And music is never tame, is it? Ah, here we are."

He guided her through the arched doorway, her hand firmly tucked into the crook of his arm. Large crowds of unknown people still rendered her momentarily mute and unsettled, her inherited shyness never totally dissipating, although after two visits to the bustling Conservatoire, she was not as nervous.

She had discovered that Sebastian possessed a quiet ease in almost all situations. He was far from loud or boisterous, his manners sedate and impeccable, and he frequently tended to remain silent as he observed those around him; however, it was not from timidity, but more from an inner self-confidence that did not require extraneous affirmation. Conversation with complete strangers was effortless on his part, a talent she did not have.

He looked at her with an understanding smile, patting her gloved fingers lightly in reassurance. His smooth, casual sauntering through the active bodies, most of them intent on some purpose that did not include idle chatter with strangers, allayed the worst of her nervousness. He nodded and smiled politely at the occasional familiar face but did not halt.

"I thought today we would first visit the opera rehearsals," he murmured, leading her to a set of wide stairs. "That is always fascinating to observe. And I can introduce you to some people I know. I can tell you right now, Miss Darcy, that the current reigning soprano leaves much to be desired. Your voice is superior." He continued in a steady stream of softly uttered dialogue, his resonant tones soothing and sentences entertaining. By the time they arrived at the large theatre where an operatic performance was being practiced, she was completely relaxed.

She did agree that the soprano practicing was not excellent but merely adequate. However, she would not agree with Sebastian's assertion that her voice was far better. He introduced her to a few of the singers and stage personnel, but the bulk of his acquaintances were in the music departments. On the one hand, she was amazed at how many people he knew based on brief visitations in the past, yet on the other, his openness and humor was magnetic—especially to women, a fact that irritated Georgiana profoundly. And considering how few women inhabited the halls of the Conservatoire compared to men, there must have been a communications network of some sort informing every last one that he was in the building!

She was fully aware that jealousy generated her annoyance, and she should have been troubled by such an unsavory emotion regarding a man she insisted was merely a friend. Luckily, the acute yearning to slap every woman who greeted him with a flirtatious, "How wonderful to see you again, Mr. Butler!" was overshadowed by her awe at the impressive atmosphere.

For over two hours they wandered from room to room surrounded by music in various renderings. Georgiana slowly relinquished the bashfulness Sebastian found so charming, conversing with students and teachers with growing confidence. A few were now familiar to her, and their welcoming attitude encouraged passionate discourse. Sebastian observed her exuberance, empathized with the happiness, and vividly related to her fervor, not realizing that some of the latter arose from female envy! Indeed, he only discerned the unique inner fire of the true artist, and in those hours, he recognized that he would give anything he owned to grant her heart's wish. If only there was some way to make it so.

Refreshed after a pot of hot tea and sweet treats in the tearoom, Georgiana and Sebastian left Mrs. Annesley to rest while they headed down a semi-deserted corridor, lined with doors marked with French names on thin wooden plates.

"Do not be intimidated by Professor Florange," Sebastian said as they walked. "He can be gruff, but he is an excellent teacher and he means well."

"Are you sure it is acceptable for me to accompany you? I could wait in the tearoom with Mrs. Annesley. I do not wish to irritate him or intrude upon your appointment."

"I assure you he will not mind in the least. I have some new compositions I wish to share with him, and I think you will benefit from hearing his instruction. Ah, here we are!"

The office of Professor Florange was blessedly devoid of females. The gray-haired man, tiny and stooped with thick spectacles perched on a beaked nose, greeted Sebastian and Georgiana with abstract enthusiasm. His office was a chaotic mess of sheet music, melted candles, ink-splotched tabletops, and leather portfolios stuffed with scribbled papers. His suit was rumpled and face stubbled, but his beady black eyes examined the compositions Sebastian withdrew from his leather portfolio with intelligent concentration. He mumbled indecipherable French as he read and then shuffled to the pianoforte, clearing away several pieces of music with deliberate care before placing the new sheets on the rest.

Georgiana stood near the door, away from the professor's desk and the pianoforte, not wishing to be a distraction, and was therefore unaware of which composition Mr. Butler had given until the opening chords. She gasped, hand rising to her heart and eyes saucers. It was their piece! Instantly, she pierced Mr. Butler with an accusatory gaze and noted his flinch, but he met her eyes unrepentantly. Anger flared, her cheeks flaming in response, yet to her exasperation, the anger rapidly dissipated as the music swirled about the room.

Professor Florange played the composition perfectly. He never said a word or glanced at either of them, his focus complete upon the written notes rendered masterfully by his aged hands.

Georgiana bit her lip, the odd man's mannerisms lending no clues to his opinion. And suddenly she realized she wanted to hear his opinion! Sebastian smiled, annoyingly pleased at her altered attitude, and winked at her as the music flowed melodically about the room. The professor reached the end, muttered a few more French sentences that she could not hear, and to her alarm, flipped back to the beginning and started over again! Sebastian only smiled wider, which should have steeled her nerves or irritated her, but only served to increase her apprehension.

Finally, he stood from the bench, startling her into near apoplexy by turning to her rather than Sebastian, his ebony gaze sharp and voice shrill when he asked in heavy accented English, "Why have you not sat for our examinations, Mademoiselle Darcy? You should be a student here with talent such as this."

"Mr. Butler wrote a greater portion, truly he did—"

"Yes, yes," Professor Florange interrupted, "I know of Butler's style and can discern his contributions. Yet there is something more here than previously seen in his work. This is better, much better, than his work has ever been…"

"Mr. Butler's compositions are extraordinary, sir, you must know this to be so!"

Professor Florange chuckled, the sound grating and unexpected. "No need to bristle, since I meant no offense to your young man here. He is well aware of what he is capable of and thus what he needs to learn. And do not let your head swell"—he wagged a bony finger under Georgiana's nose—"since I am not saying you are a genius. But there is great aptitude inside you, Mademoiselle Darcy, possibilities that should be unlocked and given wings. I can do this. I long to do this."

"Thank you, Professor. You are kind, but—"

"Kindness, bah! I am not kind at all! Just ask Butler here. I am a teacher, a very nasty one a good percentage of the time whose job is to recognize the gifted, admit them into the Conservatoire, and exhaustively drive them until they excel beyond their wildest potential. That is you, mademoiselle. Gifted and, I suspect from this"—he stabbed the sheet of music still propped on the pianoforte—"that together you and Butler could even be brilliant. So you shall take the exams and join us, yes?"

He turned away, the latter obviously not meant as a question. Georgiana stood speechless as the professor bent to gather the sheets. Sebastian raised his brows questioningly, satisfaction and pride mixed with nervousness at her reaction.

"I appreciate the offer, Professor," she stammered, "but I am afraid that is impossible."

"Impossible? What is this 'impossible'? For an artist nothing is impossible." He walked back to his desk, dismissing her objections with a grunt. "Butler, this girl is good for you. This glissando is inspired, the entire refrain beautiful. I might suggest adding a flute here to enhance the pitch…"

Sebastian nodded, bending over to jot notes onto the paper as Professor Florange continued to offer ideas. Frequently, the younger man looked up with eyes bright and warm. With a glance he tried to transmit pride and compassion.

Georgiana walked to the desk silently, watching the men interact while her emotions churned from the opportunity so cavalierly thrown at her feet. Never had she expected, even in the wildest of her imaginings, that a distinguished master of music would praise her humble compositions. It was staggering. It was overwhelming. And it was impossible despite Professor Florange's assertion otherwise.

As the moments passed, her anger reawakened and pervaded the jumbled emotions. The arrival of a student interrupted the impromptu collaboration. Professor Florange ushered them out of the office with curt gestures and fuss, the door shut with a firm thud that nearly bumped their heels. Yet before either could take a breath to speak, the door opened again, the professor's grizzled face thrust through the crack and tiny eyes fixed on Georgiana.

"In the autumn, Miss Darcy. Autumn."

And then the door was slammed again. Silence fell, except for the muted noise of a cluster of passing students, while they stared at the solid wood, half expecting it to swing open for another parting sally. Sebastian recovered first, turning to Georgiana with his captivating grin in full force.

"Did I not tell you he would love your work? With Professor Florange's endorsement your admission is a given, not that you would not pass the exams with stellar marks, but his recommendation is—"

"You planned this?" she interrupted in an incensed whisper.

"No. That is, I hoped his opinion…" he trailed off at the fury marring her features, his confusion compounded by the unbidden vision of the vehemence suffusing her face occurring in a more intimate setting. Gods! When highly passionate, even in anger, she was surpassingly beautiful!

"Are you listening to me?"

The finger jabbed into his chest brought him back to the present. Georgiana was standing inches from him, obviously having said something quite scathing while his thoughts veered into baser realms.

"Of course I am listening," he lied, mentally giving himself a shake and willing his blood to calm.

"Then how could you disrespect my feelings so thoughtlessly? How could you forget your promise?"

"I promised not to talk about it and I did not."

"You are going to parse over semantics?" She was incredulous. "You knew what I meant! I did not want this and you know it!"

He stepped closer and placed his hand upon her shoulder. "Miss Darcy, you would be marvelous here. Can you not see yourself learning more? Music is your future, I know it is."

"This is your future, Mr. Butler, not mine. Do not mistake the two."

"I only wanted you to see the possibility. It could be yours if—"

"No, it cannot."

"Are you worried what Mr. Darcy will say? You have said that he approves of your interest in music and applauds your talent. Surely he would want you to fulfill this dream?"

"If it were my dream then perhaps he would agree, but that is not the point. This dream is more of a fantasy, Mr. Butler. Yes, I love music and I love composing. I am flattered by Professor Florange's praise. If I were someone else, then maybe this would be a viable option. Nevertheless, this is not the life for me and it is wrong of you to presume that your beliefs are the same as the ones in my heart."

She twirled away, graceful and fluid even when agitated, and headed down the passageway.

"Miss Darcy, wait! Please accept my apology. I meant no disrespect, truly."

She whirled back around, Sebastian pulling up short to avoid colliding with her. He took hasty steps backward and his inhale caught painfully in his throat when he saw her face. Her mien remained one of ire but also a shimmer of wounding, the latter hitting the middle of his gut like a knife. Her next words caused the knife to twist.

"Have you so misunderstood me, Mr. Butler? Have my disclosures of homesickness, of missing my family and wanting to be in England fallen upon deaf ears? In the course of our friendship, have you forgotten that I am a woman? My desires are of hearth and home above all else."

She paused and looked away. Sebastian struggled with how properly to respond to her accusations when the only one he seemed able to focus on was the ludicrous idea that he had *ever* forgotten, even for one tiny second, that she was a woman! Before anything coherent and gentlemanly formulated, she lifted her eyes, Sebastian noting the fury but also hints of something else mingled into the blue depths. Was it fear?

"Tell me truly, sir. Would you have me stay behind, alone, living in Paris? Can you imagine how such an act would damage my reputation? All while wasting my best years on pointless pursuits that serve no purpose other than to increase my vanity?"

He opened his mouth to respond, but paused when two instructors passed by, their curious glances at the bickering duo bringing a smile to his lips.

"Are you not being melodramatic?"

Sebastian may have begun to see traces of humor in the situation, but Georgiana had not. Her cheeks flamed and jaw clenched, hands fisting at her side as she stiffened her spine and pierced him with a withering look. "Am I? Imagine how Lord Essenton, or you, would take to the idea of Lady Adele or Lady Reine behaving in a likewise fashion."

"They would not be alone, since I will be here," he countered, the underlying message that he would be there for her not transmitting as he wished.

"Somehow I doubt that would convince Lord Essenton. You have the luxury of freedom and waiting years or decades before marriage with your perfect, aristocratic wife, even then to do as you wish. I do not have that luxury."

"You speak as if in your dotage! I hardly think one or two years will render you unfit as a wife, Miss Darcy. And think of what you could accomplish here. We could compose together, brilliantly, as Professor Florange said!"

"Is this why you brought me here, Mr. Butler? Was it ever about my pleasure in viewing a place wondrous and unique or only to exert your selfish wishes for glory? Is our friendship nothing to you but a means to an end?"

Color washed over his cheeks as anger surged. He involuntarily leaned closer and pressed one palm against the wall above her head. "Never would I wish to cause you pain, Miss Darcy, whether you wish to believe it or not," he replied acidly, his eyes hard as granite. "My heart is honorable in its intention to want you to excel. Perhaps I am somewhat selfish, but only in that I desire your company and will miss our collaboration when you depart. Can you honestly say you will not miss it as well? Is that what you fear and why you insult me and cheapen our relationship with ludicrous accusations?"

Georgiana had not budged. In unconscious increments, Sebastian had drawn closer to her immobile body until his face was scant inches away from hers. His words penetrated her mind but she found them difficult to assimilate with his presence overpowering her senses. His mouth was so close, his stormy eyes mesmerizing and his masculine cologne stinging her nostrils in a most pleasant manner.

Kiss me rose unbidden to her lips and for a dizzying moment she thought she may have spoken aloud when his eyes lowered to her parted mouth and he leaned even closer.

"Butler! Is that you? Ha, indeed it is! What a surprise!"

Sebastian jerked as if scorched by a hot brand and whirled about to face the owner of the voice, his tall body hiding Georgiana, a fact she was grateful for as she needed the concealment to compose her shattered wits and frayed emotions. From the strain in his voice, Sebastian was as impaired, although he did manage to string words into a sentence which is more than she could have done.

"Lord Caxton! Unbelievable. I had no idea you were here. Teaching?"

"As always. A position was offered and I could not pass it up. I have been here for nearly two years now. I cannot stay away from home for too long,

however, and will return this summer. I heard you were touring the Continent, so I am not shocked you gravitated this direction. Thinking of enrolling?"

"I already have, for the fall session. Have no fear, however, as I shall not torture you by taking one of your classes."

"I shall be gone by fall, but my successor will be thrilled at the news. I could not pass by without greeting, but I apologize for interrupting your… discussion with the lady."

"No! Not at all!" Sebastian stepped to the side and turned toward Georgiana, extending his hand. "Please, forgive my rudeness. Miss Darcy, I have the honor of introducing you to an old friend and long-suffering instructor from Oxford, Baron Caxton of Alford Hall in Suffolk. Caxton, Miss Darcy of Pemberley in Derbyshire."

Caxton bowed, his brows lifting slightly. "Miss Darcy, *enchanté*. It is a pleasure indeed. I have had the good fortune to meet your brother on a handful of occasions and Mrs. Darcy once. Luck has smiled upon me greatly now to make your acquaintance."

Georgiana's turbulent emotions had no opportunity to recover, one glance at Lord Caxton sending them spiraling. Air escaped her lungs in a rush, the greatest of self-control required to not stammer and drop her mouth open.

Standing before her was the most physically exquisite man she had ever beheld. He was only of medium height, but brawny and possessing a face to rival the gods as personified on canvas or in marble. Nothing she had viewed in Italy eclipsed the figure standing before her. He was flesh and blood. His perfectly chiseled attractiveness was magnified by lushly curled coal-black hair, dynamic ebony eyes, bronzed skin, and a full mouth lifted in a vibrant smile.

As handsome as his person, equally impactful was his vitality. He possessed an energy within that was rawly male and charismatic, piercing her as a lightning bolt even from several feet away. She was enervated and terrified, her core shaken by an instantaneous, visceral reaction to another human being unlike anything she had ever experienced.

He stepped closer, increasing the power of his impression, and for a second she feared she would swoon! But somehow her hand was in his, being lifted toward his lips, serving as an anchor to her drowning spirit. He stopped before making contact, his warm breath feathering across her knuckles in time with the musical cadence of his voice.

"An extreme pleasure it is, Mademoiselle Darcy, my only sadness is that I have been deprived of your company these many years."

"You know my brother?" she responded automatically, her heart pounding so loudly in her ears that she barely heard her own voice and had little idea what she was saying.

The baron stared as if equally enchanted, dazzling her further. "Indeed quite well. My uncle is the Duke of Grafton, who has partnered with Mr. Darcy for some years now, as you are undoubtedly aware, and we are rabid horse enthusiasts all. I frequent the tracks and am a member of the Jockey Club, although my duties to Oxford, and now here, do not allow me to participate as I would wish."

"You are a professor?"

"I teach the violin. One of the few instruments poor Butler here could never master. Quite inept with it, I must reveal." He nodded toward Sebastian but did not remove his rapt attention from Georgiana. "Thankfully, he has myriad other talents. Miss Darcy, pray, tell me my good fortune is continuing and you will be attending the opera tonight?"

"The answer is an affirmative, my lord. I will be in the company of my uncle and aunt, Lord and Lady Matlock."

"Excellent news. You shall see me in the orchestra. I lead the string division of the Académie Royale de Musique. Do you like opera, Miss Darcy?"

"Very much."

"If my prejudice can be excused, I must say that we perform Rossini's *The Barber of Seville* extraordinarily well. You will be delighted."

"I am certain I shall."

"Your opinion is one I will appreciate hearing, Miss Darcy, if I may be granted permission to converse with you in the salon afterwards? Fresh ears offer unique insights that are of tremendous value."

Georgiana murmured a promise to render a critique, Baron Caxton's vibrant smile of appreciation increasing the fluttering in her chest and capturing her focus so thoroughly that she almost missed his next sentence. "Tomorrow evening is the gala in memoriam of Duc de Berri. Dare I hope to be so fortunate as to assume your presence there as well?"

"I have been invited and would not miss it for the world."

"Stupendous! Forgive my continued boldness upon such short acquaintance, but it would be my greatest honor to secure a dance, or possibly two, Miss Darcy? I posit that I must secure your favor now, prior to other gentlemen dominating your attention ere I locate you amid the crowds."

"You are far too generous, Baron."

"Not at all. I shall anticipate the delight of your company both evenings. Unless"—he looked suddenly to a forgotten Sebastian—"I beg your forgiveness. Is there an understanding?" He gestured between the two.

"No! Not at all," Georgiana blurted, shaking her head emphatically. "Mr. Butler and I are friends, nothing more. I would be pleased to dance with you tomorrow Lord Caxton."

"Wonderful. Well then, until tonight Mademoiselle Darcy. I will be counting the hours, I assure you. Now, I fear I must be on my way. I am already late for class and hopefully my students have decided to devote their free time to practice."

He bowed deeply, eyes caressing her face before tearing away to address Sebastian. "Butler, will you be at the gala tomorrow? Fabulous. We can reminisce then. Adieu, Miss Darcy."

He inclined his head again, this time drawing in the hand he still clasped to his lips for a glancing kiss.

Georgiana followed his progress down the hall, entranced and unaware of peripheral stimulants. At the corner Lord Caxton turned his head, smiled broadly as he waved to her, and then disappeared from view.

CHAPTER NINE

Opera:
A Dramatic Song

"No! Not at all!... friends, nothing more!"

She had practically shouted it and the words continued to pound inside his brain. The music rising from the orchestra pit and booming voices from the stage were insufficient in drowning the harsh exclamation.

Sebastian stole a glance to the box four to the right of his. Miss Darcy's profile was softly outlined in the muted light of the opera house, her eyes gazing out and down. Was it just his imagination that she was peering into the recessed pit where the musicians played? *Probably,* he thought sourly, *not that it matters to me.*

A nudge into his ribs interrupted the musings, Sebastian turning toward his grandmother. Lady Warrow fluttered her fan daintily, her eyes also staring fixedly at the stage. She was smiling, her face gay and relaxed, yet he knew she was displeased. How could she not be? Her escort had been surly and distracted since meeting her in the foyer before leaving for the opera. In truth, he had been battling a host of negative emotions all afternoon.

Sebastian had stood in the hallway outside Professor Florange's office observing the interplay between Lord Caxton and Miss Darcy while his insides churned savagely.

Seconds before Caxton's interruption he had been a hairbreadth away from kissing her. In a public passageway! He could almost taste the pleasure of her lips. The warmth of her breath caressed his face with each rapid exhale, utterly intoxicating him and wreaking havoc on his reason. The yearning had been so overwhelming that he did not know what had shaken him more—his raging lust for her kiss or his raging lust to murder Lord Caxton for stopping him! Nothing remotely similar had ever happened to him, and to say he had been unnerved would be the understatement of the century.

His composure had taken a serious hit from their heated encounter. His choler seethed alongside the wild rush of ardor, neither noticeably diminishing in the minutes after Lord Caxton's intrusion.

Then, to stand there forgotten while Caxton and Miss Darcy flirted was agonizing. He recognized the searing pain that flooded his body as uncontainable jealousy, the additional emotion compounding his distress. He was used to women responding to Lord Caxton, the man's allure a well-known fact even if other men did not comprehend it; however, watching Miss Darcy's pronounced reaction was something else entirely.

The cumulative assault rendered him physically ill.

Georgiana had remained silent throughout the ride to the de Valday townhouse on Île Saint-Louis. Whether that was from anger toward him or some other emotion he refused to name he could not begin to discover, the lump in his throat and churning bile in his stomach preventing conversation.

He had stewed all afternoon, arriving at the Théâtre National in a foul mood that did not improve when the brief encounter with Miss Darcy in the crowded salon gave him little to grasp on to. Was she remote in her welcome? Or was his imagination heightened? He could not decide which was the case, but to his mystification he seemed painfully aware of her tiniest nuance as never before.

Attending to the performance was impossible, as his grandmother's frequent subtle prods into his side proved. For the first time in his life, music did not calm him and for that alone his irritation grew. As the baron had promised, this rendition of *The Barber of Seville* was excellent—or rather those short portions he did manage to focus upon were beautifully done. Maddeningly, he discovered the words of their argument ringing through his brain with strength and clarity sufficient to drown the heavy coloratura contralto of Rosina and lush baritone of Figaro!

He pointedly avoided encountering her in the salon during intermission, that a feat easy to accomplish as the attendance for the gala performance was sold out. The recent stabbing of the Duc de Berri, nephew of Louis XVIII, on the steps of the Rue de Richelieu Opera House, had greatly upset the standard schedule of musical entertainments in Paris. While the antics of Polichinelle continued upon the stage, the heir to France's throne suffered for hours in one of the salons ere his death before dawn. None in the audience or upon the stage were aware that the tragedy had occurred, but all in Paris grieved and felt the consequences when the Emperor closed the Rue de Richelieu permanently.

The Académie de Musique floundered without a permanent home—and would for months to come—the hastily organized two-night gala to benefit opera and honor Duc de Berri becoming a special event for Parisians.

For Sebastian, the advantage of the evening laid in the crowds of people separating him from Miss Darcy, his emotions yet too raw to trust. He vacillated between wanting to seek her out and apologize to irritation for feeling he needed to apologize. His assurance that ignoring her was best warred with his dismay that she did not appear to be looking for him. Moments of mature reasoning that said their friendship was valuable and worth salvaging were smothered by the childish impulse to run away from an emotional situation he was not prepared to cope with.

A long night of sleeplessness and an endless day of pretending he was not dwelling upon the situation with Miss Darcy—when his thoughts rarely strayed elsewhere—had sapped his strength. He felt older than his grandmother when he finally entered the glittering ballroom where the gala was in full swing. Lady Warrow had chosen another escort for the evening, rightfully assuming the Marquis de Dumet significantly more charming than her grandson would be. Cheery he may not be, but Sebastian had managed to reach a measure of emotional stability by the time he crossed the threshold to be immediately greeted by friends from the Conservatoire. Within minutes of jovial converse, his mood improved. So did his confidence in restoring his friendship with Miss Darcy.

For a time, that is.

"Have you and Mademoiselle Darcy suffered a misunderstanding of some nature?"

Sebastian's hand jerked at the question but resumed its path toward his mouth, the sip of wine taken before he answered Monsieur Laroche. "Not at all," he lied. "Why do you ask?"

"You have not danced with the lady yet tonight, nor spoken one word to her, both an oddity striking in their irregularity. We have grown accustomed to the two of you in constant companionship."

"*We*? Who is this *we* encompassing?"

"Everyone," Laroche responded.

"*Everyone* is a great number indeed. I was unaware my actions were scrutinized by the entire population of Paris."

"No need to bristle, my friend. We Frenchman are notorious gossips, especially when it pertains to matters involving love."

"Therefore it may please you to learn that *love* has nothing to do with my attachment to Miss Darcy. We are friends, nothing more."

Laroche's brows lifted at the subtle churlish emphasis on the last two words. "As you wish. Thanks for the clarification to what we were speculating was an extremely poor judgment call on your part."

"There is that *we* again. How pleased I am to have provided a wealth of amused conversation to so many people. And do, pray tell, enlighten me as to my poor judgment?"

Laroche bobbed his head toward the punch bowl where Georgiana stood engaged in conversation with Lord Caxton. Sebastian winced at the sight of her beautiful face lifted toward the baron, their mutual admiration visible from across the room.

"Leaving a prospective *amour* in the custody of Lord Caxton is unwise, or incredibly foolish. Women are drawn to him as a magnet, as are a few men I could name but shall not. Personally, I am blinded to his allure but not heedless of the reality. Nor am I so moronic as to allow my sweet Flavie to be in the same building the baron is in let alone talk to him!"

"Your mistrust of Mademoiselle Flavie's devotion to you, Laroche, strikes me as a personal character flaw or failing in your relationship. And this after you boast incessantly of your lady's infatuation and crazed hunger for you," Sebastian countered, hoping to ruffle the ofttimes volatile musician and thus divert the topic away from Baron Caxton's attentiveness to Miss Darcy, a fact surely as obvious to everyone in the room as it painfully was to him. Alas, Laroche did not react as desired.

"I am merely presenting the truth of it. You have known the baron longer than anyone here so must have seen hundreds of women fall at his feet, *oui*?"

"Lord Caxton is an upstanding gentleman of London Society. His manners are impeccable with no hint of scandal or impropriety ever."

Laroche grunted. "Pathetic. What man would not sell his soul to be that handsome and to possess his power over the opposite sex? God knows I would, and then revel in the joy of endless pleasure and adoration every day until the devil takes me. Yet, he behaves as a *gentleman*! Unnatural, I maintain."

"With that attitude, I suspect Mademoiselle Flavie has the greater reason to distrust."

"Laugh all you want, Butler, and go on living with your delusions. It is true that he is a fine gentleman and respected teacher. We have yet to see him tumble a single maid or hear a whisper of an indiscretion with a female student…"

"I doubt you will."

"…but we are waiting."

"*We* again? How is it that I am not including in this infamous *we*?"

"You will be, once you are a true student… and after the initiation!"

"Initiation?"

"Never mind that"—Laroche waved Sebastian's concerned scowl away—"you will pass the test and then can partake of the betting. Yes, the betting"—he hastily nodded at the question etched upon Sebastian's face—"such as when will Lord Caxton weary of his costly visits to Madame Roux's establishment and succumb to one of the determined ladies who dog his every step, with heaving bosoms and bold solicitations freely advanced. The man is only human, is he not?"

Sebastian shook his head. "I believe you and your cronies are doomed to failure on this wager. I *have* known Caxton for years, and he simply is not a rogue. I venture your wager will remain uncollected."

"Ah, but if he were to set his gaze upon a woman? That, my friend, would be a different story altogether." Again he nodded his head toward Lord Caxton and Miss Darcy—the two now on the dance floor for the second set—leaned close to Sebastian, and whispered, "Is there a female alive who could resist such masculine handsomeness and charisma?"

The swallow of wine lodged in his throat, Sebastian gulping past the spasm that threatened to spew the liquid out of his mouth. Laroche pounded him on the back, his laughter preventing further references to Lord Caxton's mystique and Miss Darcy. Sebastian decided his burning throat, red face, and coughing fit were worth the disruption in that undesirable topic. Thankfully, before Laroche revisited the subject, they were joined by a group of fellow musicians from the Conservatoire, the lanky man in the front sweeping his eyes amusedly over Sebastian and then quirking a brow at Laroche.

"You must have told Butler about Reims. I knew he would be thrilled but did not anticipate choking to death over the news."

"We were discussing the mystery of the baron freely wooing Miss Darcy, Gaston. I had yet to mention Ambroise Guilmant-Deffayet's symposium on Guillaume de Machaut."

"Most unwise of you, Laroche, pointing out Butler's glaring error when we need him along on our excursion."

"What," Sebastian rasped, adding another cough, "the bloody hell are you babbling about?"

"The symposium. In Reims. Taught by Guilmant-Deffayet. On Machaut. Pay attention, Butler!"

"Ease up on the poor man, Gaston," piped up the man to Gaston's left. "He has lost his lady and ruined a perfectly fine swallow of Cinsaut on the same night. Let me rescue this before you spill it—adding to the tragedy—while Gaston cheers you with details on the symposium."

The speaker grabbed the wine glass from Sebastian's slack grip and proceeded to drain half the contents before Sebastian could formulate a response. Not that there was an opening to argue, since Gaston instantly did as suggested.

"It is as Anjou and Laroche have said. Guilmant-Deffayet is hosting a two-week lecture series on the poetry and compositions of Machaut. In Reims. We heard of it today and it begins in four days so, well, you can do the math."

"We know your penchant for medieval poetry and motets, religious compositions and music history," Laroche explained. "You have quoted Machaut numerous times and played portions of *Le Remède de Fortune* for Madame de la Croix's soiree so assumed this was a opportunity you would not miss."

"Besides," Anjou interjected, "you have more money than all of us combined and we are not above begging if necessary."

Gaston shook his head even while laughing. "No need to beg. Look at Butler's face! Prepare your travel bags, gentlemen. We are leaving for Reims two days hence."

Georgiana was bemused. *Yes*, she thought, *that is the word for it: bemused*. Or maybe *bedazzled* was an apt description for how she felt. The lights seemed brighter, the music especially melodious, the dancing more enjoyable, and the food ambrosial. Everything was exquisite as never before. The air surrounding her sparkled magically and tingles bounced over her skin.

Yet there was an unreal quality to the sensations within and perceptions without. It was not disturbing exactly. It was merely strange. *Strange and wonderful*, she amended as her silk-clad hands brushed over the baron's gloved palms, his thumb miraculously managing to squeeze and caress her knuckles in the seconds before the steps of the quadrille pulled them apart. Flawlessly, he sidestepped to engage the lady next in line, executing a fluid chassé while never looking away from Georgiana. She could not claim to be an adept judge of a man's behavior nor did she possess the vanity to assume men were instantly attracted to her; nevertheless, if asked, she would be forced to blushingly agree that Lord Caxton appeared to be as bemused as she.

This was their second dance together since arriving at the ball. The first, a waltz, had left her breathless and dazed. A portion of that response may have been a result of lively dancing on a crowded floor with lights blazing overhead. Undoubtedly the steady stream of conversation and questions while twirling at a fast pace augmented the breathlessness. Lord Caxton appeared relentless in his pursuit to learn as much about her as possible. This was quite flattering, of course, as was the intensity of the dark eyes that rarely left her face unless it was to scan over her figure—a fact she pretended not to notice even as heat flooded her skin—and the way he drew her closer to his body than was strictly necessary for a proper waltz. The latter greatly shattered her typical composure, and it was with some relief that she greeted the dance's conclusion.

The following hours continued to be a heady assault upon her senses. Lord Caxton was attentive and practically glued to her side for the entire evening. He filled her glass before it was half empty, secured an empty chair before she expressed a need to sit and rest, and procured sustaining treats with continual frequency. Much to her surprise, considering how flustered she felt around him, conversation flowed easily as the baron boasted a gift for drawing information in a carefree manner. Never domineering or overtly possessive, his demeanor and proximity to her spoke of his intent ere he formally expressed his wishes.

"Miss Darcy," he began, leaning closer to ensure she could hear him.

"Yes, Baron?" she responded, automatically lifting her eyes to his face. Fresh waves of warmth spread through her limbs, her mouth drying instantly at the effect of his presence so near. *How is it possible for one man to be so handsome?*

"I apologize for intruding upon your space, but even with the crowds thinning as the evening draws to a close, I fear the music and chatter combine to prevent easy discourse." He smiled, the perfection of white teeth behind strong lips and tiny crinkles appearing in the corners of his eyes increasing his attractiveness and thus her enchantment. "Alas, whisking you away to a secluded alcove is not a proper option, so I must therefore latch upon this relative privacy to ask a question of you before another group of friends descend upon us."

"Private conversation in a ballroom is nigh on impossible, I would agree. I shall do my best to ignore extraneous noises, Baron."

"Superb. And I shall do my best to be swift and pointed. If it is feasible in regards to your schedule and appealing to you, I would be honored to call upon you tomorrow afternoon. My only lecture for the day is completed at three o'clock. May I join you for tea shortly thereafter?"

"You are more than welcome, my lord."

He bowed and stepped back a pace. "I will await the hour with high anticipation, Miss Darcy. Now I see Lady Matlock approaching and since the music and dance are finished, I believe it is time to bid you a good night."

He bowed again and, in the process, captured her right hand, brushing across her palm and lightly stroking over her fingers while lifting it to his lips. Holding her gaze, dark eyes penetrating, he whispered *au revoir* and pressed a lingering kiss against her gloved knuckles. Then with a crisp pivot, he exited the room.

Georgiana stared at his retreating body, admiring his fine figure and basking in the intoxication of blatant flirting from a man as handsome as Lord Caxton. She was not so foolish or dazzled as to be unaware of how every woman in the room had observed him and in many cases brazenly sought his favor. Nor had she been so blinded as to not recognize that he ignored or bluntly rebuffed all of them, exclusively focusing on her—even when they both danced with someone else!

No, Georgiana Darcy was not a fool. But she was young and stunned by the onslaught to her sensibilities. If this were not the case, then most likely she would have noticed that her heart did not ache at his departure and that the hand he kissed hung limply at her side.

~*~

Sebastian rarely experienced nervousness. It simply was not in his nature to be unsure or fearful over mundane matters. Yet the tremble to his hand when he rapped on the door and the flutter in his chest as he stood on the stoop waiting for the butler to answer could be described as nothing but nervousness.

Later, he admitted that entering the salon to discover Lady Matlock and Lady Simone sitting with Miss Darcy and three other ladies of his acquaintance from Parisian society eased his nervousness, even if he could not ascertain Miss Darcy's opinion of him while in company. After all, Sebastian Butler naturally relaxed around women, and instantly, he sent a silent prayer to the Creator for gifting him with five sisters!

Eventually the older women left, probably fabricating pressing tasks and appointments in order to leave the youths alone. In a flash, the nervousness returned, Sebastian embarrassingly fidgeting with his coattail, shifting his feet where he stood by the edge of the sofa, and stammering like a schoolboy.

"Miss Darcy, I regret that we were unable to speak last evening and will confess in honesty that I was avoiding you at the gala. No, please! Let me finish if I may, and then I shall mutely withstand your censure."

"You are far too harsh on yourself, Mr. Butler, but proceed with your confession of dreadful doings and wicked thoughts. I will listen most attentively."

He sat—or rather fell—into the cushioned perch across from her. "You do not seem angry at all. In fact, I detect that you are laughing at me."

"I am not angry. I was, to be sure, but no longer. For some reason, it is extremely difficult for me to stay angry with you, sir. Does this ruin your well prepared speech of contrition, Mr. Butler?"

Sebastian laughed at her tease, the lifted weight from his shoulders momentarily making him light-headed!

"I had nothing prepared, being more of a spontaneous sort of fellow. I did intend to grovel, however." He leaned forward, looking at her seriously, although his gray eyes did sparkle a little. "I truly am sorry for embarrassing you with Professor Florange. I did deceive and no matter my rationale, it was wrong of me."

"Indeed, it was wrong of you. I shall not argue that point or placate your conscience, Mr. Butler. Nevertheless, I know you only meant well and the outcome is that we now understand one another with improved clarity. I do believe our friendship can withstand a disagreement or two."

"Or two? Are you presaging a future disagreement we must overcome?"

"Not at all," she countered with a shake of her head and laugh. "Nevertheless, I doubt there are many friends who do not irritate each other once in a while."

"I am relieved to hear you still consider me a friend, Miss Darcy. You were harsh in your judgment of my motives but not completely erroneous. I feared an understandable loss of good opinion."

"I am not that fickle in my sentiments. Besides, as you pointed out, I was harsh and justly deserving of losing your good opinion."

"So we are equal in our faults. Blast it all if that does not make us human!"

"Indeed! And this fallible human wishes to express her appreciation and understanding for what she now realizes was your desire to enlighten her to the broader world. I thank you for that, Mr. Butler. Furthermore, since it was I who threatened to glean all I could from you in the short time we have, I daresay it is idiotic of me to then be vexed with you for simply wanting to give me more. As it turns out, I was rewarded immensely with Professor Florange's praise. The day certainly was not a loss."

He frowned at the dreamy expression upon her face following the last statement, not wanting to imagine she was referring to anything besides the professor's endorsement of her talent. "I am relieved to hear you say that. Dare I hope that your confidence is boosted?"

"It is," she said, nodding slowly. "I know, as you do, Mr. Butler, that music is etched into my soul. It is who I am and what I love. I have faith and, yes, confidence that I can fulfill these desires to create and play, even as I live my mundane life in England."

"Somehow I doubt your life will ever be mundane, Miss Darcy."

"The life of a wife and mother is typically mundane, a state of existence I am happy to embrace. My comfort is in knowing I can pass on what I have learned, and who knows? Maybe my son will be the next Beethoven or Mozart."

He nodded and smiled despite the unease and twisting sensation within his gut. "So, am I truly and utterly forgiven? If not, I have an additional peace offering that I am sure will secure my standing within your good graces."

He retrieved the leather portfolio he had placed on the side table when he first entered the room, handing it to Georgiana with a deep bow. "A gift, my lady."

She opened the folder, recognizing the contents after one glance at the sheets of music, her smile widening with each turn of the page.

"Are these all of them?" Her voice was reverent and touches upon the sheets caressing.

"All that I have written thus far. There are many psalms in the Bible, so I judge it will take me a lifetime to compose music for all of them. These, however, are my favorites and the ones that inspired me. This here"—he leaned across the space separating their seats and tapped Psalm twenty-three—"is the first one I placed to music. Naturally."

"How old were you?"

"Sixteen or so. I have not played it for a few years to be honest, so it is probably shockingly horrid. You have my permission to embellish or rewrite at will."

"Oh no! I could never do that!"

Sebastian laughed. "We have been collaborating for some time now, Miss Darcy. I trust your insights and creativity. I sincerely believe you could improve upon many of these. Professor Florange did say we were brilliant together."

He murmured the last, biting his lip for bringing the subject of their argument to mind, but Georgiana did not comment or appear irritated. Rather, she was staring at him, her smile soft and eyes shining. In an instant, the urge to kiss her rushed through him as powerfully as it had before, the passion of anger apparently not the only impetus.

"Thank you for bringing them. Will you play one for me? Or several?"

It was impossible to look away from the pleading in her eyes, and the honeyed tones of the entreaty passing plump, moist lips entranced him. Some particle of his mind knew he was leaning closer to her and a dim voice cautioned him, but both were ignored.

What could not be ignored was the voice of the butler.

"Mademoiselle Darcy, you have a gentleman caller. Lord Caxton. He claims to have an engagement scheduled with you?"

They shot to their feet. Georgiana swayed slightly and the instinctual steadying pressure of Sebastian's hand under her elbow brought her closer to him, thus worsening his dizziness.

Lord Caxton strode in, his dark gaze skimming over the two of them and assessing the tableau in the seconds before Georgiana darted away from Sebastian's side. What his conclusion was could not be easily discerned, but Sebastian did notice a faint tightening to the corners of his eyes. Then he bowed, extending the formal welcomes as appropriate and gallantly filling the awkward scene with normalcy.

"I trust I am not interrupting?" The baron swept the hand holding his hat in the general direction of where they had been standing, Georgiana having moved some four feet away. "My class ended earlier than usual, so I hastened over for our tea engagement. I do apologize for the surprise entry, Miss Darcy."

"No need to apologize, my lord," Georgiana said in a rush. "Mr. Butler dropped by to bring some compositions I have expressed interest in. Psalms, actually."

"Psalms? How intriguing. I seem to recall your fascination with sacred music, Butler."

"More of a hobby. My serious compositions are not primarily choral. Rather, they tend to run in the direction of operatic or chamber music."

"As do most these days. Originality is sorely lacking in this generation, so it seems to me."

"Perhaps, Baron, you are looking in the wrong direction. Certainly Haydn, Beethoven, Schubert, and Czerny, to name but a few, offer the world unique styles."

"I shall take your word for it, Butler. I am unfamiliar with German composers, preferring French and Italian creations. I have heard few of Beethoven's compositions but admit to being uninterested. 'Far too German' is what the critics say with abrupt changes, barbaric dissonances, and excessive calculation. Not of my taste at all."

"I suggest you speak with Professor Reicha. Were you aware that our esteemed master of fugue studied with Beethoven?"

Caxton quirked his brow in surprise. "No, I was not."

"I daresay he might alter your opinions."

"Perhaps. This is a fascinating topic that I would very much like to pursue, Butler. I imagine your travels have given you an insight those of us mired here in France do not have. Our prejudices cloud our evaluations and stifle our acceptance. However, I am sure we are boring Miss Darcy profoundly. See, she is flushed and glassy-eyed! Please, sit, and we stuffy musicians shall talk of pleasanter matters while we refresh ourselves with tea and cakes."

"Thank you, but I am quite fine, truly. I do not find the discussion boring in the least."

"No?" the baron asked with genuine surprise. "How extraordinary. Ladies typically do. Tea?"

The baron sat at Sebastian's abandoned place and began to casually pour tea as if the activity were one he normally performed.

"Yes, thank you," she replied absently, sitting on the edge of the recently deserted sofa. She still held the leather portfolio, her grip on the edges tight to prevent the trembling that had invaded her body from betraying her discomposure and causing her hands to shake.

What is wrong with me? Why does he agitate me so?

Which "he" are you referring to?

"Miss Darcy?"

"What?" She jerked to the present, eyes lifting to Lord Caxton who was gazing at her questioningly.

"Are you well? Do you require rest? Perhaps we have strained your delicacy?"

Sebastian laughed, drawing both sets of eyes to where he yet stood next to the sofa's armrest. "Miss Darcy is far from fragile. She has outplayed me on the pianoforte numerous times, walked my feet to a state of blistered toes in the quest to see all in a museum, and I would not suggest daring her to a horse race."

Georgiana blushed but met his teasing gaze boldly. "I have never outplayed you, do not believe for a second you suffered blisters to your toes, but will boast that I beat you soundly every time we race. Forgive me, my lord"—she turned to the older man—"I was momentarily lost to daydreams of comparative analysis between German and French composers. What did you ask?"

"Only how you take your tea."

"One spoon of sugar and a fair dose of cream."

Again both sets of eyes lifted to Sebastian, who shrugged. "Sometimes two spoons if the tea is strong."

"I see," Caxton muttered. "Thank you, Butler. You have provided another answer to the mysteries surrounding Miss Darcy." He handed the cup to her but did not relinquish his hold on the saucer immediately, instead capturing her gaze and speaking with warmth, "Mysteries that I intend to devote myself to discovering, if this pleases you, madam?"

Georgiana's answer was a deep blush and duck of her head.

Caxton smiled in satisfaction, releasing the saucer and reaching for another. "How do you take your tea, Butler?"

"I"—he cleared his throat, looking away from Georgiana's rosy cheeks—"I am afraid I must return to the chateau to prepare for my departure tomorrow. I came by primarily to deliver the psalms into Miss Darcy's safekeeping for her to tinker with while I am in Reims."

"Reims?"

"Ah, you must be attending the symposium on de Machaut by Guilmant-Deffayet," Caxton guessed, ignoring Georgiana's expression of surprise and faint sadness.

"Guillaume de Machaut? Taught by Guilmant-Deffayet? Truly?"

Sebastian inclined his head toward Georgiana, smiling at the fascination and curiosity infusing her face. "Truly. And it should surprise me that you know who these men are but it does not."

"How long will you be away, Mr. Butler?"

"Long enough for you to memorize each psalm and for my brain to be filled with new facts for you to cull. Or, to put it into practical terms, two weeks and a bit."

"And you are leaving on the morrow?"

He nodded. "It is a rough road to Reims and the symposium starts in two days. We are taking a chance that accommodations can be procured"—he paused to chuckle and shrug his shoulders—"not that the gents are worried over it, since any inn with a pub will do as far as they are concerned. Fortunately, I know of several finer establishments near the university."

"Well, I am admittedly terribly envious. I have no doubt it will be enlightening and I will most certainly ask a million questions. Be sure to take notes!"

"As you command, madam."

Caxton rose at that point, blocking Sebastian's respectful bow from Georgiana's view, and extended his hand to Sebastian. "Travel safe, Butler. It is a long road, and rough as you said, so I am sure preparations are needed."

"Yes indeed," Sebastian agreed, noting the edge to the baron's voice. "I do have packing to do. I will leave you to your amusement. Miss Darcy, a pleasure as always." He bowed again, this time within Georgiana's sight, and stepped toward the door.

Georgiana stood, following after with quick paces and impulsively reaching out to touch his sleeve.

"Mr. Butler!" He halted and turned, Georgiana so close she could see the flecks of green in his otherwise gray eyes. "Please do be careful."

"I will, have no fear. And please extend my regrets to the Mademoiselles de Valday."

"Oh! Of course! You will miss the dinner party we are hosting to honor the de Valdays arrival in Paris. Mademoiselles Yvette and Zoë will be devastated."

"I promise to make it up to them with the anticipated amount of flirting and attention as soon as I return. Be sure to tell them so."

Georgiana laughed. "That will please them to be sure. And I will keep these safe." She clutched the music portfolio against her chest and patted it with her other hand.

"I know you will." He took the hand spread on the smooth leather and brought it to his lips. "Adieu, Mademoiselle Darcy."

With a dozen or so steps he was out the door, the click as it closed was strangely loud, adding fresh shivers to the ones already racing up her spine.

"Come, Miss Darcy, your tea is growing cold."

"Of course," she murmured, lifting a smiling face to Lord Caxton, who had moved to stand by her side. She walked back to the sofa, sat, and picked up the lukewarm tea.

"I am anxious to hear of Pemberley from your lips, Miss Darcy. My uncle, the Duke of Grafton, speaks highly of the stables and estate lands, but I have a feeling you will share a more personal perspective."

And from there, the afternoon passed in easy discourse of English countryside and horses and home. Georgiana greatly enjoyed herself even while ignoring the hazy sensation of melancholy and annoying tingles that spun across her knuckles and danced up her arm.

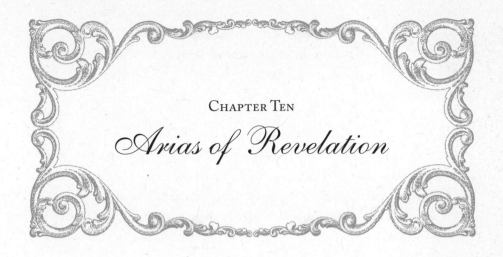

CHAPTER TEN

Arias of Revelation

THE DE VALDAY CARRIAGES rolled up the drive to their Paris townhouse at a slow and stately pace. The clomp of horses' hooves and the crunch of gravel warned the butler, Monsieur Vigneux, of their arrival and he, in turn, alerted the waiting inhabitants. However, all of this warning still did not provide time enough for Georgiana to reach the stoop before Yvette and Zoë. They embraced her as if years separated their prior visitation, enthusiasm so intense that English was not even attempted!

Frédéric approached the clot of skirts and fur and ruffles, his natural stride lazy and sensuous. He snared Georgiana's hand effortlessly from amid the chaos, bowed low while managing to maintain eye contact, and bestowed a precise kiss to the bare skin of her wrist.

"Mademoiselle Darcy, enchantress and love, my heart is whole once again in your presence."

The little speech was delivered with exaggerated emotion and facial expressions, Frédéric's sisters quickly shoving him aside and waving off his overblown dramatics with their typical teasingly deprecating remarks. Frédéric grinned and winked at Georgiana before fluidly clasping her to his side—her arm somehow linked around his—and escorting her into the house, Zoë and Yvette on each side, chattering a French tirade all the way to the sunny salon facing the rear garden.

Georgiana smiled as she listened, responding mostly in nods and holding the laughter in check. She had missed them, sorely, and within five minutes felt exhilarated. The vague sadness that had invaded her heart since the departure of Mr. Butler three days ago vanished.

Almost.

Additionally, Frédéric's bearing and magniloquence had clarified a mystery within her mind. The seventeen-year-old youth delighted her and she truly adored him, but his age and immaturity made stronger feelings impossible. Yet, from the moment she had met him in Lyon, she recognized his innate sensuality. Frédéric oozed magnetism and charisma, his aura intensely masculine if yet unseasoned. Suddenly, Georgiana imagined him as a fully-grown man, one no longer innocent of the world and the effect of his allure, and as an epiphany, she realized it was what Lord Caxton possessed.

The thought was rather disturbing. Frédéric was a tease, a naïve tease who meant no harm with his playful declarations of undying love. Someday he would comprehend his intrinsic charm, then choose how he would use this power. Would he harness it? Or would he utilize it for selfish whims?

How has Lord Caxton chosen to use his native seductiveness?

Georgiana was not sure she wished to face the answer to that question. Luckily, there was little opportunity.

"Dearest Georgiana!" Yvette gushed, enfolding her into another warm embrace. "We have been utterly desolate without you!"

"Dreary Lyon was positively lifeless when you departed," Zoë added with feeling.

"It is true," Yvette agreed, curls bobbing with each emphatic nod. "Even our charming chateau was gloomy without your presence to light the atmosphere. And not a single ball or soiree to entertain since the de Marcov wedding reception!"

"Shocking," Georgiana gasped.

"Indeed! I do believe I have forgotten how to dance!"

"Fret not, my dear Zoë. I am confident the skill will reassert itself once the music starts."

"Ooh! Are you announcing a ball?"

"Yes, please say yes!"

Both girls dropped onto the settee beside Georgiana, pleading faces on either side of her. "I am"—she paused for the squeals of glee—"but not for two days"—another pause for the groans of dismay—"and first you must suffer through a sedate dinner party tomorrow night. It is, however, thrown to honor the de Valday relocation to Paris and the guest list numbers nearly sixty souls."

This news was greeted with identical happy smiles and bobs of ebony ringlets.

"Quite perfect," Frédéric noted from his casual repose on the chaise, "as that allots us tomorrow and Wednesday to shop. I am in dire need of new cravats and a fob for my pocket watch." He pulled the glittering timepiece out of his waistcoat pocket, frowning as he polished the diamond-adorned fob on his sleeve. "And you, my lovely Yvette, have worn each of the hairpieces you own at least twice."

Yvette's hand flashed to the emerald comb embedded in her lush hair.

Zoë nodded in agreement, her face as mournful as her twin's. "Alas, it will not allot us the time necessary to acquire new gowns. We shall be the laughing-stocks of Paris wearing these woefully outdated dresses."

"Ridiculous, all of you," Georgiana laughed. "Zoë, your gown was brought to you while I was in Lyon—"

"Yes, but Parisian fashion changes daily!"

"Hardly! And the style is very similar to what I am wearing. I have no doubt you possess *something* adequate for the next few engagements until your modiste sews a new wardrobe."

"The divine Mademoiselle Darcy is correct," Frédéric declared, stuffing the shining watch back into his pocket. "The important part is that we are finally in Paris and parties await! Tell us, sweet Georgiana, who has been invited to our *dîner de gala*? Luminaries galore? A host of beautiful women?"

"The delicious Monsieur Butler, *oui*? To delight us with his stunning handsomeness and skilled hands upon the pianoforte, *oui*?"

"Sorry to disappoint, Yvette, but Mr. Butler is away from Paris at the moment."

The twins gasped, Yvette pressing her hand against her heart and Zoë covering her mouth with the back of her hand, four wide eyes staring at Georgiana as if she had just announced the end of the world.

"The tragedy! To be separated from your heart and soul when your love is blossoming and at its most passionate!"

"Oh, you brave, brave girl, to be so cheery for us when your heart is breaking!"

Georgiana rolled her eyes. "Heavens, you two are the most dramatic females

I have ever encountered! Mr. Butler is a friend, Yvette, not my 'heart and soul' so there is nothing tragic about our separation. You are very silly indeed."

"Well, I am devastated beyond repair," Zoë moaned.

"I as well," Yvette concurred, although her eyes were not as doleful. "He will return soon, *oui*?"

"In two weeks. And he wanted me to tell you both that he shall atone for missing your dinner by flirting outrageously and fawning extensively once he returns."

They brightened at that news and immediately launched into an animated discussion of attractive Parisian men. Strategies for coquettish behavior, charming repartee, and properly alluring clothing dominated the next half hour, Georgiana laughing and blushing at the same time.

Frédéric—who had remained silent—suddenly leaned forward, gazed intently at Georgiana's face, and whispered, "Mr. Butler is merely a friend you say? Hmm… I sense a different emotion lurking under your skin."

"You are as ridiculous as your sisters, Frédéric," she whispered back, the twins busily adjusting décolletages for improved bosom display and not aware of the quiet exchange.

"Am I?"

"Yes, you are."

"You deny your heart is captured? Ah"—he sighed—"you blush and divert your eyes. Telltale signs. Who is the fortunate man, my sweet? Is it the worthy Monsieur Butler or another dashing gentleman who has wrest away your heart?"

"No one has wrest my heart, Frédéric—"

"Your voice wavers," he interrupted. His tone was compassionate and eyes tender, drawing Georgiana in. "You struggle with your emotions. Unsure, you are. Why does love confuse you so? Is your heart torn between several lovers?"

"There are no lovers but—" She paused, contemplating how best to put her tumultuous thoughts into words. The urge to share was suddenly so strong, overriding her natural reticence and the dim voice questioning why she would divulge her innermost feelings to Frédéric. "Mr. Butler is my friend and can be no more, this I know. Yet, it is true that I feel… something more. Then there is the Baron Caxton who stirs me and is suitable in many respects. I…"

"This baron," Frédéric encouraged when she halted, "he is courting you?"

"No, not officially, no. We barely met. Baron Caxton—"

"Baron? What baron? Will there be a baron at our party tomorrow?"

Georgiana jerked at Yvette's interruption, her cheeks instantly scarlet, but Frédéric answered with aplomb, "Barons, comtes, seigneurs, perhaps even a marquis or duc—the possibilities for conquests will be endless, my dearest sisters. I can only pray to be as fortunate, although with Mademoiselle Darcy as the owner of my heart, I doubt if I will even notice."

Shopping, dinner engagements, dancing, symphonies, horseback rides, a promenade through Tuileries Gardens, a boat ride down the Seine, carriage tours of the city, appointments with the modiste, afternoon teas with ladies of Society—the subsequent days were a whirlwind of activity that made the prior weeks boring by comparison. Daily the entertainments changed, as did the persons accompanying her on an outing or encountered at a particular venue. Faces and names grew more familiar to Georgiana, and a few true friends were made to join the de Valdays as her closest associates while in Paris.

Another who was quickly instilled on the list of her constant companions was Lord Caxton. She was unsure how he managed it, but suddenly he was free from his teaching duties at the Conservatoire all hours of the day and night. When not joining her for whatever group venture was devised to pass the daylight hours or an evening appointment he finagled an invitation to, he requested the honor of her exclusive company.

Through it all, whether surrounded by large numbers or merely a handful of others, his concentration was clearly on Miss Darcy. This undisputable conclusion was highly flattering to the innocent Georgiana but also astonishing.

Whenever he walked into her sight after being apart, she was struck anew by his overt masculinity and pronounced attractiveness. He exuded power and confidence with every step or gesture or flicker of his eyes. The aura of perfection so overwhelmed her that every time she was again bemused and bedazzled.

She had not forgotten her revelation of Lord Caxton's potency and apprehension over whether he used his gift of captivation avariciously. He wielded his charm masterfully and with purpose, of that she could tell, but was polite and solicitous and genuine. Nothing ungentlemanly occurred to give her reason to doubt his intentions and her heart felt his sincerity. Furthermore, as the days passed, the instant reaction of scattered wits and fluttering heartbeat waned at a speedier pace.

His captivating persona did not change, but rather it was the sense of ease and familiarity that grew stronger. With each conversation and enjoyable hour, Georgiana's fondness for the baron multiplied.

"Tell me of Pemberley and your childhood there," he requested on the day they rowed and drifted down the Seine.

"But you have heard my stories! Why, I do believe you could navigate the entire park at Pemberley blindfolded!"

The baron smiled at her tease but shook his head. "I rather doubt that. Should I apologize for never tiring of hearing of your youth, Miss Darcy?"

"No," she answered with a flush, "however, I do believe it is past time for you to tell me of your childhood, Baron. I shall row while you talk."

He held the oars away from her hands. "I can row and talk at the same time, or we can drift on the current. No need to exert yourself. Now, where to start…"

"The beginning is usually best," she interjected, Caxton again smiling at her humor.

"Indeed. Well, it may surprise you, Miss Darcy, to learn that I was not the firstborn son."

He went on to talk of his siblings, the eldest and heir to the Caxton estate dying when four years of age, his parents, and the modest estate in Surrey where he had lived all his life until boarding school.

"You miss your home, I can tell."

"I do. Now, that is. Oh, I missed home before, but not to the degree I now do. Two years in France without a return visit or more than correspondences from my steward and my family is too long."

"You said when we met you at the Conservatoire, that you would be returning home soon."

"I leave in June," he replied, scrutinizing her expression as he continued. "My teaching term will be over, I have learned all the musical lessons I need for my simple desires, and the estate needs me. My steward has managed capably in my absence, since my father's death four years ago actually, and he has the assistance of Baroness Caxton—my mother," he hastened to add, quite pleased that his ambiguous word choice seemed to startle Georgiana. "She is competent and has some authority, but she is a woman, so her knowledge is limited."

For some reason, the last sentence and the tone it was delivered in disturbed Georgiana. But the conversation moved on and her worries fled. Listening to the baron talk was pleasurable. His voice was pitched higher than one might expect in one so manly and brawny, but mellow and light. He chose his words carefully, she could tell, speaking with economy and precision. In character, he was serious and constrained, short on humor, and bordered slightly on austere. Yet he was considerate and kind, very intelligent, and devoted to his homeland and family—traits that Georgiana appreciated.

As a dancer, he was superb, possessing the fluid rhythm she recognized as unique amongst those who were gifted musicians. Waltz, quadrille, allemande—all were performed with skill and verve. On the ballroom floor, his restraint vanished and this was both exhilarating and overwhelming. Dancing, forever that one activity where close proximity and touching were allowed, provided a convenient, proper place for Lord Caxton to unleash his sensual magnetism.

"Tonight, Miss Darcy, I intend to teach you the steps of the mazurka," he said as they entered the mansion where the Russian ambassador to France dwelt and where a ball was about to begin.

"The Russian dance? Oh my, I am not sure I am capable if the steps are as complicated and fast as the rumors say."

"The mazurka is actually a Polish dance brought to Russia as a sort of souvenir of their conquests. Your history lesson for the day," he added with a soft laugh, steering her cleverly through the throng crowding the foyer. "And indeed, it is a fast, powerful dance, yet not unlike a quadrille as far as the steps themselves. It is beautiful and graceful when performed correctly."

"You are well versed in the dance, I suppose?"

"Fair enough. I am also a good teacher. I am confident you shall master it and know I will enjoy instructing you."

The penetrating look as he spoke the last, along with the subtle squeeze of her arm against his side caused her cheeks to flush. Was there an insinuation in his words and tone of more than just the dance? There was scant time to reason it out, Georgiana tucking it away along with everything else he said and did for a future period of inspection.

And as she suspected, dancing with Lord Caxton was as breathless this time around as it was when they first danced together at the gala. Neither time was the rapid rhythm of the dance, even one as extreme as the mazurka, the primary cause for her accelerated body functions or scattered wits.

Georgiana knew most ladies would decide she was crazy, but distance was necessary, and she was relieved that rules of decorum dictated only two dances per gentleman. On the dance floor Lord Caxton stretched the limits of propriety. It was never to the point of rudeness, severe invasion to her space, or gross misconduct, but he did grasp onto the opportunity as a way to express his innermost desires.

Conversation was safer to Georgiana's way of thinking, and for that reason, she preferred casual activities rater than dancing. A stroll along a sunlit garden promenade offered that.

"When did you begin playing the violin?" Georgiana halted beside one of the Corinthian columns placed around the exterior of the Arc de Triomphe du Carrousel in Tuileries Garden, shielding her eyes from the sun and squinting up at the baron.

He wrinkled his brow in thought. "I am not sure I remember precisely. We had tutors frequently over the years when I was young, who exposed us to music of some sort. Along the way, I learned to play several instruments, but the violin appealed to me most. Yet it would not be until my stay at Harrow that I felt a true affinity and thus focused on it above all else."

"Your parents obviously encouraged your musical education."

He shrugged at her statement, resuming their stroll down the concourse toward the palace. "Not particularly, no. We merely happened to have tutors who possessed skills to varying degrees. My mother can play the pianoforte and the harp well enough to entertain on special occasions, and my sisters are accomplished to the same degree. Few women can boast of more than that."

"Few women have the chance to practice or receive higher learning to improve what talent they may be gifted with, unlike men."

He glanced at her face, noted the color infusing her cheeks, and frowned. "True, I suppose. Yet what would be the point, Miss Darcy?"

"Why… to learn, of course, to discover what is hidden inside and enhance their capabilities and express the joy of music that is within their heart!"

"Nothing prohibits a lady from doing any of those things if she wishes it," he responded calmly. "The females of my family have no desire to learn more nor do they have the aptitude. Obviously, this is not the case of all females, such as you, Miss Darcy. I have no doubt at all that you shall always play, much to the delight of any who are fortunate enough to listen, and will challenge yourself to master new pieces, even those written by German composers."

She smiled at his tease but stopped walking once again. "Do you disagree with ladies enrolling at the Conservatoire?"

"I neither agree nor disagree. What an individual, male or female, chooses to do with their lives is not for me to decide, as long as they are harming no one. I have seen men waste years in study that will never serve them in a fruitful manner due to lack of proficiency. That is tragic. I see the same with the women who enroll. Even those with genius eventually leave it behind for a husband and children. I often wonder if they are happier for the time they spent or unhappy when it must be left behind. I do not know."

"Do you feel as if you have wasted your years here, Baron?"

"Not at all. I came to share what expertise I had with others, and to enjoy France while I was at it. Teaching was always something I knew to be a temporary profession. I am content and quite ready to move on. And, of course, I can certainly not regret my time here since it has ended with my introduction to you."

He accented his praise with a sprig of yew torn from the hedge. "Alas, flowers are not close by, so this must suffice." He handed the fragrant branch to her with a smile and bow of his head, Georgiana dipping her head and bringing the greenery to her nose. "Now," he said, once again resuming their walk, "while at Oxford, I played in the orchestra, as a student and a teacher…"

Georgiana listened to his remembrances while mulling over his statements. It was irrational, she knew, to feel irked by his opinion when he had said nothing she had not thought herself and said to Mr. Butler.

So why the sense of sadness? Perhaps it was his detached attitude that struck her as strange. There was little in the way of passion when he spoke of his talent, as if he took it for granted and felt no sorrow over leaving it all behind. Yet had she not calmly claimed the same contentment with her pathway? *It is admirable*, she decided, ignoring the twinge of annoyance and twirling the yew sprig in her hand while listening to him talk, *and means we have even more in common.*

Equally outstanding were Lord Caxton's skills on horseback. In this he supplanted her abilities and rivaled those of her brother, whose horsemanship surpassed anyone she had ever encountered. Twice during those weeks, they met at the estates of friends living on the outskirts of Paris, grasping on to days of sunshine to join others for fresh air and exercise.

The horses and their riders walked, trotted, and cantered over the damp green fields in various sized clusters. Lord Caxton utilized the opportunity to converse with Georgiana in a one-on-one scenario, the open pasture providing nearly complete privacy while never being out of sight of at least a few of their companions.

"Are you a man unafraid of a challenge, my lord?"

"Not typically, no, but how do you mean?"

"See that cracked boulder yonder?" She indicated a massive rock jutting from the earth a good one hundred yards away, the jagged edge on one side resembling the tooth filled maw of a beast. Caxton nodded. "I challenge you to a race, the winner naming her, or his, prize."

She was already tightening her hands about the reins, the rush of adrenaline making her heart beat faster and breath hitch. Her eyes assessed the uneven turf and obstacles ahead, projecting the images onto a canvas in her mind not only for the purpose of winning but to displace the visions of Mr. Butler and her on similar races across grassy plains.

"Interesting idea," Lord Caxton responded, "however I do not think this would be proper, Miss Darcy."

She looked at him then, her brows lifted in surprise. The baron was frowning, his expression faintly disapproving.

"Ladies should not gallop, nor, I must add, participate in wagers, although I understand you meant nothing of a serious nature." He smiled and leaned across the space separating their mounts to lightly clasp her gloved hand, his voice soothing. "I would be crushed if you were to lose control of your horse, who is unfamiliar to you and much stronger, or misjudge the terrain and suffer an accident, Miss Darcy. Furthermore, those rocks are quite far and not easily seen. As greatly as I desire it, it is highly improper to be secluded with a gentleman, no matter how innocent."

He patted her hand, smiled again, and resumed their casual walking gait and conversation as if the subject had never occurred. Georgiana said no more and managed to push the matter aside and enjoy her afternoon. Yet she could not shake the feeling that Lord Caxton's remarks about being alone with a gentleman were not general or regarding him, but were a reference to her and Mr. Butler being chaperone-less and very close to each other both times he had encountered them together. Oddly, instead of feeling ashamed by his reproach and being reminded of what she could not argue was improper behavior, the incident brought Mr. Butler into clearer focus.

And that thought lay heavy upon her heart no matter how she tried to ignore it.

The days turned into weeks, the two since Mr. Butler departed and Lord Caxton initiated what could only be viewed as a serious address flowing into a third week. Each day was packed with adventure and entertainment, and in most of them the baron played a part. If Georgiana had expended what residual energy she had on contemplating the situation she discovered herself in, she would have logically deduced that separation from Mr. Butler—who attracted her but was on a different path—and constant togetherness with Lord Caxton—who offered everything any woman could possibly want—were positive developments.

However, Georgiana had limited time alone and fell into her bed each night—or in the hours immediately before dawn—utterly exhausted. Mr. Butler's portfolio of psalms lay on her nightstand forlorn and untouched, a consequence she was aware of but too weary to lament. Yet each night her eyes rested upon the brown leather, and in those seconds before sleep claimed her, she felt a sense of peace. And when she did remember her dreams, he was always there.

Sebastian Butler sat in the pub at the inn where he and his friends had dwelt for the past two weeks. It was noisy, as most pubs were in the late afternoon, but spacious enough that he managed to claim a secluded booth near the back. It was his favorite spot, mainly for the relative solitude but also because the wide window provided light. Here he could drink a pint or two of ale after the day's lecture ended while rewriting the hasty notes taken during the session.

No one needed to point out that seldom had he taken notes during a lecture, infrequently were they more than a few jotted lines of major significance, and rarer still had he recopied them! He knew it was an oddity, and he knew very well that he was doing it for Miss Darcy. The pouch of parchment sheets sitting on the table beside him was thick, would be thicker when he finished the pages he was working on, and if luck held would be even thicker if the ordered music compositions arrived before they were set to leave tomorrow. The shop owner promised they would be in by today.

He paused to flip open his pocket watch—nearly three o'clock—take a gulp from his mug, and stretch his aching neck before dipping the quill and getting back to work.

He was exhausted. The symposium had been as fascinating and educational as he had hoped, more so, in fact, because through it all, he had imagined Miss Darcy sitting next to him. Well, not literally. But in the figurative sense, he had listened to every word while imagining how he would share the knowledge with her. Better yet, he could vividly envision her face, knowing precisely how she would feel. He would enjoy the entire lecture all over again with her.

"Why are you smiling as an imbecile while sitting alone in a pub? Most unusual."

Sebastian looked up at Gaston, continued to smile, and waved at the bench across from him. Not that Gaston was waiting for an invitation, with his hat already tossed onto the seat and his bottom halfway there. He plopped a large envelope onto the table while simultaneously gesturing the barman for ale.

"I was passing by Mollet's so stopped in to check. There is your package. So now we can head home without you crying all the way."

"Thank you," Sebastian said simply, slipping the tied bundle under the pouch without opening it and resuming his task without further comment.

Gaston waited until his tankard was brought and drained a third of the way before interrupting the silence. "So, do you have a strategy or prepared speech? Something insipidly mawkish and riddled with purple prose?"

"What are you talking about?"

Gaston's initial response was a derogatory phrase that turned the heads of several near neighbors. Sebastian received the full impact of Gaston's condescending expression, flinching involuntarily at the combination.

"Spare me," Gaston said scathingly. "I have been married for ten years and happen to still love my wife—most of the time. She must be mentally deficient to put up with me, but damned if I can see it. I do, however, frequently need to pull out the romantic nonsense in order to keep her from leaving me for someone handsomer or richer." He shrugged, sitting back and draining the ale. "It seems to work, though, so that would be my suggestion."

"As fascinating as your marriage advice is, Gaston, I still have no idea what you are talking about."

"Balderdash! I prefer a stronger expletive but do not want to upset the delicate ears of yonder fellows." He pointedly glared at the group sitting closest, the three men ducking their heads for being caught eavesdropping. "The last thing in the world I want to do, Butler, is play matchmaker or give courtship advice. Curls my hair to even think on it."

"You sure you are French?"

"It's worse. My mother was Italian. I should be the most sentimental sop in the country instead of the irascible bloke I am."

"Bloke? Seriously?"

"I have been associating with bloody Englishmen for too long. The colloquialisms are rubbing off. And do not try to change the subject. I am here to beat some sense into you and give advice, since God knows you need it, even coming from me. First answer my question—do you have a plan for wooing Mademoiselle Darcy?"

"How do you…? That is, what gave you that idea?"

"You honestly look surprised." Gaston laughed aloud, again drawing the attention of the neighboring drinkers, but he ignored them and instead gestured for another ale from the barmaid, who had also turned to stare at his enthusiastic bray. "Ah, you amuse me, Butler, you truly do." He wiped a tear from his eye, continued to chuckle, and reverted to his typical French slang-laced syntax. "*Merde*, was I ever that innocent? But then I am French and Italian, so no. You, my sad, repressed English friend, are in dire need of a swift kick in the ass. Or several tumbles amid the sheets, but since that is unlikely considering your affection for Mademoiselle Darcy, I will settle for the kick. We can keep it figurative for now, unless you remain denser than a post or in denial."

Sebastian glanced around but the eavesdropping men had left and the other patrons were paying them no mind. Still, he leaned forward and lowered his voice. "Very well. No need to threaten me. I just thought I was better at shielding my emotions." Gaston interrupted with a rude sound and then raised his hand in apology, Sebastian continuing, "Apparently, I am transparent enough so for you to decipher my thoughts." He sighed. "It is not as easy as simply wooing her, Gaston. It is… complicated."

"*Amour* is always complicated. My first point of advice is to forget imagining it ever *will not* be complicated. Accept that and move forward. You want her, so go and get her."

"What if she does not want me?"

"*Oui,* that does make it tougher to be sure, but not impossible. That is where romancing comes in. Poems, flowers, sweet treats, flowery words of love! If that fails, take her into your arms, kiss her, and show her what passion really is."

Sebastian shook his head, hoping his friend was partially jesting, but rather doubting he was. The image of kissing Miss Darcy—one that was easily envisioned—made rational conversation difficult, but he tried. "I would never force my desires upon her, Gaston. Whatever I feel for Miss Darcy, and I am not so sure I even know, I am her friend and want her to be happy. It is complicated and I cannot move past that as easily as you suggest."

"How so?"

"She is to return to England and I must stay here. I cannot ask her to wait for me to finish my education, but I cannot give up this opportunity."

"What prevents you from having both? Marry her and study together. Everyone knows Professor Florange endorses her. When you have absorbed all that the Conservatoire has to offer, return to England and your estate. Problem solved!"

"She was fairly adamant that she does not want to accept the professor's invitation, Gaston. Furthermore, for me, it will never be a matter of finishing my education. Even after I am Lord Essenton, I will pursue my music and compositions. Miss Darcy longs for the stability of a home and family, nothing more." Sebastian shook his head, gazing at the dry ink lines of text on the table but not seeing the words.

"Yet you take notes and buy compositions for her. Strange habit if you are convinced she is uninterested." He smirked at Sebastian's startled expression, drained his tankard, and rose from the bench. Smacking three coins onto the surface of the table he concluded, "Butler, I have a wife, five children, a house to maintain, work at my father's pâtisserie, perform regularly with the symphony, and teach at the Conservatoire. I do all of this on an income a tenth of yours and only three servants. Excuses are for imbeciles and incompetents. You are neither. I think both of you are making it complicated. I do not know why, other than that you are English. There is no feeling in your country! Your souls scream for freedom! Here is my final advice, my friend. Search your heart without reserve. Then, once you face your truth, confront the fair mademoiselle and search her heart. Complication will vanish in the air and only desire will remain. Trust me."

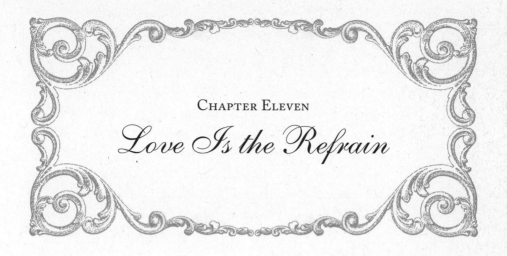

CHAPTER ELEVEN

Love Is the Refrain

S EBASTIAN WAS A BELIEVER in love. He was a composer living in
an age of romance, so a belief in love was somewhat obligatory. This
innocent, idealistic exaltation of love's power conquering the evils of the
world and giving birth to every expression of art was ingrained. His mind had
rationally yearned for the all-consuming bliss of passionate love to enter his
heart, sure that when it did, the beauty of the emotion would open his eyes and
unlock his soul. Ah, yes! Then music would have deeper understanding. Poetry
would be more poignant. Life would be richer.

Nevertheless, by the time he mounted the steps of the townhouse owned
by the Marchioness of Warrow—his home while in Paris—his opinion of love
was not as favorable.

Gaston's words echoed through his head the entire journey from Reims.
Gaston said nothing further and gave no indication of having the conversation
in the first place. This suited Sebastian just fine, and thankfully none of the
other gents brought up Miss Darcy either. In between ribald conversation and
crude jokes, there were long periods of silence with only the revolving wheels to
listen to. It was then that Sebastian ruminated on the situation.

He relived every moment spent with Miss Darcy, replayed their conversations, and summoned to mind each expression upon her lovely face. He dug into
his heart, extracting feelings and attempting to analyze. When the overlapping

impressions jumbled in his mind, melding into a solid mess of incoherences, he shoved it aside and decided to formulate a plan as Gaston had suggested.

Nothing.

Sebastian wanted to kick his own rear end—saving Gaston the duty—for having little idea how to proceed in wooing a lady. *Has my bragging of five sisters giving me an advantage been a laughable boast?* Apparently, the answer was yes. He had never been in love and never gone to any extreme to curry a woman's favor. Single-mindedly, he had focused on his professional pursuits, pouring his energy into that course alone while fighting his father along the way. He was a believer in love, but the emotion had manifested on the pages of a musical score and flowed from a piano's keys. Foolishly, he assumed true passion would leave him be until he was prepared to handle it and never imagined that he would encounter any problems when it did!

If he was being honest, he was terrified and hid behind a mask of ineptitude.

When the quiet and rocking carriage lulled him into interludes of slumber, the tumult inside led to bizarre dreams that exhausted instead of refreshed and brought him no closer to a solution. A sudden storm forced them to abandon the plan for a straight ride to Paris, causing them to spend two nights holed up at an inn before the washed-out road was navigable. For Sebastian, it was more time to agonize over the predicament with nothing to occupy his mind but how much he missed her.

The streets of Paris stirred his soul and tendrils of excitement brushed the edges of his heart. *She is here.* The thought made him smile despite his weariness. *Tomorrow I will call upon her and will trust my instincts.* As a plan it was not the best, but it would have to do.

Fatigue of body and mind assailed him. So much so that when the butler informed him that Lady Warrow was away from home Sebastian sent a rapid prayer of thanks heavenward. He felt a bit guilty about it, but talking to his grandmother at that moment was most unappealing. She was far too astute. She would see right through him and probably break her silence on the subject, Sebastian sure she suspected his attachment to Miss Darcy since she missed nothing. In truth, her ideas were undoubtedly superior to his at the moment, although knowing his grandmother, she might suggest a bold attack similar to Gaston's.

Wasting no time, he headed directly to his bedchamber. Stripping down to shirt and trousers, he poured a glass of whisky and reclined on the bed in relief. A stack of mail sat on the nightstand, Sebastian rifling through them as he sipped and relaxed tense muscles. One from his mother, his sisters Adele and Reine writing together, three from friends back home, one from his father, and the last from de Marcov.

He started to open de Marcov's, knowing his friend would cheer him with his words, but Sebastian stopped before breaking the seal. "You will also have something to say about my sister's marital satisfaction and that is not a thought I want spinning in my head before sleep," he murmured, shuffling de Marcov's letter to the back of the slack.

His sisters greatly entertained with their letters, a joy he savored so that one would wait. It was similar with his pals from school, each of the three fellows he had known since boarding school. *Start with mother,* he thought, yawning and burrowing deeper into the pillow. *Her letters are loving and safe.*

Indeed, it started out that way. Lady Essenton began with her typical caring salutation and opening paragraphs, expressing how great her affection and pride, and reminding him to be safe and cautious. He smiled at the familiar refrains, but with a flip of the page the smile faded.

Dearest son, I do pray you have chosen to read my missive prior to the one your father is writing as I pen this. Undoubtedly they shall be posted together but one never knows how the whimsies of the mail carriers, especially when traveling across water and vast lands, will affect the delivery of a letter. I hope to warn, although I can do no more than that in this message. Please know, my son, that today we received word that Lord Everest has asked to pay court to Lady Cassandra, the intent clear that he will ask formally for her hand once the necessary arrangements are documented. The reasons for the match are not proper for us to speculate upon within the indelible markings of a letter, however I am sure you can comprehend it is not a match based on affection. Your father is certain of this, not that his reaction to the news would be improved or altered if his Lordship was deeply in the throes of passionate love for Lady Cassandra. Lord Essenton applauds Lord Everest's good sense in aligning himself with a noble family of great wealth and standing. I fear his wrath is not in any way directed toward any of the persons involved in the situation here but rather firmly directed at you.

Oh, how it pains me to pass on this tragic news! My only consolation is in knowing that I will reveal in a softer tone and choice of phrase than your father shall. His anger is fierce, Sebastian. The only point that prevents him from being utterly incensed is that Lady Cassandra has vocally conveyed her displeasure in Lord Everest's suit. Of course, Lord Burrow has scant interest in his daughter's distress or wishes, but enough concern to privately appeal to your father, upon the weeping behest of Lady Cassandra, to counter the advance of Lord Everest with one tendered by Lord Essenton on behalf of Viscount Nell.

My sweet, dear son! How I regret this turn of events and wish I knew how best to advise you! I have no love for Lady Cassandra and fully understand your hesitation, nay distaste, for the lady, however I do appreciate the advantages to a union with her, dowry and estate lands and the rest compensations you are well aware of. Your father is writing this moment with a demand for you to return home and marry Lady Cassandra. One word from you will halt the process with Lord Everest. I cannot offer advice on your response, Sebastian, other than to try to repress your own temper and consider this with cool rationale.

"Like hell!" he shouted—not the first outburst flung into the air as he read his mother's letter. He scanned through the remainder, but other than a handful of lines relating mundane local matters toward the end, it was about the pending engagement of Lady Cassandra. "He can have her," Sebastian muttered, even as he reread the letter to make sure he missed nothing, "although I pity him marrying that dreadful harpy."

He shuddered then inhaled deeply before opening his father's letter. No warm greeting here, not that there ever was. Lord Essenton wrote his son rarely—wrote anyone rarely for that matter—and in most instances it was to scold. Fatherly affection was not expected.

The entire message was written on one side of the page, his father's script tidy and compact. His fury was evinced by more exclamation marks than usual and the choice of numerous colorful words and phrases. Lady Essenton's warning helped soften the blow, but Sebastian winced nevertheless. No restraint was shown, Lord Essenton blunt and brutal in his angry accusations and demands, and throughout the first reading, Sebastian was a child again, enduring another lengthy harangue while tears stung the insides of his eyes. Now, as then, he weathered the storm, eventually passed through it, and after cooling down, recognized that he was stronger and had tolerated this tirade better than the one before.

He read the letter two more times before refolding carefully, placing it onto the table with the others, and focusing on unwinding every tight muscle from head to toe. Closing his eyes, he willed his wild emotions to calm. It was a chore, but eventually he reached a place of quiescence.

Nothing had changed from his perspective. He never would have agreed to marry Lady Cassandra, and once she was married to Lord Everest, the subject would be closed. Yes, Lord Essenton would stew and rage, probably send two or three verbally abusive letters and give him hell when he did return home—no matter if it was three years hence—but one thing he could not do was force Sebastian into anything.

> *Our compromise is voided as it relates to your marital status. Fritter away your life abroad forever if that is your desire. I shall not argue the matter further as long as you come home, marry, and go about the business of getting her pregnant!*

These sentences written by his father struck a chord. "Very well, Father," he slurred in the final moments before he fell asleep, "I will do my best to marry and happily do what it takes to conceive a child."

Assuming Miss Darcy wants to marry me...

"But the weather is glorious and perfect for shopping! How can you even *think* about staying home?"

"Staying inside, even on this glorious day, my dear Yvette, is a delightful thought. Yes, above shopping."

Yvette and Zoë stared at Georgiana as if she had just proposed flying to the moon. "This is three days in a row," Zoë declared. "Are you ill?"

"Have you and the baron suffered a spat? Is your heart now broken by him so soon after being broken by Monsieur Butler?" Yvette mourned, her frown of concern as overblown as Zoë's.

"My heart has been broken by no one," Georgiana assured for the umpteenth time, sighing and walking toward the piano.

"But the baron has not called upon you for days and days!"

"It has been all of two days, Yvette, and he warned me that he needed to attend to Conservatoire duties. He will be here this afternoon for tea, if that information comforts and allays speculation."

"And Monsieur Butler? Surely he must be home by now and yet he does not visit. The tragedy increases! We shall inquire as to his whereabouts while socializing today, my dearest Georgiana. Surely someone will have news."

"You will do no such thing! Mr. Butler's business is none of mine unless he chooses to enlighten me!" Georgiana smiled at her two friends, softening her face and tone after the sharp retort. "Truly, dearest Yvette and Zoë, all is well. I am merely tired and desirous of solitude. I have missed playing. I know you do not understand, but trust me that my opting to remain home is not a reflection of internal sadness or because I do not enjoy shopping and your company. Now, hasten on your way before the best ribbons are gone."

The twins did not look convinced but they argued no further. Minutes later Georgiana was alone. Blessedly alone. Everyone in the house was gone except for the servants, who wandered about quietly attending to their tasks. Even Mrs. Annesley had gone for an afternoon by herself in the city. Lord Caxton promised to join her for tea later in the day, as soon as it was possible to break away from practice for an upcoming symphony performance, but that gave Georgiana upwards of three hours of freedom.

"Freedom," she mumbled as she spread the sheets along the piano rest. *An odd word choice*, she thought, pausing to reflect. *Am I not happily anticipating the baron's visit?* She nodded as an answer and it was true that she enjoyed his company.

But…

She ran the tip of her index finger over the symbols inked on the staff, following the lines across to the brace and then down to the lower staff. Without lifting from the parchment, she completed the circuit, tracing each clef and note sign until reaching the bottom of the page. There she paused, staring at the signature scrawled in the margin for a minute before brushing her fingertip over it.

Sebastian Cedric Frasier Albert Butler.

It amused her that he used his full name on some of his compositions while on others he only wrote *Sebastian Butler*. After a comparative study, she deduced that those psalms placed to music when he was younger bore all five, the habit disappearing with more recent pages. Why? She could not hazard a guess, but she preferred the complete attribution and if the subject presented, she planned to tell him so. She had never asked his full name. Knowing it, even with the mystery of what each name meant or why it was chosen, felt intimate somehow, as if they were connected by a secret few knew. It was comforting.

Two days before she had risen from bed determined to spend more than fleeting minutes glancing at Mr. Butler's psalms. The honor bestowed upon her when he entrusted his compositions to her was not taken lightly, and guilt consumed her that he would be back in Paris with her not having played a single note. Guilt, however, was not the driving force.

She missed him.

For three weeks he had been gone. Admittedly, during the first week she barely thought of him, her days and nights bursting with activity and the magnetic presence of Lord Caxton sparing her scant time to breathe. By the second week the vague melancholy and emptiness that had persisted since his departure surfaced from where it had been buried beneath the frivolity. Incrementally, the hole expanded until it became an ache and invaded her dreams.

Losing herself within the music brought him closer and eased her heart. The psalms were beautiful, even those written when young, thus it was a joy to play and sing. She did not mark on his paper but jotted suggestions, musings, and alternative refrains onto separate blank sheets. She played the pieces over and over, practicing her variations in places, until many of them were memorized. Then she allowed her eyes to close and fingers to automatically press the correct keys to create a swell of harmony in song.

Time passed swiftly. To Georgiana it felt as if she had barely sat down when she heard the door chime. Her eyes flew open and the music halted with a discordant peal joining her gasp of shock upon noting it was half past four! She lurched from the bench, realizing how long she had been at the activity when her legs protested and she nearly collapsed to her knees. Ignoring the intense tingles and spasms attacking blood starved muscles, she hastily stuffed the music sheets into Mr. Butler's leather portfolio and shoved it into the bench's hidden recess, turning just as Lord Caxton entered the salon on the heels of Monsieur Vigneux, the butler.

"Miss Darcy," he began, bowing deeply, "I apologize for arriving much later than I anticipated. I do pray you are not vexed with me?"

"Not at all, Baron. I was delighting in my solitude."

"Oh. Have I intruded upon you then?"

"Please, no, I did not mean to imply not wishing to see you!" she stammered to a halt, blushing at his penetrating gaze and feeling utterly foolish. Her muscles continued to ache, her neck especially in need of a rub and stretch—neither of which she could do with him in the room—and her wits remained scattered from the abrupt shift in the atmosphere.

"I heard you playing when I entered the foyer. Quite a lovely composition it was but one I am unfamiliar with. Who is the composer?"

"An obscure English composer, I do not even recall the name. Here, let me pour you some tea. How was the practice? Will Paris society once again be astounded by another Académie Royale masterpiece?"

If he noticed her evasiveness and rushed sentences he was too polite to comment. Instead, he answered her question and the conversation moved forward into common areas, allotting Georgiana the time to regain her composure. She was not sure why she avoided mentioning Mr. Butler. There was no shame in their friendship or the compositions he lent to her or the fact that she wrote music herself. Yet none of these were topics she wished to discuss with Lord Caxton. Mr. Butler and the feelings he stirred within her were private and too confusing to discuss with anyone, especially the baron.

Twenty minutes passed. Georgiana was relaxed and over her upset, engaged in the pleasantries as they sipped their tea, with no premonition that a momentous turning point in her life was about to happen. One minute they were chatting about the planned horseback ride for tomorrow, weather permitting, when in the next breath Lord Caxton placed his cup onto the low table between their seats and moved to sit beside her on the settee.

"Miss Darcy," he began, his tone grave and face serious, "it has increasingly weighed upon my heart the need to express, in a direct manner, how thankful I am to have met you and to verbalize—so as to have no misunderstanding—that these past weeks have not only been the happiest of my life but are a fulfillment of a long held hope. That is, of course, to find the woman I could spend my life with."

Georgiana was unable to avert her gaze from his handsome, mesmerizing face. His dark eyes scanned across her features like a caress, causing her heart to pound painfully inside her chest. Suddenly she could not breathe and felt drenched in a fog as the impact of his words pierced through her. *Oh God! Please do not propose!*

He relaxed his face and smiled. "Now, I see that my vehemence is startling to you. Please, do not be alarmed, Miss Darcy."

He took hold of her hands where they lay slack in her lap, pressing firmly between his warm palms—Georgiana too dumbfounded to notice—and went on, "I appreciate that you are young and perhaps not as assured of your feelings. I am not, at this juncture, asking for anything other than the honor of proceeding as we have thus far."

"I will be leaving for home in less than three weeks," she forced between wooden lips.

"Yes, I am aware of this fact, and the thought has brought me an extensive measure of distress. Part of the reason I was later than I anticipated for our tea today, Miss Darcy, was due to a meeting with the Conservatoire director to discuss my resignation date effective in April rather than late June."

"I see. Your family will be thrilled to have you home."

"Yes," he laughed, "I am sure they will, however I admit I was not thinking of my family. I was only thinking of you, or us, I should say. Miss Darcy, I have no wish to trifle with you or walk away today without my intentions unmistakable. There is not a shred of doubt in my mind that you would be a remarkable Baroness Caxton. This is my ultimate desire; however, for now I will be content to court you as is proper until formal permission can be granted by Mr. Darcy. Some say we are already entered into a courtship—"

"They do? Who is saying that? Why?"

He cocked his head and frowned while also smiling in such a way that Georgiana instantly felt the fool. *Of course it would appear as if they were courting!* She had heard the whispers, seen the jealous stares, and even been bluntly asked a handful of times. Yet, fool or not, she sensed a river of irritation rising from her belly. Was she to receive the brunt of gossip every time she danced with a man, or tied together for eternity after a few days of harmless entertainments? She withdrew her hands from his—only in that instant aware that he held them—and struggled to make sense of her churning emotions.

"It is not surprising that the assumption is being leapt to, Miss Darcy," Lord Caxton soothed. "I have been conspicuous in my interest in you and have never done so with another woman. Playing games is not in my nature. I see what I want and am determined in my pursuit. In this instance, it is you that I want."

"My Lord Baron, I am… at a loss for words. Naturally, I am flattered and not adverse to, to… you and… I…"

"And that is sufficient for the time being, Miss Darcy. All I ask, if you can see to answer one question for me honestly and from your heart, thus giving me hope for more, is this: Can you imagine yourself as a baroness? My baroness?"

Georgiana hesitated, searching his face as she searched her heart. Could she be his baroness? Did she feel affection for him strong enough for marriage? Was she in love with him?

Far inside, buried under the emotional turmoil, a rational voice proffered that if she had to ask the questions, the answer should probably be *no*. The fact that the voice possessed a musical quality in a deep baritone lent credence to the logic. Yet, the baron had asked for honesty.

"Yes," she whispered, "I can imagine this, but…"

"Thank you, Miss Darcy!" he interrupted, springing from the seat and bowing. "With that, I am content. Now, I have taken up far too much of your time. Until tomorrow then." And with minimal fuss, he was gone, leaving Georgiana standing in the familiar foyer yet feeling lost.

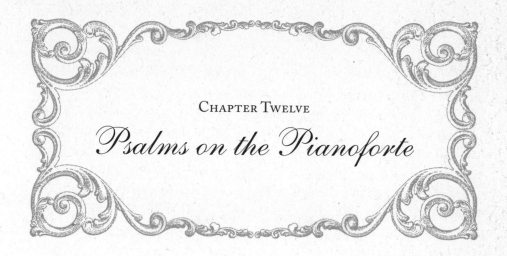

CHAPTER TWELVE

Psalms on the Pianoforte

MR. BUTLER ARRIVED AT the grand townhouse on the Quai d'Orléans on the following day with the thick pouch of copied lecture notes and purchased music sheets tucked under his arm. It was nearly three in the afternoon, two days after his return to Paris, the delay in seeking out a visit with Miss Darcy not a purposeful one.

He had fallen asleep after reading the letters from his parents with every intention of waking to visit with his grandmother before she left for whatever evening engagement he was sure she had scheduled. Instead, it was his grand-mother who bullied his valet into rousing him for a late midday meal and tea in her salon—the next day! He had slept for over eighteen hours. A hasty bath and shave was adequate to join Lady Warrow in her sunny, femininely decorated parlor, Sebastian so ravenous that the cold sandwiches, meats, cakes, and fruit were replenished twice.

They talked about his expedition to Reims and what he learned there. She talked about her exploits and some of the juicer gossip bandied about. Neither brought up the topic of Lady Cassandra and his father's wrath. Sebastian assumed she knew—his grandmother always knew everything—but he certainly did not want to talk about it. Nor did she mention Miss Darcy, a point he thought odd but could not very well broach himself.

He ached to see her. Literally ached. Eighteen hours of heavy sleep with pleasant dreams of her by his side, belonging to him, had eased his heart and cemented his purpose.

I love her.

There was no longer any doubt in that reality. It did not mean he had an agenda or prepared speech for how to go about expressing his love. He was unsure how their future together would mesh with his study at the Conservatoire or plans to pursue his music. Worst of all, he had no clue as to whether she felt anything for him greater than friendship. Yet none of this changed the simple fact that he was utterly, passionately, and with every fiber of his soul in love with her.

What did change his plan was a closer inspection of his reflection in the mirror of his dressing room later that night.

"Good God! I look ghastly! Why did you not say something?" He turned an accusatory glare on his valet.

Hendricks continued to iron the trousers laid on the table and did not bother to glance up from his important task. He shrugged one shoulder, drily responding, "I figured you could ascertain the obvious without me having to point it out. Besides, you needed to eat, since the last thing I want is you grumpy when I am trying to cut your hair." He glanced up then, putting the iron aside and picking up the trousers to fold. "You should know by now that your unruly hair cannot go three weeks without a trim, let alone five."

Sebastian grunted, but he did not argue. Hendricks was a childhood friend—a servant's son who he called "Jimmy" in those days—before becoming his valet when he left for Oxford. Lord Essenton had not approved of a close companion being one's manservant, no matter how qualified, but Sebastian insisted, another fight ensuing, and had never regretted his choice. Well, maybe at times like this when Hendricks's flippancy grated on his frayed nerves. Still, the valet was correct. Sebastian's hair needed a trim before he left for Reims, a suggestion from Hendricks that he had ignored.

"Very well," he grumbled, sitting on the stool, "do your worst."

"Not now. Tomorrow, after I wash it thoroughly. You have a pound of road dust in there," he explained when Sebastian opened his mouth to protest. "Cutting it like that is unwise. Besides, I have all this to attend to," he said as he swept a hand over the pile of clothes lying on the floor beside the partially unpacked portmanteau.

"What have you been doing while I slept a whole day away?"

"Do you really want to hear a dreary detailed report of my hours? I did not think so. Mostly I was preparing this." He picked up a jar sitting on the table and opened it to reveal a pasty cream. "This will reduce the dark circles under your eyes and remove the chafed areas of your skin. You do look ghastly after all."

"You sure you are not a girl? I could arrange a nice post as a ladies' maid for you to practice your feminine techniques."

"Thanks all the same, chuckles, but I will stick with you. I am satisfied to practice techniques *on* the maids, after which I glean tricks of the trade to keep your ugly face respectable enough to appear in public."

Hendricks was correct, again. Sebastian gave in to the inevitable, which meant a day of rest, a thorough washing, a haircut, several treatments to his face, alterations to some of his clothes, and so on. The delay in confronting Miss Darcy worried him and increased his anxiety, but by the time he announced himself to Monsieur Vigneux at the de Valday townhouse, he did feel much better physically. And since women are not the only creatures on the planet who believe appearance makes for a nicer impression, Sebastian was vastly more confident knowing he was exceptionally dapper after a day in the hands of his valet.

Monsieur Vigneux pleasantly welcomed the frequent visitor of Miss Darcy's without frowning, as he had on that first introduction, and seemed genuinely sad to inform him that Miss Darcy was not currently at home. Momentarily at a loss—not that it had not crossed his mind that she may be out—Sebastian stammered a bit, finally deciding he would leave the pouch and a note of friendly greeting.

"Poor timing on my part," he said and grimaced. "If I may request, will you see she gets these as soon as she returns? And inform her I called?"

"Of course, sir."

"Monsieur Butler! How delightful!"

He pivoted toward the voice, already registering the owner and thus not surprised to see the de Valday twins bouncing toward him down the staircase. "Mademoiselle Zoë, Mademoiselle Yvette"—he bowed deeply—"what a lovely surprise. When Monsieur Vigneux informed me that Miss Darcy was away, I presumed you were with her. My happy mistake since I am now able to welcome you to Paris as I was not able to do when you arrived."

Yvette and Zoë curtsied before him, two pairs of matching bold eyes raking over his figure before meeting his amused gaze. It was Zoë who spoke, her voice gay. "Indeed, we were heartbroken, Monsieur Butler. Of all in Paris, it was you we most desired to meet again, is that not so, Yvette?"

"It is true! Devastated we were! Then our dear Georgiana relayed your dismay…"

"And promise to flirt and fawn!"

"*Oui*, that too," Yvette agreed with her sister. "Thus our hearts were placated."

"And now you are here to fulfill your promise!"

"I shall, if you feel it is still necessary. Nearly three weeks in Paris, so you two must be weary of the constant flirting, parades of gentlemen vying for your attention, and endless streams of flattering admiration."

They both laughed and shook their heads, each grasping onto an arm and steering him into the salon.

"Is it possible to weary of such activity, monsieur? I think not!"

"After rotting away in Lyon forever we shall require years of excitement to erase the scars! Lyon is frightfully dull. Did you not find it so, monsieur?"

"Indeed. Frightful. I barely survived."

"Besides," Yvette said, her face innocent but eyes peeking sidelong at Sebastian, "we had to rescue poor Georgiana from rattling about this old house all alone, day after day. *Tragique!*"

Zoë took the clue. "Oh yes! We worried about her day and night, the poor lamb without us! Fortunately, you were here to amuse her, Monsieur Butler, and then the Lord Caxton as well."

Sebastian recoiled as if slapped, hard. "What?" he blurted, noting the shrillness of his voice but too distraught to control the tone. "How do you mean?"

Zoë shrugged, sitting on the sofa next to Yvette. "He has been most attentive. But then Mademoiselle Darcy is never lacking for companions and entertainments to choose from."

"Indeed, she has worn herself to a frazzle from continual engagements and hours of dancing. You have missed much, Monsieur Butler. The Duchesse de Saint-Aignan hosted a magnificent gala last week with all of Parisian Society invited. It was stupendous!"

"I danced until dawn," Zoë dreamily recalled, "and so did lovely Georgiana, with dozens of men."

"But only the handsome Lord Caxton was honored with two dances. She has missed you, however, Monsieur."

Sebastian searched Yvette's eyes for a clue as to her meaning, praying for anything, even the tiniest glimmer to restore his shattered hope. "Has she?"

"Of course! Why, these past three days she has shockingly refused every invitation in lieu of staying home to play your compositions on the piano. Even shopping!"

Yvette said the last with a tone and expression that left no doubt as to how incredible that decision was to her. Zoë nodded, her face wearing an identical expression.

"So I know she will be pleased to welcome you home, Monsieur Butler. She should be returning any second from her horseback ride with Frédéric, the Limoges and Tonnerres, and Lord Caxton."

"*Oui*, any moment now," Yvette agreed. "So sit, monsieur, and have some refreshments. We will divert with humorous anecdotes until the sweethearts return."

Sebastian paled further, sank into the chair, and sucked his breath through a narrowed airway. "Sweethearts? Surely you jest, Mademoiselle Yvette. They have barely met."

She shrugged, leaning to pour hot tea just brought in by the maid. "All it often takes is one look. Who can understand the ways of *amour*? Such a mystery." She handed him the delicate china cup, Sebastian taking it automatically and staring sightlessly into the steaming liquid.

The de Valday twins rambled on, Sebastian drinking tea that had no flavor while fighting to pay attention enough to offer feeble responses. They dropped the baron's name from time to time—Sebastian wincing and trying to ignore a pounding headache—but primarily related gossip in a steady stream. The clock on the mantel ticked bolts of pain into his temples for the subsequent half hour until the sound of laughter and voices from the foyer superimposed.

Sebastian jerked up from his perch and swung his eyes toward the door. Georgiana and the baron entered first with Frédéric de Valday a step behind. In an instant, Sebastian assessed the picture presented and the image increased his agony.

Georgiana wore a fine riding outfit of pale gray that accented her perfect womanly curves, and a fashionable hat perched atop the piled mass of her golden hair. Her cheeks were rosy with a light sheen of dew across her brow, ruby lips moist and smiling, and sky-blue eyes gazing upward into the face of Lord Caxton, who walked at her side holding tightly to her hand where it rested in the bend of his arm. The baron was beaming, his smile gay and eyes fixed on Georgiana.

"Monsieur Butler, welcome back to Paris." Frédéric's enthusiastic greeting rang out and alerted the enthralled pair. Lord Caxton's smile held as he added his welcome, but Sebastian only saw Georgiana.

"Mr. Butler! I am so pleased you are safe. I feared a mishap upon the road when no word of your return reached us."

She dropped the baron's arm and hastened across the space, bobbing a quick curtsy before Sebastian. Happiness infused her voice and her radiant smile was trained upon his face, Sebastian sensing a slight lessening of the band constricting his chest and becoming unable to resist smiling in return.

"I am quite well, Miss Darcy. No mishaps other than a washed out road that delayed us and then orders from my valet to rest and spruce up before appearing in public. I apologize for causing you any concern."

"All is forgiven, sir, now that you are here. We are very relieved."

"Yes, quite a relief," Lord Caxton drawled. He had trailed behind Georgiana, assuming a possessive stance, with his body as close to her as possible but a half step nearer to Sebastian. The subtle blocking between the two was not subtle to Sebastian. "Good to have you back, Butler."

Sebastian nodded and shook the hand offered. "Thank you. It is good to be back, my lord."

"We have been entertaining your guest in your absence and filling him in on the excitement he has missed."

"Thank you, Yvette, but nothing that has occurred here could possibly be as thrilling or illuminating as the lecture on Machaut. I am aflutter with anticipation, Mr. Butler."

"I have scrupulous notes for your perusal as well as some new compositions I am confident you will enjoy."

"More of your compositions? I would not have thought your schedule allotted the luxury of time to write, but of course, I will delight in hearing them."

"These are not mine. You are correct that scant time was available and the pianoforte available at the inn was a sad instrument indeed. Plus, I rather doubt the patrons would have tolerated less than a lively dance tune."

Georgiana laughed. "No, I do not image they would."

"More musical topics to discuss? I would think the subject exhausted by now." Caxton's countenance was friendly but the muscles were sight and eyes hard.

"There is no way to exhaust a topic fascinating and evolving. What I brought are pieces written by various composers but are for a six octave pianoforte such as yours at Pemberley, Miss Darcy. You will learn techniques that may inspire your compositions." He smiled with genuine warmth toward Georgiana, who blushed but darted an uneasy glance toward Lord Caxton.

"Compositions?"

Sebastian's brows lifted in surprise at the baron's inflection. "Indeed. Miss Darcy is an astute, talented composer, along with possessing an exquisite voice and mastery on the pianoforte."

"I am aware of her beautiful soprano and have heard her play a few times, but I did not know she dabbled in composing. How extraordinary."

"She is extraordinary," Sebastian stressed, not hiding his irritation at Caxton's tone of displeasure. "She is extremely talented, in fact, and her writing capabilities are well beyond 'dabbling,' I daresay."

"Well, just what the world needs, a female Beethoven. Next we shall have women running businesses and in Parliament."

"There are many women in the artistic world, my lord," Yvette said, for once her voice serious. "Novelists, poets, ballerinas, singers. Women have been queens. Why not a famous composer?"

"I have no desire to be famous, thank you very much," Georgiana said with a breathy laugh. "Thank you for the compliment, Mr. Butler. I am of the opinion you are exaggerating flagrantly; nevertheless, I do appreciate the gesture."

"I am not exaggerating! Would I have trusted my psalms with anyone else? I am aflutter with anticipation to hear how you have improved what I know are dismal renditions desperately in need of a fresh perspective." He turned to Lord Caxton. "Miss Darcy has an inspired vision that is to be greatly admired."

"I see I have been properly chastised," Caxton said with an incline of his head, turning toward Georgiana with tender regard. "Perhaps you can share some of your compositions with me, Miss Darcy? I am sure they are as amazing as you."

"I would be delighted." She looked at the baron with mild surprise, her mien gradually infusing with pleasure.

"Now I fear I must say adieu. We have our final practice tonight. May I call upon you tomorrow, Miss Darcy? I have the morning free before I must prepare for the performance. There is an exhibit of Spanish paintings at the Ferrand Museum and I would be honored to have you, Monsieur de Valday, and the Mademoiselles de Valday accompany me?"

The twins looked less than wildly enthusiastic, museums more in the "frightfully dull" category of entertainments. Georgiana agreed to the outing, Sebastian barely managing to hide his disappointment, since he had planned to invite her to tour the show with him.

Lord Caxton said his farewells and began walking toward the foyer with Georgiana alongside when he halted suddenly and turned to Sebastian. "By the way Butler, a group of gents are meeting at La Palu's Club tonight for cards, if you are interested. I know how good you are at poker, so it would add to the challenge. Some of the finest wine in the country to boot. How can you pass that up? Allison and Lignac will be there."

Sebastian smiled, intrigued despite his glum mood. "It does sound like fun. Count me in."

"Excellent! I'll drive you there, as your house is on the way. Eight o'clock sharp!"

Georgiana was not gone for long, but the interval before she crossed the threshold felt an eternity. What words of love or affection were being said? The thought soured his stomach.

Despite his depression, the following hours were surprisingly pleasant. Georgiana was gay and the de Valdays far too blithesome for gloominess to reign in the room. Conversation was neutral and their infectious effervescence combined with Georgiana's warmth lightened his heart. Thoughts of intruding barons faded in the happiness of friendly companionship, until, that is, the de Valdays excused themselves to prepare for a family dinner engagement.

"You are not invited to their family dinner?"

"No. Well, in truth I was invited but I declined. Lord and Lady Matlock are engaged elsewhere tonight, a whist tournament at the Comte d'Apchier's. A night alone sounded far more appealing. Early to bed for once and perhaps I will actually rise before noon!"

"Yes, it can be exhausting. I slept for nearly eighteen hours night before last, another reason why the delay in my visit. I am sorry for causing you anxiety, Miss Darcy."

"I knew if anything truly horrid had occurred Lady Warrow would alert us, but it is a relief to know you are well." She paused, averting her eyes from his and reddening. "You were missed, Mr. Butler," she murmured.

Emotion choked his throat, words lodging in a jumble and leaving him unsure of what to say. The vacillating sway of hope and despondency in the past hour had left him weak. Whatever vague plans of how to declare his feelings that had formulated in the recesses of his mind were shattered by the appearance of Lord Caxton. Miss Darcy's indecipherable expressions and comments gave him no clue as to how, or if, he should proceed.

"Are these your notes?" She jumped up from her chair and retrieved the bulging pouch long ago forgotten on a table by the door. He trailed her movements with his eyes, absorbed the delicate movements of her hands as she pulled out the top papers and began to scan the sentences, was mesmerized by her beauty and the elegant balance of every feature as she read the first paragraphs aloud. Then she looked at him with a mischievous glint in her crystalline eyes. "These are scrupulously written, Mr. Butler. I know your penmanship to be excellent but this exceeds my expectations for hastily scribbling during a lecture. My, your tutors must have sung praises to heaven for such a precise student."

Her tease broke the spell. Sebastian chuckled. "If only that were the case. Note taking has never been my strong suit. These were recopied, with my own embellishments added from what I gleaned during the talk."

"How very thoughtful of you! A simple thank you is insufficient. I will enjoy reading all of them, I assure you. And now that I have unencumbered hours stretching ahead of me, it is an accomplishable feat."

"Hours of well-deserved solitude that I am disrupting." He rose to his feet and bowed her direction. "I shall depart and leave you to your leisure, Miss Darcy."

"No, please stay, Mr. Butler!" She stepped toward him, her wide eyes pleading. "I have been anxious to discuss your psalms, or rather, to play a few of my favorites with you." She pivoted and walked to the piano, Sebastian trailing behind. "In truth it is difficult to pick a favorite, or two or three for that matter, since they are all so lovely."

"You are far too magnanimous," he said and laughed, inclining his head but his gaze not leaving the shimmering blue of her eyes.

"Well," she stammered, a flush spreading across her cheeks, "I did accept your challenge on a couple of them to tinker with some modification. Always jotted on separate sheets, of course!" She hastened to add when he began rifling through the stack.

"Some modifications? I see three pages of altered refrains, chords, and sequences with an added rondo on Psalm thirty-five alone." He held the sheet up, his brow arched and smile crooked. Georgiana's blush deepened, but she met his gaze with a lift of her brows.

"That one was especially pathetic and juvenile. I deserve a medal for suffering through playing it as is."

"Heartless! But I shall not argue. Very well then, do you have one you wish to start with? One you have improved upon, as I have no doubt you are capable of, or one not so pathetically written in the first place?"

"This one here is particularly wonderful with not one note requiring improvement. Psalm sixty-three. I played it until nearly memorized." She withdrew five pages from the scattered papers, handed them to Sebastian, and brushed past him to sit onto the bench.

Sebastian froze. In that second of her body passing his, one muslin-covered shoulder contacting his arm and the swish of her skirt gliding over his leg was enough to unbalance him. He inhaled and shook his head before bravely leaning over to place the music sheets on the piano rest in proper order. He prayed she was unaware of how his hands trembled, only to moments later lose his grip on one sheet when he was assaulted by the fragrance of rose water. He recaptured the slipping paper and quickly set it in place, reading the title as he did.

"Psalm sixty-three," he whispered. Georgiana turned her head when he spoke, her face so close he could feel her warm breath and a loose strand of soft hair feathering over his cheek. "I wrote the music during this past month, after arriving in Paris. The scripture struck me in a unique way and I was—"

"Inspired," she completed his sentence. Sebastian nodded, unable to speak or think coherently with her brilliantly blue eyes fixed on his. She seemed to be searching his very soul, begging for an answer to a question he did not understand, yet before he could interpret or ask the question heavy upon his heart, she turned her gaze away.

Sebastian straightened. Closing his eyes and swallowing, he pressed the back of one hand hard against his mouth, fighting to stop the sighing moan from escaping. His other hand hovered a mere inch away from the creamy skin at the nape of her neck.

Lord, help me!

Hastily he backed up, desire surging so strongly that he feared his control spiraling beyond the point of reason. *Distance, I need distance.* Woodenly, he moved to the edge of the instrument. It felt as if a bass drum was lodged in his chest and cymbals were being rung next to his ears. Looking at her was out of the question, Sebastian knowing his shredded regulation would fail, but after what felt like interminable hours of thundering silence he risked a sidelong glance.

Georgiana sat with her eyes downcast, on the keys where her immobile hands were spread. She was flushed and breathing deeply, the rounded flesh of her bosom rising with each inhalation to further upset Sebastian's control. He searched her face for some clue as to her sentiments, but she was unreadable, especially with her head averted.

He no longer denied how alive and happy she made him. He delighted in their conversations and collaboration, was consumed with desire for her, and sensed that there was a hole within that only she could fill. *Is she as affected by me as I so ardently am by her?*

She began to play the psalm. Her delicate fingers pressed the keys skillfully, the music arising from the belly of the piano heart-wrenching and vital. He studied her movements and had a sudden, vivid vision of those fingers touching his face in such a way. The sensation was so powerful that his knees weakened and his hands gripped the firm edge of the piano for support.

The ivory and ebony responded to her hands, bringing the music to life. Then she added the lyrics, wavering at first and then growing stronger. She sang of the longing for God, the thirst in one's soul while searching through a dry land, the glory in finding that satisfying love that is richest of all, and the comfort attained in the watches of the night in knowing God is holding you fast. It was a spiritual psalm written by King David to worship his God.

Yet Sebastian heard a lover's prayer in the phrases, just as he had when reading the verses and placing them to music, even if not recognizing why he was inspired to do so. He heard a desire for fulfillment, commitment, and communion that spoke to the thirst in his soul for her. His heart was open, bare, and ready to embrace what he had too long denied.

I love you, Georgiana Darcy, and I need you to be forever by my side.

The words tingled on the surface of his tongue. His lips hummed with the consuming epiphany. He was spellbound by emotion and the glory of her face, not immediately becoming aware that the song had finished.

Georgiana sat with misty eyes staring sightlessly at the keys. Her thoughts were similar to Sebastian's yet with a twist. Emotions coursed through her veins—wild and glorious and frightening. Love indeed, yes. She may have been young and innocent, bemused and dazzled by Lord Caxton, and wrestling with a momentous decision offered by a worthy gentleman that she was attracted to, nevertheless she comprehended how intense her feelings toward Mr. Butler.

I love him.

It was surprisingly easy to admit. It was also agonizing. From a very young age, Georgiana's interest and aptitude for the art of music had been recognized and endorsed. Books and compositions were purchased, Mr. Darcy housed the latest and best instruments at Pemberley, skilled musicians were hired as tutors, and dozens of performances were attended for her inspiration. She refused to consider herself a great proficient, but she knew gifted talent when encountering it. Weeks of immersing herself in Mr. Butler's compositions, this one especially, revealed a genius, a masterful brilliance Georgiana believed in whether he discounted it or not.

Knowing that a remarkable talent was loosed upon the world made her heart soar and plummet into the abyss simultaneously. *His passion is elsewhere, as it should be, not with me. My future is different.*

"I take my earlier statement back," she murmured, breaking the weighty quiet. "That is my favorite psalm. The composition was perfection, Mr. Butler. Your brilliance is astounding."

"Thank you, Miss Darcy. Uttered by you, those words are dear, even if I deem them too generous."

"Not generous enough in my estimation. After your education at the Conservatoire, I shall not possess the vocabulary to adequately praise your compositions. I, like others, will merely be blessed to listen and bravely attempt to play."

"Please, do not—"

"I see you wrote a part for the violin into this one," she interrupted, glancing upward then and across the narrow expanse of wood separating them. "Apparently, some of Lord Caxton's instructions penetrated."

"I may not be able to competently play the violin, or any stringed instrument for that matter, I confess, but I do know how to write music for them." He bent over the piano to peer at the indicated sheet, his face a foot away from hers. "Biblical references to harp and lyre necessitated the inclusion of stringed music despite my amateur status."

"You gravitated toward the piano as I have, I surmise. I can play the harp with moderate proficiency, however, thanks to Lady Matlock, and have done fairly well with the cello, thanks to Colonel Fitzwilliam. My brother tried to interest me in the violin, and I can manage basic chords but never took the time to practice."

"Similar to my story, Miss Darcy. I fear I resisted the urging of my instructors and tutors thus my incompetence is of long standing."

Georgiana nodded, once again staring intently into his eyes. Sebastian was still leaning over the piano surface and returned the frank stare. "So the baron was not your first instructor in the violin?"

"I was an incompetent before the baron got his hands upon me. He tried his best, but I fear it was useless." The reminder of Lord Caxton was not a welcome one under the current circumstances, making Sebastian's smile wan.

"How long have you known him?"

Sebastian straightened, managing to somehow keep his expression impassive. "Only for a few years. We met at Oxford."

"Were you personal friends with many of your teachers?"

"No. Lord Caxton and I were never intimates either. He is quite a bit older than I am, and teachers did not generally socialize with the students. But we both have a penchant for cards and moderate gaming, often meeting at the university gaming halls. I am not a huge gambler, Miss Darcy. I pray you do not get that impression."

She did not seem perturbed, nodding calmly and bringing the conversation back to Caxton, much to Sebastian's annoyance. "And Lord Caxton? Is he what you would consider a huge gambler?"

"No, I cannot say he ever was," he answered truthfully. "He is wise in that regard. For both of us, it was a casual pastime, the spirits and cigars as appealing as the game."

"Yes, I can imagine. Or rather I know that is what gentlemen claim. It is a mysterious amusement, ladies only allowed to spin conjectures as to what truly takes place behind the closed polished wood doors."

"I would reveal the truth, Miss Darcy, even to the point of facing being blackballed as a traitor to my sex, but trust me, it is not nearly as exciting as your wild fantasies. Best to leave the mystery intact. I will tell you that I win my games most of the time."

"Then I am surprised the baron invited you! Perhaps he does not mind losing money?"

"I think he sees it as a challenge to supplant me," Sebastian replied, wondering if she sensed the double meaning.

"Well, good luck tonight then. May the best man prevail."

"Indeed. Let us hope the battle fairly fought with the outcome as fate designs," he stressed, not referring to a game of cards.

"Try not to leave him destitute or homeless," she teased.

"I am not that fine a player. Besides, each gentleman there has wealth to spare. Their estates should be safe."

"Have you ever been to Lord Caxton's estate in Suffolk?"

"No, I have not."

"My brother has been to Suffolk, to the Duke of Grafton's estate, which is near the baron's properties I understand. Perhaps I should have paid more heed to what Fitzwilliam said about the region or paid more attention to my geography lessons. Lord Caxton said his land is beautiful and a half day from the sea. I do adore the sea. Suffolk is a huge distance from Pemberley, but London is reasonably close. Lord Caxton expresses how he misses his home, and I know he is weary of living elsewhere while a steward manages for him. He plans to end his teaching and traveling abroad, desiring to settle in Suffolk and begin a family."

She stopped her aimless rambling abruptly, refocusing on Sebastian and then reddening and averting her eyes. Sebastian stood rigid, his entire body screaming to run from the room rather than listen to her musings about Lord Caxton!

Into the awkward silence, the striking of the longcase clock was jarring.

They both jerked violently, Sebastian recovering first to latch on to the interruption to blurt a hasty good-bye.

CHAPTER THIRTEEN

Two Nocturnes

S EBASTIAN WAS DETERMINED TO have a pleasant evening gambling and socializing with gentlemen of his class in a richly appointed establishment boasting the finest cigars and liquors. He was also determined to ascertain the level of commitment between the baron and Miss Darcy. Men tended to gossip and blather as freely as women, especially when loosened with alcohol.

He wanted to despise the older man for pursuing Miss Darcy, but he was too honest an individual to falsely direct his anger toward the baron. As evidenced by his opinion and feelings, she was in every way perfect and worthy of being sought after and fallen in love with. The greater mystery is why none had tried before! Or maybe they had and Miss Darcy had not returned the interest. Whatever the case, he could not fault her for developing affection for Lord Caxton.

The truth is he thought very highly of Lord Caxton. He came from a good family with impeccable breeding and abundant wealth. Sebastian knew him to be an honorable gentleman who would make any woman a fine husband.

No, the brunt of his anger was directed at himself. If only he had not been so selfish, so blinded to his budding sentiments, and so resolute that their relationship was one of friendship only.

"If only I had listened to de Marcov," he grumbled.

"Sir?"

He jumped slightly at the question from his valet, grimacing. "Sorry, Hendricks. I am daydreaming." The valet continued with the cravat-tying project as if nothing was amiss.

Sebastian again drifted off, barely aware when Hendricks finished the task and helped him into his jacket. He did not know how he would go about it, but it was time to discover the depth of attachment between Lord Caxton and Miss Darcy. He respected the baron, but he refused to lie down and let the woman he had fallen in love with slip through his fingers without a fight!

His prime desire was to see her happy, so ultimately he would bow to her choice. Nevertheless, he cringed from the idea of watching her waltz off with another man, even if her love was firmly placed therein, and knew he would not be able to bear it.

He shook off the disturbing images and forced the anxiety aside. *There is time, I am sure of it.*

"Time for what, sir?"

Sebastian jumped at Hendricks's query to what he thought had been an internal musing. "Uh, time for me to have a bit of fun and win some money. Shall I place a wager or two for you?"

"Not this time, Mr. Butler. My purse is only fat enough to roll the dice with my peers, which I will be doing as soon as I clean up here."

"Then I shall be on my way. Best of luck to you."

"You as well, sir. Go forth and grab on to what you want."

Sebastian's eyes narrowed at the retreating back of his manservant, sure there was an odd glint in the man's eye during that last statement. *Figures, cheeky scamp.* But it did put a smile on his face, and with a freer heart, a steady resolve, and a thick pocketbook, he left.

La Palu was swank and located in the heart of bustling Paris cabarets, taverns, and private clubs catering to the younger crowd of genteel gentlemen from all cultures inhabiting Paris. At La Palu, the atmosphere was excessively masculine, and the typical entertainments of cards, billiards, and darts were enhanced by abundant flows of wine, liquors, and Italian coffee. Laughter was rampant, coarse conversation abounded, smoke swirled in a thick cloud between the polished rafters, and the constant clink of coins and shuffling cards filled in the background.

It was a difficult place to remain glum, unless losing large quantities of cash at the games, and since the fates did seem to be on Sebastian's side as far as poker was concerned, he was in a surprisingly fine frame of mind. The growing stack of chips on the table space in front of him was indicative of his luck.

He sat with five other men, including a jovial Lord Caxton, sipped a glass of fine red Bordeaux slowly, so as to keep a level head, and concentrated on the serious business of gaming. Of course, serious or not, the men did engage in a fair amount of raillery.

"Duc de Montmoron has a new mistress." So spoke the Vicomte d'Érard.

"Another one? He is tired of Madame Legard already?"

"He is now with the actress, Mademoiselle Cérise Maigny."

"Ah, understandable."

Lord Caxton shook his head, tossing another chip onto the middle pile. "That man's love affairs could easily be the plot to one of Mademoiselle Cérise's plays."

"He certainly is never bored," Mr. Allison said lasciviously. "Something you can comprehend, yes, Caxton?"

"Now be careful, Allison," Monsieur de Lignac interjected. "Rumor has it that the good baron is smitten."

"Is this true?" d'Érard asked, brows disappearing into his hairline.

"Do not look so amazed, d'Érard. Love does happen, even to the best of us," de Lignac replied.

Allison snorted. "Not everyone, let us pray. I would sooner chew glass."

"Love is it? How extraordinary! Who is the fortunate woman?"

"Unfortunate, you mean to say, d'Érard," Allison grumbled. "Butler, are you going to call, raise, or stare at your cards for another hour?"

"Fold, actually." Sebastian laid the cards down, pressing his palms onto the tabletop to still the trembling. He dared not lift his gaze to Lord Caxton's face, but every nerve tingled with anticipation, awaiting his response to the jibes.

"The lady's name is Miss Georgiana Darcy, and it is I who am the fortunate one."

"Darcy? As in Darcy of Pemberley?" Mr. O'Byrne asked, the baron answering affirmative. "My father knows him. And I was so blessed to dance, twice, with Miss Darcy at Almack's! She is quite beautiful and has a dowry of over thirty thousand pounds, so the rumor goes."

"Ha! I knew there had to be a sound reason for the carefree bachelor to proffer sudden declarations of love! Well done, Baron, well done."

Caxton trained a severe glare on Mr. Allison. "I shall excuse those remarks, Allison, as we are friends of long standing. However, rest assured my interest in Miss Darcy is honorable."

"Of course it is, Caxton," Lignac added his glare to the baron's, Allison merely shrugging and tossing in another chip.

"Nonetheless, it does inspire stronger feelings of affection if the lady in question is worthy, you must agree with that Caxton?" d'Érard asked with a smile.

Caxton nodded curtly.

Mr. O'Byrne spoke next. "I was not aware Miss Darcy was in Paris. Or is your arrangement dating from when you were in London, Baron?"

"I owe my present happiness to Butler here." He smiled gratefully toward Sebastian, who was intently stacking his chips into orderly rows. "He is a Darcy, indirectly as it were, and introduced me to his kinswoman on a day that shall be remembered as one of the best in my life."

"So, one of those whirlwind romances, eh, Caxton? Love at first sight and all that?" Lignac asked, ignoring Allison's mock retch.

Caxton laughed, pitching a number of chips into the large pot and laying his cards onto the table. "Straight flush, queen high, gentlemen. Beat that!"

The groans reverberated around the table, the slap of cards falling in disgust muffled by Caxton's gloating chuckles and sweeping of the pot.

"Unfair," d'Érard grumbled. "The baron wins the hand of cards and the fair maiden."

Lignac laughed and patted d'Érard's shoulder. "Cheer up, old friend. We married men can make him suffer by inventing endless horror stories of the dreariness of matrimony!"

"No false inventing necessary if you ask me," Allison said.

"We did not ask you," Lignac countered, grinning. "So, when is the wedding, Caxton? How long do we have to try to save you?" He winked at Allison, who grunted.

"I doubt if I would tell you, all considered. But the truth is that we have not reached a permanent arrangement as yet."

Sebastian's head jerked up at that and he cringed at the sight of the baron's elated face. But Caxton was organizing his winnings and did not notice.

"Yet?" O'Byrne asked.

"In time, my boy, in time." Caxton grinned at the youngest member of their group, Mr. O'Byrne, barely twenty and on his first adventure beyond England. "But I am supremely confident."

"Oh, do tell! This promises to be provocative."

"Again, I shall excuse your crassness, Allison, but please understand that this is the future Baroness Caxton we are discussing. And Miss Darcy is a great lady. As such, she deserves the utmost respect. This is why I have asked her permission to court her formally, if her brother approves, once I have returned to London."

"And she agreed?"

"She was speechless in her joy, and that is all I shall say on this subject at this juncture. I deem this topic exhausted, gentlemen, in honor of my lady's reputation and modesty. Now, Butler, are you ever going to stop shuffling the deck and deal?"

The remainder of the night was torture. Sebastian's luck failed him utterly, probably not because of the abandonment of any angel of fortune but rather due to severe distraction on his part. Dramatic performance had never been his forte, but bluffing skills proved to serve him beyond poker, as no one noted his inattention. Of course, alcohol may have played some part in that as well, the players in high spirits and unconcerned with one sullen member. Whatever the case, he was suddenly eager to end the gaming and revelry, longing for the refuge of his dark bedchamber where he could crumble in private. He fervently prayed Lord Caxton would be too tired or caught up in silent musings to talk, but his luck continued to fail him.

"Butler, I never have properly thanked you for introducing me to Miss Darcy. I suppose it was sheer coincidence that we encountered each other that day at the Conservatoire, but I feel I owe you a debt of gratitude nonetheless."

"You owe me nothing," Sebastian mumbled, staring out the windows into the moonlit cobblestones and wishing the sky was overcast, so he could not see the shine of happiness visible on the older man's countenance.

"She is a remarkable woman. Nearly flawless she is, if one can presumptuously assert that claim upon another human being. I am quite besotted and find I have lost all flavor for Paris. My heart now yearns for home so we can publicly proclaim our mutual affection. Pity you shall be otherwise occupied by the time we exchange our vows, Butler, since your acquaintance with the lady led to our paths crossing."

Sebastian nodded once and remained silent. Truly he could think of nothing to say, even if his throat had not been dry and constricted beyond the ability to vocalize. *God, why is this carriage moving so slowly?*

"I am also induced to thank serendipity for preventing her heart for falling for you or vice versa," Lord Caxton continued. His gravelly chuckle rang oddly churlish instead of humorous. "Nevertheless, who am I to question fate? Obviously you were meant to be the friendly conduit and nothing more. You are young, my friend, so do not lose heart. Someday you too shall know the delight of a lover's touch, her smile upon your face, the scent of her skin, the feel of her breath, her kiss—"

"You have kissed her?" Sebastian cried in genuine shock, his eyes wide and murderous when he jerked his gaze to Caxton. A rush of rage blended with a surge of nausea, the struggle to keep both under control immense.

"Not as yet. I am a gentleman above all. But once we declare our intent, and I am able to speak to Mr. Darcy, I shall ask for the honor, have no doubt. And it will be wonderful!"

Sebastian was utterly speechless. How visible the stunned expression on his face or shimmering pain in his eyes from where he sat in the shadows he could not know. Caxton did not comment on what he saw, but his eyes never left Sebastian as he rhapsodized over the fair Georgiana Darcy. He stressed her returned attachment and affection, recounted conversations, and eloquently described the sparkle in her eyes and glorious smiles as they danced. The final blow was a detailed summary of how she agreed to his courtship request.

Sebastian's heart and mind were numb long before the journey to his townhouse was over. Monosyllabic grunts and vague nods were the best he could do, while praying fervently for the trip to speed up and for the strength not to strangle the enamored baron. If once or twice a note of falsity entered the stream or a gleam of warning was directed his way, Sebastian was too distraught to grasp on to it.

Then, as he threw open the carriage door without waiting for the footman and prepared to dive head first onto the street if necessary to escape the torture chamber, Lord Caxton leaned forward and clasped onto his wrist. He brought his face near Sebastian's, eyes black and harsh in the pale light, and said in a heavy voice, "Have no worries regarding Miss Darcy, Butler. I know she is your *friend* so it will comfort you to know that I adore her and promise to protect her with all of my strength for as long as I live. *No one* shall be allowed to harm her or take her from me. I promise you that, Butler."

❧

"Amanda, may I ask a question?"

Mrs. Annesley halted her reading and lowered the novel to her lap. Miss Georgiana had not been listening to the tale of mystery anyway. For the past half hour Mrs. Annesley had been observing from the corner of her eye, noting how Miss Georgiana stared sightlessly into the mirror and brushed the same section of long hair over and over.

Finally, Mrs. Annesley thought, *the mounting tension was driving me mad!* She silently said a rapid prayer for wisdom and hope that this was the opening she had been waiting for.

"Of course, Miss Georgiana. You know you can ask me anything."

Georgiana nodded distractedly, her eyes unfocused and hand clasping the brush loosely in her lap. When she spoke it was a bare whisper but intense, revealing the serious nature of the question.

"You have told me, many times, of the love you bore for your late husband. How… that is…" She sighed and closed her eyes. "What did it feel like? How did you know?"

"May I answer by telling you a story? When I was twenty, I met a man who quite simply stole the breath from my lungs. It sounds rather melodramatic and girlishly fanciful, like something from a badly written romance novel, but that is precisely how it was. He was beautiful. Handsomeness personified. I was overwhelmed and fluttery. All the ridiculous phrases of erotic, nonsensical poetry applied to how I felt around this man. Of course, it is no longer so absurd or laughable when it happens to you!"

She chuckled in memory.

Georgiana smiled and again nodded her head. "Visceral, would you say? Beyond logical reason?"

"I daresay that is apt, but there is little in the way of logic when it comes to love, my dear. That is not to say love is utterly foolish, but I am getting ahead of myself. With this man, it was like fire, an uncontainable passion that was

175

both terrifying and thrilling. Of course, I was very young and I had no sense of restraint. I was enraptured by life in mostly the irresponsible ways and allowed my sensibilities to rule." She shrugged, a humorous smile flashing. "It was not wise at all, but extremely fun, I confess."

Georgiana had turned on her stool and was looking at her companion in surprise. Amanda Annesley had gradually become a dear friend over the years, a woman of uncommon strength, morality, and steadfastness who also possessed a dry wit and rustic practicality. Yet here she was talking of being impetuous once upon a time. It was mind-boggling but also enormously intriguing.

"*Uncontainable passion*," Georgiana quoted, her eyes wistful. "A marriage of wildness."

Mrs. Annesley laughed aloud, shaking her head and her finger at the dotty young woman. "You are creating your own fantasy tale, Miss Georgiana, and not allowing me to tell mine."

"Are you not speaking of Mr. Annesley?"

"I was in love. Besotted. Infatuated. Giddy. After two blissful months of flirting and dancing, he was forced to leave for a business trip. Oh, the tears! I was anguished. Until another man came along who captured my heart and wrest my breath away worse than the first."

She was smiling softly, gazing at Georgiana's perplexed expression with only reminiscent humor and no self-chastisement. "I was the worst form of silly girl, Miss Georgiana. So easily in and out of love that within three years I fell in love at least five times! They were decent gentlemen who returned my affections to varying degrees, but always something went awry. Usually me falling for another! Then one day, I was sitting on a large boulder in a clearing near the pathway toward my home, nursing another broken heart, when a man happened by. It was the son of the local barrister, a gentleman all of us in town knew very well and thought well of. He was a bookkeeper of respectable financial means and excellent reputation, thirty-five years of age, nondescript in appearance, and staid in personality. One could not help but have the highest opinion of him, as he was decent, kind, friendly, a fine dancer, and responsible. I cannot tell you how many times I had overheard, or even partaken briefly, in a wondering conversation as to why he remained unmarried. Yet for all his stellar qualities, he was unattached and indifferent to the machinations of many an eager mother or marriageable young lady."

Her face shone with remembered love and traces of grief. "He comforted me as a gentleman ought, asking no questions. He merely handed me his handkerchief and then began to ramble about the weather, the flowers, the clouds, the laughing children that he had encountered further up the road. I do not even recall what he said. It was the sound of his voice, his genuine concern for my misfortune while not probing or faultfinding, and his willingness to postpone whatever business he was about to tarry with a foolish girl like me that I remember most.

"Out of compassion and friendship bloomed a love that was passionate, eternal, and utterly fulfilling." She reddened faintly, fidgeting with the edges of the book's pages as she momentarily reverted to the blushing bride of long ago.

"How did you know it was he and not one of those other men? Or one yet to come?"

"In some respects, it is indefinable and most assuredly varies for everyone. I already knew Mr. Annesley's character, so there were no questions there. The surprise was in how he made me feel. With the others, it was as if lightning had struck, wild and astonishing but also rapid and without substance. A flame must have fuel, Miss Georgiana, or it quickly dies. To continue with the analogy, a sustaining fire must first begin with the tinder banked and stacked, with kindling material appropriate for the job. The blaze must have adequate purchase and replenishing resources to survive. Passionate love is like the flame. When all is laid correctly, it will exist, thrive, and be unquenchable. I knew I had that with Mr. Annesley, and he for me. We just... knew."

She looked at Georgiana then, her eyes grave. "Occasionally, as the years passed and our love flourished, I would muse on those other men who came before my Mr. Annesley. Love is not a simple emotion, Miss Georgiana. I am not a scholar, as you know, but I understand that in some languages there are many words that we translate as *love*. I have been often fascinated by this fact, but of course it makes sense. I did not love those other men the same way as my husband or with near the depth, but I did love them. Or at least held an affection and spark that may have flowered into something more. Fate worked for the best in my case, I am sure of it. However, they were generally good men who may have made me happy. Who knows? Would that instantaneous flame of passion fanned into a long-lasting blaze to stand the test of time? Or was it always destined to die a swift death, and I am lucky to have discovered the truth before the folly of an ill marriage? I cannot know, of course, but I do know that what burned in my heart for Mr. Annesley was stronger and more beautiful than what any poets have been able to put to words."

"Do you not believe there is only one man for each woman? That one person completes your soul and will bring true happiness?"

Mrs. Annesley pursed her lips. "I am not sure it is always so simple. You and I are rather spoiled, yes?" She smiled at Georgiana's puzzled stare. "I think it may depend on one's ignorance. If I had married one of those men before I met my Mr. Annesley, I would never have known the possibility of consuming love. In that ignorance, I may well have contentedly lived out my life, none the wiser or worse off for the lack. Two years after my husband died, I received a marriage proposal from a dear friend of our family. He too was a good man and I knew he would take care of me in most of the ways that count. I was sorely tempted, Miss Georgiana. I was lonely, still young enough to wish for the companionship and special joy that only takes place within the bonds of matrimony, and the practicality of financial security was certainly no small instigation. Yet, I could not do it. I knew, beyond doubt, that we would never share even a tenth of what Mr. Annesley and I possessed. I decided it was better to be alone in my memories, and wait for another man of like passion to come along, if God willed it, than to marry for lesser reasons. You, my dear friend, are spoiled by the uncommonly rapturous marriages that surround you. I could be wrong, but I fear you will never be happy until finding that person who, as you said, completes your soul."

Georgiana's head was hanging low. Mrs. Annesley waited. She had spoken, answered the questions Georgiana had put to her. Now she needed to hear precisely what the impetus was.

Finally, in a whisper, "Lord Caxton asked me for the honor of paying court, making it clear he wishes to marry me."

"I see. And what did you say?"

"I did not know what to say, and that was the most shocking aspect of the entire situation."

Georgiana rose and began to walk about the room at a slow pace. Her eyes were clouded and her hands clenched before her breast. "Maybe I should have foreseen his declaration. I certainly was aware of his regard, so a wiser woman would wonder at my surprise. But our acquaintance is of such short duration that I never anticipated matters moving so swiftly. I did not expect it, Amanda, that is true, but if asked, I imagine I would have expressed happiness at the idea of courting Lord Caxton. Of being his baroness."

She turned to her companion. "I felt the lightning bolt the first moment I saw him. My breath was squeezed from my lungs. Our hours together since have been very pleasant. I like him, I truly do. Maybe I even love him. What better way to discover the depth than to engage in a courtship? But I could not agree. And then *he*..."

She sighed and quickened her pace. Her eyes flashed and voice rose angrily. "It should not be so complicated! Should it? I know I am only twenty, but why is it that every time I think I am in love something muddles up? It feels wrong while also feeling right, which makes no sense. Why must affection be false or misplaced or weak or not returned? Why do you fall in love with the one man who does not love you back?"

She halted as if slamming into a wall. Her breathing came in harsh spurts and her cheeks blotched red. Frustration registered upon every aspect of her being as she stared blankly out of the window into the darkness. So indrawn was she that it was several minutes before she realized Mrs. Annesley was at her side with a comforting hand resting on her arm.

"You refer to Mr. Butler."

Georgiana nodded and tears shimmered in the eyes she lifted to her companion. "What you describe, the varying flames? I understand the analogy. I feel it in my heart, Amanda. Only... unlike your Mr. Annesley, Mr. Butler does not feel the same."

"Are you certain of this?"

"Today I sang his psalm, the sixty-third. When I first played it days ago, my heart was awakened. It did not touch me as a worship song but rather one of human love, of passionate love between a man and a woman. I saw that he had written it recently, after meeting me, and I hoped. But he said nothing, he did nothing." She shook her head, the tears glistening on her cheeks. "I talked about the baron, partially to search for information that might shed an unsavory light on a man who appears almost too perfect to be real, but also to make Mr. Butler jealous. Is that not awful of me?"

"No. It is natural. What did he do?"

"He left! I am sure he feels something for me, Amanda, but it distressed him. He does not want this… complication in his life. And the truth is, I understand, even as it breaks my heart."

Mrs. Annesley enfolded the confused young woman into her arms, holding tightly until she felt the slim body relax. Then she led her to the bed, silently moving through the familiar procedures of shedding the robe, plaiting her hair, and tenderly tucking her under the warmed blankets. When all was accomplished, Georgiana comfortable amid the plump pillows and goose-down counterpane, Mrs. Annesley sat on the edge of the bed and gently ran her fingertips over her friend's weary brow.

"Sleep, my dear. Soothe your mind in pleasant dreams. You are fretting when you should not. There is no reason to leap into decisions of such magnitude. Lord Caxton will understand that you are not ready for a commitment. And if he does not understand, then that is part of your answer. As for Mr. Butler, I think you may be allowing preconceived notions to rule. Yet, whatever the truth, peace and serenity are necessary to interpret affairs of the heart. Trust your instincts and trust God to lead you. Do not be hasty. Mark my words, dearest Georgiana—all will fall into the proper place if you remain calm and in control. Now, sleep."

Georgiana did sleep, although her dreams were troubled. Dark-haired men faded into blonde men, music played, and laughter rang. And she kept hearing a voice saying *I love you* but had no idea who spoke.

❧

"Sebastian?" He was pulled from his inpatient contemplation of the ceiling to eagerly look at the woman who spoke his name. Merely the sound of his name from her lips was enough to complete his soul and blanket him in peace.

A lazy, appreciative smile lifted his lips, his respirations increased, and his heart started to pound. His eyes roamed slowly over her figure as she gracefully glided toward the bed where he lay. She wore a flimsy nightgown of pale cinnamon that shimmered in the half-light. The fabric flowed over her curves as she walked, revealing tantalizing glimpses of the exquisite flesh underneath. Her hip-length golden hair shone, crowning her head, shoulders, and back as a regal veil. She was smiling, her face resplendent with happiness and hints of lust as her blue eyes swept over his unclothed form concealed only by a thin sheet of satin.

She reached the bed, joined him under the lifted coverlet, burrowed completely against his body, and released a heady sigh. She propped herself on one elbow, her beautiful face hovering above him and wavy blonde tresses a curtain enshrouding them. One hand caressed his neck and shoulder while the other traced tender circles over his brow.

"I love you," she whispered.

He captured the teasing fingers that massaged his scalp and played with his hair, drawing each tiny tip to his lips for light kisses. He grazed over the underside of her fingers, bestowed nibbles along the way, paused to reverentially kiss the gold rings on her finger, and then traveled on to her palm and delicate wrist. She moaned faintly, her eyes liquid with rising passion.

"I love you, Georgiana, with all my soul."

And then there were no more words. Kisses and caresses commenced at a languid pace that rapidly escalated as their mutual hunger consumed them. The lovely but intrusive gown was discarded. Their hands were everywhere, provoking and inflaming. Lips were not content to remain in one place for too long, although their mouths were inevitably drawn together for fervent kisses. They writhed, limbs tangled, and the entire surface of the bed was encountered at some point as they endlessly shifted in order to touch another part of the other.

He stroked over her hips and back, fingers twining in the silky hair cascading down her slender back as she swayed above him, moving in a rhythmic fashion that drove his passion to rapturous levels. Observing the drugged expression of unrestrained pleasure and love inundating her face, while simultaneously feeling each movement searing his sensitized nerves, led to the inevitable glorious conclusion. She arched her back, nails digging into his shoulder as she cried his name in ecstasy. The taut pressure in his body was on the brink of a violent release of pleasure, the groan already formulating deep in his throat and back arching when he pulled her body onto his chest, crying in purest joy as he relinquished control and gave in to the unleashed power of his love...

Sebastian jolted awake, his strangled cry of her name ripping through the chamber. The sheets were a knotted mess under his sweat-soaked skin and the damp nightshirt clung to his flesh. Ragged respirations burned painfully in his lungs. The vivid dream of Georgiana and the sweet fire of pleasure that raged in his loins consumed his thoughts. So amazingly beautiful were the images and so stunning the rapture that it was several moments before his dazed mind realized it was a dream.

"Oh, sweet God!" he rasped, drawing his knees up to ease the sudden agony. He had never been so aroused or so weak with desire, and the interrupted, enviable ending, while the dream was still so clear in his mind, created a pain unlike anything ever experienced. His body pulsated with the need to hold her tightly as the tremors of his love abated and his heart felt near to bursting with the comprehension that her presence was a fantasy. He groaned in misery, unable to calm the tumultuous seas crashing within.

Lurching to his feet and swaying, it was a moment before he was able to stagger to the dark window. He leaned against the cold stone, knees buckling and body sliding to the floor. Stars flashed before his eyes and his head swam from lack of oxygen, heartache, and confusion.

"You are a fool, Butler," he admonished in an audible murmur. "You are in love with her. Utterly, passionately, eternally, and all the rest."

Tears welled in his eyes, a faint sob catching in his throat. *And it is too late because she loves another.*

"You need not worry, Caxton," Sebastian whispered, his breath a vapor in the chill. "I am not in a place of competition, as her affections are not directed toward me. I have what I wanted. A friend." He laughed bitterly, and then covered his face with his long-fingered hands and succumbed to his misery and self-pity.

FOURTH MOVEMENT

Recapitulation

CHAPTER FOURTEEN

Dissonance Accelerando

"M ISS DARCY? YOU HAVE a visitor."

Georgiana glanced up, her eyes instantly shining in hopeful anticipation. "Who is it?"

"Miss Foster-Riggs. She is waiting in the salon."

Georgiana nodded, her face falling into the melancholy pose she could not seem to prevent when alone. She sighed, pressed her fingertips against the persistent ache inside her forehead, and closed her moist eyes. A few moments were necessary to collect her scattered emotions before feigning cheeriness before her guest.

> *We miss you, dearest sister.*
> *All of our love and devotion,*
> *William and Lizzy and the boys*

Tracing a fingertip over the signatures etched upon the letter in her hand, Georgiana fought the tears. *How I wish they were here!* But they were far away, not that their presence would change the web she discovered herself entangled in. With each passing day, she yearned for the security of Pemberley, the beloved manor's thick walls a sanctuary she dreamed of regardless how naïve the sentiment.

Entering the salon, her heart did lift at the sight of her waiting friend, genuine smiles breaking out as they clasped hands.

"Dearest Georgiana! I pray I did not disturb your rest?"

"Not at all, Josephine. You are always welcome and I have all afternoon to rest. Please, sit and have tea with me."

"If you insist, but I shall not keep you long. I need my rest as well! I intend to revel in tonight's entertainment long into the wee hours of the morn!"

Miss Foster-Riggs sat on the settee across from Georgiana, inspecting the signs of sadness and crying on her friend's face. "I am surprised to find you at home, actually. I thought sure your gorgeous baron would have whisked you off for a ride or something."

"For the thousandth time, he is not my baron. You are as bad as Zoë and Yvette."

"Well, he does occupy much of your time. We women have difficulty capturing your attention for ourselves these days. But we persist!"

"Indeed, you do and I am grateful." *I only wish Mr. Butler was as proactive,* she thought with an angry scowl. "You should know that I delight in my hours spent with you and the others as greatly as in the company of a man."

Josephine laughed, waving her hand airily. "I am not so convinced of that! Nor can I blame you for seeking the baron's company. And, in light of the desire to charm and devastate at a glance, I have come on a purpose." She began peeling the layers of satin fabric away from the bundled she held in her lap and continued her narrative. "Your enraptured baron shall need to join the collection of gentlemen unable to resist you. Remember, I spoke of the perfect hair ornament to complement the gown you have chosen for tonight's ball? Well, here it is."

Lying within the folds of white satin was a narrow circlet of gold finely wrought in a design of numerous thin strands curved and woven together with inlaid lapis lazuli and blue chalcedony. The deep, violet blue of the lapis lazuli blended stunningly with the milky-blue of the chalcedony, the polished pieces delicate and integrated beautifully.

Georgiana gasped. "Oh, Josephine! It is exquisite! And perfect! But far too fine for me to be comfortable borrowing. What if something were to happen to it?"

"Pish! It shall be securely nestled amid that mass you call your hair—which we all envy with a jealousy most evil in nature—so where could it go? But you have nothing to fret over anyway, as I am giving it to you as a gift. No, spare your breath! With my hair and complexion it was a horrid choice in the first place." She patted her lush locks of fiery red, the porcelain skin that forever appeared faintly blotched with red veins and bright freckles, no matter how thick she powdered, instantly flushing as if knowing it was being discussed. "What my great-aunt Sylvie was thinking I'll never know, but now she has parted this world, God rest her soul, so she will never know that I have given the hideous thing away."

The "hideous thing" was placed onto Georgiana's head, perching precariously at an angle atop the smooth daytime chignon, but regal and splendid nonetheless. The twinkling gemstones of varied shades of blue accented the multifaceted slivers of blue in Georgiana's pale eyes, lovely even with her day gown of canary yellow.

"There," Josephine declared. "You are a vision. The baron shall fall to his knees in devotion, laying his life at your dainty feet. Every woman will be green with envy, myself included. And Mr. Butler will be cursing his stupidity for not snapping you up sooner."

Georgiana jerked. "You and your delusions, Josephine," she denied with a shaky laugh. "No one will notice me at all. And I doubt if Mr. Butler will be attending. He is quite busy these days." She said the last faintly, using the excuse of rewrapping the circlet to distract and busy her trembling hands.

Josephine shrugged. "Too bad. He will be missing the event of the winter. The de Valdays throw the most divine galas."

"You exaggerate outrageously, dear Josephine. Nothing could compare to the Fercourt or the Lauraguais extravaganzas. And I am yet recuperating from the Chamilly affair. This will be sedate in comparison."

Josephine gasped dramatically. "I certainly pray not! I intend to dazzle and dance until my feet bleed."

"Monsieur Sainte-Mesme is agreeable to this? His feet are up to the task? Or does he plan to allow other gentlemen free access to his fiancée?"

"He is enraptured and will do whatever I desire," she declared with a toss of her head, and then dissolved into girlish giggles. She clasped on to Georgiana's hand. "I shall so miss you, my dear friend. Our time has been far too short. Why, oh why must your baron take you away?"

"For the last time, he is not my baron, and I am returning to England with my family, as we have planned all along."

"Yes, yes. But you will marry and burrow into life as a proper English wife, and I shall never see you again!"

"I have no intention of marrying anyone in the near future, Josephine. And worry not, as we will keep in touch, write letters, and surely Monsieur Sainte-Mesme will escort his new bride to London next year. Besides, you will be the devoted, proper wife long before me."

Josephine frowned, gazing intently at her friend. "You seem sad, Georgiana. In fact, you have not quite been yourself for over a week now. Have you and Lord Caxton quarreled?"

Georgiana sighed, her fingers reaching to rub her temples. "No, we have not quarreled. All is well, I suppose. I am not as convinced as he is regarding our relationship and am growing weary of having my caution dismissed."

"He does not mean to push, Georgiana, I am sure of it. Lord Caxton is a good man and deeply in love with you, any fool can see that."

"I know. He is a wonderful man and I care for him very much. It is just so fast and overwhelming. I need time, Josephine, and perhaps distance." She shook her head, smiling wanly. "I am making no sense, I am afraid. And I am sounding like a petulant child."

"You are homesick."

"Yes. And tired, with a headache and persistent ringing in my ears."

"Then you must rest," Josephine declared authoritatively. "Sleep in a darkened room will restore your vigor and prepare you for tonight. Do not fret so, dear Georgiana. Everything will be just fine, you'll see!"

Minutes later, Georgiana sluggishly climbed the stairs toward her bedchamber. *Everything will be just fine.* The same advice offered by Mrs. Annesley. Yet she did not feel as if *anything* was fine. Her heart ached more than her head, the weariness that consumed her one of the soul as well as the body.

Mr. Butler had apparently disappeared. He had not returned to the de Valday townhouse since the day he shared his hymns. She still had the leather portfolio in her possession, the music and lyrics of each one now memorized from uncounted hours poring over them. Yet their composer was nowhere to be found. He never appeared at any of the functions she attended and offhand comments by others conveyed the same curiosity regarding his absence elsewhere. The lively presence of the Marchioness of Warrow proved that nothing serious could have befallen him, allaying Georgiana's worst fears.

Georgiana was alternately torn between sobbing dismay and fits of anger. It was unconscionable to abandon a friend in such a manner, and she had her moments of extreme vexation when vivid images of delivering the tongue-lashing he deserved would give her an odd strength. But primarily she felt grieved beyond the words to describe. She was unbelievably hurt at his apparent indifference, crushed by feelings of inadequacy and doubt in her judgment.

The terror of having her deepest fears confirmed—that is, that she was entirely wrong regarding his friendship—prevented her probing the situation. She knew that discovering he was happily passing his time elsewhere, with someone else, would devastate her, so she avoided Lady Warrow's presence, ignored the troubled glances the marchioness sent her direction, and did not inquire amongst their mutual friends.

And with each passing day, the sense of profound loss escalated.

Then there was the matter of Lord Caxton. He maintained his constant attention but did not press her to formalize their arrangement, of which she was thankful. However, she was not sure if that was due to understanding deference or because he presumed her acquiescence. His subtle phrasings and assumptive familiarity pointed to the latter.

She enjoyed her hours with the unfailingly humorous gentleman. His masculine presence never failed to move her, his handsome virility breathtaking. Yet twice, he had leaned in as if preparing to snatch a kiss, Georgiana pulling away, not out of alarm at the improper maneuver, but because of the image of Mr. Butler that jolted through her mind.

She cared for Lord Caxton, she was certain of that. So why did she experience flares of annoyance when he fervidly expressed his affection? Eventually, she realized her anger was not directed at him but at the persistent feelings for Mr. Butler that interfered with total relinquishment to the passion and future Lord Caxton freely offered.

"Damn you, Sebastian Butler!" she muttered to the air. Sinking into the mattress and already succumbing to the beginnings of sleep, the questions continued to swirl.

Is my love for the baron not able to flourish because I am madly in love Mr. Butler? Or do my emotions toward the dashing older man simply not run deep enough?

The constant strain of trying desperately to figure it out while nursing an aching heart and maintaining a pose of frivolity amid the nonstop entertainments wore on her. A long, drugged-like nap, followed by a cleansing soak in water hot enough to redden her delicate skin, could not erase her dulled senses. She dressed in her new gown, stared at her reflection as the maid coiffed her waist-length hair into an elaborate array with the circlet a crowning glory, and left the room a vision of beauty.

It was all a daze.

Her brain was addled with clouds obscuring lucid thought. The pressure behind her forehead and ears had escalated, a faint buzzing sound further disturbing her concentration, and her muscles ached. Some tiny part of her rational mind knew she was sick, but drive and determination forced her onward. The de Valdays had planned this soiree to honor their dear English friends, Lord and Lady Matlock and Miss Georgiana Darcy, as a farewell spectacular. Very soon, they would be returning home and Georgiana did not know whether to leap for joy or cry.

The carriage belonging to the Marchioness of Warrow rattled along the busy streets of nighttime Paris. The marchioness sat on her seat, the layers of fabric elegantly swathing her lush figure draped perfectly to prevent wrinkles. Her posture was one of serene dignity, her lined face composed, but her eyes displayed a pronounced concern as she stared out of the shadows toward the fidgeting young man across from her.

"Thank you, my boy, for agreeing to escort me tonight."

Sebastian Butler nodded, not removing his gaze from the passing scenery. "Of course, Grandmother. It is my pleasure, you know that."

Under other circumstances she may have smiled and teased at his use of the word *pleasure* when his tone so manifestly lacked anything remotely joyous, but she saw no irony in the situation. The marchioness was an old woman, but one who counted keen discernment and mental acuity to the gift of physical vigor granted by the Almighty. Nothing missed her penetrating gaze and inclusive ear. And when it came to matters concerning her family and those she loved, her assiduousness was formidable.

Therefore, she knew about the labyrinthine love affair her grandson was embroiled in probably better than the persons involved did. She also knew how stupid they both were being on the subject. Unfortunately, her long life and numerous romantic entanglements had taught her that such matters were best left alone, meddling generally making it worse. Still, she was not above a wee bit of interference. Besides, watching her dearly beloved grandson miserably lock himself away in the music room while Miss Darcy looked like she was perpetually ready to burst into tears was interrupting her gaiety, and that was very annoying!

"It will be a delightful party, I am sure, since the de Valdays are masters of entertaining. Nevertheless, we would have been remiss not to attend, as it is our kin who are the guests of honor."

Sebastian remained silent, only a slight increase in his tension and a shifting in his seat giving voice to his frame of mind.

Lady Warrow continued, "I ran into Lady Matlock and Miss Darcy at the modiste's two days ago. It was an appointment for final fittings for tonight's affair and Miss Darcy's gown was stunning. Oh, to be so young and beautiful again! To have one's figure soft and toned and perky in all the appropriate places," she said and sighed dramatically. Pretending not to notice the longing inundating Sebastian's face, she went on in a thoughtful tone, "She was quite the vision of loveliness, as you shall see tonight, I daresay. Yet something was amiss."

Sebastian jerked his eyes toward his grandmother, concern and possibly hope now added to the visible desire and love. "How do you mean?"

She shrugged, picking invisible lint from her gown. "Oh, I do not know. Just not as cheery as she generally is. Naturally, she was the epitome of politeness and kindness, dear girl, but an air of sadness surrounded her. Nothing that I am sure a dance or two with my handsome grandson will not cure."

He grunted. "I imagine her dances will be taken by Lord Caxton."

"Good heavens, Sebastian! You know as well as I that a young lady unspoken for cannot limit herself to one dance partner! The scandal of it! Why, people would assume they were betrothed or formally courting!"

"But... I thought... that is—is not their arrangement a known fact?"

"What arrangement? Have you heard something I have not, Sebastian? That would be highly unlikely, considering the horrid gossip that I am. Please tell me!" She leaned forward, her face so precisely set in avid curiosity that Sarah Siddons would be jealous.

Sebastian stammered, "Lord Caxton himself told me they had an arrangement. That Miss Darcy had agreed to his courtship. And Miss Darcy confirmed it."

Did she? Or did you assume it? He frowned, shaking his head against the abrupt onslaught of conflicting viewpoints and emotions.

Lady Warrow waved her hand dismissively. "Well, I have heard nothing other than that the baron continues to pursue while Miss Darcy evades. Interpret that how you wish. Oh, we have arrived! Hand me my fan, will you, dear boy?" Sebastian automatically did as requested, the marchioness using the device to hide her satisfied smirk.

They entered the glittering reception hall of the de Valday townhouse, Lady Warrow regal and stunning even in her seniority. She clasped her grandson's arm lightly, always thrilled to be the center of attention and at the side of an attractive man years younger than her, even if he was kin.

Sebastian stood tall and elegant, wearing garments of the finest cut and weave, the black ensemble with maroon waistcoat a striking contrast to his fair skin and light-golden hair. He had pulled himself together, superior breeding and decades of training proving to be an asset against the throbbing in his heart and clash of thoughts swirling through his brain.

His eyes scanned the crowds searching for the only face he truly wanted to see, yet he was frozen in nervousness as to how he would react when he saw her. *How will she react to me?* Fortunate for his nerves, he had little time to dwell on the idea, as he was speedily surrounded by dozens of friends sincerely delighted to see him. Bare minutes passed before his native charm and gregarious personality managed to supplant the anxiety. Quickly caught up in the merriment of lighthearted conversation and music, his eyes continued to dart amid the press of bodies and shifting gaps for the particular figure and graceful carriage that he would recognize instantly.

Easily a half hour passed, as he surrendered to the joy of laughter, discovering the atmosphere a welcome balm to the turbulence within. Freedom from the aching yearning to see Georgiana—*Where was she?*—and the fear of pain to be caused if she arrived on Lord Caxton's arm was not attained, but for the present he was somewhat calm.

He stood near the massive staircase that led to the upper level, one hand resting casually upon the ornately carved wooden railing, chatting with a group of students from the Conservatoire when everything changed.

Sebastian would never know what captured his attention and caused him to look left, upward to the gallery above. His fanciful nature would forever say his soul felt her presence, but whatever the reality, he glanced upward and instantly lightning struck deep into the marrow of his bones.

All he could do was stare.

Georgiana wore a gown of three shades of blue, falling in gossamer layers of silk over a lacy petticoat. The cinched, wide sash of gold-threaded cobalt rested just under her full bosom and fell in a cascade over her bottom to the floor. A diaphanous strip of palest blue loosely surrounded her slender neck and edged her décolletage, providing some modesty while accenting the feminine flesh encased inside the bodice. The blazing light highlighted the sheen in her abundant hair, each tress artfully arranged with the circlet of gold and blue stones the perfecting accent. Her pale skin was slightly flushed, her blue eyes glossy, and her plump lips curved into a soft smile.

For Sebastian, the room faded and the hum disappeared. For that moment, in that instant, everything melted away. All of the doubt, the pain, and the unknowing vanished. It was only Georgiana and how utterly he loved her. He did not even try to prevent the radiance of his emotions from diffusing over his face.

The minutes leading up to her entrance, Georgiana had not struggled with emotion but with a body determined to fail her. Alone in her room with both windows open and a cool breeze flooding the air to revitalize her feverish mind, she had perked up a bit and deluded herself into believing she was well enough. Then she entered the hall, it already warm from an abundance of lights and people, and the restorative quality vanished.

Traversing the passageway took an eternity, the balcony railing a blessing of solidity under her hand. She scanned the moving crowd below as she slowly walked toward the stairs leading to the foyer that was awash with human bodies, and spied Mr. Butler mere seconds before he lifted his gaze to her.

She paused to observe him where he stood tall and handsome, relaxed and smiling at the bottom of the steps. Peace washed through her as she studied his attractive profile, the squared line of his jaw, the broad expanse of his shoulders under the dark suit, and the long fingers lying atop the balustrade. Love in its purest form speared her, and for a moment the clouds and haziness of pain vanished.

I have no choice. I only want him.

Then he turned and those gorgeous eyes of stormy-gray alit upon her face. His countenance broke into a spontaneous display of unfettered joy and unleashed brilliance. *He loves me!* It was written transparently upon his face and in the eyes that caressed her. The knowledge of returned affection both weakened her muscles and lent her the necessary strength to quicken her pace. Her decision had been reached in those heartbeats before he looked upon her, but knowing that he loved her only made it sweeter.

With her gaze locked with his, she crossed the short span to the stairs, beginning her descent gracefully but with an accelerated tempo. The hunger to hear his voice and feel his soft touch spurred her on and kept the tendrils of weariness and pain at bay.

Sebastian watched her countenance transform into the vision of the Georgiana in his dreams, a Georgiana who was his wife and who loved him. His heart leapt, performing a musical crescendo in his sudden joy at the expression spreading over her dainty features. The flair of happiness shining from her eyes electrified every nerve and he could not breathe, but it was precious agony.

Eyes never leaving the glory of her face, he shifted his weight to head toward her when abruptly the magical revelation was ripped apart.

The baron strode into the scene, marching directly in front of Sebastian. The baron's brawny body invaded the minuscule space between Sebastian and the staircase riser, forcing him to step hastily backward and break eye contact with Georgiana.

Everything thereafter occurred in rapid succession.

Georgiana's step faltered with the unexpected severing of the invisible chord that had anchored her to Sebastian. Her focus shifted to Lord Caxton, mainly due to his body blocking the view of the other, and the brilliant smile still lighting her face was directed at him.

Sebastian recovered his balance, stepped to the right, and looked past the baron to see Georgiana's radiant smile and shining eyes fixed upon the older man. *It was never you, fool!* His jaw clenched in anger, pain assaulted him with the power of a physical blow, and he turned his stiffened body away from witnessing the lovers' greeting.

Lord Caxton ascended the stairs, Georgiana's smile fading at the hardness to his dark eyes and harsh set of his face. She backed up a step and leaned onto the railing, glancing away from his cold smile just in time to witness a furious Sebastian pivot away.

Sadness enveloped her as a wet blanket. Every ache and pain resurged through her head and muscles with renewed force. She shivered and gasped, clutching onto the banister as the room began to spin wildly. The epiphany reached just seconds previous was as absolute as ever, but coherent thought suddenly became mixed with fantasy as the wispy edges of shadow intruded.

She looked back to the baron, who was now only four steps below her. The urge to speak the truth and shout her feelings aloud raged within, the hoarsely croaked plea bursting through her lips.

"Please, Lord Caxton, I need you…"

But the remainder to that sentence, the declaration that she needed him to understand that her love was firmly fixed elsewhere, was left temporarily unspoken. Instead, her knees buckled as a wave of furious heat struck her flesh, unconsciousness wrapped around her, and she tumbled forward into the arms of Lord Caxton.

❧

Please, Lord Caxton, I need you… Lord Caxton, I need you… I need you… I need you…

The words rang over and over inside Sebastian's head, causing him physical pain, and the terrifying vision of a senseless Georgiana lying in the baron's arms would never be erased.

Chaos ensued. A physician was called for as Georgiana was whisked off to an upper room. Sebastian stood stunned at the bottom of the staircase watching the woman he loved being carried away by another man. Word rapidly spread to the gathering mass of friends and family, many of them forgoing the party to collect in the library and wait for word.

Sebastian paced, the vigorous movement necessary to bear the agony slicing through him. The ball recommenced and, although dimmed in its merry fervor, the strains of music reached the hushed room. Sebastian found no solace in the refrains from the orchestra. Rather it wore on his nerves. So he paced.

"Sebastian, dear, please sit down! You are giving me a headache and wearing a hole in the carpet will not speed up the doctor's appearance."

He strode to the dark window, released a huge sigh, clasped his hands behind his back, and fruitlessly willed the frantic worry and ache to ease. He ignored his grandmother's sympathetic gaze resting upon him, her concern indicative of his distraught appearance no matter how hard he tried to hold himself together.

The door opened, every eye swinging to the portal in hope and dread, but it was only a servant relating word from Lord Matlock that Miss Darcy was currently being examined by the physician and that she was unconscious and burning with a fever.

The waiting recommenced. As did Sebastian's pacing. *Why has Caxton not returned?* Sebastian knew it was a bit childish, but the thought of Lord Caxton standing vigil near the stricken woman while he was relegated to the lower chambers was infuriating. Jealousy was one more emotion to add to what ate up his insides.

Eventually, Lord Matlock arrived to update the worried guests, accompanied by a clearly disturbed Lord Caxton.

"The doctor diagnosed her ailment as influenza and is currently working to reduce the fever," Lord Matlock said. "She has rallied briefly but is confused and extremely weak. An apothecary has been sent for as well with prescriptions ordered. For now, however, we can only pray. I suggest, as difficult as it may be, that we rejoin the ball and present a face of confidence and ease. Miss Darcy would not wish for her friends to fret over her and not enjoy the entertainment."

"But your lordship! How can we dance and be gay when dearest Georgiana is abed and in dire straights?"

"Out of respect for her sensibilities and her selfless desire to please others, Mademoiselle de Valday. She will applaud your bravery when she recovers. Now, if you will excuse me, I am going to see if anything else is needed upstairs, and then I too shall rejoin our guests."

Silence fell after the thud of the door behind Lord Matlock, but it did not last for long.

"My lord, what is your opinion? How did she appear to you?"

Lord Caxton answered with a growl, "I was banished to the passageway moments after laying Miss Darcy upon the bed. Then the earl insisted I come downstairs with him. I know only what you have been told by Lord Matlock."

He muttered a curse under his breath, whirled about, and stomped out of the room and onto the terrace. Sebastian watched him disappear into the shadows beyond the window and then followed. He was not sure what he wanted but some impulse prompted him.

The baron was leaning against the wall with his hands over his face. Sebastian did not hear crying, but the man's whole body shook. He hesitated, even began to take a step backward when Caxton dropped his hands and turned an anguished glare upon him.

"Come to gloat have you?"

"No," Sebastian began, truly surprised at the question.

"No? I would if the situation were reversed. I should be up there, damn it all! I should be sitting beside her, holding the cool cloth to her head, whispering of my love and lending strength. I would be if not for these bloody rules and ridiculous notions of propriety that keep me out of her room simply because we are not formally engaged as yet!"

"Yet?"

"That's right, Butler! Yet!" He yelled it, pushing off from the wall with force and stalking toward Sebastian, who held his ground and returned the glare. "I told you how it is between Miss Darcy and me. Formalities may stand in our way, but nothing else does!"

"You are that certain, are you?"

Lord Caxton paused. The two men stared at each other defiantly, measuring and evaluating as conclusions were drawn. Caxton broke the tension first, his voice calmer if still as forceful.

"I know you care for her, Butler. I am not a fool or blind. I can empathize with how you are feeling, since I know how wretched I would be if she did not return my affection. I truly am sorry for that, but you must accept what is."

"And if I cannot accept what is?" Sebastian choked.

"You must. Your persistence and presence benefits neither of you. Miss Darcy is pained to see her friend's unhappiness and I cannot fathom how tormenting it must be to see us together."

He stepped closer to the rigid Sebastian, laid one hand on his shoulder, and said, "For what it is worth coming from me, do not torture yourself needlessly. Take comfort, if you can, in knowing she is loved, deeply, and let it go. My advice? Stay away from what can only cause you pain."

Caxton squeezed his shoulder and re-entered the library, leaving Sebastian in the dark and cold of the night. Yet the external was nothing compared to the black and ice inside his heart.

B Y THE NEXT AFTERNOON, Georgiana's fever had broke. Word
of this reached her many friends, all of them tremendously relieved.
Sebastian received the report from Lady Warrow, nodded once, and
went back to writing the letter he had been working on when she knocked
at his door. His relief at the news was immense, but it changed nothing. His
plans remained the same and the next several days were going to be focused on
carrying them out.

For Georgiana, those days following her collapse were tumultuous. Youth
and stamina were in her favor. Rest, copious fluids, healing herbal teas,
and bolstering foods were efficacious. The constant nursing by a gaggle of
concerned de Valdays aided in her recovery.

Lingering fatigue and persistent dizziness plagued her for days, but worse
were her muddled memories. With each passing day, as her head cleared, she
realized how disorderly and foggy she had been for nearly the whole week prior.
Had Mr. Butler looked at her with ardent love? Was he standing there at all?
And where was he now? Why has he not visited or sent word?

Fretting over these questions, striving to reconcile fever-induced illusions
with facts exhausted her. However, real or imagined, her feelings regarding the
two men in her life were crystalline. Mr. Butler's absence, while painful and
worrisome, was beyond her control at the moment. Furthermore, it changed

nothing in regards to the wholehearted, irrevocable love she bore him. Nor did it change her decision.

"Are you certain you are up to this? You can barely sit up without the room spinning!" Mrs. Annesley frowned as she arranged the quilt about her companion's legs, assuring complete modesty as well as warmth.

"No, I am not certain. But I do not think it shall be any easier a week from now." Georgiana sighed, rubbing her aching temples. "The poor man has been haunting the downstairs rooms for the last two days. I cannot bear causing him further distress."

"He is not exactly going to be leaping for joy after you speak with him."

Georgiana groaned, hiding her face within her palms. "What else can I do, Amanda?"

Mrs. Annesley sat beside, pulling her into a warm embrace. "Forgive my irritability. My insensitivity is unpardonable, even if it does arise out of recent frightful events and my concern over you aggravating your recovery. Of course this is not easy for you, and you are very brave to confront the matter boldly."

"I am positive bravery has nothing to do with it as I am terrified. I have tried to rehearse the words, but even if my wits were not addled, I do not deem there is an easy way to tell a man who loves you that you do not feel the same."

The door opened before Mrs. Annesley could reply, admitting Lady Matlock. She crossed to her niece, laying the back of her hand clinically against her forehead.

"If your fever was returned, I would forbid this interview. Are you sure you are up to this, Georgiana? I can speak to him for you."

Georgiana smiled wanly and shook her head. "Thank you, Aunt, but this is something I must handle myself."

Lady Matlock frowned, clearly not convinced. "Are you still resolved to speak to him privately? I should stay just in case—"

"I will not humiliate him additionally by having an audience," Georgiana interrupted softly, continuing in a subdued, pleading tone, "but, please, stay close, both of you. I am not ashamed to confess that I will need comforting."

"Of course," they agreed simultaneously, Lady Matlock continuing, "I will fetch him then, if you are ready?"

Georgiana used the intervening minutes to murmur a prayer for strength and wisdom. Her hands shook and she clutched the fringed edges of her dressing gown's tie tightly to still them. Inhaling deeply in a vain effort to settle her stomach, she gazed around the familiar environs of her bedchamber. The comfortable chaise, crackling fire, and casual atmosphere lent a peace she desperately needed.

The knock on the door caused her to jerk even though she expected it. Surprisingly, her voice was steady when she granted him entrance, but her heart constricted to see the sincere, relieved smile that blazed over his handsome features.

"Miss Darcy!" Lord Caxton rushed across the room, kneeling onto one knee beside her and clasping a hand. "I have been frantic! Reports only placated partially. I needed to see you for myself and daresay you appear quite well and breathtakingly beautiful."

"That is kind of you, my lord, but an exaggeration to be sure."

"Not in the least! But tell me truthfully, are you recovering as expected?"

She nodded, smoothly extricating her hand from between his palms under the pretense of securing her robe. "Please have a seat, Baron." She indicated the chair positioned purposefully near her feet. "I remain fatigued and with a slight headache and ringing in my ears that causes dizziness if I move too swiftly. But the doctor assures this is normal after a fever."

"You are young and healthy. I am sure your total recovery will be swift. Nevertheless, it does my heart good to lay eyes upon you for reassurance. Thank you for allowing me entry into your private chambers." He glanced around the room quickly, returning to pleased contemplation of her face. "I fear I have been quite a pest. Lord Matlock, by rights, should have tossed me out on my rump, but mercy prevailed."

"He would not have done that, Baron."

"No, I suppose not, especially knowing of our relationship."

Georgiana cringed, praying the reaction did not invade her face. This was the opening waited for, but before she could gather her thoughts he went on, apparently oblivious. "Of course, I was not the only visitor who sought information as to your condition. I am surprised the bellpull did not break!"

Georgiana blushed, ducking her head modestly. "I have been overwhelmed by the extravagance of well wishes and expressed concerns. I guess I did not comprehend the wealth of friends I have made in Paris." Her voice fell, eyes involuntarily closing in pain at the marked absence of the one friend she most desperately wished to hear from.

The baron misinterpreted her expression, scooting his chair closer and grasping on to her hand once again. "Are you feeling unwell? Should I call for your aunt?"

"No. I am fine. It is simply humbling, and dismaying, to have caused so much angst among those who care for me. It has been unexpected and somewhat embarrassing."

"You have dozens of friends here, Miss Darcy. They love you genuinely." He smiled, squeezing her hand. "It is easy to love one as kind and wonderful as you."

His voice lowered into a soft caress, one thumb beginning to trace tenderly along her knuckles. He cleared his throat, preparing, she knew, for a repeat declaration or renewal of his address—the request for a formalized courtship that she continued to evade. "Miss Darcy—"

"Lord Caxton," she interrupted, forcing her eyes to engage his and again extracting her hand, "I wanted to see you today for a dual purpose. I know you have been troubled over my well-being, and this anguishes me while it touches me."

"Indeed, I have been troubled, but it is a paltry price to pay for the happiness I derive from your company and my feelings for you."

She winced. "Please, Lord Caxton, I beg you to allow me to finish before I lose my will. You have honored me, immensely, with your suit and constancy. Even in the face of my indecision, you have been the soul of patience. I truly do not deserve your regard, my lord, and pray you will believe me when I tell you it does break my heart to decline your entreaty for a deeper commitment."

"I do not understand," he interjected harshly.

"It is entirely my fault for not being bolder. I have been confused and unsure of my sentiments, but now I know. Please forgive me, Baron, as I never meant to cause you pain."

"I have rushed you and been overbearing. I apologize. But, Miss Darcy, this is what a courtship is designed for! An opportunity to grow closer and learn about the other and to clarify one's affections. You know, surely, how strongly I feel for you? I love you and have no doubts about us. However, if you require time I shall be more patient—"

"I do not require time." Her tone was slightly shrill and she faltered, swallowing and inhaling deeply to calm the rapid pounding of her heart.

Lord Caxton looked as if he had been slapped. His cheeks flared with color, lips pressed together firmly, and dark eyes smoldered.

"I am so sorry. This is awful!" She pinched the bridge of her nose between her fingers, begging the dizziness and ringing to disappear. "I am saying this wrong and creating a muddle of it. Perhaps I should have waited until I felt better. But I refuse to procrastinate further, thus protracting your suspense and worsening the disappointment. Lord Caxton, I—"

"Does this have to do with Butler?"

She should have anticipated this, but the surprise knocked her breath away. Treading too close to the tangled situation with Mr. Butler was nearly more than she could tolerate, the mere mention of his name sending shivers of longing up her spine. The epiphany of her consuming love for the absent musician, whether returned or not, had indeed cemented her decision. Her decency and ethics would not allow her to marry one man while her heart was firmly fixed upon another.

Nevertheless, there was a voice sequestered into a hermetic chamber that wondered. Was she making a terrible mistake? Could she eventually fall passionately in love with the baron? Should she be so hasty and concrete? Was she sentencing herself to decades of loneliness and regret?

She did not know the answer to all the questions spiraling inside her brain except for one. Looking into the baron's stormy visage and hurt eyes swelled her pity and remorse, but that was all. She did not love him.

"Mr. Butler has nothing to do with us," she replied firmly.

"I am not unaware of your affection for him, Miss Darcy. Trust me when I tell you he does not return your interest. Do not close the door on us because of a one-sided infatuation without a future. Mr. Butler is one of those men who waste their lives on pursuits that have no lasting benefit. He is driven, which is admirable, but prevents caring for anyone outside himself."

"Whether I agree with you regarding Mr. Butler or not is irrelevant, and it is a topic I do not care to discuss. I am honored by your request, my lord. My sincerest hope is that you will not hate me for being immature and capricious. I truly never intended to"—she paused, struggling to find the right word—"lead you on. You are a decent, good gentleman—"

"Enough! I do not want to hear how wonderful I am followed by assurances of finding a more suitable mate. I want you! I choose you!"

He lurched to his feet. Gazing at her with arrogant command and faint undertones of sympathy, he declared, "You have been unwell, Miss Darcy. I shall impose upon you no further today. We can discuss this matter when you are restored to full clarity and health. I am confident that you will see our relationship in its proper light."

"Please, do not expect me to change my mind, Baron! I know my heart and this is my final answer. Please try to understand and accept my sorrow over hurting you!"

He stiffened and his eyes flared. "As you wish, madam. I will trouble you no further with my unpalatable presence. Bear in mind, however, that I am not a fool. Do not expect me to run back when you realize your error in judgment. Good day, Miss Darcy."

And with a smart bow, crisp pivot, and swift stride, he was gone, Georgiana's whispered apologies and wrenching sobs dampened by a slamming door.

~❦~

Sebastian knew he was a coward. The idea of leaving, probably to never lay eyes on her again, was ripping him apart one thread at a time. Therefore, facing her and attempting composure as he lied about his reasons for quitting Paris were beyond his ability.

With this reality in mind, he rode into Île Saint-Louis at a quarter hour before nine on the night of an exhibit of paintings by Théodore Géricault, Lady Warrow having commented that Miss Darcy was finally well enough to attend her first public appearance.

Suspicions as to his grandmother's motives for sharing this news gave him pause, but lack of trust in his self-control did not overrule common decency. Miss Darcy may not love him, but she did care for him, this he knew. The friendly note telling of his departure to Vienna for an impromptu educational program at the Gesellschaft der Musikfreunde was secure in his pocket and would have to suffice.

The butler greeted him formally and admitted him without question.

"Sorry to disturb, monsieur, but I shall be quick. I need to retrieve a portfolio of music I left with Miss Darcy some weeks ago. May I search the music room?"

"As you wish, sir. Did you wish for me to inform Miss Darcy of your presence?"

Sebastian drew in a sharp breath, his eyes darting about the foyer before he could reassert control. "She is at home?"

"In her room, sir. Resting."

"Ah, then no. Please do not bother her. She needs her rest. I will be only a moment."

He hurried into the room, intent on grabbing the folder containing his psalms, leaving his letter, and departing. If the compositions were not there, he would sacrifice the work gladly to prevent having to face her, such was his state of mind. He knew talking to her would cause the fragile remains of his heart to shatter completely.

But he was not prepared for how his senses were bombarded by merely entering the music room and laying eyes on the piano. *All the hours spent at her side, happier than I have ever been while witlessly denying my emotions. You are a fool and deserve to suffer.*

He ran his fingers lightly over the keys. His leather portfolio sat upon the lid with several of the psalm sheets propped on the rest and scattered over the gleaming wood. The crisp pages written with the distinctive boldness of his notes showed numerous slight curls along the edges and faint smudges from tiny fingertips indicating her frequent playing. He rifled through the parchments, collecting the psalms from among the compositions written with her delicate strokes. There were at least a dozen songs that they had collaborated on, the pages filled with notations and music in both their penmanship, each sparking a crystalline memory.

Moisture stung his eyes and he shook his head violently to dispel the images. *Enough!*

Fury rushed through him and angrily he gathered the sheets and stuffed them haphazardly into the folder. He snapped the case closed, slapping it harshly against the rim of the piano before shoving it under his arm. Reaching into the inner breast pocket of his jacket, his fingers brushed the folded letter but stiffened seconds later.

"Mr. Butler! I did not know you were here."

His head jerked backward, every muscle twitching as if a knife had plunged between his shoulder blades. He froze, his hand falling to grasp the edge of the piano.

"I did not wish to disturb your rest. I came to retrieve my music," he whispered, harsh and rasping without the slightest hint of warmth.

"Oh. I see. I apologize. I should have returned them long ago. Please forgive me."

He closed his eyes, rigorously willing his body to not betray him. "There is nothing to forgive, Miss Darcy. I hope you enjoyed them."

"I most assuredly did, very much. I confess I shall miss having them in my possession, but as I have memorized all of them, I suppose it does not matter. Thank you, again."

Her voice was soft, tender even, but with a hint of confusion that he detected with tremendous remorse. Relaxing slightly, he turned to face her. He glanced briefly into her gorgeous eyes, noted the sadness therein, and quickly looked away.

"You look well, Miss Darcy. Are you fully recovered from your illness?"

"For the most part, yes. I have a residual weariness that I cannot seem to shake and my memory of that evening is hazy at best." She stepped further into the room, drawing closer to him. "I recall seeing you there, Mr. Butler, by the staircase, but cannot be certain. Were you there?"

"Yes," he murmured, reluctantly meeting her eyes and holding the gaze. "I was there. Very near Lord Caxton, your rescuer," he finished with a bitter twist to his lips and low snarl to his voice.

She was frowning as if sorting through a puzzle. There was a question within her eyes, as if she were begging him for something, but he did not know what.

"Did you see me? Before my rather dramatic entrance, that is? I thought… that is, for a moment it seemed… but I am not sure."

"Yes, I saw you," he whispered.

"I was unsure and have wanted to ask, but our paths have not crossed. Until now."

Sebastian's mind was blank. Her words were spoken lightly but he sensed her encouraging for an explanation. The pain was threatening to overwhelm him and he had a sudden, savage need to escape.

"I apologize for my disassociation, but under the circumstances it is for the best. Pardon my intruding upon your solitude, Miss Darcy. I… I must be going."

He ducked his head and lurched forward in a rush to pass her body, but she impulsively reached out and grabbed on to his forearm. Her grip was not overly strong, yet it halted his momentum as surely as a noose thrown about his chest. He gasped, his jaw tightening as the sensation of her touch pierced through him.

"Please! I beg of you, please tell me what I have done, what I have said to lose your friendship! I cannot bear it, Mr. Butler. I thought, I thought that you cared for me, that our friendship was real and—"

"I cannot be your *friend*," he snapped.

She dropped her hand, stunned. "But…"

He lifted his head, piercing her with eyes dark from agony and suppressed passion. "I cannot be your *friend*. I will not be a *friend* when I want so much more! I will not watch you with *him*… God, Georgiana! *I love you!*"

And then he clasped her face between his palms, closed the small gap, and claimed her mouth in a hard kiss.

Georgiana stiffened in momentary shock. The declaration and impetuous movement startled her, but the feel of his warm, soft lips, even in the wild roughness of his attack, was intoxicating and amazing. She melted, pressed into him, and grasped onto his forearms for support. Instinctively, her mouth responded, her lips parting slightly and softening.

His crazed longing took advantage and with a groan he plunged his tongue between her lips. The kiss became more demanding while strangely tender, the grip about her face relaxing as he explored every aspect of her mouth. Then she opened wider, tentatively meeting his seeking tongue, Sebastian moaning as he sensed all control spiraling wildly beyond his reason.

The squeeze of her hands on his arms and soft curves pressing against his chest penetrated the haze of his passion. He wrest out of her grasp, releasing her lips with a strangled cry of pain. Desire was instantly replaced with numbing recrimination. *I have forced a kiss from a lady who belongs to someone else!* It was unconscionable. Shame nearly buckled him. The assault of emotions rendered him unfit to interpret her eager response for what it signified. He could not look at her, instead running a trembling hand over his face and stammering incoherently as he stepped away.

"I… I am sorry."

Georgiana stood immobile long after the reverberating thud of the slammed front door was gone. She raised her fingers to touch her swollen lips and ruddy cheeks, both of which tingled from his touch. She was shivering uncontrollably, breathless, her heart pounding a soaring rhythm in her ears. It was glorious! The single most incredible moment of her life!

Already she knew she was lost, addicted, and desperate for more of him. In that instant, she suddenly comprehended precisely why her brother and Lizzy were continually drawn to touch each other. She also finally understood what Mrs. Annesley had meant by her analogies of unquenchable fires burning within. Merely from the touch of his lips, an inferno raged through her insides, ignited unknown places, and infused her with life as never sensed before.

This fire was nothing close to the simmers felt when in the presence of Lord Caxton. Suddenly, every shred of doubt evaporated and her fate was utterly sealed. All from three simple words and one kiss.

"It was not a fever dream! He does love me!"

Slowly, a beaming smile spread over her face and a deep laugh erupted from her throat as she performed an uninhibited pirouette with her arms waving freely. Then, after three exuberant twirls she abruptly stopped. She saw the truth behind his absence over the past weeks, his withdrawn posture and cold indifference in sharp contrast to the warmth prior, his desperation and agony as he kissed her, and mostly his references to Lord Caxton. Suddenly, the scene from the ball flashed through her mind clearly as if an act in a play.

"Oh, Sebastian," she cried, dropping into a chair. "We are the biggest of fools, you and I!"

Her heart was freshly pounding but not from desire. That he was suffering with the false impression that she loved another caused all air to vacate her lungs. Panic rose within her chest. She had to talk to him… *now*! He had to know the truth of her feelings, so they could end this craziness.

She launched from the chair prepared to run the miles to his residence if need be. Damn propriety! But voices and laughter of the Matlocks and de Valdays entering the foyer halted her. The thought of Mr. Butler hurting for even another second was intolerable, but she must be sensible.

"Aunt Madeline will know how best to proceed," she whispered, the uncontainable smile breaking out again. "Be patient, my love. Soon I shall be yours."

❧

Like Lady Warrow, Lady Matlock was aware of the tangled web her niece and Mr. Butler had unconsciously woven, watching the unfolding drama as patiently as possible. A large part of it was speculation on her part, since Georgiana possessed many of the typical Darcy traits so expertly wielded by her brother. Deciphering the thoughts of one who so adequately hides them behind silent composure is a difficult task. On several occasions, Lady Matlock felt that Georgiana was close to divulging, only to have her taciturn nature exert itself. Questions were deflected, conversations were vague, and replies were noncommittal. Georgiana made light of the situation, but the spoken hints and observed actions were enough for Lady Matlock to know that her niece's heart was captured by the young musician, and Lady Matlock was convinced he was equally enthralled by Georgiana.

Georgiana's pyrexic mumblings confirmed Lady Matlock's suspicions. When confronted, Georgiana elaborated on their meaning to the sympathetic Lady Matlock, Lady Simone, and Mrs. Annesley, the full story thus revealed. Lady Matlock's advice was to seek the aid of Lady Warrow, judging that she could solve the puzzle of Mr. Butler. Georgiana balked at this; her natural timidity and insecurity regarding his feelings paralyzed her.

"I quail at the image of his rejection, Aunt. To hear my worst fears bluntly confirmed will devastate me! I cannot bear it, not now."

The older ladies accepted Georgiana's pleas for the present, her health precariously perched and not strong enough to handle that degree of shock. Georgiana did ask for guidance in how to handle Lord Caxton, however.

Lady Matlock was against her niece having such a conversation with her persistent weakness and lingering symptoms, but Georgiana insisted on dealing with that situation immediately. There truly was little choice since the worried gentleman visited the townhouse a dozen times a day! The Matlocks grudgingly agreed to Georgiana's demands, and there was no consolation in being proven correct when the stress endured did lead to a short relapse.

Georgiana's spirit improved with that drama no longer hanging over her head, but her physical health was slower to catch up, so it was judged best not to tell her of Lord Caxton's return two days later. Lady Matlock felt for the man's obvious anguish, but his belligerence when requests to see Georgiana were denied erased some of her pity. Richard had been incensed and close to calling the baron out, but Lord Matlock managed to restore peace long enough to evict the crazed baron, who clung to the belief that they had an agreement.

Despite the serious nature of Georgiana's influenza, the family speculated that her prolonged lassitude was not entirely physical. Upon returning from the exhibit it only took one glance at the incandescent glow upon her face and buoyant skip to her steps to confirm the theory.

"I cannot pinpoint the moment I knew I loved him," Georgiana softly answered her aunt's query. "My feelings of friendship evolved of their own volition, it appears. Nor do I have any idea when he recognized his love for me. It is a question I intend to ask, merely for my own curiosity," Georgiana declared with a gay laugh.

The ladies sat in the cozy salon of the de Valday townhouse drinking warm beverages and snacking on hastily supplied treats while Georgiana recounted the past months' interactions with Mr. Butler, culminating with the encounter in the music room.

"I was amazed when he kissed me," Georgiana went on, blushing furiously. "I pray you are not angry with him, Aunt. Mr. Butler is a gentleman in every way that counts, but is it not desirable to allow the soul free rein upon occasion? Music is about stirring the soul and passionate feelings. I delight in this and cannot fault Mr. Butler for expressing his emotions in an active manner."

"Absolutely not!" Yvette blurted. "It is so romantic!"

"Was his kiss divine?"

"I shall not answer that, Zoë," Georgiana gasped, but her expression and physical reaction to the remembered kiss gave her away, the twins laughing gleefully.

"We have been tremendously foolish, Aunt," Georgiana resumed once somewhat composed. "I have been certain Mr. Butler wished for no more than friendship and that his musical pathway too important to complicate with romance. I have no desire to interrupt his study and am determined to wait for him as long as necessary."

"Do not fret over that aspect of the situation, Georgiana. Honestly, I doubt if Mr. Butler would consider his music more important that you."

"I hope you are correct. Oh, but those concerns are not what bother me most!" She jumped up from her seat and began to pace. "It is what to do now! Yes, we have been foolish and probably deserve to suffer as a consequence of our stupidity if for no other reason than to never err so idiotically again. Nevertheless, I cannot bear that we remain apart a moment longer! What he must be thinking right now is too wretched to tolerate! Please, tell me what I should do?"

"It is a simple matter, my dear. Tomorrow we will call—"

"Tomorrow? How can I wait until tomorrow? I abhor the idea of his sadness continuing. I need"—she inhaled deeply, closing her eyes as she fought for serenity—"I need to see him and tell him… everything."

"You have no choice. It is nearly eleven o'clock, and to be honest, even if it were noontime I would suggest waiting so you can collect yourself."

"But—"

"Trust me in this, Georgiana." Lady Matlock clasped the agitated girl's hand and yanked her onto the cushioned ottoman. "Tomorrow, we will call upon Lady Warrow. I suspect the perceptive marchioness has suspicions of her own and will happily accommodate your need for a private audience with Mr. Butler."

Georgiana's smile burst forth at the vision conjured with that statement. Her body shivered, the remembered sensation of his lips upon hers assaulting her control. Desire mingled with anxiety and happiness with sadness.

Lady Matlock squeezed her hand tighter and leaned closer. "Breathe, Georgiana," she ordered softly. "Go to bed and rest. I promise that everything will be fine. Think only happy thoughts for an untroubled, revitalizing sleep. Tomorrow, we will focus on Mr. Butler and all will be well."

Chapter Sixteen

Crescendo

GEORGIANA WAS HUMMING AND had been all morning. Surprisingly, she had fallen asleep the night before as soon as her head settled into the pillow. A blissful, deep sleep replete with passionate dreams of the gorgeous blond Mr. Butler leaving her refreshed and smiling upon waking with the dawn. She had purposely left the drapes open, so that the first rays of sunlight filtering through the glass would wake her. Absurd as it was, Georgiana wanted the morning hours to prepare for what promised to be the happiest day of her life.

This is the day my life will begin. When Mr. Butler, my Sebastian, will know that I love him.

She basked in the joy of it, danced about the room, pressed her lips in remembrance of his kiss, and frequently released breathy sighs. Her mind replayed every moment they had spent together since meeting in the de Marcov reception line at Chateau la Rochebelin in Lyon three months prior. Scene after scene of artistic discussions, casual touches at the piano, laughter while partaking in innumerable activities, dances, creative heads bent over parchment music sheets, and so on, all rolled together into a moving montage. The memories rang with incredible lucidity, the power of her love energizing so that even with the future yet uncertain, she felt no fear. Recollections of his eyes upon her, the caress in his voice when he spoke to her, the fervency of his declared love for her, and the passion of his kiss were all the surety she needed.

By eight o'clock, she was at her vanity brushing her hair until it glistened and crackled.

"I shall wear the blue gown from the ball," she said to Mrs. Annesley. "I know it is vastly inappropriate for a daytime visitation but I remember how his face glowed when he saw me in it."

"I doubt it was the dress, Miss Georgiana."

"Hopefully it was not merely the dress!" she countered with a laugh. "Perhaps it is silly but I want to look my very best."

"You could wear rags and I doubt he would think differently, but the blue gown it will be."

Mrs. Annesley disappeared into the wardrobe to confer with Georgiana's maid. Georgiana resumed her susurrate humming and brushing while mentally rehearsing how she would approach him with proper phrases reflective of her heart until a knock at the door interrupted the pleasant reverie.

"This was delivered for you, mademoiselle," the maid stated, handing the folded missive to Georgiana and bobbing a curtsy.

Georgiana murmured her thanks and swung the door shut, absently unaware of anything but the familiar bold penmanship of Mr. Butler. Her heart lurched with a thunderous boom of joy before settling into an erratic tempo. *He should not be writing to me.* An awful foreboding washed over her and with trembling hands she ripped through the wax seal imprinted with the scripted *E* for the Essenton house.

Miss Darcy,

The irony of begging your forgiveness for my unpardonable behavior by compounding my sins in sending a letter unsolicited is not lost upon me, I assure you. But at this point, I have discarded every shred of decency, of knowing what is right and proper. I do beg for your forgiveness, not just for my beastly actions yesterday, but for everything I have done to hurt you. Yet, I know I do not deserve it and that you are justified not to grant me any mercy. I cannot explain my actions adequately. I have tried, dozens of times, but each page is balled upon the floor. Georgiana—please, allow me to address you informally just this once—I will not burden you further with my desires. I only wish you to know that I will eternally count our time together as the happiest of my life. My affection is and always will be real. My true prayer is for your happiness. Lord Caxton is a good man and will honor you, as you richly deserve.

Please try not to think ill of me. And do not fret that I shall disturb your tranquility. This morning I will be departing the city, so you will be free to enjoy your final weeks in Paris without interference.

Be well, my friend. Follow your dreams and do not ever cease exercising your inspired, incredible gift for music.

God bless, SB

Rather than crumbling from fear or simple lack of oxygen due to it being squeezed from her lungs, Georgiana was spurred into action. She whirled about and tossed the letter to Mrs. Annesley, who returned from the wardrobe in that instant and dropped the dress in her mad scramble to catch the fluttering piece of paper. Without breaking stride Georgiana dashed into the closet barking orders in an uncharacteristic harsh tone.

"Amanda, I need a carriage prepared, now! There is no time to waste."

Her dressing robe and nightgown fell to the floor. In her wild haste, she did not feel the bite from the cold on her bare skin and grabbed aimlessly for the first gown encountered. Fortunately, it was a thick woolen walking-dress, maroon with silver trim, long-sleeved and high collared. She threw it over her head, not bothering with a chemise or petticoat, haphazardly buttoning up the bodice. She rushed to the chest where she kept her stockings, extracting a random pair of cotton hose and lacy garters, and returned to the bedroom just as Mrs. Annesley finished reading the letter.

"Miss, I—"

"No matter, Amanda. Just call for a carriage. I must try to reach him before he leaves! Hurry!"

"Should we talk to Lady Matlock?"

Georgiana grasped onto Mrs. Annesley's arms. "I understand your concern, but I cannot waste the time and Aunt Madeline is still asleep. I am sure she would encourage me to stop him. I must stop him. If I am too late..." She shuddered and gasped, the pain in her chest increasing. "No. I will not lose him! Now go!"

Mrs. Annesley agreed with her companion's logic and need, even if propriety warned against such crazy action, so argued no further. "Very well, Miss Darcy. I shall call for the carriage. Get dressed and be sure to grab a warm cloak and boots."

It only took fifteen minutes for the coachman to hitch the cabriolet and bring it to the front door, but to Georgiana it felt like years. After a quick hug from Mrs. Annesley, she climbed hastily into the carriage, ordering the driver to travel as speedily as possible. Unfortunately, the shortest route to the stately manor where Lady Warrow resided with her grandson, although largely residential, also contained a portion that passed through a business district. The commercial streets of Paris, even early in the morning, were busy with traffic. Voices rang as drivers called friendly greetings or swore instructions, street vendors loudly hawked their wares, and servants cluttered the sidewalks in conversation and purchasing. Carts, carriages, and horses maneuvered along the wide, cobbled avenues, often precariously avoiding collisions. It was dangerous and fruitless to attempt speed.

Georgiana bounced on the seat, craned her neck out the open window as if determination alone would part the sea of bodies and vehicles, and flipped the lid on her pocket watch to assess the passage of time roughly every thirty seconds. She truly felt as if riding a snail might be faster, but in fact they were moving along at a steady clip. After what seemed like hours, Georgiana glimpsed the ivy-covered brick and iron wall that enclosed the first mansion edging the marketplace. It was distant, two blocks away yet, but her eyes fixed on the tree-shrouded barrier as a beacon drawing her nearer.

Sebastian lives less than half a mile beyond.

She glanced toward the muted sun where it attempted to shine through the cloudy sky. It was barely over the horizon, just reaching the cracks between the buildings. Surely he would not be gone yet!

She shivered, partly from nervousness and partly from cold. Spring rapidly approached with fairer days occurring, the temperature raising enough to fool some plants into releasing early buds and new growth, but Paris still remained primarily in the grips of winter. That day, it was overcast with threatening gray clouds thickly dotting the sky. A bitter wind blew from the north in sharp gusts, bringing the prickly tang of rain although it was dry as yet. People were bundled against the cold, heads wrapped with scarves and gloves protecting hands. Georgiana glanced to her own bare hands fisting in her lap atop the flannel cloak. Not the best attire for dreary weather and showers, but it was too late now.

A sudden powerful gust of wind blasted through the window and struck her square in the face. The biting cold slapped against her fair skin as a lash, stinging her eyes and searing her throat when she gasped in shock. At nearly the same moment, the carriage rocked violently and came to an abrupt stop, the jolt slamming Georgiana against the seat cushion. She heard the driver swear from his perch outside while the horses exclaimed protests of their own. He called to them, reasserting control before jumping from his seat—the carriage again swaying from the motion—his voice lifted in rapid French laced with curses to someone on the street.

Georgiana shook her head to rid it of the mild dizziness and exited the carriage in a panic. *We must keep moving!* Any disagreement with another driver was inconsequential as far as she was concerned. But her vexation and ready tongue-lashing turned to plunging despair at the sight that greeted her.

The blast of wind had slammed into a tented produce seller, the canvas acting as an umbrella, lifting and launching the entire structure into the air. Several vegetable- and fruit-laden tables had fallen over, scattering boxes and edibles across the road. Frightened, unbalanced shoppers had bumped into those tables fighting for stability, causing further damage as the tables lost the battle and caved, adding their goods to the general mess accumulating on the stone surface.

As she stood next to the carriage assessing the damage and helplessly watching the worsening drama unfold, two oxen-drawn carts slid in the sticky, wet debris and crashed into each other. The stubborn animals refused to budge, but it did not matter, as the drivers were too concerned with screaming at each other and pointing to the splintered wood and cracked wheels.

Passersby took advantage of the mayhem and flocked to the scene, gathering the produce that was now considered free for all. Of course, the vendor and his helpers did not concur with this attitude, with fights both verbal and physical breaking out.

Less than a minute had passed. Georgiana stood on the clear sidewalk examining the unsurpassable obstacle on the street and instantly came to a conclusion.

She lifted her skirts and ran.

Dimly, she heard the driver calling to her but she ignored him. Dodging in between dozens of milling people and leaping nimbly over scattered debris, Georgiana reached the brick wall and did not pause as she plunged onward. The silence of the slumbering avenue of homes was welcome after the commotion behind her. Now the sound of her heels striking the stones, her rapid breathing, and the rushing wind that was escalating in intensity assaulted her ears. Leaves swirled over the manicured lawns and immaculate street, the sight of multi-hued dances on air quite beautiful if she only had the time to enjoy it.

The chill blast stung her cheeks and whipped her hair into her eyes. Drizzling raindrops increased the discomfort, but she refused to acknowledge the pain. She rounded a corner, spied Mr. Butler's house at the end of the road, and ran faster. There was no activity visible on the street, no waiting carriage, and the drapes remained closed. Her heart constricted in uncertainty of whether the apparent serenity of the townhouse was a good sign or bad sign.

She reached the doorway, clutched the knocker, and rapped strongly in time to each gasping respiration.

God, where are they? Answer the door!

She wondered later if she actually did shout out loud, since an irritated voice urged the demanding visitor to be patient. Then finally, the door opened to reveal the housekeeper. Her French face was pinched indignantly, but melted into shock at the sight of a disheveled Miss Darcy wheezing on the doorstep.

"Mademoiselle Darcy!"

"Please," she panted, "I need to speak with Monsieur Butler. It is urgent. Can you inform him that I am here?"

"My apologies, Mademoiselle. Monsieur Butler is not at home."

Georgiana shook her head slowly. "No, please. You must be mistaken. Please, can you check for me? Please?"

"I am sorry, but his coach left an hour ago. Mademoiselle? Are you well? Pardon, how stupid of me! Please, come inside out of the cold. I shall announce you to the marchioness. Mademoiselle?"

But Georgiana was no longer listening. She stumbled backward down the steps with the housekeeper's pleas a faint humming devoid of substance. Her whole body was numb and her limbs heavy. Her eyes were wide but unseeing.

Tears pooled and glimmered upon her icy cheeks. Shivers wracked her body. The intermittent wind flipped her unbound hair and loose cloak crazily.

She felt none of it.

In a stupor, she slogged down the street, unaware of the direction and with no purpose in mind. Her dulled wits experienced no great surprise at finding herself a dozen houses away, on the narrow bridge spanning a tiny creek. She halted, frozen hands gripping the cold rocks forming the railing, and gazed into the sluggishly eddying water below. She knew this bridge, as they had passed over it several times. The street led from his house to other parts of the city, including the quaint park visible through the trees and edged by the shallow stream. They had walked there from his house just a half mile behind her, usually with friends but once alone, talking and laughing.

The memory brought fresh tears and a single sob escaped. So many hours and days, each of them burned into her consciousness with stark clarity and understanding. So many looks, his striking gray eyes tenderly caressing her and speaking of the emotion buried inside.

She was paralyzed. A small voice warned of the cold and encouraged her to return home to the wisdom of her aunt, where hope might be found. But she was detached, mesmerized by the currents in the black water, and temporarily lost to grief.

She did not feel the raindrops when they mingled with the tears running down her cheeks. She did not notice when her cloak blew open, falling from one shoulder to leave her upper chest exposed. She did not feel the cold seeping into her core, since it only joined the iciness already there.

She did not hear the clatter of horses' hooves or the rattle of wheels. She did not hear her name being called. She did not feel the first tentative touch upon her sleeve. It was not until the hand brushed the tangled strands of her hair away, warm fingertips covered with supple leather fleetingly stroking along her jaw, that she gasped. Or perhaps it was his breath, sweet and hot, and the frantic tremor in his tone as he spoke close to her ear that pierced through her shell. But she was forever certain that it was the rough pivot about, his grip tight with worry on her upper arms, combined by the dazzling beauty of his face fraught with anxiety that restored some of her coherency.

"Georgiana, what in blazes are you doing standing here? You have been ill and now you"—he swore, releasing her only long enough to tear the thick overcoat off his shoulders and throw it over hers. It was warm from the heat of his body, the aroma of spices and tobacco locked into the fabric assailing her nostrils. She closed her eyes and inhaled deeply.

He roughly grabbed her hands and shoved them into his flesh-heated and too large gloves, all the while muttering in a voice pitched low in fury and distress. "What are you thinking? Come. Let me get you inside the carriage. Your skin is like ice." He rubbed her cheek with the back of his bare hand, frowning deeply and not aware of the instant flush that arose at his touch. He threw one arm over her shoulder and drew her close to his side, steering her toward the vehicle while trying to button the voluminous coat one-handed, fumbling with the task and releasing several frustrated curses.

Giggles bubbled in Georgiana's chest, since she never heard him utter a profanity. She tried to talk or smile or laugh but her teeth were chattering so violently that the muscles would not obey. How he had found her, why he had returned and happened by, was a mystery. For the present, she was incurious, her mind captivated by the glory of his presence, her senses enthralled by the solid strength and heat of his body, and spirit content to bask in the glow of happiness warming her insides.

Numbly and with his assistance, her uncontrollable trembling and shivering worsening when he removed his arm from around her, she settled into the seat and submitted to his fussing over her.

Sebastian had not met her eyes since the harsh glare on the bridge, but she saw his furrowed brows and heard the stream of mumbled scolds as he busily arranged the coat snuggly around her and then reached into the space under the seat for several thick furs. He half-knelt, his tall body taking up the narrow space between the benches as he set about laying the blankets over her legs, tucking as he grumbled under his breath. Gradually, she noted the catch in his voice, the whimper within the words, the jerking motions in his normally graceful hands, and the harsh respirations that misted the minuscule space between them.

She was not aware that she had leaned forward until inches from his lowered head. Neither was he, until she spoke, and touched him.

"Sebastian."

He froze. Her voice was velvet, musical, sensual, and tender. For the first time in their acquaintance, she uttered his Christian name. She whispered it, intimately, precisely as he had imagined in his dreams, rolling it off her tongue as if having familiarly done so thousands of times. Her tiny fingers brushed over his right ear, burying into the windswept hair behind and playing casually.

"Sebastian, I cannot be your friend either. I will not merely be your friend because I too want so much more. I love you."

He lifted his head slowly. Wonder and shock played over his face. His eyes were liquid, sparkling with hope and astonishment. His hands had stilled on her blanket-draped ankles, his body tense with disbelief.

Long moments passed in silence. Georgiana smiled, continuing to run her fingers gently through the silky hair by his ear, and leaned closer until he could feel her breath tickling his face.

Their lips were less than an inch apart, eyes sliding closed in anticipation of the joy to come when the coach stopped with a jolt and the driver knocked on the roof to announce they were at the Warrow townhouse. The interruption was jarring. They pulled away, each noting the desire and irritation shining in the other's eyes. Sebastian smiled before remembering the state she was in, a frantic frown creasing his brow and setting his jaw.

Georgiana's trembling had increased, although she thought it was largely due to him rather than the cold. Nevertheless, she could not deny that she was freezing. The spits of rain had been enough to dampen her garments and hair, adding to the discomfort. Suddenly, the thought of a blazing fire and hot tea was very appealing.

Sebastian hopped lightly from the coach, turned to assist her clumsy efforts to discard the pile of blankets, and then lifted her into his arms. "We must warm you up. If you become ill again, I shall never forgive myself," he murmured, clutching her tightly against his chest and striding briskly into the house. She snuggled into his body, arms locked about his shoulders and face pressed into the silk cravat surrounding his neck. She smiled, inhaled the comforting scent of his cologne, and rejoiced in his protectiveness. Not for a second did she consider the inappropriateness of their proximity.

His voice rose into a commanding tone, "Madame Laroque, hot tea and coffee immediately. Food too. Monsieur Godenot, send a note to the de Valday house informing Lord and Lady Matlock that their niece is safe. Ah, Grandmother, good."

They entered the salon and Sebastian crossed to the unlit fireplace, carefully depositing Georgiana onto the cushions laid before the hearth. His reluctance to release her from his arms was obvious, the sensations so glorious as to be almost painful, but she needed a fire. Lady Warrow followed, wearing a dressing gown and a face creased with anxiety. Georgiana cringed, suddenly consumed with guilt.

"Oh, my dear girl! We were frantic with worry! You just disappeared, Madame Laroque said, walking in the rain and wind. Thank the Creator Sebastian happened along. I would never forgive myself if you came to any harm."

Georgiana wanted to apologize, shame crushing her, but fresh shudders were wracking her body and her teeth clattered so loudly she could not think. The void left without his warmth surrounding her was profoundly gaping and raw.

"Later, Grandmother. Please see to the orders I left, will you?"

He shared a look with the elderly woman. Lady Warrow nodded in understanding and a bright smile flashed over her face. She patted Georgiana on the shoulder, bending for a soft kiss to her cheek.

"Very well. I shall see to it. All will be well now, Miss Darcy, all will be well." And then she left, Georgiana certain that Lady Warrow's words of encouragement were not just referencing her immediate need for warming.

Sebastian removed his jacket and rolled the sleeves of his shirt to the elbows, setting to the task of lighting a fire and competently establishing a roaring blaze in no time at all. He knelt on the hearth less than a foot away, but said nothing as he worked, and his face was inscrutable. Once he was satisfied with the results, he turned toward her, hesitating and quickly glancing away from her adoring eye.

"Here, let me help you remove these," he whispered, moving closer and reaching unsteady fingers to unbutton his overcoat and the damp cloak. Pulling the latter from around her shoulders he paused again, frowning and cocking his head before beginning to laugh.

"What is it?"

"Did you have assistance dressing this morning, Miss Darcy? Or is my female fashion sense truly superior to yours?" He looked into her eyes then, mirth dancing in his eyes and crooked smile broad.

She tore her eyes away from his with effort to scan over her clothing, truly seeing what she had on.

"I think perhaps you do," she agreed with a laugh.

He tossed the thin garment of lavender to the side and then brushed his fingers along the unevenly hooked row of buttons on her maroon dress. He continued to chuckle, eyes twinkling with amusement.

"I was in a bit of a hurry. It is fortunate I thought to dress at all. I do think my shoes and stockings match." She lifted her skirt to check—they miraculously did—and missed the expression that crossed his face. "Your letter drove rational consideration from my mind," she finished with a catch, swallowing and looking at him with questioning eyes.

Sebastian's eyes, however, were trained on her silk-covered legs and even though he visibly winced at her words, he did not raise his eyes immediately. Instead, he slowly scanned upwards over every inch of the figure easily discernible beneath the damply clinging dress. While she watched, his expressive eyes paused at the gaps in her poorly buttoned gown that revealed small patches of the naked skin underneath, lingered over the unsupported fullness of her breasts, and studied the unbound golden hair that tumbled crazily over her shoulders and back.

Innocence did not prevent her comprehending the burning passion visible upon his face. She also recognized how the mixture of love and desire and guilt and nervousness flustered him. It was easy to recognize since she felt the same.

"You were leaving," she whispered to break the tension.

"To Vienna," he mumbled, answering automatically and dazedly meeting her eyes. "The Gesellschaft der Musikfreunde is offering a short session on Italian renaissance music, focusing on Palestrina."

"That sounds… amazing."

"I am sure it will be."

"Then you were not leaving just because of me?"

"Yes, I was leaving because of you," he answered truthfully in a tone half sober and half bemused, "but the educational program would prove enlightening as well as diverting. I needed to be diverted. It has been… painful. I would not have left otherwise."

"Then what brought you back?"

"Fate," he answered with a smile, "and the portfolio containing my concerto pieces that I forgot sitting on my bed. I was not thinking rationally today either."

Her eyes welled with tears. "I am sorry to have caused you pain or driven you away."

He shook his head, reaching to tuck a loose tress behind her ear and then capturing a long curl around his finger. "Do not apologize, Miss Darcy. It was my error and my choice. Under the circumstances, with... Caxton... it was what I needed to do. I caused far more grief by my actions than you have."

"Lord Caxton is no longer an issue." Her voice was vehement. "And my name is Georgiana."

He paused with his fingers lightly resting upon her hair and ear. "Georgiana," he repeated in a husky timbre that sped fresh shivers up her spine and reignited the tremors in her muscles. "You are still chilled," he said.

Before she could think of what to say to correct his misinterpretation, he rose onto his knees and reached over her body to retrieve a quilt from the sofa behind, his chest brushing her face in the process. The final threads of coherency fled with his proximity, heat radiating into her skin and masculine cologne drifting into her nostrils. She inhaled his scent, turned her cheek to press into his shoulder, and stifled a moan that in the next breath became a gasp when his resonant, musical voice vibrated through her.

"You meant what you said in the carriage?"

His voice was soft and awed. So were his hands as they draped the quilt about her, lingering and caressing her arms.

She blinked her eyes and shook her head in an effort to clear the dizziness. "Yes and no," she teased, smiling wider at the perplexity flashing over his face. Reaching one hand to stroke lightly over his jaw, she went on, "You are wrong, you know. We are friends and always will be. Wanting more, needing more, loving each other does not supplant the friendship we have. You will forever be my friend, Sebastian, my dearest friend in the entire world."

He traced one fingertip over her lips, voice husky when he spoke. "And will I be more?"

"As much as you wish. You already are, you know."

"I wish to be everything. Your friend, lover, husband, musical collaborator, muse." He smiled, natural humor mixing with the earnest timbre. He leaned close and cupped her face within his hands. "Will you allow me the honor of being everything to you? Will you marry me, Georgiana Darcy?"

"Yes," she responded, but the word was lost against his lips.

Oh God, such a kiss!

Fire blazed instantly, eradicating the residuals of chill even to the marrow of her bones. It was passionate and hungry, longing and fervency ruling completely in those dizzying initial minutes. In less than a heartbeat, their arms were locked about the other and she was willingly drawn onto his lap until their bodies were pressed together.

Instinct consumed. Potent love and yearning took over. The kiss was driven by mutual desire with the awareness of their surroundings or propriety vanishing. Life depended on their connection, the need to erase the anguish of the past weeks as vital as breathing. Passion and a generous allotment of lust spurred their actions, but primarily it was the beauty in having barriers broken and their love expressed that intoxicated them both.

The wickedly grinning Marchioness of Warrow waved the tray-wielding maid away, gingerly closed the salon door behind her, and leaned against it. For several minutes, she deliberated her next move. Her inclination was to lock the door and instruct every servant in the house to go about their business and forget that two people were alone inside. From what she had briefly observed, it was doubtful Miss Darcy's health was any longer an issue! Her grandson was doing an admirable job in heating the young woman, and the natural conclusion to their activity was sure to cure any ills besetting her, as the marchioness well knew.

Personally, she had no qualms with breaking rules of morality that said lovemaking should only be within marriage. Unfortunately, most folks did not agree with her liberal attitude. As bursting with happiness as she was for the young couple who had obviously resolved their stupid misconceptions, she knew that no matter how great the pleasure attained if left undisturbed, they would regret it later.

So, after waiting for a span of time deemed long enough to allow certain liberties without crossing irreversible barriers, she cleared her throat, lifted her voice with fabricated instructions, and generally caused a racket the entwined lovers surely could not ignore. She would always assume that her interruption kept the couple undefiled and pure, but she was wrong.

The astounding kiss gradually slowed after the initial furious burst of passion. The glory of this unique intimacy was sustained in stages, growing softer, their lips caressing and exchanging gentle pressure. The wonder of breath on sensitized skin, the thrill of brushing noses together, the tenderness of kissing facial features, and the sweetness of inhaling the natural scent of skin were marvelous exercises.

The moderating in their pace was not due to a declining need or conscious thoughts of propriety, but rather a burning ache to touch tenderly and share the wonder of their emotions.

"I have admittedly been quite dense of late," Sebastian whispered, pausing to bestow a tiny kiss to her lower lip, "and I do not wish to leap to conclusions, but I assume you are saying yes to my proposal?"

"I said yes but think it was lost against your mouth."

"You may lose any words against my mouth whenever you wish, dearest Georgiana."

He felt her cheek flush against his cheek and delighted in the sensation but longed to see the becoming blush. Opening his eyes and withdrawing mere inches, he was overcome by the waves of emotion that poured over him at the sight of her radiant, passion-filled face.

"My God, you are so beautiful, Georgiana! I cannot believe my fortune! Is it true? You said yes? You are mine? You love me?"

"I love you. Yes, again and again, yes! I am yours and you, Sebastian Butler, are mine. Do not forget that part of the bargain."

"No, I shall certainly not forget." He smoothed the snarled hair, embedding his fingers into the tangled tresses. "Promise me something else?"

"Anything."

"Never call me 'Mr. Butler' unless you absolutely must. My Christian name, as you speak it, fills me with surpassing joy. I shall never tire…"

He stopped, looked toward the door, and then erupted in chuckles. "I believe my grandmother is alerting us. Do not blush, dearest Georgiana. She highly approves of you and has been trying to tell me for weeks that I was blind and a fool. Whoever said the elderly do not understand the young? Frankly, I am surprised she has not locked the door and left us to our own devices. My grandmother has a flagrant disregard for proper behavior and forgets, at times, that true gentlemen and ladies exist. A kiss and embrace, no matter how passionate, will barely register as worthy of notice to her and expressing our affection is nothing to cause embarrassment. That, of course, is excellent, since I intend to frequently kiss and embrace you, my love, as often as feasible. If you do not mind, that is?"

Georgiana shook her head, laughter bubbling. All through his speech, he had been gently removing her from his lap, settling her back onto the cushions, straightening her skirts, and replacing the fallen quilt over her shoulders. His hands, so deft and artistically adroit, lingered and caressed firmly while spreading fresh shivers through her body.

"Are you still cold?" he asked with a frown, fingering the rapidly drying fabric of her dress.

Her blush deepened but she met his eyes and smiled, cocking her head in amusement. "You are being blind again, Sebastian."

He knit his brow, confusion lasting for several heartbeats before comprehension dawned. Then the smile that blazed anew was dazzling—and slightly smug—conjuring a fresh web of magic around them that was seconds away from sending them spiraling into another interlude of passionate kisses. But the door opened, shattering the spell along with the entry of Lady Warrow and two maids bearing trays of food and warm beverages.

Sebastian rose smoothly to his feet and bent to clear a spot on the low table.

"Refreshments!" Lady Warrow sang. "Nothing like warm liquids and sweet pastries to drive away a chill, although it looks like my grandson's efforts have warmed you up nicely, Miss Darcy. You look positively flushed! Very proficient in laying a fire, is he not? And the quilt was a wise move. We must not allow you to relapse, my dear girl. Yes, Stella, pour Miss Darcy a hot cup of tea, lots of sugar and lemon. These rolls are my absolute favorites, as they are thick with honey and plump raisins. The perfect remedy to all ailments."

She prattled on innocently, seemingly unaware of heightened color to cheeks, ruddy lips, and glazed eyes. The idea of the Marchioness of Warrow knowing of their recent improper conduct was embarrassing for Georgiana, no matter Sebastian's assurance that the older woman would relish the behavior, so she was calmed by the older woman's apparent ignorance.

Sebastian was not fooled in the least, knowing his grandmother very well, but he said nothing. The quizzing would come later, and he was fine with that, having no desire to hide his happiness, but for the present he would remain as serene as he could manage. It was best to let Georgiana recuperate and take the lead in announcing their understanding.

"Thank you, my lady. I do indeed feel much better and am plenty warm. I confess to being famished, however, having ran from the house prior to breakfast," Georgiana said, and then flushed and ducked her head to take a sip of tea before glancing to Sebastian, who looked slightly pained.

Lady Warrow laughed gaily. "Oh, to be so young and impulsive again! Youth allots for such whimsies, Miss Darcy. Sebastian remains distressed, I can see, but vigorous constitutions are made for recklessness and overindulgences. Live, I say, while one can!"

"Miss Darcy has been ill, Grandmother. There is reason to fret."

"Indeed, but look at her now. Why, she is glowing! The picture of health and happiness!"

Sebastian did look at her, and she looked back. His smile softened, the worry fading in light of her obvious radiance and profuse joy.

The diminutive marchioness sat on the sofa behind Georgiana, arranging her frilly dressing gown and appearing every inch the aristocrat she was even in bedroom attire. Serving herself some tea with four spoons of sugar, she continued in her breathy voice, "I, of course, am vastly experienced in foolhardy behavior. The frivolities of my juvenescence are the stuff of legends! As time passes, my dear, I shall entertain you with my youthful exploits."

"Youthful? Did I not just one month ago have to save you from the claws of Duc de Fallais's mistress who did not appreciate your brazen flirting with her *amour*?" As always when speaking to his grandmother, Sebastian's tone was tender and imbued with amusement.

Lady Warrow snorted indelicately, waving a hand breezily. "Competition is a good thing. Young upstarts such as Mademoiselle Ablis need to be reminded of the lure of expertise to the male population." Her mouth was prim as she sipped her tea, but the twinkle in her eye and saucy wink toward Georgiana left no question as to the "expertise" she referred to. And, despite the logic to the contrary, Georgiana had no doubt that Lady Warrow's aura of lush sensuality and zeal, along with a voluptuous body and stunning beauty that defied the aging process, meant she could likely make good on her threat to lure.

"The point is," the marchioness continued, "audacious recklessness is healthy for the soul, keeps one alive, and provides the best tales to tell the grandchildren. Sebastian pretends to find me outrageous, but he loves my stories."

"I have been taught it is polite to pacify one's elders, a duty to bear as a gentleman and selfless kinsman."

"See how he delights in teasing me? Ungrateful child!" she declared with theatrical suffering. "Years of professed mortification, yet now he creates dramas of his own! Manfully enduring romantic torment, running hither and yon, rescuing the fair maiden from inferior suitors, and bursting through the door with a fainting damsel in his arms. Where did he learn such colorful escapades if not from me?"

"I read books," he answered dryly.

"You two have a story to tell, I daresay. Of course, it is none of this old woman's business. Probably too ancient to remember such blazing emotions," she said sighing dramatically and ignoring Sebastian's sniff. "I may die at any moment and never hear the end of the tale."

"Old, ha! You shall be dancing rings around me at my own wedding, Grandmother. I am sure of it."

"And when might you be having a wedding?" Her brows rose in a precise imitation of guileless questioning, but Sebastian merely chuckled and shook his head.

"Lady Warrow," Georgiana spoke, her voice dulcet and hesitant, "there is a story, as you surmise. Not always happy but replete with angst, drama, and foolishness. I fear I have behaved badly and caused your grandson a great deal of grief."

"No, Georgiana, please do not take it upon yourself!" Sebastian protested.

"But I must." She turned to the marchioness, leaning toward where she regally sat and impulsive clasping on to her tiny hands. "I know how dear Mr. Butler is to you, and thus must beg your forgiveness and understanding. Please believe that it was innocently wrought and that I now intend to do all in my power to reverse the damage."

Lady Warrow chuckled, shaking her head. "Oh, my dear child. Have you not been listening? What is life or love without some heartache and sensationalism attached? Makes a dreary existence far more agreeable and appreciated. I would worry more if you two did not have an intriguing, suspenseful tale to tell! How bland would that be?"

"Well, I suppose we shall not disappoint then. I am not sure about being sensational, but there has been a fair portion of suspense. Fortunately, like all good stories, it has a happy ending." She paused, extending one hand to Sebastian, who instantly clasped it tightly.

"Grandmother, Miss Darcy has confirmed the reciprocation of my love and has agreed to become my wife."

"Well, about time! I was beginning to believe Lady Matlock and I would need to bash your heads together to restore some sense." Lady Warrow laughed happily, tugging Georgiana up onto the cushioned seat next to her. "I am thrilled for you both. I knew you were perfect for each other from the start! You could not do better than my grandson, and I am pleased to see you finally realized that, my dear. However, Sebastian is the luckiest of men to have found you."

"Be sure, I am abundantly aware of the fact, Grandmother. My great fortune is immense, and I know I am receiving the higher prize within this arrangement."

"I disagree most vehemently!" Georgiana declared with a laugh. "It is I who have been rewarded supremely."

"Very good," Lady Warrow interrupted with a sage nod. "Always best to start a relationship with an argument. Maintains the spice and equality. Now, Georgiana, do not forget that I am quite excellent at planning weddings. I am a close, personal friend of the Archbishop of Canterbury, so a special license would be no problem. Any cathedral in the country can be arranged if you wish."

"Grandmother, please! We have been betrothed less than an hour, and even that is precarious until I speak with Miss Darcy's guardian and then Mr. Darcy. We have yet to discuss our wishes or even think of wedding details!"

"Oh, Sebastian! How many sisters do you have? Have you not learned that young ladies begin planning their weddings from the schoolroom?"

A knock at the door halted Sebastian's retort. Lady Warrow continued to chuckle, Georgiana smiling at Sebastian but shaking her head slightly in the negative.

"Miss Darcy's carriage has arrived, milady," the butler announced with a bow.

"Yes, you should return home, my dear. You need to bathe and dress properly, and I know Lady Matlock must be beside herself with worry. Oh, do not frown. We have an afternoon date already arranged, if you recall. So you shall be back in no time at all. I am quite sure I can persuade my grandson to dine with the women."

The butler then turned to Sebastian. "Pardon me, sir, but Hendricks was requesting instructions as to what to do with your packed bags?"

"Return them to my room, but tell him not to bother unpacking since we will be leaving soon enough."

Georgiana gasped and jerked, ice crushing her heart to a stuttering stop.

Tears stung the wide eyes fixated upon his startled face, and her voice rose to a hysterical pitch. "You are leaving after all? Why? I thought we…?"

She stuttered to a halt, bit her lower lip, and closed her eyes against the sudden panic. Unreasonably, she felt a horrible cloud of doom descend. Maybe the whole morning was a dream? The alarm grew, her heart pounding, even as a rational voice told her she had no right to upset his education.

The agony lasted a mere half dozen racing heartbeats before he was there with hands firm under her elbows. He drew her to her feet.

Neither heard Lady Warrow exit the room.

"Georgiana—" he began.

"Forgive me," she interrupted, voice anguished and face grief-stricken. "I should not expect you to stop… Your studies are very important, I know, and a chance to study Palestrina in Vienna is incredible. You were planning to spend the summer there as it is, I remember, so…"

He lifted her chin, halting her declarations with a brief, firm kiss. He pulled away infinitesimally, cupping one cheek in his hand and drawing her closer with the other about her waist. He smiled, infusing the gesture with the full force of his love. "You are a silly girl, Miss Darcy, if you think for one second I would leave you now. As appealing as Vienna and Palestrina may be, neither is as appealing as you! I was only going to escape and now I have no reason to escape, to my everlasting joy."

He engaged her lips for another long kiss, saying more in the following minutes than in hours of conversation. Finally, though, he did release her to explain. "My reference to leaving soon relates to my accompanying you to England when you depart. After all, I believe I have a vital appointment with your brother, do I not?"

"I do not wish to encroach upon your purpose."

"My purpose was radically arrogated the moment I laid eyes upon you, Georgiana, even if I was unaware at the time. Our fates are entangled now. The specifics can be discussed later, but I am not worried as long as you are by my side."

Her relief was audible, a long sigh followed by a droop against his body. Sebastian did not argue, taking advantage and embracing her gently against his chest, his face embedded in her fire-warmed hair. He whispered into the disheveled tresses covering her crown, "You are my purpose now, Georgiana. You have accepted my proposal and I do not intend to allow you to renege!"

Georgiana tightened her grip about his waist and shook her head against his shoulder. "And to further clarify, nothing is more important than you, and you have every right to expect my loyalty and devotion. Not that you have anything to worry about, as I aim to smother you with love until you beg me to desist in order to preserve your sanity."

Georgiana mumbled into his chest, "No chance of that."

"How happy am I to hear it."

She looked upward into his face. "I apologize for my reaction. It is silly of me, but I think I am having some difficulty believing I am no longer caught up in a fever dream."

"Does this feel like a dream?" He bent his head for a kiss, a firm but short one that nevertheless left her smiling and flushed.

"Yes, it does feel like a dream, but real at the same time. Like yesterday when everything became clear." Sebastian smiled at her words and brushed light fingertips over her lips. "I was anguished at your misconceptions regarding my sentiments," she whispered against his fingers. "I empathized and was distraught. I wanted to rush over instantly but Lady Matlock cautioned waiting until today. I had it planned. I would hunt you down, in your own house if necessary, and force you to listen to me. I practiced being brave and bold. I wanted to wear the blue dress from the ball now that I knew your reaction to seeing me in it was not a dream."

"It was not the dress," he told her huskily.

"Be that as it may, I planned to be stunning and irresistible, not windblown and mismatched."

"You are beyond stunning and wildly irresistible." He scanned slowly over her body. His pale-gray eyes had darkened to stormy slate when they returned to her face.

"Thank you," she whispered. "Sebastian, I practiced boldness and honesty. Part of that is telling you that I spoke with Lord Caxton days ago and informed him finally and firmly that I did not love him and could not in good faith or decency continue on with our acquaintance or accept his advances."

"I can imagine he did not accept this news with ease." Sebastian was unconscious of how he reflexively squeezed her waist, but Georgiana bore it. "It cannot be easy to have the person you plan to… marry"—he swallowed, his grip tightening more—"tell you that she has changed her mind."

"I do not... What do you...?"

"Georgiana, I need to know. Forgive me, but I must hear that your heart is completely mine and not partially, even in the smallest particle, still belonging to him."

"No! Not at all!"

"Understand that I am not going to let you go, Miss Darcy. I will fight for you to my dying breath, but I will wait and woo you as I should have in the first place, if that is necessary to erase any residual feelings you have for him." His voice had risen and he was now grasping her elbows in each hand and staring into her startled eyes with a return expression bordering on frantic.

"My feelings for the baron were never more than infatuation and respect and fondness, Sebastian. My heart has belonged to you since Lyon, I now know. You must believe me!"

"But he told me... Did you or did you not have an understanding with him?"

She watched his eyes change from frantic to surprised to confused to angry in the space of three sentences. Her own emotions underwent a similar flow. "I never had an understanding of any kind with Lord Caxton. He wished for one and asked to court me, and presumed more than was granted I came to realize, but I never said more than that I would consider the idea."

"He lied to me." Sebastian released her, walking away a few steps before turning back to face her. "I thought... well, he convinced me that you and he were... He lied to me."

Silence fell. It was Georgiana who broke into their thoughts, speaking calmly. "I see we have much yet to clarify. Our mutual misconceptions run deep, apparently. Are you disappointed with me or angry?"

"I am angry with myself for being such a blind fool, dearest Georgiana. And I am quite angry with Caxton! But I am not angry with you, or disappointed." He crossed back to her, cupping her face between his hands. "You said you loved me since Lyon?" She nodded. "I have loved you since the moment you knew who Moscheles is. We are a pair of like souls, Miss Georgiana Darcy. Passion for music binds us."

"I feared your passion for music too great to allot space for me and that your gift would suffer if distracted by romantic entanglements. I never wanted to disrupt your education."

"Yet during your plotting to hunt me down and force me to listen, you no longer held any consideration about disrupting my education?" He laughed lowly and gently tweaked her nose.

"I confess I did not."

"Because you trusted that my choice would be you. That we are fated, yes?"

"Yes," she whispered. "I knew that you loved me, which I did not know before. Furthermore, after last night I thought only of being in your arms and tasting your kiss again. Does that shock you?"

"Not in the least." His voice was nearly inaudible, rough and clipped, his lips hovering a hairbreadth from her mouth. "I am happy to oblige, but before I do, I am required to remind you that you, Miss Darcy, have already been granted a place in the Conservatoire. My education will not be disrupted in the least but will, in fact, be enhanced with my personal muse learning along with me as Viscountess Nell. And before you recover your voice, I am going to grant your wish and kiss you."

This he did for a good long while. The repossession of sanity and decorum was sluggish. Even as the frenzied kiss subsided, they remained glued to each other, breathing erratic and hearts palpitating.

"Georgiana, my beautiful Georgiana. I hate the very idea, but I must send you home. As desirable as you are in your current state, and perhaps in part due to how fervidly I desire you right now, you need to change out of this inappropriate garment. We shall have plenty of time, all of our lives, to discuss these past weeks, if we even choose to. I abhor leaving the sanctuary of your arms, but you need to get home to a hot bath and fresh clothes. I need to prepare myself for an appeal to Lord Matlock and Colonel Fitzwilliam."

Sebastian bundled her in his thick overcoat. "Another reason for you to return in a few hours," he offered with a crooked grin. He guided her to the waiting carriage, halting first in the foyer so she could express her thanks to a clearly euphoric Lady Warrow.

He stood on the step and settled her on the seat, tucking quilt edges about her legs. Georgiana leaned forward, clasping his hand.

"I will see you for tea. Two o'clock precisely, no later."

"Yes, madam. As you wish." His voice dropped lower, eyes penetrating. "Say it again, Georgiana."

She ruffled the hair by his ears, eyes equally penetrating. "I love you, Sebastian Butler."

His smile was brilliant. He kissed each palm and then the wrists, squeezing firmly. "And I love you, Georgiana. Forever."

Codetta

June 1820

"LADIES AND GENTLEMEN, IT is my honor and privilege to formally present to the assembly, for the first time of a multitude to come, Viscount and Viscountess Nell!"

The Earl of Essenton swept his arm high in the air and stepped aside as the double doors were simultaneously pulled open by two livery garbed footmen. Nearly two hundred people bowed and curtsied in unison, those proper genuflections quickly followed by cheers and applause. Sebastian and Georgiana Butler walked through the gaping doors attempting to maintain a pose of stately decorum but failing miserably.

How could they not smile ridiculously and walk with jaunty steps?

This was their wedding day!

Of course, Sebastian and Georgiana had been beaming and treading on air ever since that rainy April day in Paris. They glowed and laughed during the journey back to England, ceasing their perpetual giddiness only because they were forced to separate. Georgiana diverted to Hertfordshire to meet her family and attend the wedding of Kitty Bennet to Major General Randall Artois. Sebastian parted from the woman he loved reluctantly and would not have delayed the required formalities with Mr. Darcy except that he deemed it wise to speak with his father first.

Lord Essenton, to put it mildly, was less than pleased with his son. The earl had fumed and lectured for hours over the Lady Cassandra incident; she was already married to Lord Everest. Sebastian wisely opted to remain mum while his father released his pent up anger. Once that was out of his system—Sebastian granting him two days to punish with silent scowls directed at his son—Sebastian requested an audience with his father and delivered his prepared speech culminating with his betrothal to Miss Darcy.

He tried to gloss over the fact that, at least to his way of thinking, the engagement was not official until Mr. Darcy agreed. Colonel Fitzwilliam and Lord Matlock had given their approval and this was technically adequate since the former was Miss Darcy's legal guardian equally with Mr. Darcy and the latter was granted guardian status when Miss Darcy was left in his care while in Europe. Sebastian was respectful to the rules enough so as to need Mr. Darcy's blessing, but not so old fashioned as to claim certain rights of the betrothed, that primarily being the honor of stealing the occasional kiss. Ships provide excellent dark cubbies to hide in for lengthy kisses, the voyage across the Channel exhilarating for the young couple!

Lord Essenton, however, latched on to the minor point as a major loop-hole in the agreement, tossed every available titled lady into Sebastian's face, and recited dowry amounts as if reading from a ledger. Eventually, sheer will-power and the figurative beating down of the earl's stamina when Sebastian refused to budge won the day. At least Sebastian liked to think his strength of conviction and backbone in the face of a vigorous assault swayed his father and that it was not the size of Miss Darcy's dowry—that having increased dramatically with additions from Lord Matlock, Colonel Fitzwilliam, and Dr. George Darcy.

Whatever the case, by the time the entire family met at Pemberley in June, Lord Essenton was as polite and warm as he could manage. Miss Darcy was accepted, and although Sebastian knew his father would never admit that he was charmed by her and impressed by Mr. Darcy and Pemberley, it was obvious to Sebastian.

Confronting the reputedly formidable Mr. Darcy was a walk in the park after Lord Essenton, but Sebastian was a nervous wreck nonetheless. His greatest concern was not whether Mr. Darcy would permit Sebastian's request to marry Miss Darcy, but rather how he would receive the news that his sister was accepted as a student at the Conservatoire in Paris. To his surprise and relief, Mr. Darcy was overjoyed and swollen with pride at the idea. On top of that, Mr. Darcy was pleased with Sebastian as Georgiana's chosen man. In fact, he was ecstatic! Everyone on Georgiana's side of the family was ecstatic and with the exception of his father—who was rarely ecstatic about anything—Sebastian's family felt the same way.

With the final formality attended to, all that was left was to plan the wedding!

The combined forces of Lady Essenton, Lady Warrow, Lady Matlock, Lady Simone Fitzwilliam, and Mrs. Fitzwilliam Darcy set to the task with vigor. At times, Georgiana felt superfluous, and in the face of such extreme enthusiasm, she struggled to exert her wishes or thoughts. All in all, however, the wedding plans proceeded as Georgiana and Sebastian desired.

The noontime ceremony was held at St. Giles-in-the-Fields in the London Borough of Camden, an elegant yet modest church that fit Sebastian and Georgiana's preference for an intimate wedding. The Essenton family worshiped at St. Giles-in-the-Fields upon occasion, but Sebastian especially loved the church's pipe organ and the moment Georgiana laid eyes on the instrument and heard the organist play, she agreed this was the sanctuary for them to be joined in holy matrimony.

Due to the numerous close, personal friends of the Marchioness of Warrow the choices for where to hold the wedding dinner and soiree were myriad. Yet as soon as the estate of the Earl of Mansfield was mentioned, Sebastian and Georgiana gasped, no other options then considered.

Perched on a high ridge overlooking the lake and lush grounds of Hampstead Heath, Kenwood House, the white brick, Ionic columned neoclassic villa belonging to Lord Mansfield of Scotland boasted a sloping garden of extraordinary beauty. It was onto the cultivated lawn that the newly married Viscount and Viscountess stepped, arm in arm exiting the flower-encircled, glass-paned doors of the orangery to greet their friends and family.

The celebrating continued long after Sebastian and Georgiana waved adieu from the white-ribbon- and flower-adorned carriage; their departure, timed as the setting sun cast a ruddy glow across the landscape, was lavished with high fanfare and well wishes shouted until they disappeared from view. For several minutes, the newlyweds dreamily stared at each other while relishing the quiet, serene atmosphere of the enclosed coach. Neither could say they were exhausted, but it had been an eventful day with constant bustling since dawn, so it did feel wonderful to relax and breathe.

Sebastian moved first by lifting Georgiana's hand to tenderly plant an abundance of kisses starting with the finger adorned with three gold rings. With his other arm he encircled her shoulders and drew her body closer to his side.

"Was your day everything you have ever dreamed of, my lady?"

"More, my lord. I do not believe my imagination is vivid enough to dream a day as perfect as today was."

"And it is not over," he whispered into her ear, his lips gently caressing the sensitive region.

Georgiana instantly reacted with a gasping sigh and limp droop into his arms, her brain buzzing pleasantly and vocal cords only able to emit a weak murmur. "The song you played was… indescribable. I am not sure I thanked you adequately or conveyed how deeply it touched me. I will treasure the memory and composition forever, Sebastian."

"As I will your song to me." He pulled away from her neck, smiling into her eyes. "You realize, do you not, that our surprise gifts to each other was our first performance together?"

"No, I actually had not thought of it that way! And we received our first encore request!"

"Indeed we did. Your choice of Psalm sixty-three was excellent other than the fact that I grew misty-eyed and struggled to contain my professional composure. That psalm will forever belong to you, dearest wife."

"I think we should have all three printed and framed for posterity sake."

"Marvelous idea! Ah, Georgiana, I love you so! I am the happiest man in the world and this day has been the finest in my life."

"And it is not over," she repeated his previous phrase, blushing at the implications of that sentence even while her heart began to pound.

"No, it is not over by a long shot," he replied, the hand stroking over her jaw and cheek holding her fast as he bent to deliver a searing kiss.

It was not the first intense kiss they had shared, not even the tenth or twentieth for that matter. This particular kiss would end when they reached the palatial townhouse of Lady Warrow, where they were to spend their wedding night, but the promise of greater fulfillment of the surging desire that they had carefully bottled for months would soon be attained, adding a dimension to this kiss that was breathtakingly beautiful while also slightly overwhelming.

Georgiana broke the kiss, Sebastian simply traveling on to other parts of her face before resuming his oral investigation of her neck and shoulders. His boldness and tactics were new, rendering Georgiana breathless and dazed. She felt an uncontrollable urge to rip into the clothes keeping her from his body, an urge dizzying in how it exhilarated and frightened her.

"What were you and Lord de Marcov in deep discussion about that had you flushed?" she blurted, not even sure where the question came from but needing to say something to restore her scattered wits.

He chuckled against the skin at her collarbone and shook his head. "I am positive I cannot repeat most of it to a lady. Let's just say he was offering me wedding night advice."

"Oh."

"Adrien has only been married a short while, but his knowledge of what constitutes a successful wedding night is vast."

"He was telling you… specifics?"

Sebastian looked at her shocked expression, his face amused. "Some specifics, yes. Being French means de Marcov is not as inhibited as I. He loves to harass me, if you have not noticed. Good-naturedly, of course, but since his experience does trump mine when it comes to this topic, I figure it is good to listen. Within reason."

"What did he say?"

"Mostly things designed to fluster me rather than assist, hence why I was flushed. But he did remind me that a new bride is to be handled with tenderness and selfless focus to her needs, but that in the morning she is to look 'properly ravished' as he puts it. I rather like that term and shall do my utmost to ensure the reality."

Georgiana had no response, other than to blush to her toes. The images such a phrase conjured increased her palpitations and shortness of breath.

"Trust me, dearest wife," he spoke softly, "my urgency to make love with you will not overrule my senses. You have nothing to fear or be nervous about. I promise tonight will be as wonderful as today and as fulfilling to whatever dreams you may have."

She remained rosy and trembling, but smiled at the sincerity on his face.

"I trust you and never could fear what we have together," she assured, both of them remembering every kiss and embrace they had enjoyed since the combustible exchange when he proposed before the fire in Paris.

"Indeed, I believe we have proven the ardent nature of our connection." He stroked the back of his hand down the slope of her neck and brushed across her décolletage, Georgiana sighing and pushing her chest against his hand without conscious thought. Sebastian grinned and chuckled with satisfaction. "Yes, we shall be marvelous together, Georgiana. Nevertheless, I did choose to spend tonight at my grandmother's house rather than the Essenton townhouse in Kensington so we would be alone. Since I was young, I tended to stay there when in London without the rest of my family for a reason I am sure you will appreciate."

After that cryptic remark he bent to kiss her, within seconds Georgiana weak and heated so that she welcomed the carriage stopping at Lady Warrow's house so she could breathe the fresh air of the evening.

Other than the butler, who greeted them with minimal fuss, they saw no other servants. Lady Warrow planned to stay at Kenwood House for the next several days, allowing the "young lovers to have their way without interference" as she told Sebastian. She went on to covertly hint of the best places within the house for secret trysts! When she reached the point of describing one bedroom with a cushioned chaise possessing a nice springiness and situated in the room so as to view the sky while "engaged in the act of love," Sebastian choked and with a strangled *thanks, Grandmother* dashed from the room! Of course, later he had sought out the chamber and chaise she mentioned, just in case.

Arm in arm, Sebastian led up the stairs and down the passageway, his voice light and relaxed, putting Georgiana at ease. Pausing at the end of the corridor, he turned toward her and clasped her hands between his, placing them against his heart.

"This door leads to your dressing room where your maid is waiting to assist you. I shall be in the room beyond, probably pacing anxiously for you to return to me," he said as he laughed, kissing her hands. "Seriously, take as much time as you need, my love. I only have one request."

"That is?"

"I have a fantasy. Well, I have several fantasies, but one is to release your hair myself. Will you leave it up for me?"

"Here I thought you were going to ask something difficult," she teased.

"Thank you. Now I will let you go, as painful as it is, the sooner to have you back with me. Take your time but hurry."

A half hour later Georgiana heard music. Piano music. Her fingers stilled at her neck, the rose-scented perfume soaking into her skin and smile spreading over her face. Suddenly, she was in a rush to complete her toilette and join her husband, excitement warming her belly and driving away the jitters.

"Just pin it loosely," she instructed her maid, "so it will be easy to let down. Use these clips here." She handed a trio of combs prettily decorated with an array of colorful flowers and gems, the wide accessories adequate to hold her thick tresses temporarily. Satisfied with that, she excused her maid, waiting until alone to examine herself one last time in the mirror.

With Lizzy's assistance, she had an extensive trousseau fit for a new bride. Lacy undergarments and gauzy gowns galore! Each garment was exquisite, this one blue silk with gathers and ruffles and trimmings designed to draw attention to her figure while covering little of it. The sheer robe provided infinitesimal assistance in concealment but enough to provide a particle of modesty. Yet despite the flush to her cheeks, Georgiana did tarry a moment longer to perkily adjust her breasts inside the bodice and slip the neckline an iota lower.

Sebastian had barely begun the second piece when she opened the door to view the comforting scene. The bedchamber was enormous, richly decorated in ivory, gold, and pale greens. It was dominated by a massive bed of ash, the mauve and gold counterpane folded neatly at the foot of the thick mattress, white sheets and plump pillows inviting. Candles burned, their numbers adequate to dispel most of the shadows and accent the golden highlights in her husband's blond hair.

He sat on the bench of a beautiful pianoforte with his back to the threshold where she stood watching him play. The song was one of the compositions they had worked on together, from start to finish, a lively tune written in one after-noon while they were in a silly mood more intent on laughing than composing anything earth-shattering. His hands moved over the keys fluidly, his body relaxed and swaying with the rhythm. Georgiana marveled, as she always did, at how casually he played even the most intense musical score. Never did he seem the slightest bit anxious or worried. It was incredible.

Smiling, the internal flutters of nervousness abated in the soothing flow of music, she closed the door silently and padded on bare feet over the plush carpet. His jacket and waistcoat were off, the muscles of his shoulders discernible under the linen shirt and thrilling to observe, but it was not until she sat onto the bench beside him with her back to the piano keys that she realized his cravat was discarded. Her eyes dropped to the open collar of his shirt, scanning the strong lines of his neck down to the skin below his throat, where strands of tawny hair the color of his eyebrows were visible.

A man without cravat and waistcoat was not a totally new phenomenon, but seeing a field worker or her brother partially exposed was vastly different than the man she was wildly in love with. It affected her in several astounding ways. Mesmerized, she was not aware that the music had stopped until his fingers stroked over her jaw.

"You are utterly breathtaking."

She lifted her gaze to his face, the depths of love and desire shining from his eyes reigniting the quivers of nerves. Or perhaps it was largely desire that rushed through her torso. Clearly, they were both equally affected and lost in enchanted contemplation of their casual attire and the hints of bodies revealed for some time, until she broke the silence.

"Only you would have a pianoforte in your bedroom."

"When I was eleven my grandmother purchased a pianoforte for me and placed it into this room so I could play whenever in the mood," he explained, speaking softly. His gaze left her face to follow the trail blazed by his hand sliding down her left arm to where her hands lay in her lap. "It was a way to circumvent my father's restrictions and a prime reason I chose to stay in this house whenever possible. Fortunately, this house was purchased by Lady Warrow independently, after her third husband, Lord Warrow, passed on, so Lord Essenton had no grounds to refuse my visiting." He tickled his fingertips over her knuckles and fingers while he talked, tingles shooting along her skin and up her arms, finally slipping under her right hand and drawing it to his mouth, warm breath stimulating the fine hairs to rise as he concluded, "He never knew of the pianoforte."

"I think Lady Warrow enjoys breaking restrictions," Georgiana shakily asserted.

"Noticed that, have you?" he asked with a laugh, kissing her palm. "In this case, I am abundantly thankful. I cannot recollect how often I woke with a score playing in my head and was able to immediately play it and jot it onto a sheet. It is convenient, to say the least."

"I wish I had thought of the same at Pemberley."

He kissed the bounding pulse in her wrist. "In Paris, I have my piano in the parlor attached to my bedchamber for easy access. I can play whenever I want and wearing whatever I want," he finished hoarsely, delivering a sucking kiss to her pinkie and then pressing her hand firmly against his heart.

Georgiana gasped at the heat scorching through the linen covering his chest, her eyelids fluttering and instinctively leaning closer. "A piano nearby is a nice idea, but I am glad it is in a separate room, so if you get a two in the morning inspiration you can pound away without waking me."

"And vice versa," he murmured, his free hand encircling her neck and pulling her toward his mouth. "I like how readily you accept that my bedchamber is now yours."

"Am I presumptuous? I should not have…"

Sebastian halted her words with an open kiss delving deeply into the glory of her mouth for long enough that Georgiana had almost forgotten the topic of conversation when her released her. "I love that you are presumptuous, Georgiana! My preference is you never leaving our bed. Never. Somehow I doubt I will be separating from your warm body no matter what brilliant tunes may be running through my brain. Now," he went on briskly before the mental images augmented by the sensual cast to her face drove rational thought away, "I have another song I wrote for you, one meant for your ears only."

He kissed her again, short and chaste, delivered a smoldering gaze over her body, and transferred the hand he still held tight against his chest to rest on his thigh. Patting the back of her hand, the message clear that he wanted it to stay there, he then sat straight and turned his attention to the pianoforte keys.

Georgiana's senses reeled. Her head spun from the blood surging through her heated veins. How many bars were played before she could concentrate on anything other than the feel of the hard thigh muscle under her palm she never knew. The sonata augmented the delirium that was rising by the second due to his closeness, the feel of his muscles, and the smell of his spicy cologne. The beauty of Sebastian's smooth notes and the romantic lyrics sung in his melodious tenor penetrated through the haze, and as she listened, her emotions soared.

The euphonious tones were played in tempos ranging from a slow andante to moderato, the lyric ballad meant to soothe and move the heart. Each stanza was of a fixed meter, not perfectly rhyming but with an identical rhythm. Alternating in French and English, Sebastian sang of their unique courtship from the perspective of his evolving emotions for his bride. He sang of how his admiration and respect grew to friendship before then escalating to love and passion. He sang of his denial and despair and joy. He sang of his hope for their future.

Through the entire sonata, he kept his eyes steady upon her face. Every line was uttered as a direct message of his heart delivered to her via music. And when he ended the last word and removed his fingers from the keys the final chord was still echoing around the chamber as she entered his embrace and hungrily sought his kiss.

She could not say how long it was when he pulled away from her lips and arms. She did not have a chance to feel bereft because he quickly rose from the bench to stand behind her, grasped her under the elbows, and lifted her to her feet. As if by magic the bench no longer separated them, Georgiana supported in his arms with her back pressed against his chest.

"Sebastian," she moaned, melting into his body, her head resting on his shoulder.

"Did you like your song?"

"Yes," she breathed, shivering at the exquisite impression of his tongue and lips tasting the skin around her ear.

"I have titled it *My Friend and My Love*, Georgiana, as a reminder of all that you are to me. My friend, the woman I love, and now my wife. I love you more every day I pass with you, and after tonight, I know my love for you will surpass every imagining and expectation."

Georgiana closed her eyes and gave in to the myriad sensations bombarding her. Pleasure radiated from dozens of places inside and outside her body, and every one was generated by Sebastian in some way.

One of his strong arms encircled her waist with long fingers caressing her hip. He held her gently but firmly against his body, Georgiana able to discern each respiration and heartbeat. The flex of his muscles, press of his lips, and prod of his hardened manhood were easily detected by her sensitized flesh. His other hand stroked across her belly and up her side to then brush the outer swell of her breast. Traveling as leisurely as possible, he skimmed under her arm, slipping between their bodies to run up her shoulder blade and across to eventually cup her jaw and turn her face toward his, bending to bestow a searing kiss.

Time faded and so did the room around her. Georgiana no longer had any concept of reality beyond Sebastian and how he dazzled her wits and stoked her internal fire to a blaze of desire. *Overwhelmed, oh so blissfully overwhelmed! Fiercely alive and breathlessly hazy all at once*, she mused in wonder. She clutched onto the arm round her waist and lifted the other hand to hold fast to his head, pouring her soul vigorously into the kiss and pressing her whole body forcibly backward.

Groaning from the depths of his chest, Sebastian broke the kiss and rested his forehead against her cheek. His harsh breaths gushed down her chest, goose bumps rising and her nipples hardening more than they already were. Her body screamed for *More! More!* even while her mind, whirling at the onslaught of sensations, needed a respite. Thankfully, perhaps, he offered that by withdrawing minimally, although still holding on tightly just as she was.

"Time…" he wheezed, pausing to swallow and raggedly inhale. "I want to… It is time to release your hair, love. These combs are lovely but not as lovely as your hair. God, I love your hair, Georgiana!"

The three combs were removed one by one and tossed onto the piano bench, Sebastian releasing his hold about her waist to embed both hands into the thick tresses at the nape of her neck, his fingers splayed to capture the silky curls in between. Sighing contentedly, he buried his face into the lush locks spilling over and falling midway down her back. Fresh shivers cascaded down Georgiana's back as he repeatedly raked through her hair and lifted handfuls aside to kiss her neck. Devotedly, he played with and teased each curl, her legs weakening from the bliss engendered from this simple act.

"Sweet scent of rose water. Beautiful," he murmured, his voice thick with awe and lust. "I want you, precious wife. Can you tell how fervid my hunger for you?" Georgiana was unable to manage more than a feeble nod, although a verbal answer was not necessary since it was impossible to mistake his ardor and physical response.

Blurrily, she hoped he recognized how powerful her desire for him, even if the intensity of her passion threatened to buckle her knees and shred her final vestiges of coherency. Seconds later, her fears came true when his hands suddenly left her hair and cupped her breasts, each thumb rubbing over her rock hard nipples and sending a bolt of pure sexual electricity straight through to her core.

"Oh God!" she gasped as her body sagged and would have crumbled to the carpeted floor if Sebastian had been slower to react.

"I have you," he said with a gravelly chuckle. His clench was solid around her waist and under her bosom, one palm still warmly encompassing a breast with the thumb pressing against the nipple. "Perhaps we should take this to the bed. I think I have moved too fast, have I, my love? I know I could use a moment before I lose control. No need to rush what promises to be a perfect night. Come. Let me help you relax. How does a glass of wine sound?"

While soothing in his melodic timbre, he steered to the bed, turning her around to face him for the first time in what felt like hours of sensual play. His smile was radiant and smug, cheeks ruddy, and eyes glistening silver. Georgiana knew she presented a similar picture and not just because she could see her reflection in his brilliant eyes. Yet her thoughts were only on his countenance. As abruptly as her senses had lurched when he touched her breasts, they now leapt anew.

He is stunning! Handsome. Desirable. Mine!

"Kiss me."

He did.

Slowly. Softly. Tenderly. Leisurely.

Gentle caresses of his tongue across her parted lips and tiny nibbles with his teeth. Sedately, he stroked the flushed flesh of her neck and shoulders, the gauzy robe sliding off her shoulders and fluttering to the floor just as she wilted and crushed her breasts against his chest.

"Sweet merciful heavens," he rasped. "I do need to lay you down before you fall. Or before we both fall. I think we need to breathe. Let me plump these pillows. Climb on in, love. It is a very comfortable bed. Are you cold at all? No? Then just the sheet should do. There. Scoot a bit so I will have room beside you. Is this better? Excellent! Now, how about that glass of wine? A Sauvignon Blanc from France that I know you love."

He knelt onto the bed with one knee, bending near to kiss her forehead and lightly stroke her chin. "I will only be a minute," he whispered, smiling as he began to pull away.

"Wait! Take your shirt off!"

Sebastian's brows rose, his eyes glancing at the hand cinched around his wrist then back to her startled eyes and white teeth biting her lip. The blush spreading from chin to forehead revealed her shock at the impulsive command, Sebastian grinning crookedly and chuckling.

"As you wish, my lady. I am yours to command and please in any way you deem possible."

No disrobing fanfare other than to randomly chuck the garment into the air, and he was kneeling on the mattress with bare torso inches away from her gaze. His grin widened as she boldly scrutinized the fair skin covering his straight, broad shoulders, the lean but defined muscles scattered with tawny hair leading in a thin trail down his flat, hard abdomen to then disappear underneath the band of his pants. The physical evidence as to the degree of his arousal was clearly noticed as her blush deepened to crimson, although she did not remove her gaze as rapidly as he may have suspected she would. When she did lift her eyes to his face, the mixture of embarrassment and brazen appreciation caused him to laugh.

"Now, some wine."

Georgiana could not have torn her gaze from his figure if her life depended on it. In fact, it felt as if her life depended on keeping him in her sight, and studying him in the process. She would be lying if she said her mind had never imagined his unclothed physique. Those speculations were birthed as far back as Lyon with the de Valdays and only grew alarmingly stronger and frequent as their wedding night approached. Yet he was superior to her feeble fabrications. Far superior.

Then he turned from the table with a glass of wine in each hand, sure-footed and graceful as he crossed the short space. His skin and hair gleamed in the candlelight, handsome face and stupendous body filling her view and looming large as he came closer. Abruptly, she heard the voices of the de Valdays—*yummy enough to eat... kiss, touch, squeeze... think of all the wonders to be enjoyed with such a man...*

Only it did not sound like the de Valdays but rather like her own voice!

"What did you say?" Sebastian asked, his brow quirked and crooked grin in place.

"Nothing!" she choked, grabbing the wine from his hand and gulping half the liquid in one swallow.

"My mistake. I thought I heard something about kissing, but it was probably my thoughts ringing inside my brain. The wine is delicious and to your liking, I presume."

Georgiana knew he was teasing, she having obviously spoken aloud, and she was both embarrassed and amused. Hiding her flaming face behind a curtain of hair and sipping steadily to squelch the threatening giggles, she nodded an affirmative.

"I happen to enjoy a nice white wine from time to time," he continued, speaking casually as if discussing the weather, "but in general my palate prefers a more robust Cabernet. Or once in a while a light claret is appealing. Port I cannot abide, a point de Marcov likes to tease me about since it is considered a manly option."

During his calming exposition, he settled onto the bed beside her, reclining against the pillows with his right side touching hers. Stretching his long legs underneath the sheet, he entwined his feet with her smaller ones, toes tickling and caressing. Lastly, still without breaking stride in his speech, he enfolded the hand lying slack on her thigh, fingers lacing between and curling around.

"I remembered your expressed preference for Corcelles-en-Beaujolais Sauvignon Blanc so purchased a case before we left France…"

"You did?" She raised her gaze to his in surprise. "How thoughtful! Thank you."

"You are welcome, love. I wish I could say it was an onerous task and thus earn greater respect for my efforts, but alas, it was easily accomplished." He smiled, lifted her hand to kiss the back, after which he returned them both to their place on her thigh, took a sip of wine, and resumed in the same conversational tone.

"The bottles are safely stowed and will accompany us on our journey north. Ah, Georgiana! I hunger to show you my home! Staffordshire is similar to Derbyshire, so I know you will love the countryside. There are innumerable places of interest and sharing them with you will be a delight. Then to culminate our holiday at Whistlenell Hall will be a pinnacle of satisfaction for me. It will appease my heart to know you have dwelt in your new home for a spell before we return to Paris."

On he spoke, his lush tenor enthusiastically describing his ancestral country and the manor house he was born in. He painted vivid pictures of the hills and rivers, small boroughs and large cities, historic places and modern marvels of

Staffordshire. The estate grounds and Tudor-style Whistlenell Hall came alive in her mind.

It was certainly not the first time he had talked about his home. Nothing he said was new, and Georgiana found her mind lulled and body unwinding. Unconsciously, she slumped against him, her head falling onto his shoulder and drained wine glass rolling out of her hand to lay forgotten on the mattress.

Contented minutes passed before Georgiana's numbed mind gradually awoke to several considerations. First was the shocking realization that she was pressed tightly against his body with a gorgeous naked torso begging to be investigated! Second, as her eyes focused anew on his flesh and scanned downward, was that the prominent bulge previously noted—and felt—as an unmistakable indication of his desire to make love to her was significantly diminished.

Dismay pierced her heart followed swiftly by fierce irritation. The anger was directed wholly at herself. She knew what he was doing, dear wonderful considerate man that he was. In a selfless effort to calm her nervousness, Sebastian was dampening his need.

The next consideration, fueled by infuriated recriminations, was that the last thing she wanted was for their wedding night to end with her foolishly falling asleep or childishly shrinking away from what she logically knew would be a glorious consummation. All of it combined to fan the flame of her passion into a sudden inferno that blazed even higher when he jerked and gasped seconds later at the simple maneuver of her hand brushing boldly across his upper chest.

"Sebastian," she whispered, looking into his startled eyes, "thank you for understanding my nervousness and soothing me. But I do not want to hear about pastureland or architecture. I want to be your wife."

Then she kissed him, deeply, while simultaneously stroking down the middle of his chest and abdomen, over the edge of his pants to firmly press her palm onto his groin.

His response was astounding! Every muscle twitched, shivers rippling head to toe. Instantly, the flesh under her hand hardened and expanded, the shape defined to her seeking fingers even through the fabric. His arms encircled and grasped her, pulling her into his body. The kiss wildly escalated, groans and hoarse pants lodging in his chest.

It was crazed, fervent, and animalistic.

And Georgiana wanted more.

Careful, conscious thought was gone. Passion and instinct drove them. Yet as ferocious as the subsequent interlude, it was also beautiful, tenderly loving, romantic, and magical.

Georgiana would forever remember every movement, sensation, spoken adoration, impulsive exclamation, and involuntary cry.

She marveled at the heat of his skin, it soft and mildly ticklish from the hairs gliding underneath her palms while the muscles underneath were solid. In amazement, she perceived the intensity of his reaction to her touch and it emboldened her to explore and mimic his maneuvers. If her excitement was increased by his hand stroking under her gown up her bare leg, buttocks, and hip until reaching her sensitive female areas for direct stimulation, then she assumed he would enjoy this as well.

Sebastian immediately comprehended her intent and assisted with the hasty removal of his trousers, his sigh of relief from the uncomfortable confinement melding into a guttural groan when she wasted no time in carrying out her own direct stimulation. Within seconds his arousal significantly multiplied, Georgiana exhilarated by his wild writhing and panting and furious resumption of his exploration to her body.

A heartbeat later she was astride his hips, reflexively swaying and rocking against the pressure of his arousal. It was pleasure unimaginable. Then he removed her gown, both of them naked and blissfully entwined, his mouth and tongue accompanying his hands and fingers in a concerted effort to rouse.

Oh, how well it worked!

The last vestiges of rational thought evaporated from the fire of lust scorching through her body. Her only thought was the craving for more of him, all of him, to ease the ache of need.

"Please!" she rasped, opening her eyes to dazedly meet his. "I want… you, Sebastian. Please, now."

He nodded, his eyes drunk with passion and immeasurable love, and groped around the bedside table until encountering a jar she had not noticed. "This ointment will help with the pain. I do not wish to hurt you, dearest."

She opened her mouth to reassure him, but the words were lost to a gasping moan when, with a simple shift of his hips, he was poised and began the incredible process of making her his wife. Slow at first, then gradually in paced undulating movements, she accustomed herself to the strange but marvelous feeling. It was stupendous.

Yet it was not nearly enough.

Georgiana felt his body shaking. His brow was furrowed and the hands encircling her waist trembled with the effort to avoid losing control.

"There is no reason to hold back, my love. I am not a china doll and I want you."

And with that proclamation she grabbed hold of his face, initiated a fierce kiss, and plunged downward hard until he was fully encased within her. Searing pain burst through her belly but she had anticipated this. Her cry of distress was stifled and drowned by Sebastian's unrestrained shout of ecstasy. The damn burst and his efforts to proceed cautiously disappeared. Tenaciously, he clutched on to her, thrusting deep and fast again and again, each stroke igniting rivers of pain but also surges of euphoria.

Georgiana ignored the throbbing and focused on the joy of being one with him. The unmasked rapture he was experiencing lifted her soul above the pain. And miraculously, just as his manic pace started to ebb and she detected twinges of awareness in his eyes, the pain was no more than a vague discomfort superseded by exquisite pleasure and revived sexual fervor.

"I love you," she whispered into his ear, her fingers teasing over his ears and twisting through his curls. "Please... do not... stop..." she moaned between sucking kisses across his jaw.

Then she leaned back, her hair falling as a cloud down her back and waving over her breasts as they swayed with each quickened movement.

"It is my dream coming true," he muttered in awe. "God, I love you, Georgiana! With all my soul!"

Ensuring neither would be left wanting, as in his unfulfilled dream months ago when he thought she was lost to him, Sebastian matched her tempo and augmented it with intimate caresses until, like in his dream, she arched her back and cried his name.

"Georgiana!" he shouted, propelling himself one last time, until he was buried as far as possible, and releasing the pent-up pressure violently as rapturous bliss shot through his entire body.

In the aftermath, they clung together in a pliant heap, wits and muscles slow to recuperate. Peace blanketed their hearts, and for a long while they were content to wallow in the gratification and residual ecstasy flowing through their veins. Sebastian's mind was wrapped firmly in a state of utter paradise with hands lazily caressing when Georgiana lifted up from where she had collapsed onto his chest. She pushed the errant curls away from his face, smiling as she fondled his parted lips, and broke the silence.

"So, have you adequately done what you intended? Do I look 'properly ravished'?"

His jubilant laugh echoed through the bedchamber, Georgiana helpless but to join in. Only when he rolled over with her pressed under his body did the laughter abate to bubbling snickers behind their kissing lips.

"I would wager we both look properly ravished. Heaven knows I am blissfully satisfied." He smoothed the tangled hair back from her forehead, smiling even as he intently searched her face. "I love you, Georgiana. You are breathtakingly beautiful. I am as happy as I have ever been in my life and am overwhelmed by you, by us, and by this night we have shared. I…" He hesitated, swallowing and blinking away the mist. "I love you and need to know you are… How do you feel?"

"Happy. Joyous. Bursting with love for you," she answered emphatically, after kissing him and squeezing his body tighter against her chest. "Tired and weak and sleepy. Quite pleased with myself, if you must know. Smug, I suppose. I am wildly and wantonly satisfied, to use your word. It is amazing how I feel at this moment! The joy in understanding fully how stupendous our physical relationship is, and will be, is immeasurable. And yes, I am sore, since I know that is primarily what you are fretting about"—she rubbed the faint furrows between his brows—"but it is bearable, will diminish in time, and is outweighed a hundredfold by the love and euphoria. Oh, Sebastian! I love you so!"

The kiss that followed was lengthy, penetrating, and racing toward reanimating the desire lurking perpetually under the surface of their skin that had only been mildly slaked by one time making love, no matter how extraordinary. Their hands succumbed to the plea to explore naked flesh, excitement arising with every touch. Georgiana was more than willing to give in to her newly awakened power and Sebastian's response to her stimulation was evident. Halting the mad desire to rush headlong into the realm of pure bliss for a second time required restraint Sebastian did not know he possessed.

"Well," he groaned, diverting his kisses from mouth to safer facial features, "between words and actions, I conclude that qualifies as properly ravished. Indeed, we are both satisfied, dearest wife. Yet as anxious as I am to extend the ravishment, I have other plans for you. Let me pamper you as you deserve, and by morning your great fortune in marrying me will be indisputable!"

His crooked grin and pompous chuckle were infectious. Georgiana laughed and mockingly nodded in agreement with his arrogant tease even as anticipatory shivers flickered to life. Whatever he meant, she trusted that their first night of marriage would be as stupendous as promised.

Hours later, Georgiana floated through the layers of a lovely dream in which she was nestled within a warm cocoon of softest silk and down feathers. Her hazy memory could not recollect a dream where peace was as tangible. So real were the feelings of her dream that she carried them with her when passing the final barrier between sleep and awake, the serenity preventing her from experiencing the tiniest twinge of alarm by the unfamiliar bed or sight of a man's bare chest inches away from her nose. For five minutes or more, she dazedly observed the steady rise and fall of firm muscles as he breathed, the dim light of pre-dawn casting the fair skin into shadows. Gradually, her awareness extended to note a large hand resting protectively on her waist and a heavy thigh lying across her leg. Blinking to wipe the film from her eyes, she swept her gaze upward, happily smiling and sighing as reality reasserted itself.

My husband Sebastian.

He remained soundly asleep, lying on his side with a hand folded under the pillow by his cheek. Golden stubble dotted his jawline and chin, thick lashes fluttered with the faint movements of his closed eyes, and dense blond curls spiked in a mishmash pattern. She had never beheld him in sleep, but the vision he presented at this hour was not the only reason she was abruptly pierced with a surge of emotions so extreme that breathing became labored and tears clouded her sight.

God, how I love him! The cry came from the depths of her soul, followed in the same mental breath with the question: *How could I have ever imagined loving anyone but him?*

She rarely thought of Lord Caxton. It was as if years had passed since their last encounter after her illness. When she did think of him, it was only to ponder in amazement the mystery of how his presence had once affected her when the mere thought of Sebastian was enough to send her senses spiraling a hundredfold beyond. Once acknowledged and sanctioned, their mutual captivation exploded, the barrage of emotional and physical zealousness overwhelming while wondrous at the same time.

And now we are married and I have felt the power of your love. I am intoxicated.

Gently, she pressed her fingertips to the skin over his heart. Tenderness mingled with aching desire as she scanned over his upper torso. Heightened senses perceived those unseen parts of his strong, vital body touching her skin under the bed coverings. Vividly, she visualized a great percentage of his figure, since she had studied as much of him as possible before they fell into exhausted slumber. Yet as titillating as the images, it was her heart that swelled with longing.

For an hour after his comment about pampering, he had done precisely that. Starting with a bowl of warm fragrant water and soft towels he had carefully washed away the telltale evidence of her virginity. Georgiana had blushed crimson at the idea, but within seconds his light touch and humorous commentary had dispelled the embarrassment. Besides, the harsh truth was that she did ache amid the satisfied tranquility, and the aromatic water followed by a gentle but comprehensive massage with a scented oil lotion was therapeutic.

His generous ministrations also provided ample opportunity to examine her new husband at length since he remained naked the entire time! Of course, so did she, another minor embarrassment she rapidly forgot in the thrill of observing his masculine perfection and the blatant enjoyment he obtained from observing and touching her. Innocent she may still be to some degree, but his aroused state left no doubt how affected he was, but despite her attempts to take the activity into another more intimate direction, he insisted on caring for her.

Then he commanded her to turn onto her stomach, so he could focus on her backside and the next moment, she was waking up to a faint sunrise seeping in through the drapes and a downy-haired chest before her face!

Taken as a whole, the urgency to wake him up immediately and see what could be accomplished first thing in the morning was powerful. *However,* she reasoned, *he selflessly checked his passion so I could sleep and recuperate, so it is only polite for me to do the same.*

In time, she would discover that Sebastian vastly preferred she *not* be polite when it came to wanting to make love! Yet for the present, she opted to slither out of his loose embrace, recognizing as she moved that a visit to the water closet to freshen up was a capital idea.

Returning to the bedchamber after attending to physical necessities, and taking the time to tidy herself and stretch muscles that were tight, but not as sore as she would have expected, her eyes alit first on an unmoved husband. The defined outline under the sheet and exposed parts of his body wreaked havoc on her resolve to be polite, so she quickly shifted her gaze to the pianoforte.

Wrapped in a blanket found folded at the end of the bed, Georgiana sat on the bench and picked up the sheets of music and lyrics from the song he had written and sung for her last night. Softly, she hummed the tune, marveling afresh at how brilliant he was even with a simple ballad and moved to tears at the beauty of his love poem to her.

"I thought we had a bargain not to leave our bed or play piano while the other is asleep. Was I dreaming that, Mrs. Butler?"

"I have not touched a single key and only left our bed for personal requirements."

"Yet you remain there and not here, with your bereft husband, and your poise is suspiciously like one about to pound out a tune."

"Circumstantial evidence, Lord Nell, leads to wild conclusions."

He threw back the sheet, laughing as he rolled out of the bed. "Very well, I concede my error." He sat next to her, leaning for a light kiss to her lips. "Good morning, beautiful wife. You slept well, I trust?"

"Very well. You?"

"Never better. Waking was not as I anticipated, however. But thankfully my panic was brief when I saw you here. You like your song?"

"No. I love it, adore it, will treasure it forever, and think it is the greatest song ever written or that ever shall be."

"High praise from a composer of your caliber, Viscountess. I am humbled." He cupped her face between both hands, this kiss intense and extended. His voice was rough when he asked, "May I request you play the song for me, my love? I want to hear it from your fingertips while I serenade like a lover should."

The subtle differences in the music as played with her smaller hands and delicate touch did not diminish the effect. Sebastian sang in a lower key, his timbre subdued and husky, all the while staring at her face. He did not touch her while she played but direct contact was not necessary.

It was distracting in a thrilling way, Georgiana missing beats and losing the cadence a number of times. The final bars were rushed through, the last chords ringing in the air when she turned to him and slipped her arms over his shoulders.

"Now I have a request: take me back to bed so we can create beautiful music together."

Sebastian hastily scooped her into his arms, chuckling as he walked to the bed. "Create beautiful music together is it? Interesting idiom, love. I like it! I believe we can designate that phrase as our standard. The Butlers, creating beautiful music together in every imaginable way."

"Yes," she agreed, the word uttered as a sibilant sigh against his lips.

It was a promise and a prediction.

Coda

G EORGIANA STOOD BEFORE THE floor-length mirror turning side to side and leaning in for close viewing, the final inspection a ritual of sorts that aided in the calming of her nerves. Then with a deep, cleansing breath and nod at her reflection, she completed the necessary custom and left the room.

As always, her husband greeted her with a smile. He interrupted the conversation he was having with the Marquis de Marcov and excused himself politely, even though Adrien waved him away and winked at Georgiana from across the room. Sebastian unhurriedly strolled to her, Georgiana amazed as she always was at his utter lack of nervousness.

"You are stunning, my lady. If I had my way in planning your wardrobe, you would never wear another color but blue. Are you satisfied that you appear divine?"

His tease was not lost on his wife. He knew of her anxiety and the routine she went through each time in order to ease the worst of the tremors.

"I am satisfied that each ruffle and strand of hair is where it should be," she retorted. "That is as good as it gets. Have you checked…?"

"I have checked several times," he answered the familiar question before completed, "most recently not fifteen minutes ago. In addition, I asked Lord de Valday to lend his practiced eye. Duchesse de Bourgogne's *chambre de concert* has proven to possess excellent acoustics. Do not worry, my dear."

She opened her mouth to express additional concerns as Sebastian anticipated and had his prepared responses for—the game was as sure as the rising of the sun—but this time his teasing placation to settle her jitters was unnecessary.

"My dearest Georgiana! How extraordinarily beautiful you are! Your gown, lovely friend, is elegance supreme!"

"It is of the latest Paris fashion created by the fabulous dressmaker Baronne Zoë de Valday-Farrenc whose designs are all the rage."

Zoë fluttered her fan and mimed embarrassment at Georgiana's praise. "Such sweet words you say. Why look at me, I am blushing!" She patted her well-rouged but otherwise ivory cheeks. "I have not conquered all of French fashion as yet, however, and the *Journal des Dames et des Modes* has only featured my gowns sixteen times!"

"Ah yes, but you were on the cover twice and last month honored with a full spread, Baronne," Sebastian reminded her. "Few others have scored a coup of this magnitude. Every Parisian modiste must be green with envy."

"Oh, they are! Positively rotting! *Merci, monsieur*, you always cheer my gloominess."

Sebastian bowed. "Delighted to be of service, Baronne. We would never wish for you to be gloomy," he said, stressing the last word with a humorous inflection. Zoë coyly slapped his arm with her fan, understanding his jest. The Baronne de Valday-Farrenc was perpetually gay, as they all knew.

"Pardon the intrusion, but my lady has sent word that I am requested to join her and take our seats. More than likely, there is socializing required beforehand, but I shall bow to the marquise's commands." Lord de Marcov inclined his head toward Zoë and Georgiana, lingering with the latter. "Georgiana, because I am certain your stifled English husband has inadequately verbalized how sublime your beauty and radiance, especially in this resplendent garment created by the equally resplendent Baronne de Valday-Farrenc, allow me to eloquently do so." And then the marquis launched into a two-minute adjective-laced declaration so purple in prose that Georgiana's cheeks were flaming even as she laughed until tears stung her eyes.

"Well done, de Marcov," Sebastian congratulated when his friend finally exhausted himself. "Indeed, it was better than this stifled Englishman could accomplish."

"Thank you, Adrien. Your praise has accomplished what pounds of rouge could not." She lifted on her toes to kiss his cheek, de Marcov following with a courtly kiss to her fingers.

There were few men Sebastian would ever allow to flagrantly flirt with his wife. Adrien de Marcov, his oldest and dearest friend and husband to his sister Vivienne, was one of them. The other joined the gaily chatting quartet at the same moment that the Marquis de Marcov departed to join his marquise.

Frédéric de Valday glided forward, his sensuous gaze trained on Georgiana as it did on every woman he met. As always, her hand was captured by his with adroitness truly awe-inspiring to behold, and then his husky voice smoothly pierced through to momentarily render the group silent and mesmerized.

"Beautiful lady, my heart suspends the rhythm of its beats at the first glance into your eyes and gaze upon your loveliness. Magnificent, splendid enchantress Georgiana! All Paris falls at your feet in awe and—"

"Frédéric, my dear friend, time is short and my nervousness extreme, so I must stem the tide of adoration, as delightful and appreciated as it is under normal circumstances."

"*Pardonnez-moi!* Imbecile I am, fair Georgiana, to forget your persistent anxiety! You have no reason to harbor distress, as you shall be brilliant as always!"

"As I assure her each time, and since it continually comes true, one would imagine she would believe it herself. Thank you, my lord, for the support. You can forestall the inevitable question by telling us that all is in order on the stage."

"*Oui.* I personally inspected the scene and ensured that nothing had been disturbed."

"Are you ever nervous, Frédéric?"

"*Moi?*" His brows rose above eyes wide with genuine astonishment at Georgiana's query. "Never! With talent as prodigious as mine, why in the world would I be nervous? Inconceivable!"

"Georgiana!"

As one, they turned to the singsong voice, smiling in unison at the enchanting woman bearing down on them with a mysterious combination of stateliness and verve remarkable to witness.

Georgiana dropped into a deep curtsy. "Your Grace."

"Pish! Bother with such nonsense! Yvette I am to you, my friend, never 'Your Grace' or the Duchesse de Bourgogne—unless we are in public, of course," Yvette finished with a satisfied smirk and chuckle. Then she tossed her head, ebony curls bobbing. "Transcendent you are in Zoë's gown. Exquisite, my sweet sister," she gushed, leaning to kiss her twin on the cheek. "I see another plate in the *Journal des Dames et des Modes* after tonight! Now"—she turned back to Georgiana and Sebastian—"all is ready and our guests have taken their seats. Oh, the ripples of excitement! Duc de Bourgogne and I shall be the talk of Paris tomorrow and for months to come! Perhaps years! And my Zoë and Frédéric too! And you two of course!" She grasped both their hands, enthusiasm visibly oozing from her pores. "I know you will dazzle once again! I have an introduction prepared that will be in every newspaper in France! Come"—she gestured to her brother and sister—"it is time."

"Am I not to stay behind stage for your glorious introduction?"

Yvette patted her brother on the cheek. "No, *petit frère*. Your time will come later. Trust me! None shall doubt the eminence of your superb tenor and the timing will increase the excellence of the evening. I shall explain! Now come!"

And with a flurry of skirts and blown air kisses, the Duchesse de Bourgogne imperiously led the parade out of the room, the Vicomte de Valday and Baronne de Valday-Farrenc as regal as their sister.

Sebastian and Georgiana stared after the trio affectionately until the door closed behind, leaving them alone in the quiet room.

"Her Grace certainly has a presence about her, does she not?"

"They all do," Georgiana agreed with a laugh. "When I first met Yvette, she told me she would be famous and marry the grandest duke in France."

"She has succeeded, I daresay." He looked at his wife and reached to toy with the ringlets of golden hair hanging at the nape of her neck. "Of course you know the introduction will be wildly overblown?"

"We will have much to live up to once Yvette is finished."

They walked to the door separating the waiting room from the de Bourgogne *chambre de concert* and peeked carefully through the crack. On the large raised platform sat two shining grand pianos. Enormous bouquets of flowers lined the edges of the stage, but otherwise the space was empty, with the instruments the focus. The hall extending away from the stage was filled with padded chairs in precise rows, all two hundred and fifty rapidly being taken by the elegantly dressed luminaries invited to the performance. A vast majority of the guests were known after years of periodically dwelling in Paris. Yet what made this particular event special to Georgiana and Sebastian were those who had traveled with them for this journey abroad.

Georgiana's eyes rested on the front row. Her brother Fitzwilliam was there with Elizabeth, sitting side-by-side as they forever had, bodies as close as possible without touching. At the moment William was leaning to his left and in conversation with their sons, Alexander and Michael, while Lizzy's head was bent to better hear the words of her right-sided seatmate, Lady Simone Fitzwilliam. Colonel Fitzwilliam, Lady Simone's husband and Georgiana's beloved cousin, sat to the right of his wife and was laughing at what was probably a joke coming from his stepson Hugh Pomeroy. Georgiana's uncle, Dr. George Darcy, was also laughing at the mysterious quip, the broad grin then turned toward his wife in the chair next to him, the latter glowing with love as she listened to her spouse repeat the jest, her laughter added to the noise. Georgiana's one-time companion, the former Mrs. Annesley, now Mrs. George Darcy, blushingly accepted the tender kiss her rebellious husband planted on her lips, the two sharing a brief, passionate glance leaving no doubt as to the fiery nature of their marriage.

Georgiana scanned over the crowd, as did Sebastian, both pleased to share this time with those they loved. Lord and Lady Matlock, the Marchioness of Warrow, three of Sebastian's sisters, the Dowager Countess of Essenton, Major General and Mrs. Artois, Mr. and Mrs. Charles Bingley, and a number of younger cousins, nieces, and nephews claimed the first several rows.

Silence gradually fell as the duchesse ascended the steps and walked to the exact middle of the stage.

"Here we go," Sebastian murmured into his wife's ear. "Want to place bets on how long this will take? Your nervousness will disappear because you will be falling asleep."

"Madams and messieurs! Tonight you will be delighted with a musical extravaganza unprecedented..."

"What did I tell you?" He chuckled, earning a *shush* from Georgiana, but she too released a short giggle.

As Sebastian predicted, Yvette had barely begun! The introduction was not horribly long, but the prepared phrases had Sebastian and Georgiana shaking with suppressed laughter, not that her Grace was wrong in anything she said, just exceptionally flowery.

"…graduates with the highest honors from Paris's most prestigious Conservatoire de Musique… renowned composers performing in grand palaces and concert halls of the world… favored musical performers to kings and queens in capitols across Europe… England's celebrated stars of music…"

"She surely will run out of adjectives and continents soon."

"I would not count on it!"

Sebastian lifted Georgiana's face to look at him. "Are you ready, my precious wife?"

"As ready as I shall ever be."

"You are beautiful and amazing, and I am eternally grateful for your talent and inspiration these past years. I love you, Georgiana."

"I love you, Sebastian."

"…and now it is my great pleasure to share this esteemed partnership and awe-inspiring musical collaboration in a concert promised to touch your heart, renew your soul, and delight your spirit. Please join me and welcome my friends. The Earl and Countess of Essenton!"

"I believe that is our cue. Shall we, Countess?"

Sebastian bent his elbow, offering the arm to Georgiana, who slid her hand inside to then rest on his forearm.

"Yes, my lord husband, I believe we should."

And as another required tradition before a performance, they spared the time for a kiss, only then able to open the door and walk onto the stage, thrilled to do what they adored: sitting together and playing music.

Read on for an excerpt from

Loving Mr. Darcy

BY SHARON LATHAN

Now available from Sourcebooks Landmark

E LIZABETH DARCY STOOD NEXT to Georgiana on the massive portico before the main doors to Pemberley. They were dressed in their traveling clothes and were waiting patiently for the Master of Pemberley, who was currently speaking with his steward, Mr. Keith, while the grandest and plushest of the Darcy carriages waited in the drive.

The warmth of May in Derbyshire had set in full force, making the days radiant with bright sunshine until late into the evening. The vast gardens of Pemberley were responding to the weather as Mr. Clark and his staff diligently engineered the grounds, which were now bursting in nearly eye-piercing splendor with every color of the rainbow. Every species of tree indigenous to England, and many that were not, enhanced the landscape with diverse shades of green and leaves in a multitude of shapes and sizes. Lizzy had regained her strength and mobility by traversing the miles of pathways weaving through the varied gardens. The by-product of her wanderings was a familiarity with and a deepening love for this place that was now her home.

Lizzy dreamily mused at how tremendously she had changed in the nearly five and a half months since she ascended the steps to Pemberley as a nervous bride. Outwardly, her entire appearance was drastically altered; gowns, jewels, and furs beyond her vaguest imaginings six months ago were now typical. Her hair, even in its traveling coif, was superior to anything she had ever fashioned previously. She was largely unaware of it, but there was a serenity and grace to her bearing that had not been present before. She would forever laugh spontaneously and carry a ready quip on her lips, but her character was notably more refined and softened. The minute gestures and vocal intonations associated with the social etiquette of the upper classes had permeated her being unconsciously.

Inwardly, she recognized a happiness and contentment that anchored her soul. Although there remained an enormous amount of Pemberley's management and the Darcy business affairs that she did not understand, her role as Mistress of Pemberley was a comfortable and accepted one. Her place in the household and the community was firm, and her confidence was secure. This massive house, which had frankly frightened her to death initially, was now home. She no longer walked through the endless halls with feelings of paralyzing awe and unworthiness. In five short months, she had grown to love the manor and its surrounds with a devotion transcending anything she had ever felt for Longbourn. Already she missed the library and bedchamber and sitting room and, well, all of it! The approximately six to seven weeks of their planned absence stretched before her as an empty sadness despite her excitement to see her family, and it was necessary to exert every ounce of self will to not rush inside for one last glance.

At that moment her husband strode out the door with the purposeful and powerful gait uniquely his own, mien intense and serious as he imparted a few last minute instructions to his steward. He paused as Mr. Keith commented about something. Lizzy smiled in admiration at the picture he presented. Commanding all to attention as he stood with shoulders back, masculine six-foot-three-inch frame erect, and impeccably dressed, he was elegant and regal, with sonorant voice authoritative. Pure, potent love and incredible pride burst through her as a wave. All that she had become in these past months was due to him. His love for her, his devotion and respect, his loyalty and faith in her capabilities, his steadfastness and latitude, and mostly his intuitive comprehension of her temperament, perceptions, and requirements encouraged her to blossom into the woman she now was.

He nodded in finality, shook the steward's hand, and turned to his sister and wife. Instantly his face lit with a beaming smile, and although no less noble or masterful, his countenance softened considerably.

"My dears, are you ready?"

"Waiting for you, brother."

"Come then," he said, offering an arm to each of his two favorite women in the entire world. He assisted Georgiana into the carriage first, made sure she settled comfortably, and then turned to Lizzy, inquiring with deep concern, "Are you well, beloved?"

"I am fine, William. Do not fuss so." She patted his cheek and took his offered hand.

Leaning close and wholly indifferent to the hovering servants, he kissed her forehead. "I will fuss whether you wish it so or not, Mrs. Darcy. Therefore, you may as well own to any discomfort you have immediately to save me perpetually questioning!"

He assisted her into the carriage, following behind, as she laughed. The truth was that she had been increasingly indisposed for the past five days. She had attempted to hide her infirmity from Darcy, but this was a fruitless endeavor. His eagle-eyed scrutiny and intimacy with all matters regarding his wife penetrated any guile she ventured. The physician had examined her yesterday and confirmed that which they had presumed: She was definitely with child. Despite previously harboring little doubt, the Darcys greeted the valida-tion with jubilance. Although her queasiness and extreme fatigue prevented her from actually jumping for joy, her heart was leaping. Darcy was nearly beside himself with euphoria and only Lizzy pleading with him to enlighten their families first kept him from informing all of Derbyshire.

The doctor had given her a clean bill of health, assuring them both that her symptoms, albeit difficult, were totally standard. He guessed that the worst of her nausea and lethargy would pass in a month or so, at about which time quickening would occur. He had spoken to them both at length and bluntly as to what to expect. As for the trip itself, he saw no reason to postpone or cancel, merely urging them to take it slowly. In light of the occasional mild headaches Lizzy suffered as a lingering effect of her trauma, coupled now with pregnancy, it was wise and essential not to overextend.

With this in mind, Darcy had plotted the normally one-day trip to Netherfield as a two-day journey, departure planned for mid-morning, when Lizzy usually felt better. So here they now were at nearly eleven o'clock and finally pulling out of the long Pemberley drive. The two carriages with their luggage, Samuel, Marguerite, and Mrs. Annesley had left earlier. A courier had been dispatched to London the week prior to prepare Darcy House and another to Hertfordshire for the Bingleys and Bennets.

Lizzy sat close to Darcy, gazing out the open window until Pemberley, with Mr. Keith and Mrs. Reynolds waving their adieus, completely disappeared from view. With a heavy sigh she nestled under his outstretched arm and he hugged her tightly. "I miss it already," she said.

"I always feel that way too," Georgiana replied, "until I get to London. There is so much to entertain! The symphony, the plays, the park across from our townhouse, the little paddle boats on the lake…"

"The shopping," Darcy interrupted with a grin.

Georgiana blushed, "Yes, the shopping as well, although it is you, dear brother, who insist I obtain new gowns and the like. In the end, you buy more for me than I acquire for myself!"

Lizzy laughed. "Somehow that does not surprise me."

Darcy was unfazed. "I shall not apologize in providing for and spoiling the women in my life."

"Elizabeth, you will so enjoy the shopping. We can purchase baby items! Oh, how wonderful it will be." Georgiana glowed and clapped her hands in enthusiasm.

The elder Darcys smiled indulgently, Lizzy too weary and queasy to visualize tromping through the clogged, odiferous streets of London as anything less than horrible. In truth, she was taking this entire excursion one step at a time. Currently, she only focused on seeing her family and proudly being squired about by her handsome husband. As shameful as the emotion was, she experienced fresh surges of vanity at how wonderful he was in every conceivable way—as far as she was concerned—and how amazing that he belonged to her. She glanced up at his face as he exchanged pleasant conversation with his sister, his lush voice vibrating through her body where she pressed against his side. Six months ago she thought her love for him stronger and deeper than her heart could contain, yet it was as a single star in the array of the endless heavens compared to now.

He met her eyes, smiling sweetly as he stroked her cheek and then kissed her briefly. He repositioned his body slightly sideways, long legs stretched completely across the spacious carriage interior, so she could recline onto his chest. She dozed for short spells throughout the journey, snacking sporadically from the generous provisions while Darcy read.

The trip was uneventful, their carriage arriving safely at the inn Darcy had secured near Northampton. From the unrelenting sun and jostling, Lizzy had a moderate headache which she had successfully hid from her husband for the past hour. However, when she exited the carriage, Darcy aiding her, a flash of light reflecting off a glass window of the inn pierced her brain as a bolt. She cried in pain, reflexively released Darcy's hand to press palms to throbbing temples, and crumbled to her knees.

"Elizabeth!" She was in his arms within the span of a heartbeat, Darcy barking orders that sent servants dashing to obey. It was all rather a daze to Elizabeth, her head hammering and stomach churning. In record time she found herself lying on a plush bed with a cold compress over her face, a frantic Darcy at her shivering side.

"Here, my love, drink this. I do not believe you have consumed enough fluids today. An error of mine that I shall not repeat. Marguerite," he said, turning to Lizzy's maid standing nearby, "please retrieve Mrs. Darcy's blue gown and robe." He assisted Lizzy with the glass, unbuttoning her dress as she drank.

"Darling, I will be fine in a moment," she began shakily, but he halted her by pushing the half-empty glass against her lips.

"Hush now, Elizabeth. You need to rest. Drink. That is an order. And then, you must sleep. I will have dinner brought to us later."

"No, William! I will rest here as you wish, but you go and dine with Georgie. Spend the evening with her as we planned. Marguerite will stay with me." He started to protest but she interrupted. "It is merely a headache from the light. My own stupidity for not shutting the shades is to blame. It will fade quickly, these headaches always do. You need to eat a complete meal."

He argued further, but Marguerite assured him she would send for him if needed, and as Lizzy was already slipping into a doze, he reluctantly relented. By the time he returned several hours later she was awake, had eaten a hearty dinner, and the headache had dissipated. She sat on the balcony gazing at the stars when he joined her. She nestled onto his lap, cuddling contentedly, and they talked in hushed tones. She appeared rested and in her usual lively humor, but he remained anxious for her health, internally chastising himself for not lowering the shades.

He kissed the top of her head where it nestled so perfectly under his chin, his arms tightening around her body. "As delightful as it is to stargaze with you, I insist we retire. You need your rest for the remainder of our journey and I will not risk the health of you or our child."

"You worry unnecessarily, my love. The headache has vanished, I slept, so am well rested, ate an excellent dinner, and am currently blissfully embraced by my handsome husband. What more could a woman possibly want?" She smiled up at his anxious face, wiggled closer, nestled her face into his neck, and bestowed a light kiss. "Actually"—another kiss—"I do have a marvelous idea"— sliding one hand under the hem of his shirt—"for a final activity"—nibbling on an earlobe—"to fully restore my health"—slipping the tip of her tongue into his ear.

"Elizabeth," he sighed, eyes shutting in pleasure, "we should wait until"— he gasped as a nipple was grazed—"settled at Netherfield... please..." Moans interrupted words as she firmly situated his hand on a breast, while lips traveled deliciously along his jaw. "Your headache could return, beloved, listen to me..."

Lizzy stopped his voice by seizing his lower lip and sucking gently. Darcy moaned again, unconsciously rocking a burgeoning arousal into her bottom and rubbing her breast.

"You talk too much, Fitzwilliam."

"No one has ever accused me of that!"

She smiled and began seductively stroking and kissing him. He earnestly struggled to dissuade her but to no avail. Lizzy's obstinacy was manifest in a myriad of ways, and one was when she desired him. Of course, Darcy never strived to avoid romantic activities with his wife so was not well experienced in how to do so!

Lizzy laughed at his stammering opposition and met passion-darkening eyes. "I want to love you, Fitzwilliam, any way you desire. I crave your touch on my skin and your body on mine. I hunger to bring you pleasure and show you how ardent my love for you is." She kissed his eager mouth passionately, overwhelming his senses with her breath and insistence. Pulling away finally, she whispered, "Take me to bed, my lover."

Acknowledgments

As always I would be lost without the Internet and the vast resources of the World Wide Web. Perhaps I should thank my Internet provider, Yahoo DSL, for rarely letting me down and running fast, as well as the makers of Mozilla Firefox for an awesome browser! Among Wikipedia, Google Books, and the wealth of websites, blogs, and historical archives, I am able to learn about far away places, long ago eras, and unfamiliar subjects from the comfort of home and with minimal expense.

For this novel I must thank my friend and music expert Jeff Rosbrugh for allowing me to pick his brain on musical terms. His helpful illumination on sonata form gave me the understanding to structure *Miss Darcy Falls in Love* as I have. Thanks Jeff!

Huge thanks to Simone van Lingen for perusing the text and correcting my poorly translated French. I wish I could have used more phrases or had more time for her to look over the entire manuscript. I love you sweetie and owe you for more than just the French!

Special thanks to my editor, Deb Werksman, for sticking with me, pushing when I need it, advising and mentoring, and simply being who she is: the best editor around! To my copyeditor Gretchen Stelter: A million thanks for being available to work on my novels, for tracking down my errors, and catching those annoying tense issues I never can get straight! What would I do without both my editors?

In the day-to-day I know none of this would be possible without the support of friends and family: Steve, Emily, and Kyle are my rocks at home, my sister Janis, my Calvary Chapel church family, Abigail Reynolds and the Austen Authors, the TSBO Devotees, my buddies at the hospital NICU and L&D, my local romance writers group, and the ever-increasing readers of the Darcy Saga. Collectively they keep me sane and inspired to excel.

Above all I give credit where it rightfully belongs: to God. "I can do all things through Christ who strengthens me." Amen.

About the Author

SHARON LATHAN IS A NATIVE Californian currently residing amid the orchards, corn, cotton, and cows in the sunny San Joaquin Valley. Happily married for twenty-five years to her own Mr. Darcy and mother to two wonderful children, she divides her time between housekeeping tasks, nurturing her family, church activities, and working as a registered nurse in a neonatal ICU. Throw in the cat, dog, gecko, and a ton of fish to complete the picture. When not at the hospital or attending to the dreary tasks of homemaking, she is generally found hard at work on her faithful MacBook Pro laptop or iMac desktop.

For more information about Sharon, the Regency Era, and her bestselling Darcy Saga series, visit her website/blog at: www.sharonlathan.net or look her up on Facebook. She also invites everyone to join her and other Austen literary fiction writers at www.austenauthors.com. If you live in California or simply love the Regency Era, you are welcome to participate in the Fresno Area Regency England Fellowship—visit the website at www.fresnoregency.com.

MY DEAREST MR. DARCY

SHARON LATHAN

Darcy is more deeply in love with his wife than ever

As the golden summer draws to a close and the Darcys look ahead to the end of their first year of marriage, Mr. Darcy could never have imagined his love could grow even deeper with the passage of time. Elizabeth is unpredictable and lively, pulling Darcy out of his stern and serious demeanor with her teasing and temptation.

But surprising events force the Darcys to weather absence and illness, and to discover whether they can find a way to build a bond of everlasting love and desire…

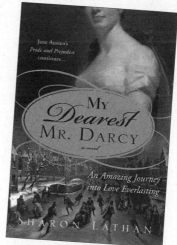

Praise for *Loving Mr. Darcy*:

"An intimately romantic sequel to Jane Austen's *Pride and Prejudice*…wonderfully colorful and fun." —*Wendy's Book Corner*

"If you want to fall in love with Mr. Darcy all over again…order yourself a copy." —*Royal Reviews*

978-1-4022-1742-5
$14.99 US/$18.99 CAN/£7.99 UK

In the Arms of Mr. Darcy
SHARON LATHAN

If only everyone could be as happy as they are...

Darcy and Elizabeth are as much in love as ever—even more so as their relationship matures. Their passion inspires everyone around them, and as winter turns to spring, romance blossoms around them.

Confirmed bachelor Richard Fitzwilliam sets his sights on a seemingly unattainable, beautiful widow; Georgiana Darcy learns to flirt outrageously; the very flighty Kitty Bennet develops her first crush, and Caroline Bingley meets her match.

But the path of true love never does run smooth, and Elizabeth and Darcy are kept busy navigating their friends and loved ones through the inevitable separations, misunderstandings, misgivings, and lovers' quarrels to reach their own happily ever afters...

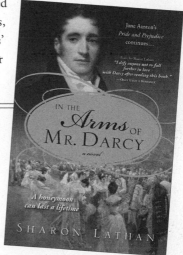

"If you love *Pride and Prejudice* sequels then this series should be on the top of your list!" —*Royal Reviews*

"Sharon really knows how to make Regency come alive." —*Love Romance Passion*

978-1-4022-3699-0
$14.99 US/$17.99 CAN/£9.99 UK

A Darcy Christmas

Amanda Grange, Sharon Lathan, & Carolyn Eberhart

A Holiday Tribute to Jane Austen

Mr. and Mrs. Darcy wish you a very Merry Christmas and a Happy New Year!

Share in the magic of the season in these three warm and wonderful holiday novellas from bestselling authors.

Christmas Present
By Amanda Grange

A Darcy Christmas
By Sharon Lathan

Mr. Darcy's Christmas Carol
By Carolyn Eberhart

978-1-4022-4339-4
$14.99 US/$17.99 CAN/£9.99 UK

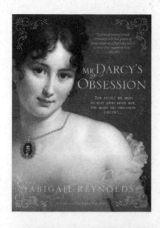

MR. DARCY'S
OBSESSION

~

ABIGAIL REYNOLDS

The more he tries to stay away from her, the more his obsession grows...

What if...ELIZABETH BENNET WAS MORE UNSUITABLE FOR MR. DARCY THAN EVER...

Mr. Darcy is determined to find a more suitable bride. But then he learns that Elizabeth is living in London in reduced circumstances, after her father's death robs her of her family home...

What if...MR. DARCY CAN'T HELP HIMSELF FROM SEEKING HER OUT...

He just wants to make sure she's all right. But once he's seen her, he feels compelled to talk to her, and from there he's unable to fight the overwhelming desire to be near her, or the ever-growing mutual attraction that is between them...

What if...MR. DARCY'S INTENTIONS WERE SHOCKINGLY DISHONORABLE...

978-1-4022-4092-8 • $14.99 U.S./$17.99 CAN/£9.99 UK

A SEXY, COMPELLING
PRIDE & PREJUDICE "WHAT IF"...

The TRUTH ABOUT MR. DARCY

SUSAN ADRIANI

THE TRUTH ALWAYS HAS CONSEQUENCES...

Mr. Darcy has a dilemma. Should he tell the truth about his old nemesis George Wickham in order to protect the good citizens of Meryton from Wickham's lies and deceits? Doing so will force Darcy to reveal family secrets that he'd prefer never come to light. The alternative is keeping the

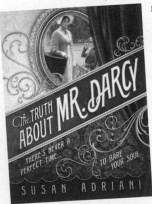

man's criminal nature to himself and hoping he leaves the area before doing significant harm.

But as Wickham's attentions to Elizabeth increase, Darcy knows if he's to win the one woman he's set his heart on, he's going to have to make one of the most difficult decisions of his life. And what he ultimately does sets in motion a shocking train of events neither he nor Elizabeth could possibly have predicted.

978-1-4022-4613-5 • $14.99 U.S./£9.99UK